Still

A

Man

Robert Molden

ISBN   978-0-6151-9364-9

Four Star Publishing
www.fourstarpublishing.com

TABLE OF CONTENTS

You're Still A Young Man

In high school, I thought I was the man. I had a little muscle on me; the six pack abs, the whole nine. I worked the four to eight shift at Buster Browns in the mall and had what I considered a pocket full of money so I wouldn't have to ask my parents for any. I was Vice President of my class three years running and I made good enough grades to skip the twelfth entirely. I had an early admission to UCLA where I planned to study criminal justice. I had so much going for me I had girls calling the house all hours of the day and night. I had my pick of chicks from the freshman to senior class. I wasn't a dog though. When I was going with someone, I was all about her. I was a parents dream. Or so they thought. I got a lot of action for someone everyone considered a fine upstanding young man.

If you asked me then I'd tell you I didn't have a single flaw or character defect. Hindsight being 20/20 I have to admit I had a boatload of them. I was too cocky for one. Another big one, I hate to admit, was I had a Gheri Curl. I got it my junior year.

My curl was long in the back, trimmed on the side, and hanging down my forehead like the mullets you see the country music artists wearing today. They're about twenty years behind the times. Black folk have already been there, done that, got the t-shirt, and moved the hell on.

In defense of my year with the curl, I was a child of the 80's and the times dictated how I wore my hair. Gheri Curls were what the ladies liked ever since Morris Day and Ready For the World busted onto the scene. I wasn't high yellow like Morris but I worked that hair like I was one of the original Rude Boys. Even though curls were 'in' me having one was a major flaw because I d never wanted a curl in the first place. I really liked the shag semi-fro I'd cultivated for years. I got the curl because that's what I thought the ladies were looking for.

These days I cringe at the pictures my mother insists on bringing out almost every time I go for a visit. In every picture, whatever piece of furniture I was propped against was slicked down from the juice of my curl.

My older brother Jeremy managed to escape the fad due to his age. He wasn't trying to follow the trends of the teenage crowd. My little brother Johnny got away without one because he was too young to con our parents into the hundred or so bucks it took to get a curl done right. Moms told him I'd paid for my own out of my paycheck and she wasn't about to shell out the money it took to get one and then all the extra money for activator and moisturizer. She said if he wanted a curl so badly, she could get a box kit for ten bucks and hook him up. My high-school campus was littered with horror stories of home curl tragedies; burnt up scalps. People walking around with the slick look but burn spots sprinkled here and there on their domes. I convinced my little brother that he should stick to his high and tight instead of risking what Moms could possibly do to his head.

Just like getting the curl I hadn't wanted I was always doing shit I didn't really want to do to please other people, usually a girl. I went out of my way to act and be like whatever I thought would get me the girl. And whenever I had a steady girl, I'd tell all the other honeys to cool out on calling me. Just in case my current "Ms. It" happened to be over, I didn't want to have to explain why this or that girl was calling. I wanted to prove that I was all about the one on one action.

But with all the studying, the school council, the early graduation, everything I did to make myself the perfect boyfriend, for some reason I couldn't understand at the time, I couldn't seem to hang on to a girlfriend. They'd come up with the craziest excuses to break up with me.

One girl, in my sophomore year, told me she'd sinned with me and couldn't see me anymore. I had one girl tell me, that her parents had found the condom wrapper in the trash out back and she couldn't go out with anyone anymore.

It happened so many times my buddy Kevin used to joke that I was trying to get through every fine girl in school before I hit UCLA so I could start all over again there. He thought I was the one doing the breaking up and I didn't correct him.

I hooked up with a girl from the student council in the middle of the year. She was a senior and planned to attend UCLA to study public administration like me. I thought it would be cool to already have a girlfriend once we got there. I'd dated a lot of girls before Karen but none of them had me sprung like I was over her. She was a triple threat. Body, beauty, and brains! The first time she let me hit it I became her love slave. The girl had it going on! I was addicted. Whipped! Nose wide as all outdoors. I was telling everyone about me and Karen would be together forever! We'd go through college together, grad school, get married, have kids. I had our future life together all mapped out three months after we started going out.

Then one day out of nowhere Karen broke me off. She and I were eating lunch in the grassy area of the quad by the cafeteria. I'd just asked her if she had gotten her dress for her prom. Karen wouldn't look at me for a long moment. She put her lunch aside and looked at me with sad eyes. I knew the look well.

"Marc, you are really nice and I care about you a lot. You were almost, like, my first, you know what I mean? But I don't think this is going to work."

I put the bologna sandwich moms had made me down and sighed heavily. I really loved Karen. Normally when a girl broke up with me, I'd be fine and start scoping the scene for the next one. But this time was different. "Why?" I asked. It was the only thing I could think of to say.

"It's just, I mean you're nice and everything," she made 'nice' sound like 'boring'. "But I think I need a more mysterious, unpredictable kind of guy, a bit more edgy." she told me, picking up her sandwich and taking a bite as if she had just told me she was going to drop a class or something. But she was dropping me!

Ain't that some shit? I wasn't edgy enough? What did that mean anyway? I found out a few days later. After Karen and I broke up, she started dating Mr. edgy, unpredictable. He was a ticking time bomb. I called her a couple of times to check on her but she never returned my calls. She started showing up to school late and eventually dropped out. I heard through the grapevine that she had gotten bopped upside the head by mysterious man on more than a couple of occasions. The saddest, I learned from one of Karen's girlfriends, was that even though she had decided to break things off with 'edgy' she got pregnant. I never saw Karen again. I assume she is living the life she'd seen growing up. Living off the County and popping out babies from different daddies in her quest to find her perfect thug.

Coincidentally, the two people I spent most of my time with were rough neck thugs in training; my brother Jeremy, also known as 'Catfish', and Kevin, my running buddy since grade school. They both acted as if they were trying to win some kind of Mack of the Year award that existed only in their heads. Jeremy was nicknamed "Catfish" in junior high because he was a bottom feeder when it came to girls. He had no taste buds and didn't care if they were blind, crippled, or crazy. I can remember at one point Jeremy was dating four girls at once and two of them were so hideous they wouldn't need costumes on Halloween.

Now Kevin, he had good taste when it came to girls. He always managed to use the right lines to convince the finest girls in the neighborhood to hang with him. The problem with Kevin was he wouldn't let anyone get too close. He'd give a girl the boot before she had a chance to start with the "I love you" line. Kevin would date a girl for a few months then just dump her and start dating someone else. When it came to dating, both Kevin and Jeremy were a father's worst nightmare. Fathers despised them and the daughters loved them! Go figure.

Here I was being a stand up kind of guy but I get dumped for being 'too nice'. I was crushed and pissed all at the same time and it showed. I walked around the house mad at the world. I wasn't myself and everyone could tell. I'd stomp around the house slamming doors, cabinets, anything that would make a bang mumbling under my breath, 'Too nice! Not edgy enough?' Then I'd go upstairs to my room to get away from any conversation and play my 'she done me wrong' music. I've always lived the good and bad times in my life to a musical soundtrack. It was moms and pops that recognized what was going on, pulled my coat, and taught me a little about love.

I was lying down on my bed in my darkened room, jumping up every time the song ended to put the needle back on the same song to play it again. I could feel my man's pain. Cameo had a way of speaking to a man's soul. As the vocalist wailed about being lonely and wondering why he'd lost his woman I lay on my bed feeling sorry for myself.

On about the 10th repeat of the song Mom came into the room, without knocking, and shouted, "Turn that screeching woman off! What is wrong with you boy?"

Of course, I told her nothing was wrong but Moms is no fool. She seemed to lose her anger at the blaring stereo and the wailing "woman" and came to sit on the bed beside me.

"Baby, I know what's wrong and I can't stand to see you hurt by these fast ass girls you keep running around with. When are you going to learn that if you keep putting yourself out there to be falling in love at the drop of a hat you are going to always be setting yourself up for heartbreak?"

I tried to brush her off. "Mom, I don't fall in love at the drop of a hat" but it sounded kind of weak as she counted off about six girls I had dated since the ninth grade, all of which I claimed to be 'in love' with.

"Marc, you've had girls calling this house all hours of the night and your father is getting fed up. I can't even keep track of all the names but I know wasn't no Karen in the bunch of them." I never realized that Moms was paying that much attention.

"Bottom line, Marcus Haley," Moms was serious when she called me by my full name; "every nice pair of legs and set of 36 C's ain't worthy of a Haley Man's love. You give it away with no discernment, honey. No discretion. As if it wasn't worth nothing at all. You don't wait to see what somebody is all about before you go declaring yourself 'in love'. And if you treat your heart like its trash then that's exactly how them…. them ho's you like to run after are gonna treat you. Just like a pile of stinking trash!"

At first, I was surprised she came at me like that, but I can't lie; what she said hit home. My mom has this ability to see right through the bullshit. She's always dropping her old school wisdom on how to fix a problem. Bottom line, Karen wasn't worth my time. She'd chosen her path and I had to stay on mine. Mom's advice helped me see that.

Just in case I missed the lesson Pops came at me a few days after I'd given up on the moping and was back to normal. Mom had obviously enlisted him in talking some sense into me. He called me into his study when I got home from work around 8:30 one night. It was back to school week at the store and I was tired from fitting all the kids into new school shoes. I needed to vent some pent up frustration over all the demanding parent's asking me for this or that shoe in this or that color so little junior or juniorette could have just the right shoe for the first day of school. I called Kevin from the store and told him to meet me at my house so we could go play some one on one up at the gym as soon as I changed clothes.

The second I walked in the door pops called me into the den where he was sitting eating off a TV tray and watching the news.

"Yeah Dad?" I stuck my head in the doorway.

"Your mother tells me I need to have a talk with you about girls." He said.

I laughed. "That's okay dad. I still remember how everything works from our very first talk."

When I was ten years old, he came to me, turning off the Atari Space Invaders I was playing and said, "It's time for us to have a talk about the facts of life." Then he handed me a book called, "Hey! What's going on down there?" and walked away muttering, "If you have any questions you can come ask me," It was painfully obvious he hoped that I wouldn't have any questions. I didn't. That book became my little resource book for a couple years. But it still makes me laugh to know Pops was too embarrassed to talk to me about sex.

"I'm cool Pops," I tell him, trying to spare him having to go through this again. I moved away from the doorway on my way upstairs to my room.

Dad looked at me as if I had stolen something off the plate of food in front of him. "Boy, get your narrow ass in here!" I must have been really bad off the past week for Pops to break down and talk to me about the way I'd been acting. Every once in a while Pops reminds my brothers and I that he's still the big dog in the house! When he makes up his mind and gets juiced up to talk about something, we have no choice in the matter but to listen.

Kevin had met me at the front door when I got home and followed me into the hallway. I motioned with my head for him to go up to my room and wait for me. He pointed at me, laughing silently in a 'your in trouble' gesture before turning the corner and going up to my room.

"Yeah Dad, I'm listening, but really, I'm fine. I ain't tripping off funky as-, I mean uh, funky Karen no more. Really!"

Pops kept talking as if he hadn't heard me. "That mess you went through over her is just gonna keep happening less you change up, boy!" I cocked my head to the side to indicate I was really listening. Might as well listen to the sermon and get it over with.

"You gotta be a young man, son." He told me. "Don't let a girl break you down. They got to know you can handle yours or else they'll walk all over you." I nodded to show that I was listening and understood.

Pops wasn't finished. "Your momma done told me how ya sniffing around these lil' fast ass girls like a puppy, bending over backwards for em! Your even spending your hard earned money on em with absolutely no discretion." Did my mom really say that about me? Damn! Pops continued, "You can be as twisted or as sprout as you want…. but don't show it man! Keep your cards close to your chest and let THEM wonder what the deal is with YOU! Be a young man not the doormat, son. Cause if you lie down at their feet they will most assuredly wipe their feet all over your back before stepping on! Be the young man I raised you to be, Marcus, and stop letting these little wild gals get you off track!"

"'Sprung' Pops." I interjected.

"Huh?" Pops wrinkled his face.

"*Sprung*. Not sprout." I told him.

"Well what the devil difference does that make to the lesson I'm trying to teach you boy? I know you understand that a hard head makes a soft ass don't cha? Don't interrupt me again boy either, I'm teaching you something about life."

"Sorry Pops" I replied.

"Alright then!" Pops got up and came to stand about three feet in front of me. He stabbed his finger on my chest to punctuate each word, "Then all this moping and moaning and loud music has got to stop Marcus! Don't you forget whose house this is boy, you understand?"

I replied, "Yeah Pops I do." I could hear my brothers in the other room burst out laughing. This will be one of those stories I will hear at Thanksgiving twenty years from now.

Pops stepped back and said in a quieter voice, "God gave you a lot Marcus. He gave you book smarts! And you look like me so you know you're handsome!" Now you know which parent I get my modesty from.

Dad paused for a moment lost for how to get his point across. Then, he put his arm around my shoulders like he used to do when I was much younger. More quietly now he said, "Act like you got the sense God gave you boy! Stop throwing away your gifts on undeserving women. And for God's sake son, don't be afraid to be by yourself for awhile. There is nothing wrong with having the patience to wait for a good woman instead of rushing to fall "in love" with someone who ain't about nothing. And if you're lucky enough you'll find a good woman like I did. Your momma and I have been together twenty-five years. Just remember you're a young man. You have plenty of time. Don't rush it."

I left the den, headed upstairs, and walked into the room trying to be nonchalant. Kevin wasn't having it. "Man what did you *do*?" He asked me, laughing. "I ain't ever heard your old man come at you like that!"

"It wasn't anything. He just wanted to make sure to remind me to make sure I keep up with my chores and stuff. We gonna play ball or what?" I asked, changing the subject as quickly as I changed out of my work clothes into gym shorts and t-shirt.

"Uh huh", Kevin was skeptical. "Whatever, man. Don't tell me! Lets go hit the court!" He grabbed the ball and rushed downstairs and out the door. I took my time tying my shoes, reflecting on what pops had said.

Between him and mom pulling my coat twice in one week, I had no choice but to take what they said seriously. It took sometime and some trial and error but I would always hear their advice ringing in my head after I'd graduated and went on to college. I stopped having serial monogamous relationships and concentrated on quality over quantity. I learned not to be so open right away. To be patient. Wait to see what a woman was all about before I took the plunge and declared my love. I had it all covered.

However, recent events have taught me I hadn't learned those lessons as well as I'd thought. Twenty years later and I'm just now realizing that I hadn't really learned a thing. I look back at the years between "the week of love advice" and now and realize that just until recently when I didn't have a special woman in my life I still felt the void from the absence of female companionship. I wasn't rushing to jump into a new one right away but still I felt the void like a physical ache. Because of that, maybe I've still been doing too much just to have a woman in my life. The difference now is I don't rush to fill the void with just anybody. Nevertheless, when I do have a woman in my life I sometimes wonder if all the damn drama is worth it. When it's "right" though, hell yeah, it's usually worth it, even if it doesn't last. It is to me anyway. Everyone has to decide on their own what they will or won't do to have love in their life. Like Bobby Caldwell crooned so long ago, your friends can wonder what's wrong with you, you act like you are in a daze. It's that love thing. Gets you every time. Makes you do for Love what you would not do. Makes you do for love what you would not do.

Lately

I graduated from college fifteen years ago and it seems like yesterday. Looking back, I think I had the freshman blues when it came to love because I was falling in and out of love every other semester. The word love rarely entered my vocabulary and with most of the women, I just "kicked it" until she or I didn't want to anymore.

I've yet to find that kind of love that lasts forever. I was definitely on the prowl and looking back Valerie started it all off. I dated her right out of college and she was a beautiful woman. I'm not really sure why she and I parted ways. Melody was after Valerie and every time I think about her, it makes me happy then blue.

Melody was the one that got away. She didn't leave me and I didn't walk out on her. Actually, she and I spent all our time together. In the two years she and I were together, we never even had so much as a disagreement. Melody and I worked for the Sheriff's department but she wasn't happy and was searching for something different. She ended up enlisting in the Marines. Melody went off to boot camp and for awhile we managed to talk on a daily basis. Every other weekend, I would drive down to Camp Pendleton and we'd hangout walking the waterfront exploring beautiful San Diego as we talked about life after boot camp.

Two weeks before basic training was due to end Melody didn't call as she usually did. She didn't call the next day or the next and suddenly a week had gone by since I'd talked to her. Melody had no family for me to call to see if they'd heard from her. I tried to get through to her commanding officers but only got voice mail and no returned calls. I'd had enough. I drove to Camp Pendleton and demanded to know what was going on.

Apparently, the military only gives out information to immediate relatives and, as close as she and I were, I wasn't Melody's family. I called the base operator trying to locate a friend Melody had mentioned the last time we'd talked. He was in her unit and saw her daily. I was able to get his number and left a message for him to call me at my hotel. Finally, that Sunday night before I was scheduled to leave, I got a call from her friend. He apologized for not getting back to me sooner. I told him my predicament and there was silence on the phone for a second. To cover my increasing horror at the situation, I half-heartedly joked, "Bruh what's up, where's my girl? Did she get sent on some black ops mission or something?"

Melody's friend spoke quietly into the receiver, "Her funeral was Saturday."

I felt as if someone had ripped my heart out of my body, sucked my soul from it, and then replaced it back inside my chest, beating but still dead.

He continued on, "She was training with our squadron doing night propelling exercises from the helicopter and the chopper went down. It was the pilot's error but they managed to live through their injuries.

Melody…" he paused and my entire body shutdown as I waited for him to continue. "I'm sorry bruh, she died on the way to the hospital. I'm sorry, Marc. I think she had you listed as her next of kin but the number she listed was for her own house and no one knew how to reach you. I'm so sorry. she was an incredible woman and all she could talk about was you."

I hung up the phone hearing his words echoing in my head. I drove to the gas lamp district and walked up and down the streets for what felt like hours. I finally settled down in the Juke Joint because I heard blues being played from outside. I found a corner in the back where it was dark and cried for the loss of my Melody.

I mourned her loss by living like a monk for the next year. I didn't go out. I didn't want to even be in the company of some woman who wasn't my Melody.

About a year after Melody was killed along came Donna. She made me forget about my self-imposed monkish life-style. Donna made me forget about every other woman. I'd met her at a co-ed softball game about 7 years ago. She was the pitcher on the opposing team. There were about 15 of them and Donna was the only woman on the team.

They all worked for the same bookstore. The one where you can get a cup of coffee, grab a book, and sit uninterrupted and read the whole damn book without paying for it if you have the inclination and the time.

Her team was good, considering they were all the bookstore nerdy type. But since it was their first year in the league I think they got nervous when they found out HiCi had won the tournament the previous year. When I saw Donna out there pitching it made me almost (I said, *almost*) not want to hit the ball but you know a brotha can't go out like that. I hit my homerun and ran around the bases thinking about her body in the tight uniform that showed every curve. And she was beautiful as well? Good body, athletic, and good looking. MMMPH! Her jersey number was my lucky number seven. Her hair was pulled back so you could see those Debbie Morgan dimples. She had on those gray baseball pants with two gloves sticking out of her back pockets. I was focused on the booty as I rounded second, third and headed home. The other fellas on the HICI team weren't concentrating on the game either. All eyes were on Donna.

After that first game, Donna started showing up in the stands whenever we played. I eventually went over and talked to her. "So you are stalking me right?" I asked by way of greeting.

She tilted her head to the side and cut her eyes up at me. "If I am, are you gonna turn me in?"

"If you don't go out with me I'll be forced to." No smile on my face or in my voice.

As if thinking through her options she finally said, "Umm, blackmail huh? Well I guess I better agree to go out with you then, eh?"

"Are you Canadian?" I asked.

"Huh," she gave me a bizarre look.

"Nothing. A lot of black folks who aren't from Canada say "eh" at the end of their sentences." My voice and face showing I thought exactly the opposite.

Donna gave up trying to follow that line of talk. "So where are you taking me then?" She asked me.

I stared at this beautiful woman who'd been coming by to see me play for the past few games. I'd mourned Melody long enough. Time to see what could be with the living.

I said, "It's ladies choice as long as you choose correctly."

"Is that like "freedom of speech, just watch what you say?"

"Exactly like that." I said and gave her a quick wink. I love a woman that can hang with some verbal sparring.

We exchanged numbers and agreed to meet at the Plantation, a soul food joint, at 7:30 pm.

As I walked away Donna said, "Don't be late Marcus."

I replied, "I won't. I will be on time. See ya in a few."

I rushed home to shower and change. While the hot water was washing away the sweat of the game I imagined Donna's ass with the gloves sticking out. Apple bottom. MMPH! I definitely wanted to see if it felt as good as it looked. I dressed to impress and went to meet her at the Plantation. Donna told me she loves soul food and the brotha's at the Plantation brought their cooking skills to Sacramento from deep in the heart of Louisiana. I couldn't lose.

I parked my ride under the streetlights because the Plantation may have been serving the best tasting soul food in the city but it was, in reality, a hole in the wall on the outskirts of Sac town's closest thing to a ghetto. When I stepped out of my car, I saw Donna waiting at the screen door to the place. She'd dressed with care as well. A simple black floral print sundress, heeled sandals, a gold anklet on the left leg and a thick gold necklace with two silhouette faces turned in opposite directions.

A Gemini. Look out! Earlier she had been flirtatious and witty. Was the other face of Gemini going to appear tonight, I wondered?

As I approached her with a smile I called out, "I love a woman that can follow orders." She looked at me with B-girl attitude, put her hand on her hip, and threw her neck back. "EXCUSE ME!" She called to me as I approached.

I smiled, "I told you it was your choice as long as you chose correctly. You did well." I said with a wink as I placed my hand on the small of her back and opened the door for her. One of the owners of the Plantation is my frat bruh. He saw me walk in as he stood behind the kitchen counter and nodded to me slightly. I knew the food tonight was going to be off the hook and they'd treat Donna like a queen.

We were seated and offered menus. Donna said, "I've been wanting oxtails for, like, ever! Nobody cooks em like my big momma except the brothers here."

Donna ordered the greens and oxtails with a mac and cheese on the side. I ordered the string beans with half a chicken. I blessed the food and we dug in. Everything was perfect.

Donna and I talked about everything that night. We had a good time. I told her about growing up in Benicia, an uppity neighborhood with only a handful of our people, and how hard it had been to navigate the waters of staying true to my people. I told her how hard it had been to stay 'true to the game', especially considering all around me, there were people who wanted me to just lighten up and be one of the boys. One of the white boys! They wanted me to just forget who and where I came from. It wasn't going to happen. I wasn't about to end up being a "Black surfer dude" from Benicia.

Donna told me about her family. How her mother had wanted her to go to college and get herself 'some education' so Donna wouldn't have to rely on a man like she'd had to do all her life. She told me about her pops who had worked for the railroad since he was 16 years old. He had to drop out of high school to support Donna's mother, who got pregnant with Donna in her sophomore year of high school.

Over dessert of sweet potato pie for me and peach cobbler for Donna she told me, "You know, I owe them so much. They gave up a lot to have me. I mean moms could have just gone to a clinic somewhere and took me right out of her body before I was even a small bump in her stomach. She and my dad could have gone to college but instead they got married when they were still teenagers. They gave up everything. For me! I owe them. They were so disappointed when I didn't go to college and went to work straight out of high school. I feel like I need to makeup for that somehow."

As we were getting ready to leave I said, "Donna, sounds to me like your parents made choices they wanted to make. You don't need to live your life being grateful to them for having you. They made their choices and you need to make yours too. I'm sure they will love you no matter what you do or what choices you make."

Donna gave me a snorting laugh. "I don't know if they would love me if I chose all the things I want to." I didn't know what that was about so I let it lie.

We'd reached her car. I wanted the evening to last a bit longer and asked her if she wanted to go to a club and have a drink. "Thank you, Mr. Haley, but I think I will take my full belly home and hit the sack before I explode. I'm going to have to do an extra hour of palates to work off that meal." She told me with a demure smile.

Of course, I was disappointed. I'd wanted the evening to end with her and I in my bed. I wanted to test my apple bottom theory. I played it cool though. "Well, how about I call you in a bit to make sure you get home okay."

She smiled and said, "I'll be expecting your call, Sir."

She sat down in her sporty gold convertible Cavalier as I reached down to kiss her cheek goodnight. "I'll call you in about an hour. Be good." I told her.

Donna smiled up at me and said, "I'm *always* good, Marcus. You'll see." She winked at me as she drove off into the night.

Hell yeah. That's what I'm talking about! Just because it didn't happen tonight doesn't mean that baby girl wasn't feeling me. She was probably doing one of those, 'I can't go out like that' first date things.

I drove home thinking about Donna's face and body and consoled myself with the certainty that next time she'd be asking to come home with me.

We went out a few more times after that fateful baseball game where she decided to break from her stalking ways and come straight with a brother. Somehow, we never progressed further than a goodnight kiss on the cheek and her rolling off into the sunset. It seemed to me that the 'you'll see' she'd given me after our first date was all talk. On the other hand, maybe she'd just changed her mind.

We did, however, remain in close contact. She'd come by my place and we'd chill or vice-versa. I started to feel like Donna only kept me around because she had to front for her parents so they would think she had made up for her grievous error in skipping college by bringing home a bona fide "educated" brother to maybe be a son-in-law. It was quite apparent that the "skins" was definitely not happening.

I'm a patient man. I waited. Somehow, a few dates turned into a few weeks then a few months, then a few years! I released my testosterone on any number of willing women while I waited for the prize.

None of the other women had that *thing* that Donna had that made me want to just give everything just to spend time in their company.

Donna, for some reason I couldn't quite understand, had put me into the friend zone. She'd tell me everything about herself from the cramps she got around the 20th of every month to the way the men at her job were always jocking her.

Kevin would ask me from time to time if I'd hit that yet. For awhile, I'd tell him no but then one day, after I'd had enough of his questioning, I told him, "Yeah I hit it." My conscious was playing tricks on me but I continued. "We've been keeping it on the QT."

Kevin smiled and said, "Shit I knew you were hitting it a long time ago. Took you long enough to admit it, bruh."

Little did Kevin know but Donna was my girl and it didn't matter if she wasn't feeling me like that. She was good people and just great to be around. So far as I could tell she wasn't kicking it with anyone else so I waited and played it the way she wanted it played. Either way, I got to spend time with her. I was slightly obsessed I guess. In retrospect I guess I always knew that something in Donna was just wired differently. I wanted to think maybe she was following Dr. Laura's prescription and waiting the required 3 to 5 years before becoming intimate with a man. Maybe it was something else entirely.

But it finally happened. One minute we were laughing and joking as we usually did when we watched TV. That night it was the first season of Def Comedy Jam on DVD. We were laughing hard at something Martin Lawrence said and the next minute Donna grew silent, looked around the cozy living room with the muted lights, the fireplace going, me sitting on the opposite end of the couch. Her face held the look of someone who had just had an epiphany and didn't know how to deal with it.

I turned Martin off because obviously something more important was going on here. Donna asked me in a hushed voice, "Did you ever wonder if we would be this close if we had continued dating when we first met, Marc?"

"No Donna, I really don't wonder. Why? Are *you* thinking about it all of a sudden?" I replied in a quiet, hopeful voice.

Donna hopped up and went in her bare feet to the kitchen to refill her wine glass. "Do you want another glass of wine Marc?" She asked me.

I know a stall tactic when I see one. "No thank you." I replied. I was about to turn the TV back on instead of trying to figure out what had just happened with Donna. I'm never up for playing cat and mouse.

I reached for the remote as Donna walked back in holding a glass of merlot. She'd ditched the small glass she'd been using and filled up the large wine goblet. Liquid courage.

"Marc. Don't turn that on k? I think we should talk." I tossed the control back onto the table and sat back on my sofa. I gave a deep sigh but said nothing. "I was just sitting here thinking that you have become my best friend. We hang out all the time. We enjoy each other's company. The only thing we don't do is have sex."

I broke my silence. "Woman, when we first started going out five years ago your behind put the brakes on all that by saying 'I'm not ready for a relationship right now', so I think that was pretty much your call". When she'd told me that I felt for a moment like that same wet behind the ears kid I'd been in high school

"Do you still want me Marc?"

Did I still want her? Of course I still wanted her. I would always want her. I'd just been waiting for her to come to her senses and realize what a good man she was passing up. That's what I was thinking. What I actually said was, "I don't even think about you that way anymore Donna. That's how you wanted it. Remember?" My whole body was getting tense. Was she finally willing to give the whole thing a shot?

"I want to see if being more than friends will work Marc. I'm not worried about us losing our friendship. I know we can make this work! My parents already love you. They can't understand why we aren't a couple.

And the more I think about it the more I realize I can't understand why we aren't a couple either. All the elements are there. You are very attractive. The only question is are you willing to give me a shot and leave them hoochies on the curb?"

I didn't jump up and go WOOOOOHOOOOOOOO! I rubbed my chin and looked at Donna. Sexy, uncertain, Donna.

I thought about the hundreds of times we had gone out or just hung at her home or mine. We'd had disagreements and misunderstandings but still, here she was sitting on my couch drinking wine and watching Def Comedy. Honestly, I couldn't think of anyplace I'd rather be than with her right now, hoochies not withstanding. I touched her hands that were folded into her lap. She cut her eyes up to me with that sexy way of hers. She started a slow crooked smile as I put my other hand on her chin and gently pulled her face to mine.

After that first kiss, Donna and I launched into a marathon of tangled legs, muted moans, and breathless cries of ecstasy. Everything I'd been holding in during the "friend years" I unleashed with a vengeance. Donna matched me in intensity. The girl was incredible.

It was good! Hell, it was great while it lasted. Donna and I did the exclusive thing for almost a year before she dropped that L bomb on me. We were good together as a couple but little things started creeping in. I started to be suspicious.

We'd be together out on a stroll on the beach in San Francisco and she'd point out some chick with a good-looking ass or big breasts. At first, I thought it was cool as hell. However, as time went by I grew suspicious. I even asked her outright is she was attracted to women. That's how I found out about her temper. I thought I'd seen it during the friend years but man she brought it out with a vengeance when I questioned her orientation.

Donna denied it and accused me of not appreciating a woman with any hang-ups about her man looking at other women as long as he was only looking.

Then she broke my heart. A few months after that argument we were laying in bed, I was about to drift off when she said quietly, "Marc, I lied to you baby. I'm so sorry." I lay there in the darkened room with my eyes wide open. I knew immediately what she was talking about. I guess I'd always known.

Donna softly told me she was attracted to a woman named Sheila. Apparently, Sheila was already in Donna's world that first night we'd had sex but they were only acquaintances. They met at the gym and it took a long while before they progressed beyond brief eye contact and nods to each after aerobics class.

Her epiphany the night we were watching Def Comedy suddenly made sense to me. She may have always been attracted to women in general; something she knew would disappoint her parents. However, when her attraction turned from the general to the specific she must have really freaked out about how her parents, and probably everyone else she knew, would take it. She'd used me to stave off her inevitable foray into a lesbian relationship. That's one big ass pill to swallow.

Donna sat up in bed and looked at me with earnest eyes, telling me she was attracted to Sheila but hadn't acted on it. Actually, she said they hadn't acted on it *yet.*

Apparently, both she and Sheila were curious. My woman was coming to me for permission to be with another woman but it didn't sound as if either she or Sheila wanted me up in that mix. Did she just want me to wait and let her have her taste of lesbian life and then decide which she liked better?

Much as I loved Donna, as long as I'd waited for her to want to be with me, I wasn't going out like that.

I played it off as if best I could. "Well Donna, you gotta do 'you' don't you? If you've got an itch to scratch I won't stand in your way. I think you need to go ahead and get your stuff from over here, go home and, you know, learn to deal with your new life. I wish you the best."

I guess I had to be glad she told me about it at all. She could have just hooked up with ole girl and lied about it. I wasn't happy though.

After that late night confessional, Donna took most of her belongings back to her house the next day. She and Sheila obviously acted on their curiosity and discovered they preferred homo to hetero. They were two black sistahs in love and didn't care who knew. Donna's parents were devastated with her news but stood by her. They still call on me from time to time like the son-in-law that never was.

Last year I thought Donna was "the one." Turned out I didn't have the right plumbing for her. Sheila is her woman now.

I've never met Sheila and never seen her up close but I've spotted the two from a distance quite a few times this past year at the grocery store, at the gas station, book store, etc., and they are always hugged up.

They don't care when people stop and stare at the black lesbian show. I can't hate just cause I can't have her but I sure wanted to. I guess it's just hard for me to understand why two beautiful and sexy sistahs are on a lesbian trip. And in Shelia's case, it's more like beautiful Amazon. She's 6-3, curly hair to the middle of her back, 38D's, six pack abs a pierced belly button, with an apple-bottom to round it all off to perfection. Of course, this is according to Donna. I haven't seen her close enough to make the determination myself.

Donna being my latest and greatest, I sometimes wonder if I had come at her stronger or played the He-Man act a bit more things would have gone differently. No way to know. Besides, I can't be someone I'm not hoping to get my woman to stay with me. Pops taught me that.

After Donna's devastating news, I remembered momma telling me every woman ain't worth the trouble. I fronted like it was cool to family and friends, as if I was unfazed by the sudden disappearance of Donna from my life.

I was playing basketball with Kevin last week when he asked if I still hear from her. "Yeah we talk every once in a while, usually when she needs something." I told him.

He grabbed the ball to stop the game action for a second and asked with a sly grin, "They ever let you play, man?"

I grabbed the ball back from him and sunk a sweet shot. "Man, I ain't trying to be in the mix with them crazy broads. I like my action one on one." I told him.

Kevin laughed. "Negro, your ass ain't lived till you've done two at a time." He and I were on different tracks. He wanted the bachelor life forever. I let it go and finished whooping his ass on the court.

It's a Thin Line Between Love & Hate

According to the chirpy, valley girl, news anchor that popped up on the TV screen in the darkened room, waking me up, it was a cool 35 degrees outside. I rolled onto my stomach and stared blurry-eyed at the clock on the table. It read a couple of minutes before 5 a.m. I reached out and hit the off button so it wouldn't go off at 5 a.m. and turned over onto my back with my forearm resting on my face.

I stayed in that position for a little while, staring at the ceiling, waiting for inspiration to hit before I could jump out of bed and begin my usual routine. Get up, shower, watch the news while getting dressed, eat the usual two eggs, two slices of bacon, two slices of wheat toast, and have a few cups of coffee. My Monday through Friday routine has rarely varied in ten years. Before that though, as a detective with the Sacramento County Sheriff's Dept., the only routine I could count on was one given to me by the dept. The hours were erratic, and the work was crazy and dangerous. Add being passed over for promotion one time too many and I'd had enough of that life. That's why for the past ten years, ever since quitting the force and opening my own agency, I revel in my *routine,* particularly the morning work day one. It's the most relaxing time of day. I took a few more moments to enjoy the warmth of my bed as I continued to think back on my life. I guess knowing I'd be turning 35 in a few months had me wanting to take stock, see what was working for me and what I needed to work on.

Ultimately I had to admit, life has been pretty good overall. I've been blessed. I've had my share of disappointments, of course, but who hasn't? My motto is "treat others the way I want to be treated" and for the most part, I've done this. I'm no different than the next guy. Okay maybe the next guy who has his stuff together not the next guy who is turning 35 still living with his momma, still blaming the man for why he can't get anything going.

I've had my ups, downs, twists and turns just like everyone. I take the good with the bad and play the hand I'm dealt without complaint. Well, without too much complaint anyway. Sometimes you just gotta say something to the dealer about the shitty hand he keeps dealing you. But I've learned in the last thirty five years that sometimes what I thought was a horrible deal turned out to be the best thing that could have ever happened to me.

For example, when I first started working for the Sheriff's department out of college, I was assigned to the coolest Captain in the department. She liked my work and promoted me at the earliest opportunity at the earliest possible time. I moved to an undercover assignment. Little did I know that what I took for a blessing, being promoted, turned out to be a curse. I went from working for the coolest captain to having the king of all asshole's as a boss. For the next few years he and I bumped heads like bulls in the same stable. It was alpha male against alpha male and since he outranked me, it was his say so that caused me to be passed over for detective three times due to his yearly evaluations of my work. Understand this, I was an excellent undercover officer. But the Lt. would put shit on my eval like, 'questions superiors orders' and 'difficult to get along with'. The only person I had difficulty getting along with was him, because I was the only one who wouldn't kiss his ass.

I worked my ass off and never once received a citizen complaint. I had an impeccable record and exemplary service. While working undercover, I bought and sold drugs like I had grown up working the streets. In actuality, I'd gone to a practically all white high-school deep in suburbia and attended an elite college. Therefore, for the third year running when I was passed over for promotion for some big boobs whose service record didn't even come close to mine I walked away and didn't look back.

I took my anger at the system and used it to fuel my struggle to get my agency going. It worked. Funny. The *department* now comes to me for work they need done that a badge would just get in the way of. Screw the department. I'm piling up money and favors for their short-sightedness in letting me walk.

Even though I've been successful, thanks in large part to the work the department threw my way; I just have a funny feeling that my 35th year was definitely going to be my most successful year ever. The big four zero is going to bring me success beyond everything I've achieved so far. I could feel it in my bones.

With that positive affirmation, I stopped dwelling on the past. Time to seize the day! I jumped out of bed ready to kick ass and take names. Then I jumped right back in bed. Maybe right now wasn't the time to be seizing anything. I pulled the covers up over my body. It was freaking 35 degrees outside, I remembered hearing. The house was pretty cold. Maybe I ought to start wearing pajamas so when I get out of bed I won't turn into a block of ice.

I normally sleep butt naked because I have heated blankets and that's the most comfortable way to sleep. Pajamas are just not necessary. I keep the temperature on the blanket around 78 degrees which is nice and toasty. Getting out of a comfortable 78-degree bed and stepping bare-assed into a cold room is not the most pleasant way to get the morning started. I thought briefly of Melody as I always did at times like this. She'd have had me so hot after her usual good morning hello that when I stepped naked out of bed I couldn't feel anything but the warm afterglow of making love to my woman.

I put that thought aside. Tried as I always did to bury it in the past where it belonged. Enough procrastination! It's time to get up. Bare-assed and swinging I jumped up and ran to put on my robe hanging on the back of the bathroom door. While belting the robe I headed straight to the heater. "Its cold as a witch's tit in this camp!" I said out loud to myself. I pushed the buttons on the thermostat to turn the heater on.

Once the digit's read 80 degrees, I went back to the bathroom and turned on the shower full blast. I use only hot water so it will steam the room up. It keeps my skin smooth and keeps my fern green. I can't stand a cold house. If I had a floor heater, it would have been on full blast too.

If I ever had the opportunity to trace my lineage beyond slavery, I'm sure I'd find my folks in the hottest of the hot African regions. I can see it now. My great, great, great, great, great grandfather, King Marcusofa, walking around the village soaking up the UV rays, sipping on some African spiced Lion juice from a gourd, listening to the music of kids and animals playing together in the sun. Over there? That's my great, great, great, great grandfather Marcobi walking a rhino trying to look impressive for the ladies sitting under the giant baobab tree shading themselves. My desire for all things hot is in my blood. My birthright.

While the shower was heating up, I walked over and turned the TV off. Normally I would watch the morning madness on the news while the shower starts steaming up the bathroom. For some reason today was different. I wasn't in the mood for who got shot, who is sleeping with who, why professional, rich, as hell athletes are striking again, or which politician was about to meet his downfall because he was caught with his hands or cigar in the wrong cookie jar.

Switching up, I grabbed the remote for the stereo system built into the wall unit, pushed the button for disc 10 and Maxwell's smooth voice came crooning out of the hidden speakers. This was the first time I'd heard this old cd in a long while. Brother said he was reborn when he was broken…I hear you Maxwell, work it all out this lifetime. I felt that shit.

I'd 'been reaching out for something better than I had before', too. Damn, that Negro can sing and he better be glad I'm a man cause if I were a woman I'd stalk his ass just to get him to sing to me. I am *passionate* about good music, good food, and good wine. I walked downstairs singing to myself, "I can let my life pass me by" Swore I sounded just as good as Max. In the kitchen, the coffee was brewing right on schedule.

"I can move to the light, Oh if I take it one day at time, Oh spread my love out and fly…."

Just as I passed the front entranceway crossing into the kitchen, the damn doorbell rang, interrupting Maxwell and I as we crooned. Hmm, now who in hell is out in this cold this early in the morning to see me? It could be a neighbor in trouble. Could just be trouble all by it's lonesome. I grabbed my 40-caliber pistol out of my coat in the hall closet and headed to the door.

That bum-rushing the door, home invasion robbery shit ain't happening here. I pulled my combat boots out of the entranceway closet just in case I have to put my foot in someone's ass. The bell rang again. Impatient robber I guess. "Hold On!" I called out irritably. I slipped on the boots and tied my robe tighter. If trouble was out there on my doorstep, it was about to meet trouble's daddy.

"Who is it?" I yelled. I didn't hear anything except a low mumble. I gripped my troublemaker. Ready to use it if I had too. "Yo speak up! Who the hell is at my door? A female voice called through the paneling,

"It's me Donna. Open up, Marckie."

Marckie? Donna's my ace still, but what's up with the Marckie' shit? I'm not feeling that one bit. And after a year of only hearing her voice on the phone what the hell is she doing showing up out of the blue so early?

I opened the door and put the gun in the pocket of my robe.

"Hey *hey*, whatcha doing in my neck of the woods this early?" I said, while giving her a one armed hug.

Donna smiled and cut her eyes at me tilting her head slightly like she does when she is flirting. You know that look. It's a look that says, 'Come get me'.

"Well obviously I came to see *you*, Marc."

I stepped back and allowed her to walk in. As she passed, I gave her the once over. She was wearing a tight trench coat, pumps, and black stockings with a seam up the back? It's all of 5:30 in the morning and she's dressed like Jessica Rabbit on my doorstep? I asked, "What's going on D?"

Donna turned around like the models that do the half turn on the runway and opened up the trench coat.

I was like a deer in the headlights. My eyes briefly popped out of my damn skull before I regained composure. I didn't speak though. I stood in the doorway of my home at 5:30 in the morning with a gun in my robe, Maxwell coming through the sound system, and my friend and ex standing there in a peek-a-boo outfit that would put Frederick's to shame and me playing a mental game with junior, trying to keep him in check. I chuckled and rubbed my goatee but couldn't move. My heart started beating faster and faster as I soaked up the vision of her bad ass body in the negligee.

I forgot the door was open. Donna said, "You trying to get my high beams going? It's cold Marckie!" I chuckled again and closed the door.

"Sorry about that. You know how to come in with a bang, don't you D?"

I'm not ashamed of the trance I went into when she went into her striptease.

I mean Donna had an ass like 'POW', her breasts were like, 'WOW', and the whole package together was about to bring the freak out in me. It had been a long LONG time since I'd seen Donna this way.

Remember that old cut, "Break up to make up?" That song was written for Donna and I, no doubt. Looked like she was in make up mode right now. What else could she be doing at my spot dressed like that?

Once the blood started going back to my brain I started thinking this wasn't like Donna to just show up without calling. She wasn't the type to just go at the drop of a dime. She was all about making plans. Some weird control thing I guess. Donna believed in setting up appointments, making reservations, and calling to confirm before doing just about anything. I've actually heard her call the gas station and say, 'Hello, this is Donna, are there any lines at the pumps and what's the price on your unleaded today?'

So knowing this about Donna I said, "Donna, what's up, everything okay?"

It was a little awkward to have this conversation when her nipples were calling out to me from behind the lacy see through material.

"Marc, I know this isn't me. I normally don't show up without calling. She picked up her coat and put it back on while walking towards the sunken living room. "This is totally out of character for me. Um... I was on my way to work and the damn tire blew? The tire on my car?"

She gave me this little devilish smile, as if hoping I would buy her damsel in distress story and put on my shining armor to rescue her.

I kept my mouth shut and my eyes focused on her face. I wasn't playing whatever game she wanted to play today.

"Wow Marc, aren't you happy to see me? It's been so long plus I knew you'd be up and I just thought I'd surprise you okay?" she said with a deliberate pout.

Ignoring the obvious come on I said, "On the real now, come for real." Got me stuttering, ain't that some shit? "What's up with the", I gestured to the lacy outfit, "and the striptease?"

I walked over and pushed Donna's shoulders so she was sitting. Then I sat on the glass table in front of the sofa and looked her in the eyes.

"Is that a gun in your pocket or are you just happy to see me?" Donna said with a cheeky grin, still trying.

"It's a gun." I tell her, as if to let her know I am unaffected by her game.

She stared back at me and tried to keep the flirty thing going. Her eyes went from the top of my head, then slid down my chest and rested on the "magic stick" which was about to tent pole my robe.

Oh it's that kinda party? Well hell, I thought, we *are* both consenting adults.

I got a vision of 50's video in my head. "I've got the magic stick, I know I can hit once I can hit twice." Though my face betrays nothing, my imagination has me working Donna over, bumping and grinding on the floor right here in the living room.

I snapped out of it when she leaned forward and got to her knees in front of me. She was jump-starting my fantasy so why stop her? Maybe cause I know Donna too well. This was some weird shit she was pulling. She put her hands on both my thighs. Before I lost the power of reason, I grabbed her chin and forced her to look at me.

"DONNA! Seriously, what's up? You trying to come back? You trying to give me a birthday blowjob? What's up? Cause all this mystery isn't necessary. If you wanna fuck just tell me."

She gave me a fake smile and even faker laugh. But the harshness of my words got through to her, I think. She scooted back up and sat on the edge of the couch.

"I don't know what I'm doing Marc." Donna got to her feet and started playing with the belt of her coat but wouldn't look at me.

At least I wasn't Marckie anymore. Donna looked on the verge of tears. I hadn't seen her do this kind of flip-flop of worrisome emotion in the 7 years we've known each other. I already know the, "I need to borrow some money" look, and the "I need a place to lay my head" look. This one was awkward. It hit me in that instant how much she must be hurting right now to come to my spot with the act she had just performed. She better be glad I think with the head on my shoulders. Otherwise, I might have taken her up on her offer and asked questions later.

Donna started doing her signature "I'm in distress" move. Rubbing her scalp at the back of her head. I didn't press her and she didn't speak.

She caught herself telling on herself and put her hands in her lap, tossed one of her beautiful dimply smiles and opened her mouth to speak but closed it again and slumped onto the couch instead and went back to rubbing the back of her head.

I had to get that outfit off my mind. I tried to focus on the neurotic head rubbing woman and the real reason for this visit. All the right stuff was being pushed out of my head by visions of whip cream, banana split's on tight bellies, hot oils, nipple rings like Janet's. All the things I could do to that body. The memory of her and I together was working on me to make it happen again. I was ready for some action.

I got up to switch on the fireplace because it was cold. I could tell that Donna had goose bumps cause she kept rubbing her arms. Damn if I didn't see those high beams after all, poking through the nightie and imprinting on the trench coat. The freak in me was ready to come out. I began thinking about what I could be doing right here, right now. "Yeah, yeah...get it get it, don't stop, get it get it." How quickly my thoughts went from supportive friend to my own satisfaction.

Again, I focused back on what brought Donna to my house this morning because the look on her face was making me worry. It didn't help, either, that Maxwell was playing and it was all about emotions and shit, I focused back in on her; waiting for her to tell me what the hell was going on.

Took too long! I flashed and it was all about me again. Donna wasn't helping me stay focused on her problems when she said, "Damn you got Maxwell playing, coffee brewing, the shower going. Can I join you? I smiled like a kid in the candy store. But just as quickly as she turned it on, she shut it back down, "Oh wait! I'm sorry did I interrupt something, do you have company?" Ain't that something? She knew the answer to that question because if I had company I wouldn't have opened the door. Donna gave me that devilish smile cause she knew she interrupted the mental image her words had created.

"Did I open the door for outside company when you were my inside company?" I asked her. She gave me a crooked smile and closed her eyes as if remembering all the times she'd been here and we'd ignored everything outside that door. Last summer we'd kicked it so hard, the doorbell would ring when she was visiting but I pretended as if I hadn't heard it. We could have been just playing cards or snuggled up watching a movie. It didn't matter.

"Look Donna, I'm going to run upstairs and turn the shower off. Get your story together about why you are here because I want to hear it when I get back."

I walked over to the closet and put my boots away then stashed the gun back in my coat. As I was heading back up the stairs I called down to Donna, "By the way, the coffee is in the kitchen. You know where everything is so help yourself. I'll be right back."

I walked up the three flights of stairs slowly; halfway hoping with each step I took that Donna would be taking steps following me, taking off what little she had on. As I continued my climb, I was visualizing Donna right behind me taking off the jacket, panties, bra, lace stuff, heels, and leaving a trail on the stairs as she followed me up to my bed. When I got to the top of the stairs I could hear her downstairs humming to Max.

Donna the Diva is one of those people that make other people just want to be in her company. She's my girl regardless of her orientation.

She's good people and it just didn't work out for her to be "the one". Good thing I never gave her the ring I'd bought her.

I turned off the shower, tossed my robe on the bed, and slipped into some comfortable pj's. I knew I wouldn't be going into the office on time. Donna was at my house in a negligee and I'm sorry, that's worth going in late each and every time. If I could get to the bottom of what prompted all this I might just play along.

I sat on the bed and dialed the office to check my messages. "Hello, You've reached Haley, Inc., Confidential Inquiries. Sorry, our office is now closed. If you know your party's extension..." I still have a hard time believing it all. I'd worked so hard to get it going and every time I hear my Personal Assistant's greeting, I get a fresh feeling of euphoria just to realize this professional, almost sensual voice on the voice mail works for me! This is my business! Yeah, momma, your boy did something good. Haley, Inc. Confidential Inquires ' is often referred to as "HiCi". I like the way that sounds. It's got a good ring to it. Anyway, I obviously wasn't alone in liking Ashley's voice so much. A lot of clients ask about her after she transfers them to me. Some have even been brave enough to come down to the office just to see the face behind the voice. I left a message for her to screen my calls and let me know if something important came up.

I made my way back down the stairs and watched Donna doing a slow sensuous dance to Max in the middle of my living room. Damn I'm jealous. I wish I could sing like him and make the ladies just warm up inside. I can hold a tune but I'm no vocalist. I'll leave the singing up to Max and Ruben and the others to set the mood right for me. Like the mood right now.

Donna had poured me a cup of coffee prepared exactly as I like it. I sat on the couch, sipped my coffee, and watched her sway.

Okay Donna, the jig is up. What's the deal?

Out loud I said, "So you show up after all this time...damn near naked...get a brotha's nerves all out of sorts and still haven't said what the hell you are doing here. Talk to me!!" Donna sat down and looked at her hands for about five minutes, quiet as a church mouse. She'd open her mouth to say something and close it again with a big sigh. Put her head back and roll her eyes up as if hoping the words she wanted were written on the ceiling. I waited with an expectant, enquiring look on my face. But even while I was being forceful about her telling me what was up I couldn't help reminiscing about the times she and I had shared.

"Marc?" I snap back to the here and now once again. Donna finally seems ready to talk.

"You and I have known each other for a long time. I've always been able to tell you things I can't share with anyone else. You have always been there for me."

"Buuuuuuuuut?"

"Hush. Let me finish now that I finally know what to say. Anyway, through the ups and downs we have always been good friends, eventually lovers, able to hang tough no matter what."

What the fuck is going on was what I wanted to know. Is this a kiss off? I love you but I can't be your friend anymore? Nah, if that's what she was going to say why the sexy get up? Plus, we'd only spoken on the phone several times during the last year, we hadn't seen each other there wouldn't be any need to make a big goodbye speech. All she'd have to do is just stop calling. I certainly wasn't going to try and track her ass down.

What the hell? It's too early in the morning for this shit. All this is going through my head but other than clinching my jaw tighter I remained silent. I'd never known Donna to be this erratic. Flirty and sexy one second, on the verge of mute tears the next, then rambling about how much I mean to her.

As if she couldn't hold it anymore Donna suddenly wailed, " Sheila is seeing a MAN and now she's pregnant! I don't know who else to go to Marc. Nobody else understands!"

She put her head in her hands and sobbed so hard her shoulders shook. "Shit! She's pregnant! Why would she do that to me! God I hate her!"

I don't know what I was expecting but it certainly wasn't that. So maybe she came over here dressed like that trying to play a game of tit for tat? All this drama over some revenge sex? And why in hell did I stop her?

Trying to readjust the situation in my head, I watch Donna as she, obviously in pain, continues to sob into my sofa. She must really be in love with Sheila. I don't remember a single tear during our time together.

"Awhh damn, that's rough, Donna. I'm sorry this is happening to you." I told her. As much as I would have liked to have seen Donna be completely heterosexual, I know it wasn't going to happen. For her to come here acting like this, I don't even know what to think. Should I be flattered? Should I be pissed? I'll figure it out later.

"I'm sorry," I tell her. "Are you sure?" I asked, no response. "Sheila's pregnant?" I asked again, "Cause you don't have any sperm." I have an amazing ability to inject humor where humor is most inappropriate. I opened my mouth for another one liner and Donna shot me a tear stained 'fuck you' look.

"I wish I did have sperm! And it's not f-f-unny Marc so stop joking about my FUCKED UP LIFE!!" Donna shouted and slouched further into the couch crying even more loudly.

All my pity dried up in an instant. I got a taste of bile in my mouth. The taste of hate. Ain't this some shit? Far as I know Donna has never cried over me! I thought men were supposed to be cold but this was stone cold ignorant shit. When her ass left outta of my life a year ago she had to know it wasn't an easy thing for me. We had been hanging as friends for years and lovers for the last one. All of a sudden, she is off exploring her new life and Marc is the last person on her mind. I didn't tell her it broke my heart that I wasn't what she was looking for or needed. But she knew. She had to have known.

Now she comes over here dressed to fuck and is crying over some damn woman? There are limits to every friendship. I'd just found the limits to mine and Donna's. This ride is over. Now.

I was just about to bum rush her up out of my spot when she looked up at me with so much hurt in every unshed tear in her eyes. I closed my eyes and inhaled deeply then swallowed my pride. I'd definitely tell her about herself later. I'd tell her about how horrible it was to find out your significant other didn't want you anymore. Later. Right now, I'd be the friend I used to be.

"How do you know all this is true, Donna? Maybe you misinterpreted something innocent"? I asked her quietly while trying to control the emotions going to war inside of me.

In a tight, trembling, bitter voice Donna spoke as if reliving it all over again. "Marc, I had the late shift at the book store last night. I usually don't get home until after two in the morning on my late nights." She paused; looking as if she was about to break down all over again, took a deep breath and continued. "We finished closing out a whole lot earlier than normal for some reason and Marc all I could think about was snuggling up close to Shelia. I practically skipped my happy ass home cause I was two hours early and I thought maybe we'd have time to pull out the stupid toys and play." My brain went to that potential scene for a second before I got it under control.

"Marc," she's whispering now, "I walk in the bedroom and Sheila is laid up there in MY BED with some buff Mandingo Negro. They were buck ass naked and wrapped around each other like this wasn't the first time they had been lying together like that. Like they are up in a hotel room or some shit." Donna continued bitterly. "I was in so much shock I couldn't believe it. I wanted to rush in and snatch that bitch bald and cut his dick off!" Now that was the Donna I knew. I was hoping she didn't really do it though. I would hate to see Donna caught up in a legal case she was sure to lose.

"Marc, I just backed away quietly and closed the door." I breathed a sigh of relief. She went on, "I went to the guest bathroom to try to calm myself down. I was crying so much. I was sitting on the toilet and using handfuls of toilet paper to blow my nose and wipe my eyes. I had a pile this high!" She indicated a space from her lap to the middle of her stomach. "I picked it all up, mad at myself for being such a pussy. Soon as I had it all, I leaned over to the trashcan beside the toilet and noticed a box peeking out from another mountain of toilet paper. I pulled it out, Marc. It was an EPT." I held my breath as Donna continued in a hushed voice.

"I knew I hadn't bought the shit and with Sheila up in there with this goddamn nigga I knew exactly what I would find.

"Sure enough, rapped up in more wads of toilet paper was the test strip. It had a little plus in the window. You know what that means, right?" I nodded.

"Damn!" was the extent of what I could offer right now. I know if I had walked in on my non-existent woman in my bed with her lover I'd probably end up in jail for busting caps in both their asses. I certainly wouldn't have politely closed the door and backed away and out of the house as Donna had done. She said she checked into a hotel that night and hadn't spoken to Sheila since.

However, Donna has a temper. One that is quick and fierce. After her initial burst of anger runs out, she is usually contrite and apologetic as all hell but when that temper first rears up look out! It occurred to me maybe that Donna didn't just back away and leave the two cheaters sleeping in each other's arms. Maybe she was trying to drag me into some real serious shit that fierce temper of hers got her into. Did she kill them then come over here to try to seduce me into helping her get rid of the bodies?

Damn. I had to laugh at myself. I've been in law enforcement and worked around low life criminals too long. Everybody's a cold-blooded suspect before proven guilty in a court of law. Maybe I won't convict Donna of a crime of passion right this second.

I stood up and grabbed Donna's hands, pulling her up to a standing position. "Come here woman." I said, giving her a long rock solid bear hug. "Stop all that crying now. Every person you have a relationship with is not worthy of your tears. Don't shed a single tear for someone who treats you wrong, woman!" It seemed to be working cause the sobbing turned to small whimpers. I continued, "She brought someone else into your bed. That makes her unworthy of you, Donna. Maybe you ought to be glad you found out what kind of person Sheila is before you all did something crazy, like get inseminated or adopt a baby like you've been talking about."

Donna's whimpering turned into heavy sighs. I could tell my momma's wisdom cut through the bullshit and hit it's mark, even in this new age of *alternative lifestyles*.

I continued to calm my girl down. I had to utilize some mind control over junior because all of a sudden it struck me how little there was separating me and Donna, my robe and her thin coat and lace thong. Somehow, I managed to block out the sexual connotations of our situation and just continued to hug and shush Donna. It had been a long time since I'd held her in my arms like this. It felt good. It felt like home. Except, it wasn't.

FOOL OF ME

I pulled a bit away from Donna and wiped the tears from her cheeks. She looked at me with those huge eyes and forced a smile. "Marc." Donna said softly. "I'm so sorry! I'm sorry for busting in on you, trying to trick you into some crazy idea of revenge against Sheila. Its not even like she'd care, anyway." Shrugging her shoulders, Donna sat down again as if in surrender. I remained silent but sat down beside her and put my arm around her shoulders. Donna rested her head in the crook of my arm. I was at war with myself. Maybe now that she'd had a taste of the other side of life she was ready to come back to the hetero team? Then again, did I really want to put myself out there for her again like that?

"One thing is for sure," Donna said, "I'm through with Sheila. There are plenty of other women out there, right? I'm gonna go confront her ass and pack my shit." She had another epiphany. Donna animatedly asked, "Can I hole up here with you for a few days while I sort out what I'm going to do about a place to stay?"

Immediately, I thought about how torturous it would be for me to have Donna in my home, in the guest bed next door to my room, or even the one downstairs, and not really 'have' her. And I know Donna. In the middle of the night, she'd get up, say something like she was cold or lonely, and want to crawl into bed with me *just to cuddle.* She'd be making sure I took care of her needs and never stop to think about what taking her was costing me. She was just like that. Not intentionally cruel but just totally clueless sometimes.

Donna had basically just let me know in no uncertain terms that she wasn't thinking about trying to be with a man again so why should I allow her all up in my world again. Then again, I had given her my blessing to go off into her new life without ever telling her how much it hurt. I'd fronted like we could be friends. If it were my boy Kev or one of my brothers, I'd let them shack for a few days without a second thought. Time to fake the funk again, I guess.

"Yeah Donna," I told her softly. I laid my cheek against the top of her silky hair. It smelled of mint and jasmine. I was struck with the memory of that smell combined with the sweat we'd generate when we used to work each other out like it was a vendetta. But I had to realize that the memory of that was all that I would have of Donna from now on. I would let her stay but it had to be on my terms.

"You can stay for a few days. I'll even have Ashley help you look for a place in your price range." I cleared my throat. "But hey, since this could get weird, lets have some ground rules, yes?"

I looked down at Donna as she straightened up from her resting place in my arms. "What is it Marc? I'll do anything just so long as I don't have to go back home to Sheila."

"It's just uh," I cleared my throat, "well, I know this is going to be a tough time for you. I will be here for you as I would any of my friends."

Before I could continue, Donna squealed and rapped her arms around my neck. "Marc, you are the *best*. What would I do without you?"

I cleared my throat again, determined to let her know that I wasn't going to be her pit stop between women lovers. "Okay but here is the deal Donna. While you are here, you need to be thinking of what you are going to do from here on out. There's not going to be anything else between us but friendship." Donna looked at me with round, innocent eyes. I knew what was coming next. Or I thought I did.

Bam! Bam! Bam! A mutherf$^@$*@ was trying to kick my front door down!! It sounded so loud it had to be two or three people. Whoever was out there was determined to get inside. Bam! Bam!

I hissed into Donna's ear "Go upstairs. Now!" She wasted no time in rushing past the front door towards the stairs and squealed again as the banging continued.

I smiled to myself as I quietly opened the closet again and grabbed my 40 and slipped my boots back on. With all the drama suddenly going on in my world, it was obvious someone just didn't want me to have a nice, quiet, morning. Cause whatever was going on was going to take a while to clear up, of that, I was sure. I am always down for some foul and rough play!! What crazy ass thinks they can bust their way into Marcus Haley's house? What asinine *FUCK* thinks I'm gonna put up with this shit!

I position myself on the side of the door and waited for the lock to bust open from the force of all that banging. Sounded like metal meeting wood. As soon as I got positioned damn if my front door didn't swing wide open with the door handle flying into the living room!

Wow!! After the door swung open and hit the wall, into the foyer here comes this big ass, 6 foot 5 burley mannish woman. She was wearing sweat pants, sweatshirt, Nikes, a beanie cap, and starter jacket. I could only tell it was a woman from the huge breasts straining against the sweatshirt.

Good thing I'd clicked off the lights when I stood beside the door. My eyes had time to adjust to the absence of light. Hers obviously had not. I knocked her in the head with the gun instead of shooting her cause I'd already quickly run through all possible scenarios and surmised what this was all about. It wasn't worth a bullet in the ass.

She fell to the floor unconscious. I quickly peeked around the corner to see if this crazy broad had gotten back up. My neighbor, Stanley, was looking out from his porch and I yelled, "Everything is okay, just an old buddy stopping by." He gave me the "damn Marc, its too early for this shit look" and closed his door.

Once his door was closed, I said loudly, for Donna's sake, who was still upstairs waiting on the outcome, "Now, who the hell is this? I know I never made love to a woman big as Shaq!" I looked up the stairs at Donna peeking behind the wooden balustrades on the second floor landing. As I spoke, I saw Donna's eyes go wide with terror!

As I've said, I'd never met Shelia personally and Donna and I had rarely discussed her during our infrequent phone calls except the time she gave me the detailed description of her new woman. But in spite of the dim light, I recognized Donna's significant other without a doubt. Donna crept down the stairs holding rail with one hand and covering her mouth with the other.

"OH my God its Shelia!!" She squealed, rushing down the stairs two at a time.

"No shit? So this is Big Shelia, eh?" I said, borrowing Donna's speech habit. "Awwwwh Shit!! You got a big ass she-man, Donna!" I said and giggled. I couldn't help myself. This situation was too crazy for words!

"It's not funny Marc, what did you do, did you shoot her? Help her!" Donna reached down to the immobile bulk on the floor and looked back up at me. "Did you kill her? Fuck Marc, I'll never forgive you for this!" She screamed at me.

I peaked out the busted door to make sure my neighbor didn't reappear. No sign of him.

"I knocked her ass out for kicking down my door!! Shit!" Ain't this some shit, a fool kicks my door down and now I'm suppose to be sorry I knocked her out? Damn!

Donna was softly checking out the quick growing knot upside Sheila's head and looking at me helplessly as if I were supposed to do something. If this had been anyone else but Donna, I'd have whooped the intruder's ass a little more and dragged him or in this case her out to the street. Instead, cause Donna is my girl, and I'm sure she hadn't wanted it to end exactly this way, I went into my study and grabbed some handcuffs and stopped in the bathroom to get a wet rag. I came back around the corner and started to reach down and hand it to Donna then pulled up short.

"Hey!" I said, "I am not the one to pamper someone busting down my door. And speaking of 'my door' how in the hell did she know where my house was?" I asked, angry for real for the first time.

"I'm sorry, Marc. I'm so sorry! I drove by one evening to show her the kind of house I liked, and told her it was yours but that was a long time ago."

"Donna! You are trippin! You know I can't be having just any ole body knowing where the bat cave is!" I told her as I reached down to check big ass Shaq/Sheila's pulse. "She's alright. Maybe her ass will think twice before knocking somebody else's door down but she'll live." I told Donna in as a controlled voice as I could manage. This shit was ludicrous.

I mean *DAMN*! Here I was one minute trying to rearrange my frame of thought to allow Donna to stay with me for a few days without allowing her to get under my skin again, next minute I have Donna and her lesbian drama all up in my living room and a busted door to boot!

I tried to readjust to this new age thing. Being a friend, imagining this was Kev or a frat bro or some other male friend in the middle of some crazy drama, I gave her the 'you know I don't like that shit look but quickly followed up with a its gonna be okay grimace.' I figured we'd get Sheila to wake up, send her on her merry way, and then figure out how Donna was going to fix her life. Without Sheila.

I finally handed Donna the wet rag with one hand. When she took it and began to carefully tend the knot upside Sheila's head I leaned over to handcuff her.

"What the hell do you think you are doing, Marc?" Donna looked at the cuffs then at me as if I were an intruder in my own home.

I strained to remain calm. I don't know if I achieved it. "I'm cuffing her big ass because when she wakes up she might try to get funky, and have to get another ass whooping. Why you bugging on me Donna? She broke into my house. She cheated on you and got pregnant by some *MANDINGO! REMEMBER*? Or is all forgiven already?" I asked in disgust.

"Marc!" Donna was begging. "Please don't cuff her, I'll talk to her once she's coherent, she won't trip I promise. I'm not with her anymore but please just don't cuff her! Its too much!"

I dropped the cuffs to the floor. "Whatever." I said to Donna as I straightened and walked away. I could see in her eyes if I cuffed the "big one" Donna would never forgive me. I walked away leaving the two on the floor of my entranceway.

When I woke up this morning, all I was thinking about was breakfast, work, and turning 35. Now, just an hour later, I was mixed up in some crazy drama. I was trying to help a friend by lending an ear, offering a place to lay low for a while. What did I get for my trouble? Donna, looking at me as if I'd suddenly grown horns; like I was some kind of woman beater. Hell, when Sheila burst through that door I didn't know if she had a gun or a crowbar or anything. I had the right to protect my home against any intruder. Admittedly, on closer inspection of Sheila once she was unconscious I realized Sheila wasn't as burly as I'd originally thought. She was wearing a mans jacket, maybe two or three sweat pants, 2 hooded sweatshirts, and a damn beanie covering her thick hair. Why in hell was she wearing all those clothes? Maybe she expected the thick padding to absorb the shock if blows were thrown. Hell, I'm not going to try to figure that crazy bitch out.

I walked into the garage got some tools, screws, and spare hinges to fix my front door. Good thing I'm good about keeping my toolbox well stocked. Never knew what could happen or when you'd need to fix a door knocked down by an Amazon.

Back in the living room, Shelia was moaning. Guess she was awakening from the bonk I served up on her. It must have been a pretty good pop on the head because she appeared to be puzzled and shocked at her location as she struggled to sit up. Donna sat there with the cool towel to the back of Shelia's head. I shook my head in disgust. Well, I guess the least I could do is offer up one of my ice packs.

I put my tools and screws and hinges on the side table on the other side of the door, and went to the kitchen. I got one of the frozen plastic covered blue ice packs I use to keep my beer cold when I'm out on the water trying to catch salmon or whatever else was in season. I covered the ice pack with a kitchen towel and walked back to the two women on my floor.

Donna appeared to be caught between a rock and hard place. She was trying to figure out what to do in this awkward situation. There she sat with her lover who just received an ass whooping from her best male friend for trying to break in. She looked at me and just continued to blink her eyes as if to try to say something but unable to find the words.

"Don't trip. It's all good. I'm not mad at you and your girl can stay as long as she doesn't act up." I told her.

I could see the relief in her eyes after. I handed her the ice pack and Shelia, sitting with her arms on her knees and holding her head down with the cloth to the back of her head looked at me clearly for the first time. "I'm gonna kick your ass when I get up." She told me.

"You're lucky I didn't shoot your big ass. I should call the cops and have your dumb ass arrested." I turned away then and started to examine my busted door handle.

Donna barked, "You two please! I've been through enough shit today." She's been through enough shit? Whatever. I proceeded to fix the door. Here I am, fixing my door with the 'perp' who broke the door getting all the sympathy. I knew I should have taken my ass to work early this morning.

While working on the door, I realized how flimsy the door must have been to have yielded to a few bangs from a woman. A BIG woman, no doubt, but still a woman. I guess when that adrenaline is flowing you get strength you didn't even know you had. I'd be at Lowe's to get a stronger door this afternoon. I did what I could with the busted lock and it would have to do for now. At least now, Stanley wouldn't be peeping at the scene from behind his curtains. I was almost sure he was.

"Get up off the floor. The living room is warmer." I don't know why I cared about their comfort. Guess home training never goes away.

I looked at the clock as I headed into the living room and surprisingly it was only 6:45. Felt like hours since I'd hopped out of bed singing with Maxwell. All the positive energy I'd felt was gone and now I was exhausted. I felt every one of my soon to be 35 years.

Donna and Sheila were on the sofa hugged up with an ice pack still on the back of Shelia's head.

"I'm going upstairs *ladies,*" I told them. I needed to put some space between us and gather my thoughts. "Close the door behind you and don't break anything else on the way out."

I knew Donna was going home with Sheila. I don't know how she could forgive her after the shit Sheila did but it was apparent she had. I also don't know how Shelia knew to come here looking for Donna unless Donna had lied to me.

She told me after seeing the pregnancy test she left the house right away and hadn't contacted Sheila since. Obviously, she'd left a note saying where she would be though. Maybe she hoped Sheila would come looking for her and find Donna and I in the same compromising position Donna had found Sheila and her Mandingo. She probably didn't expect what actually went down but it felt to me like I'd been set up. Again,

Donna didn't think things through to every possible conclusion. Didn't think about how selfish she was being by placing me in the middle of her troubles with Sheila.

On the second floor landing, I looked down into the living room. Sheila looked up at me and gave me the middle finger. I started to say something but I didn't want to prolong their leaving any longer than necessary. I'd already knocked her ass out once, no need for round two.

In the middle of the second floor stairway there is a blind spot, I could see them, but they couldn't see me due to the design of the house. I watched them for a moment staring at the silence and awkward tension between the two of them. I shook my head and continued on to my room.

I lay down on the bed and flipped the remote to start Max singing again. My mind was running back and forth from Maxwell to what had just occurred and how it was so damn strange. If I had called anyone and told him or her, they wouldn't even believe me. Well Stanley would because he'd witnessed most of it. Kevin would have a ball with this story when I told him about it later. He didn't know it but he was going to be helping me replace my door this evening.

I grew tired of Maxwell singing his love and reached for the remote. Me'shell Ndegeocello's heavy, sultry voice came on. She's a lesbian too. Damn, guess it's just a gay morning for me huh? I chuckled to myself as Me'shell started singing about being made a fool of just as I heard the front door banging shut. Sheila's parting shot, no doubt. Well Donna, I thought, fool me once…

Forget it. It's over and done with. I jumped up and hit the shower I should have had over an hour ago. It's been one helluva morning. I showered, dressed, and ate and it was now 8:30. I hadn't received any calls from the office and I was glad. Normally, if I was late going in I'd have at least two or three calls from Ashley updating me on what was going on at the office. Thankfully, this morning I'd been given a small break. I could put my game face on before having to face anyone else this morning. I went out the front door, grimacing as I heard it dragging, got in my car and headed into work.

I GO TO WORK

Haley Inc., Confidential Inquiries is a private investigative firm. I started out assisting insurance companies paying out workers compensation claims to clients. I'd go over their list of payees, do some background work into their claimed injuries and determine which ones seemed to fall into the category of fraudulent claims. I'd set up surveillance and report back to the companies when I found out this or that claimant who couldn't work anymore due to a bad back (it was almost always a bad back) was building a deck on their house or sailing every weekend, bowling, whatever. It all amounted to fraud. If you can do those things, there is nothing wrong with your back. It was a lucrative business, however, it was the same thing day in and day out. It paid the bills and allowed me to gradually build up my staff.

I started this company with me, myself, and I. It's hard to start a business when you really don't have any major cash or collateral. All that rhetoric and hype about applying for small business loans was a crock of shit because the banks weren't even listening to me. I applied for loan after loan after loan, and a black man in California with an idea and no money, is just that a black man with an idea. You can have the best idea, invention, investment, speculation or whatever but if you don't have the cash it will never get off the ground or worse, someone will beat you to it while you are still scrounging around for the money to get things going.

There are thousands of rich black people in California. You'd think, like other races, we'd support each other in our individual quests for the American Dream. For some reason I'll never understand it seems that sometimes our people don't want to help others achieve what they have. As if other black millionaires diminish their own achievements somehow.

No, for the most part the black folks with money do business and socialize with other rich black folk. The middle class are just trying to get by paycheck to paycheck and don't want to hear about a *future* return on their money when they need every cent they make just to keep things status quo. Poor folks don't even have two nickels to rub together to even start thinking about investing as a way out of poverty.

No, I was on my own when I decided I was just going to jump out there and create my own opportunity to work for myself. And I did just that. I was reaching, I know, but I placed an ad in the help wanted section of the paper. The problem I had was when job seekers called and I told them that I needed someone willing to work for free for the first month, most of them went *off!* However, I was just keeping it real. I let them know they'd have the chance to be an associate in a start-up business that had the potential to be very profitable.

I told the truth hoping to pull some hard working, ambitious people to help me, and in turn I'd be helping them get in on the ground floor. Something I'd pay quite well for when jobs started coming in. Needless to say, I got few interested prospects. Those that were interested after they knew the deal I knew I couldn't work with. I could barely pay for the supplies when I started the company. I assured potential employees by the second month they'd receive double what they would normally have gotten for a months work. I heard some interesting advise from callers about what to do with me job offer.

One lady said, "Who the hell is this, the IRS trying to trick me? Hell no I'm not coming in for an interview. Leave me the hell alone!" and slammed the phone down in my ear. Another lady I'd returned a call to cursed me for at least 30 seconds after I told her the deal and then said, "you have a nice day, and God bless."

Most of the men who inquired about the ad I'd placed laughed and said "yeah right." and hung up on me. There was one real strange call though the guy started crying on the phone when I told him about the first month with no pay. He got violent, threatening me on the phone. Telling me how he would kill me. I hung the phone up on that one. I started to go there with him, but people today are a trip and need I say anymore about that?

It always worked in the movies, a man talks about a great idea, yells to his co-workers, "who's with me? Come on!! We can do this people!! Then someone volunteers and takes on the challenge. Well not for me! The only person that actually had potential was a white guy who told me he had enough in savings to last the month. Tyler Stephens, like me, had just left what he'd thought was going to be a life in law enforcement because reverse racism, reverse sexism, all the isms, kept him from being promoted. I had to admire a guy who would be up front with a black man about being passed over for somebody of color based, so he claims, solely on color. He was honest and didn't appear to be racist. And he was hungry. Like me.

I worked day and night with very little sleep to open and close my first case. Tyler worked long hours and did grunt work without complaint. I'll never forget him for that.

It was rough but after I'd saved that one small insurance company countless thousands in workers comp payments to a fraudulent claimant everything snowballed. My second month I was able to hire a secretary, freeing Tyler up to leave the office and work on surveillance, which I didn't even have to train him to do. The next month I was able to hire another investigator. HiCi was doing okay, I kept my employees well paid, and they worked hard for me.

They work hard because they are paid well. Two years into running my own business, HiCi hit the mother lode.

After so much hard work to just get the company going and taking jobs from insurance companies and local police agencies, I just lucked into the "creeping" line of investigations.

The CEO of a large computer firm contacted me about my services. I advised him that HiCi normally took on cases relating to insurance fraud.

"Your ad says you make confidential inquiries and that's what I need. Is there a problem with that?" He asked me.

"Not at all sir, I'm willing to listen to your proposal. I just wanted you to know what this firm normally does. That way you can make an informed choice."

" I appreciate your candor, Mr. Haley I'll be in your area at 3:00 this afternoon. Will you be free to meet with me?" I told him to stop by. I figured the job would probably be too big or complicated just due to the wealth of the man. But I figured if I couldn't help him, I'd point him in the direction of some of the larger firms.

When Mr. Washington walked in, he was all business. He was in his mid 40s but kept himself fit. Wearing a thousand dollar suit, Bruno Mali loafers, and hand stitched silk tie, he'd dressed to show me how powerful he was. I was unimpressed. I treated all my clients the same. When Ashley showed Mr. Washington into my office, I waved him over to the chair in front of my desk and finished the phone call I was on. Mr. Washington looked impatient but business is business. I needed to finish my call. "Go ahead and take what you've got to the company, Tyler, from what you've told me you have more than enough proof that injury is a fake."

I hung up the phone and reached across the desk to shake Mr. Washington's hand. He started right in. "Mr. Haley, I believe my wife is having an affair. I need to uncover the affair in order to divorce without giving up half of my wealth. The pre-nup indicates no alimony in the case of her infidelity."

"You know, Mr. Washington, you don't have to pay someone to find out for sure. Just take a day off and follow your wife. If she is cheating on you, you'll know." I told him.

He replied, "Mr. Haley, I run a multi million dollar business, I have neither the time nor inclination to take up such a task. If you can't handle this type of investigation, recommend someone who can. I have no time for further research and can't trust this request with anyone else in my life."

I was a bit offended by his arrogance and subtle insult of my abilities but I decided to keep my opinion of Mr. Washington to myself. I held my hands up to stop him from saying anything more. "I never said I couldn't handle it Mr. Washington. I was merely trying to save you a few dollars. May I ask how you learned of our company?"

"I have a friend very high up in the Sacramento police department. I told her I needed someone to make discreet inquiries and she gave me your name. Moreover, might I add it is worth considerably more than a "few dollars" to have evidence of my wife's infidelity Mr. Haley. I'd be willing to pay you $40,000 for the first month of service. That shall cover it, I believe? If you require longer than a month we will meet again to discuss further payment. However, I really would prefer that this whole affair take no longer than 30 days."

I immediately thought 'What in the hell did he just say?' but I played it cool. Of course, I'd had transactions in this amount before, but not for a little job uncovering something that was probably easily found out. It would probably only take a couple of days tops to find proof of his wife's cheating. In my experience, by the time a spouse starts to suspect something is going on that something has probably been going on for quite sometime.

"Mr. Washington I will handle your case personally." I said, standing up to shake hands with him as he prepared to leave.

Having finished his unpleasant business to his satisfaction Mr. Washington barely shook my hand. "I had no doubt you would handle it. I don't want to be shuffled off to an associate. What account would you like the money wired to Mr. Haley? ."

I ignored his pontification and supplied Mr. Washington with the deposit information for the company. I added, "And from here on out, please call me Marc." I believe once a relationship has been established between my clients and I, the formalities of mister and misses can go out the window. Especially now, since the issues I'd be discussing with Washington were not superficial niceties. This stuff would cut him to his soul and being on a first name basis with the bearer of bad news might make it somehow more bearable. In addition, once transactions of this amount are involved, there is definitely a relationship expected on both ends.

Mr. and Mrs. Washington were my groundbreaking case into creeping. His wife had it all, or so it seemed. As part of my initial investigation, I had Mr. Washington disclose his assets. I had to know what was at stake for him. He was worth 290 million dollars. He owed no one and his money made money. Why Mrs. Washington decided to creep was confusing to me. She stood to loose so much.

The morning I started the case I sat down with Arthur Washington to get background information; what were his wife's specific actions that led him to believe she was cheating. Mr. Washington could only say that, at one point, they were making love at least twice a week and now it was down to once a month if he were lucky.

I listened to his justification. In my personal life, I may bite my tongue in order to avoid unpleasantness but for work, I have to tell it straight. My bread and butter depend on me shooting straight from the hip. "Arthur, just because the lovemaking slows doesn't mean that there is an affair-taking place. There could be any number of reasons why the love making slows." I told him, "Have you considered maybe you and your wife aren't sexually compatible? Do you use all of your passion and enthusiasm for work and come home with none left?"

I expected him to explode at my temerity but I was just trying to get some answers, figure out where to start on my case. Arthur brushed aside my comment with a wave of his hand. "Marc, she is cheating. You find evidence of that and I don't get taken to the cleaners. End of story."

I believed he was leaving something out. Nonetheless, I jotted down a few notes without comment. But I couldn't bite my tongue in the matter. I was being paid good money to find the truth and I needed to get into Mrs. Washington's head. "Arthur, are you an aggressive lover or do you wait for the woman to make the first move?"

He leaned back in his chair blustering, "I hardly see where that is relevant Marc." He cleared his throat and slid his horn-rimmed glasses towards the end of his nose to study me more clearly. Arthur said nothing for a few seconds and then, quietly, as if disclosing a dirty secret "I've never been an aggressive lover. Normally my wife lets me know when she wants to make love."

I jotted this down and Arthur leaned over to see what I was writing. Then out of the blue, Arthur said, "You know, Marc, my penis, when erect, is only 4 inches long." I almost sputtered 'what the fuck did you say man?' but I somehow remained professional.

Arthur's confession seemed to open the floodgate. The businessman was gone. He began pleading his case, as if I were judging him. "In spite of natures cruel joke, Marc, I've been told I'm a wonderful lover by everyone I've made love to, including Mrs. Washington." His earnest expression begged me to believe that his "shortcomings" were not the cause of his reduced sex life with his wife.

"Mr. Washington, I'm not here to judge you or your sex life. I'm simply trying to find out why your wife cut you off. I want to know why you believe she is having an affair. We both know the size of a man's equipment doesn't necessarily make him a good or bad lover."

In my mind though, I wrote, 'little dick' and put a big check next to it. Hell, it didn't take a scholar to know this could be the source of his wife's disinterest in initiating sex. He'd already disclosed that they hadn't had sex before they were married and after they were married he always had to use battery operated means to bring his wife to orgasm.

He and I sat and talked for about two hours. It was on his dime and I let him ramble. It was obvious to me that while he truly believed his wife was creeping he hoped in his heart he was wrong. "My wife was a virgin when I married her. She is 20 years my junior and her religious beliefs prevented her from having premarital sex." There were tears in his eyes as Arthur continued. "I valued the gift of her purity on our wedding night. It was something I never even thought about or knew I wanted but it was important to her so I obliged Rachel's belief system. I did, however, insist on a short engagement. I may have my 'shortcomings' but I'm no monk." He stopped talking for a moment lost in thought then continued. "You know I didn't even believe a pre-nup was necessary. I truly believed that if Rachel had saved herself for 25 years then there would be no way she'd break our marriage vows."

"So what made you finally decide to get a 'get out of jail free' contract then?" I asked softly.

Arthur chuckled at the reminiscence. "It was my brother, Ben." He told me. "Ben is also my lawyer. He's the only person I trust implicitly. I told him there was no way I would entertain the idea of a pre-nup. Thought it would be insulting to Rachel. It was only when Ben threatened to quit as my lawyer that I agreed."

"For the first year of our marriage Rachel seemed satisfied with our love making. Then on our anniversary, she introduced dildos. I was excited about it at first. However, after witnessing the difference in her pleasure when compared to just making love with me I realized I wasn't satisfying her. My pride was insulted and I eventually refused to allow them when we made love. That's when she gradually started to pull away."

I sat and let the silence float through the room for a moment before interrupting his reveries. "And now you think that she, in fact, has broken her vows to remain faithful to you. You are certain of this?"

All of a sudden, the self-important businessman re-asserted himself. He stood to gather his coat. "Yes well that is the question I've hired you to answer isn't it Marc?" he said as he walked across the room.

Just as he was about to walk through the door I said, "Arthur, you can be assured that as relevant information surfaces I'll contact you right away.

Arthur acted as if he had never admitted that he was walking around with a schlong the size of a shorty's. That he truly loved his wife and would be heartbroken that his virgin bride was cheating on him. Now it was all business again. It's something about rich men. They always feel the need to be in control of every situation. To let you know they have power over you.

He paused with his hand on the doorknob and turned back to me. "No, Marc I think you'll be calling me every two days to check in." As though this gives him the upper hand, I thought.

I sat back in my chair and thought about it. Power and control belongs to those who have the ability to know when they are indispensable. I'd listened to his tale of woe and realized how very important it was for him to settle the question of his wife's infidelity. I knew that he did not want to go through an interview process again or search for another investigator.

I looked directly into his eyes and said, "Your call but that will cost you an additional $10,000. That is not how I normally operate. It's an inconvenience I will gladly put up with but it increases the cost of my services."

Arthur gave a curt nod, turned, and walked out the door. I assumed my increase in price was acceptable.

I knew all along the case would yield quick results. My initial consultation with Arthur, the multimillionaire, took place on a Wednesday afternoon. By Thursday 6am I was doing surveillance on Mr. Washington's home. I sat all day watching the house and tracking Rachel Washington as she shopped, got her nails, hair, and toes done. I followed her into Macy's and watched from a distance as she selected sexy intimate apparel. I knew she wasn't buying for Arthur's pleasure. She went home that night looking as if she was prepared for an evening of hot sex with her husband. Just as Arthur pulled into the drive, I pulled away from the curb where I'd parked when she got home. I knew that sexy lingerie was going to be on display soon. But not tonight and not for Arthur.

The next day just as Arthur left the driveway I pulled along the opposite side of the street and parked ready for the down time of surveillance, the part I never liked when I was a cop. It can get very boring waiting for movement. I wanted a door to open, a visitor to approach, her to leave, or something to keep me sharp. Time was ticking slowly.

Thursday, and Friday passed as I observed Mrs. Washington's activities. I let Tyler cover anything that cropped up at the office.

Arthur worked 12-hour days. I hid on or around their property as soon as he left in the morning observing his spouse's comings and goings.

Late on that Friday afternoon, a few hours before Arthur was due back from work, and, according to his stipulation, I had to check in with him to give an update on my progress, I got the break in my first creeping case.

Around 3 p.m. 'Brown' came to deliver a package. When the truck pulled up to the curb on the opposite side of the street from where I sat watching. The driver, a blonde Adonis type, jumped out of the truck with flowers. "The damn UPS man?" I said aloud in my quiet car.

I rationalized to myself that maybe Arthur had ordered the flowers for his wife. I was actually hoping that he had.

Up to the door walks this young All American, stud. He appeared to be around 23 or 24 years of age and the kind of character you'd see on that show where the guys line up on TV and beg for some woman to marry them. The Bachelorette, I think. I don't know for sure. That's some white people show. I don't watch but I hear Tyler and Ashley talking about it from time to time.

Brown makes his way to the door. I think of him as 'brown" because of the clothes he wears. He switches the flowers from hand to hand and wipes his palms on his brown shorts. He rings the doorbell. Click. My zoom lens camera captured his furtive look as he glanced around to see if anybody was watching. He actually looked directly in my vicinity for a moment. Fortunately, for me, my car has tinted windows and you can't see inside. The make of my vehicle wasn't at all out of place in this posh neighborhood. No reason to suspect anyone inside was watching from inside.

Brown placed the flowers behind his back just as the door was opened. (Click) Bam here we go! I knew this case was easily made even though I hoped I was wrong. Rachel Washington opened the door butt naked!

I had to readjust the lens to make sure I captured them both in the shot. Damn, if Arthur's wife, the woman who had so little interest in sex lately, a demure virgin when she married, answered the door at 3pm in the afternoon naked. From the goodies I could see through the telephoto lens I could see why Arthur was bereft without his wife's physical affection. The lady was built to last.

Rachel greeted Brown with a kiss (click) and he smiled from ear to ear. (Click) Rachel reached down, grabbed his crotch (click, click, click), and pulled him into the house with an arm around Brown's shoulder and her teeth tugging his earlobe. (Click) The door closed. (Click). I put the camera down and settled in for the duration of the tryst occurring just yards away.

Well, hell, doesn't take a rocket scientist to figure out what was transpiring inside that house. My phone rang as I was checking to make sure the surveillance camera I'd installed behind the roses, with Arthur's approval, recorded everything my telephoto camera might have missed. I didn't answer the call. The camera had recorded perfectly. My job was almost done.

I got comfortable in my seat. No telling how long this would take. It took about 40 minutes. At 3:40pm, Brown exited. Mrs. Rachel Washington, still naked, kissed him goodbye, rubbing his crotch as if, it seemed, an invitation to come back inside for a repeat. Brown mouthed something I would pick up later from the recordings of the camera in the rose bushes. He gestured to his watch and, impulsively pulled Rachel to him roughly and kissed her with uncontrolled passion (click) before setting her away from himself and, smiling from ear to ear, and loped back to his truck.

I sat there thinking about this scandalous heifer getting her groove on with the damn UPS man in the house where she and her husband reside, probably on the same bed in which she gave him her virginity; or so she claimed.

I initially thought to call Arthur, but I decided to make some notes and sit on the information for a while. As I made entry notes about the activities of the day, I grabbed my late lunch from the back seat and turned on some tunes.

I enjoy listening to jazz while eating. There's something about jazz that makes me chew slower, savoring the flavor. It was around 5 pm when I'd finished my lunch that the pool cleaning service truck showed up. A woman stepped out of the van and removed cleaning supplies from the back. She walked up to the door and greeted Mrs. Washington, now fully clothed and respectable, (click, click) and headed to the side of the house towards the pool. The pool lady stayed about 30 minutes, I noted in my surveillance log, before gathering her tools into the back of her truck and driving away. (click, click) I wanted to give Arthur a good idea of how Mrs. Washington arranged her priorities and appointments.

The call I received when I was in the middle of recording the damning evidence against Rachel was Arthur; I learned when I checked my voicemail.

He said he'd grown impatient waiting for me to check in and wanted to know the results of my investigation as soon as possible. I returned his call and was advised that he was in a meeting but would contact me once the meeting adjourned.

I sat listening to the Urban Knights CD waiting to see if there was going to be any further incidents to report to Arthur. Around 7 pm, I concluded there would be no more surprises. I knew Arthur typically came home by 7:30 pm. Even if his wife managed to squeeze in a quickie between now and then, I already had recorded evidence of her infidelity.

I decided to call it a day. On my way home, Arthur called again and asked how the case was going. All of a sudden, I felt sorry for the poor guy. I hesitated. "Arthur, are you ready to hear what I have to say?" There was silence on the line. I continued. "Its not good news, Arthur. It can wait until we are face to face." Still silence on the other end, "Arthur? Mr. Washington are you there?"

Finally, Arthur replied, "Yes...I am here. Sorry." his breathing was deep and loud.

"Mr. Washington I can't say for sure that your wife is having an affair, but she did kiss, grab the crotch, and invite into your home a UPS delivery driver. Arthur, she also answered the door naked."

Silence for a moment then Mr. Washington quickly asked, "How long was he in my home Marc."

"Approximately 40 minutes, sir.'

There was complete silence on the line for a few seconds. Then I heard the unmistakable sounds of crying but tried to pretend as if I didn't. I didn't interrupt his heartbreak at the validation of what he'd already known in his heart was true. This was a volatile and sensitive moment for any man. To find out that your wife was making love in your home with another man? Damn! It would definitely make me want to hurt somebody, tear off some of their DNA. However, this wasn't *my* situation.

After several minutes passed with me listening to Mr. Washington cry, then try to gain control of himself, I asked, "Mr. Washington are you okay?"

"How would you feel? Shit! That's a very unintelligent fucking question, Marc, but I'll be okay." As if realizing how he sounded Arthur added, "Its not you Marc. I'm sorry." The phone line severed.

It didn't bother me that he'd lashed out considering the news that I had just given him. My line rang again. I picked up but before I could greet him, Arthur, once again every bit the businessman, said, "Thank you for the information Marc. We, uh, must have been disconnected accidentally." He cleared his throat to cover his lie and continued, "I expect visual proof of my wife's infidelity in the morning, Marc. I want full details. I want you to know that your thoroughness in clearing this matter up so quickly will be reflected in the deposit I make to your account in the morning." With that, Arthur disconnected the line again.

I sat listening to the ether of the silence. I knew without a doubt Arthur was struggling to maintain his prized self-control while his world was crumbling around him. I drove home in complete silence. No jazz. No talk radio. Nothing. I wondered if it were me, would I have the restraint Mr. Washington was displaying or would I have went home and cleaned house with bullet placed in appropriate guilty parties vital organs? I'm not a violent man by nature but as I've said, when that jones has you fully in its grasp and you find out some shit like Arthur just did, people sometimes do things they never believed themselves capable of.

I put on hold the productivity of my company for two days to show Arthur Washington that I was at his service. I had a hunch that his say so would catapult me into realms of business success that had eluded me since I'd started the company and I was right. Once he'd readjusted his ego and pride Arthur was singing my praises to his friends and business associates. His word of mouth advertisement on how he'd caught his cheating spouse within two days of retaining HiCi brought others seeking the same service to our door. Today its well known in the social circles of divorce attorneys that if HiCi is providing Investigative services, it is best to settle. My clients usually don't end up in court but set the parameters of the divorce decree and settle out of court. Now I have the luxury of picking and choosing who I do business with. Only 7 digit incomes and up can afford the retainer fees and other expenses associated with hiring my company. It keeps the bills paid and the employees happy and loyal.

LETS GO CRAZY

I called Kevin when I went into work the morning Donna and Sheila had shown up acting a fool. I gave him the run down. It was hard to get the whole story out because every time I said a few words Kevin would break into wild laughter. "I told you that bitch was crazy man!" Kevin finally was able to get out between fits of laughter.

"Yeah, yeah,," I said, "tell me something I don't know. Anyway, I want you to come by later and help me put up a new door. I could do it myself but with two people it will go faster." I told him.

"Yeah whatever black man. I'll stop by around 4 or so. What you got going later? You up for a little b-ball or did your little ménage a trios use up all your energy?" He was still laughing.

I lowered my tone even though my office door was closed. I normally don't use street language at work but Kevin brought out the street in just about anybody. "Fuck you nigga," I said quietly into the phone. "Don't forget who helped you get your car to the shop the day Janet decided she'd had enough of your trifling ways and busted up your shit then put sugar in the tank. And what about the time I let you lay up in my spot for a couple weeks cause Denise and her peeps were checking out your pad waiting to kick your ass for doing her wrong? Huh? What about that Mr. Funny man?" I laughed to myself.

Kevin started laughing all over again. "Yeah I guess you've done me a good turn or two. Damn man! I said I'd come by! Why you bringing up old shit?" I laughed and hung up the phone.

I'd arrived late at work due to the foolishness with Donna and Sheila this morning. Now, as I played catch up, I looked over a few existing files, checked my e-mail, and then checked the new client files. Nothing interesting there. Then I checked the inquiry files.

One was very intriguing. An older woman involved with a younger man. This in itself wasn't that unusual but in this case, the older woman was black, and the younger man was white.

In this line of business, you don't see that combination too often. I couldn't see why an established and beautiful (according to Tyler's sketchy notes) multi millionaire married a white out of work nobody. This guy had absolutely nothing to offer the relationship as far as I could tell from the notes in front of me was concerned. He wasn't rich and couldn't even hold a job. I just couldn't understand why this fool could possibly be cheating on his wife. He had stumbled onto a sugar momma and he could be set for life if he just waited her out. Tyler's notes indicated the wife was well into her sixties.

The day ended with nothing much major going on at work. Jamal, a junior investigator who worked under the supervision of Tyler came in as I was leaving. "I got the goods boss!" He shouted to me as I was leaving.

"Which case was that again?" I inquired back to him.

"You know the one where the lady hired us to uncover dirt on her man before the firm he hired uncovered her dirt? I beat em to the punch.

Everybody was dirty and we got the goods first. Guess I should be in line for a bonus or something huh?"

I laughed as I walked out the door. "Or something!" I called as the door closed behind me.

I decided to go pick Kevin up just in case he tried to flake on me. At Lowe's I found the thickest, heaviest door they carried and Kevin and I put it into the truck we'd rented, and drove to my house. I pulled up in the driveway and saw my neighbor standing outside pretending to be working in the yard. I wasn't about to scratch the bed of my truck up, so I rented one at Lowe's for $19.99.

It's interesting how Stanley manages to always be outside working on his yard whenever I get home but he's never dirty or sweaty and the yard always looks exactly the same. All the gardening equipment lying around his front yard looked brand new; as if they'd never touched grass or shrubs. Either Stanley was another Felix Unger or his 'gardening' was a front to watch his neighbors, particularly me, without seeming to. Stanley's ole lady was black. Another crazy match up on the surface but she is just as country as he is so I guess it's not that crazy after all.

I missed my old neighbor; a nice older woman who had moved into a retirement home a couple of years back. Stanley and his wife, Ramona, moved in just after Donna and I broke up, and ever since then, I felt like I was living under a microscope. The funny thing is the two had managed to successfully raise 4 kids about my age, according to Ramona. I guess they keep trying to make me a surrogate son because theirs are scattered all over the country and obviously don't visit as often as the couple would like.

Kevin and I got the door out of the truck and went up the front walk. I nodded at Stanley but didn't speak, hoping to encourage him to do the same. No such luck.

Stanley grinned ear to ear, revealing everyone of his teeth, then gave me his signature two thumbs up. He rushed over. "Here let me help you fellas with that. Looks like it's pretty heavy Marc. Should take a licking and keep on not getting knocked down huh?" He laughed at his own lame joke. Kevin gave me a crazy look behind Stanley's back.

"Yeah Stanley, it should do just that." I replied. Stanley turned around, dropping all pretext of helping with the door.

"Hey Kevin, I guess Marc told you he had it pretty rough this morning with his two women huh?" He stood there grinning with his hands on his hips.

"Nah man!" Kevin got in on the act. "He ain't told me nothing about no two women! Why you holding out huh Marc?"

"Shut up." was all I said. I noticed a crowbar lying almost hidden underneath the brush by the front door. Guess that's what Sheila used to help bust my door down this morning.

Stanley was talking to Kevin. "Well, I ain't one to be telling tales out of school, but I heard a commotion this morning and got up to see what was going on. And I see this big burly woman banging on Marc here's door." Stanley got warmed up and told his version of events to Kevin who punctuated the story with 'What!' and 'Get out of here! For real Stanley?' I let the two of them carry on, as they seemed to be doing a fine job of getting my door fixed without my help. I went into the kitchen, grabbed a beer, and took my time drinking it, while I looked through the paper. When I finished, I grabbed two more bottles from the fridge and returned to where Kevin and Stanley were finishing up

"Hey, two cold ones for my hard working, gossiping buddies!" They both took the beer from me

"Hey, Hey, Marc, its gotta be pretty rough having two women love slaves show up at the same time huh?" Stanley called as he walked across his yard, leaving his gardening equipment where it lay.

"I know Marc, I know!" Kevin started before I even said a word. "I just can't help messing with that crazy white man." He laughed and gave me Stanley's two thumbs up. "WOOWEE, Marc! Two love slaves, huh? Huh? How do you do it bruther?"

Laughing, I said, "I told your ass to shut up. Now come on so I can drop your ugly ass off and go get some dinner."

"Sure its dinner you're getting and not some more loving from your slaves?" Kevin jokingly asked as we climbed back into the Lowe's rental truck. Before I dropped him off at home, we made plans for some late night basketball at the gym. I dropped the truck off and went to pick up a bottle of wine.

I wasn't in the mood to cook or wait for an order to be delivered. I don't eat out too often because I prefer to cook for myself. I managed to pay attention to moms while growing up and I know how to burn in the kitchen. On my way back from the beverage warehouse, I stopped at the store and bought a few lottery tickets. Why do I play the lotto? I guess it's just because the thought of actually winning and what I could do with that amount of cash. They better not ever let me win that thing!

At my last stop, Clarence's Steak House, I ordered a smothered steak with onions and a green salad. Clarence has figured out a way to make steaks better than anyone in the business. The meat just melts in your mouth giving off blasts of southern flavors. Clarence handed me my order. I shouted, "Ooh-wee! Clarence you a bad man! I can *smell* how good this food is gonna taste!" Leaving Clarence chuckling behind the cash register, I drove home quickly. I could barely wait to get at that steak. The aroma coming from my bag was enough to make me want to pull over and eat it there on the side of the road.

Parking in the driveway, I walked up the front passageway. I hadn't even seen him anywhere but all of a sudden, Stanley is standing behind me with a huge grin on his face. "Hell yeah! Hell yeah!" There he is! Play on player! You are the man! WOOEEE! Stanley shouted, pumping his fists in the air. I couldn't help but laugh as I walked into the house ignoring his crazy ass. Had he really known the circumstances of what went down this morning, I'd still be outside talking. Stanley is a good neighbor, in spite of his spying. He claims he has to live vicariously through me since he's been married 'since kindergarten'. Otherwise I'd be out there giving you a run for your money with the honeys good buddy.

I put my food on the table and hustled upstairs to change out of my suit into some jeans and a T-shirt. If it wasn't so unprofessional wearing jeans and T-shirts at work, I would definitely do so because there is nothing more comfortable than a worn out pair of jeans and a T-shirt. I ran back downstairs and headed into the kitchen, opening the Beaujolais, poured myself a healthy portion, grabbed the food, and sat down on the couch and began eating. I was so excited about eating I forgot I had wanted to watch the game. Grabbing the remote, I clicked on the TV and started flicking through the channels trying to find the game.

Perfect! I found the NBA Pass on TNT. Lebron and Kobe were playing against each other. The new high school phenom and the old hype, Kobe, battling to see who would reach the NBA finals.

I devoured the steak and watched the game. A couple of hours had passed and the game was ending. Kobe managed to pull a win out of the hat just as my doorbell rang. Clicking the TV off, I sat still. This was probably the only time ever I wished it was the Jehovah Witnesses calling on me with their bikes parked neatly behind them. But I knew it could only be one person. I am not answering the door. I'm tired. My day has been long enough.

The doorbell sounded a few more times. I sat there stubbornly refusing to answer. It finally stopped. Good!

I'd had about three-fourths of the bottle of wine, and had a nice mellow buzz going. I poured the rest of the wine in my glass tossed the food containers in the trash and headed up the stairs. I reached the top stair and the damn doorbell rang again. I had to tell Donna off at this point because she obviously couldn't read the sign outside the door that said, 'no soliciting.' Whatever she was selling, I wasn't buying.

Ding dong, ding dong, ding dong diiiiing doooong. I stomped down the stairs, indignant that my buzz was leaving. I grit my teeth when I reached for the door, ready to release my frustration on Donna for disturbing me day and night when I hadn't heard from her for so long before today. I yanked the door open and practically shouted, "What the fuck you want D…"

My verbal assault stopped short. Sheila was standing there obviously shocked as all hell at how I'd opened the door. Then an unattractive grimace came on her face. "You thought I was Donna huh? Is that why you didn't answer your door?"

Shelia was dressed as if she'd just come from an Ebony photo shoot. I was shocked and apparently the 'dog really had my ass' because I didn't know what to say.

I stood there holding the door open and stared until Shelia blurted out in a rush, "Hello Marc. I'm sorry for bugging you and ringing the doorbell so much. I knew if I didn't do this now I'd never work up the nerve again. I figured you were home cause I saw your car in the driveway." That'll teach me, I thought. Should of put the car away as soon as I got home.

"I know this is inappropriate and I *know* I shouldn't be here after what happened this morning but I felt so bad about your door and everything. I brought this as a peace offering." She said in a 'please forgive me' voice. I took the bag and looked through it. She'd bought me a brand new dead bolt lock, screws, and a Home Depot gift certificate for 200 dollars.

Even if she had an ulterior motive for showing up, that's a hell of a good will gesture. I invited Shelia to come in. "Would you like something to drink?" I asked her, then, thinking about the EPT rolled up in toilet paper I added, "Juice, or water? I've got plenty of both."

"No thank you, I'm fine." Sheila walked into the living room and sat on the couch she'd nursed her head on this morning. I wasn't about to ask if she was feeling better. "Marc, I just want to tell you…"

I interrupted. "Look, I'm sorry for knocking you upside your head when you busted my door down." Sheila had the good manners to look shame faced for her actions.

"Marc, I'm so sorry for that!"

"Yeah, yeah, it's all water under the bridge. The door is fixed; you've paid me back. No blood, no foul, right?" Good thing there was no blood because then she'd probably be up in here with a rug doctor trying to get the stain out. What an about face! Given her association with Donna and her actions this morning I wasn't about to give her the benefit of the doubt that her apologies were sincere. She wanted something, no doubt.

The whole deal with her Mandingo and Donna was burning to be talked about so I had to ask, "Shelia what is the deal with you and Donna? Donna said that you are pregnant. What's up with that?"

Shelia looked up towards the ceiling as if to fight back tears of embarrassment. She studied the tiles on the ceiling for a few seconds then looked directly in my eyes. "Look Marc, I love Donna. She has been good to me. But she and I started out our relationship with both of us experimenting. I've had more than my share of shitty relationships and before she and I got anything going I was coming out of the shittiest one to date."

I didn't respond. Sheila didn't know it but she was about to enlighten me on how she'd pulled Donna from a loving monogamous heterosexual relationship into live La Vida Local with a chick.

"Marc, before Donna and I hooked we'd been flirting for months. I never really thought anything would actually happen but one day she just walked up to me and suggested we meet after the gym. I panicked but by the time I decided to back out it was too late. I didn't have anyway to reach her and I couldn't just leave her hanging. So anyway, we met up at Linda's Bar and Grill. When I got there, we just talked about our lives and the relationships we'd been in. She didn't tell me about you until we'd been together for about six months. We got drunk and she convinced me that we could just have a little fling. You know? Just to be able to say we'd been with a chick once. That one drunken time turned into twice with no alcohol involved. Next thing I know we were seeing each other everyday."

It fucked me up that Donna was the one to initiate things between herself and Sheila. Donna had led me to believe Sheila was the one steering the ride. I wanted to ask specific questions about time frames and when the hooking up actually happened. I wanted to know if Donna had lied to me when we broke up about not having acted on her female attraction yet.

Sheila kept talking. "After a few months we both decided to just fuck it all and be with each other. No one understands how to please a woman better than another woman. That was the best part. Even though I took a lot of heat from my parents, I didn't care. I didn't care about anything. Not the religious implications, not what other people said. I was doing my own thing and things were going great."

Twice in the same day I sat on my glass table listening to a woman tell me about her lesbian lover. Why they wanted to confide in me I had no idea. I was pretty sure the other shoe was about to drop though. I remained silent.

"Anyway Marc, about two weeks ago I ran into an old flame from college at, of all places, the bookstore where Donna works. One thing led to another, we had coffee then met later to talk about the good ole days. Billy was the only guy I'd ever been with who didn't fuck me over one-way or another. The only reason we broke up is because he flunked out. We just lost touch.. But I realized I still had feelings for him and he told me he still loved me too."

Brother was probably hoping to get some double chick action, I thought but didn't say. Sheila kept on going like the Energizer Bunny.

"We met in secret for awhile. I didn't know what to do about Donna because I realized I loved her too! It was driving me crazy trying to live a double life. I got careless, and now Donna knows everything! But shit…I don't *know*. You know? Now there's a baby involved. I swear Marc I didn't do this to hurt Donna! When Billy and I were together in college I went with him when he got a vasectomy and during the years we were together I never got pregnant!" Sheila put her hands over her eyes and wailed, " Damn It! Damn it all Marc! Even with the vasectomy and pulling out, obviously there's no 100% guarantee." She looked at me as if I should understand her predicament. Sure, your lesbian lover catches you in the buff with your old flame. Sure, he's supposed to be neutered but somehow knocked you up! Sure, I'll be your priest and absolve you of any wrongdoing. Say twenty Hail Mary's and call someone else in the morning.

This was too much. Without a word, I got up and went to the kitchen to grab another bottle of wine. I need to be anesthetized to deal with this crazy mess. I was expecting some half-ass excuse, not the truth.

From the kitchen I called out, "Look I know you can't have wine but I'm going to have a glass. Are you sure I can't get you anything?"

"Yeah, I'll have a diet coke or anything diet that you have."

I grabbed a diet Pepsi sitting in the back of the fridge and headed back to the couch for some more information. Watching her low carb diet in the middle of all this drama...now, if that didn't sound like some emotional type woman behavior, I don't know what the hell is.

I returned with the drinks and sat back on my trusty table, the same way I did when Donna showed up trying to get revenge on the person now sitting on my couch.

I expected Sheila to continue her sob story and finally get to the real reason she was here. Sheila had other things on her mind.

"So Marc, tell me, what's your story?"

"I don't have a story. " I told her.

"Oh but you do! You are single; you live in this big ass house by yourself. You're successful, intelligent, handsome, and probably still fucking my girlfriend from time to time. This couldn't be the story of your life. Tell me your story. I just spilled my guts, what are you all about Marc."

Like a lightening bolt to my ass, I was struck and stuck. Here she was telling me about how she was so conflicted about trying to come back to the straight team and the next minute she's pulling a dyke move. I can read between the lines. I knew she was really asking me why Donna decided to come to me the moment she caught on to Sheila's cheating ways. Come to think of it, I wondered about that myself. Maybe Donna and I weren't a settled thing after all. Maybe she'd seen the light and was ready to move on past her 'crush' and give things another shot? Would I even want her again after all this? I couldn't imagine forgiving, forgetting, and just taking up where we'd left off. I didn't have time to fully consider things with Sheila sitting there like the cat that ate the canary. I ignored her question and asked about her baby and if she knew when the due date was.

"I haven't been to the doctor yet so I don't know the due date. But, really, Marc tell me about yourself please. You already know pretty much everything there is to know about me. Fair is fair." She just wouldn't give up. Sheila settled back on the sofa and got comfortable, as if she had all the time in the world for me to spill my guts.

I don't owe this bitch a damn thing. Just like Donna this morning first she was ashamed and contrite, the next she was trying to be my interrogator. But I wasn't on trial.

Still, even if she had reasons she'd yet to divulge Sheila had pretty much just broken herself down for me. She'd cleared up some misconceptions I'd had due to Donna's lying ass and for that, if nothing else, I was grateful.

"What is it you want to know about me, Sheila?"

"All the things I just mentioned," she answered.

I wasn't one to freely share information but I could feel the wine loosening my tongue.

"Okay Mr. Secretive, lets start with you explaining why were you fucking my girlfriend behind my back?"

What in hell? What did Donna tell her when they'd left this morning? Through my rejuvenated buzz, I found myself not minding too much if Donna had embellished our current relationship to even things up between herself and Ms. Cheater here. But now, Ms. Cheater was on my couch, in my space, demanding answers. Even though Donna had a lot to answer for, for some strange reason I found myself not wanting to blow her cover just yet. How in the hell did I get myself in this awkward ass position?

"Look Bi-Polar, how are you going to come up in here all ladylike and apologetic then flip the script as soon as you tell me your sob story? And by the way, Sheila, Donna and I have been close friends for a long time okay? She and I go way back before you ever showed up. But just cause you came on the scene didn't mean I had to give up being cool with my girl." Let her figure that shit out. Shelia sat there watching me through slit eyes, trying to read me.

I wasn't about to back down from Sheila in my own pad. This is my stomping ground! "Listen woman this ain't no poker game and I got no reason to lie to you. But you know what? It bugs the fuck out of me that you come at me with this bullshit when your living foul on both sides of the fence. Pick a side and stick to it why don'tcha?" I said, laughing. The damn near two bottles of wine I'd had was starting to tell on me. Ebonics flowed freely once I went past mellow buzz.

Shelia, unfazed at my departure from politeness matched my Ebonics with a bit of her own ghetto-ness. "Yeah, you right Marc this ain't poker. If it was I'd be calling your GOT damn bluff cause your ass is full of shit!" She leaned toward me and twisted her neck b-girl style. All that was missing was a finger snap in the air. I was starting to enjoy this.

I took a sip of wine and set the glass back down, savoring the flavor of the fermented grapes on my tongue for a few seconds before swallowing. Sheila was turning out to be kind of fun. I turned it up another notch.

"Let me tell you three things, ma. First, you can't always believe what you hear from ole girl, especially since you've only known her for a short time. Girl has layers upon layers it takes years to peel through to get to the real deal. Second, your big ass better not ever, ever, ever, ever, try to come up in MY spot disrespecting me and accusing me of shit without having your facts straight. I'll pull a Martin on your ass in a second and have your ass stepping. And third, (I held up two fingers) if Donna and I were sweating at the same time you and *the love of your life* Billy were, then that just lets me know you and Donna didn't really mean shit to each other in the first place. So deal with that shit!"

Shelia sat and marinated on what I'd just tossed her way for a moment. I sipped on my wine.

I thought Shelia had surrendered; that the line of questioning was over but this girl wouldn't give up! "Okay, what about everything else, Marc? You still haven't told me anything about yourself!"

"Look baby-girl," I was in my stride now, the wine had me talking in my mack voice, deep and low. "This is not a 'lets analyze Marc' night. This is about you and Donna not me. I ain't got to answer for shit."

"Marc, Donna told me you two have been fucking the whole time we were together! So, this is about Donna, me, and you! I already know why I fucked up. I wanna know why she did. Why did she keep coming to you when she had me?"

This shit was funny. My first inclination was tell her to get out of my house. But I can't lie, something about Sheila kept me giving her half answers and answering questions with questions. She had me curious. Or she did until she said, "Marc, are you like a closet homosexual, having a piece of ass on the side to show off to keep the fellas at bay but you really like men, right?"

With all the wine I'd had, I couldn't even begin to wrap my head around this new tack Sheila was taking. It's a funny thing about homosexual people. Seems like they want to pull every straight person into their mix so they won't seem like they are out there in the minority. They want to believe every straight had some hidden homosexual tendencies so they won't have to acknowledge that most of the rest of us never, *ever* wanted to even put a toe over the line to the other side.

I looked at Sheila in total amazement. First, she accuses me of fucking her girl then she accused me of being gay? "Let me give you a fourth thing to think about Ms. Sheila. Number four, (I held up three wavering fingers) you don't get to ask dumbass questions about my sexual *orientation.* But to answer your burning curiosity, hell no, I am not gay." My face twisted in disgust at the thought. "If your big ass wasn't pregnant... never mind."

Sheila wanted to believe what she wanted to believe. "You don't have to huff and puff. It's okay if you are a homosexual because I'm all about men and women expressing their sexuality. At least I am now." She said, grinning at me. I just looked at her without answering. She got the drift. Strictly bona fide he-man up in this motha.

"Okay Marc, just one last question and I'll be through for the evening. Well actually it's a two part question."

"Woman, what is it? I'm about ready to kick your ass out any minute now."

Shelia choked on her laugh and took a sip of her drink, set it down, then settled back into the couch. "What I want to know is, do you find me attractive and why are you alone? If you aren't fucking Donna, and my guess is she lied about that, it just seems strange to me that a BMW like you doesn't have a woman."

Did she just call me the ultimate driving machine? What the fuck was that about? What, exactly, had Donna told her?

Her question was deep though. Not the part about whether I found her attractive (yes! More and more by the second) but the part about me being alone. I found that I actually liked Sheila in spite of myself. I liked the attitude. I wasn't about to tell her that though.

"You know what Sheila?" I began.

"No, actually, I don't know what. That's why I asked." Sheila was quick to reply.

"Well I'm gonna tell you what. Then you need to leave cause I've had a long day and plus I'm more than halfway to drunk. The answer to the first part of your question is *yes* I find you attractive. When you broke down my door this morning and I had to bop you upside your thick head, I thought you looked like a man because of the way you were dressed. So, hell no, I didn't think you were attractive then. But now you've shown up showing off all your assets, I'm guessing, to counteract my impression of you this morning. What I still can't figure out is why you bothered. You got shit coming out of both ears, Sheila. You got Donna. You have Billy. You have a bun in the oven. Why does it matter whether I find you attractive or not? Seems like you got enough on your plate without throwing me in the mix."

Shelia looked shocked by the honesty of my response. I guess she thought I'd tell her that a woman dressed to attract didn't attract me. I was on a roll though, "The only reason your ass is still on my couch is due to the fact that you are physically pleasing and a little bit intriguing. But Sheila, make no mistake, no amount of wine will make me forget who you are and the situation you are in. And to answer that question about why I'm alone, I've been involved with more than a few women but not too many that I'd call my woman. Haven't found that many that meet my standards. When I am in a relationship it's a one on one deal because I believe in monogamy not just fucking around like a dog in heat." I kind of contradicted myself there a bit but what the hell, even if it didn't make sense to anyone else, it made sense to me.

"I've loved unconditionally and been loved in return by one woman in the past 15 years. Her name was Melody. She died. It broke my heart. That's over, she's gone, and there's nothing I can do about that. I thought...I'd *hoped* that maybe Donna could replace Melody in my heart but it's painfully obvious to me now that Donna doesn't come close to filling those shoes. It's quite possible no one can and that is why, even though it's none of your business, I'm alone right now. That's the only part of my story you are going to get, Shelia. Now it's time for you to go. See yourself out."

I got up, picked up the glasses, and headed to the kitchen. I even managed not to sway when I walked. Shelia was sitting there stunned when I left the room. I heard the front door open and stepped out of the kitchen. "Drive safely Sheila. Take care of yourself. And if you ever bust down my door again your ass will be in jail so fast you won't know what hit you."

Sheila walked towards me and I thought she looked ready to throw a punch. Instead, she gave me a quick hug. "This isn't over." She whispered in my ear before turning to head out the door.

"Yes it is!" I called to the closed door. From outside, I heard Sheila shouting, "No its *not*!" A few seconds later I heard a faint, 'Wooohooo, Marc is the man!' Damn Stanley's peeping again.

I went upstairs and lay down on the bed fully clothed. The red light from my cell phone was blinking. I checked my messages. Kevin's voice came through loud and angry. He called over an hour ago.

"Nigga, where you at? I been waiting for half an hour! Are we gonna play or what?" I'd have to call him in the morning and explain what had taken place this evening. I already knew he'd totally misunderstand this turn of events.

I was awakened by the sound of loud jazz floating up to me from the living room. I smelled breakfast food. I rolled over on my back and inhaled the smell of bacon, eggs, pancakes, coffee, and toast. Melody's cooking breakfast, I thought. Then I realized my mistake. Had to be Donna. I smiled and then instantly became confused because her ass definitely shouldn't be in my kitchen after what happened yesterday. But for some reason, I was comfortable and just lay there in bed taking in the smell and listening to Norman Brown.

I took me a few minutes to realize the situation was all wrong so I started to get up to investigate. I wasn't too worried. I knew it couldn't be burglars breaking in to listen to my music and cook me breakfast.

As soon as I threw the covers off to crawl out of bed, in walked Shelia wearing a red see through robe, thong underwear, and carrying my food on a breakfast tray. I sat up as fast as I could. I didn't remember putting on pajamas.

I put on my angriest game face even though I was kind of pleased she'd used the key to the deadbolt we'd installed last night to get in and surprise me. Guess it wasn't over just like she'd said.

"What are you doing here? Why are you practically naked? How did you get in?" My mouth sputtered out questions my eyes already gave me the answers to. Sheila, bearing food, wearing that outfit, could have only come for one reason.

As I sat there staring, My mind was telling me to make Shelia leave but the devil on my shoulder was saying, 'wait a minute dawg. You sure you wanna kick this honey out? Look! She brought food!"

While I was sitting there fighting with myself, Shelia had set the tray down and climbed on top of me. I made a feeble attempt to push her off. The girl was strong. I couldn't control her. She stuck her tongue so deep inside my mouth it felt like she was trying to reach my esophagus.

Beep, beep, beep, beep. The alarm clock went off. I woke up hard as a rock but as soon as I stood up in the cold room that was no longer a problem. I felt like I hadn't rested at all.

TRUTH IS

A few weeks passed and it was business as usual. I didn't hear from Donna or Sheila and I was glad. At the office, new clients continued to pour in and my employees continued to work enormous amounts of overtime. It was time for me to hire again just so I could give my staff some back up so they weren't spread so thin. The overtime didn't bother me because the clients paid HiCi extremely well, but the investigators and office staff were swamped in paperwork and getting behind on surveillances. I called Ashley and told her it was time to run the same help wanted ad we'd used before and put it on Monster.com as well as in the SacBee.

Just under a month after all the drama with the lesbian dynamic duo had rocked my world for a minute, I sat at my desk signing payroll checks. There was a quick tap on my door. "Come in." I called out.

It was Tyler. "Can I sit down for a minute?" he asked. "I want to run something by you."

I gestured for him to pull up a chair and gave him my undivided attention. "So what's up, man? We haven't touched base in a little while. What's going on?"

"Well" he cleared his throat and continued, "You know I accepted the case from the wealthy older African American woman seeking to investigate the goings on of her Caucasian husband, yes?"

"The rich older black chick and the possibly cheating young white stud? Yeah I remember that one from the prospective files." I told him.

"Uh, yeah, that one." Tyler said, clearly uncomfortable with my politically incorrect version of his case. He was such an uptight man! I tried to loosen him up every once in a while by going for drinks after work but it hadn't worked.

"That's just what I've come to talk to you about. I'm having difficulties keeping up with her husband and I need some help on this one boss. Maybe I could pull one of the junior investigators away from the insurance or PD gigs to help out? It sure as heck would make a lot of sense, dollar wise to have someone else working with me on this because she is paying top dollar to nail this guy as soon as possible."

"Look Tyler, I've just gone over everyone's timesheets and there is no one I can really spare for you. This seems to me like a classic case. Follow the man, get the goods, and send the client the final statement. What's the problem?"

"I know it seems like an open and shut case but I haven't been able to get the goods. That bastard is slippery as a eel! One second I've got him in my sights the next thing I know his trail is cold as a winter in Chicago."

Tyler had been with me from the start. He'd worked his ass off for me when payment for his services was uncertain at best. Even though he still hadn't loosened up around me, I knew he was the best investigator I had. If he said he needed help, I knew this was no doubt a difficult case to crack.

"Tyler, I trust your instincts and I value your work here. But like I told you everyone else is busy."

Tyler made to move out of his chair. "I'll keep at it then boss." He said.

"Sit down, man. I'm not finished!" I told him. I was beginning to think I'd been too far out of the game; too much about the money, if he thought I'd just turn down his earnest request and send him on his way just because some of the newbies were tied up in other cases.

I hadn't been out there in the field for a good number of years and Tyler knew it. He assumed because the other investigators I had couldn't assist he'd have to go without help. Guess he forgot he was sitting across from the investigator that started the damn company. I'd already decided to be his back up on the case.

"Look man, if you need some help nabbing this dude, I'm your man. I haven't been out there in awhile. I need to keep my skills honed anyway."

Tyler looked at me in disbelief. "*You're* going to be *my* back up?" He said and I could tell he was holding back a laugh.

"What? You think I could do it ten years ago but don't have the chops for it now?" I dared him to tell me 'yes'. He didn't. My pride reared up, the spirit of Marcufosa was standing beside me. "Listen man, HiCi was built on my instincts on how to find the dirt. No one else is available. You trying to say you don't think I can back you up?"

Tyler turned beet red but laughed as he walked towards the door. For the first time, I could tell he was beginning to thaw towards me. "I know you got the chops, boss. I just didn't think *you* knew you still had them. I'll meet you at Wynona's Waffle House at 5 am tomorrow morning. The client is Cerise Ivan, and she wants this case cracked ASAP."

Five o'clock in the damn morning? Maybe I was too old and too far out of the game for this shit. Marcusofa mumbled to himself about having to much to do tonight to get up that early with me and went back to sit under a tree. I was on my own.

But hell, once I started thinking about getting back out there doing some real investigative work instead of sitting behind my desk dealing with the administrative side of the business, the more excited I got about being in the field again.

A small voice inside me asked what in hell I thought I could do if Tyler couldn't break the case himself. He *was* my best investigator since I'd pulled myself out of the game. I hadn't been in the field since Arthur Washington came calling eight years ago. Tyler had come to me with tons of experience and he was still my hardest working employee. There'd been times I'd stop by the office on the weekends to pick up something I'd left behind and I'd find Tyler there; reviewing files and checking equipment. He had never asked for back up on a case so now that he had I wanted to make sure he got it.

Another workday ended. I was full of preparations to start the next morning of surveillance. I grabbed my brief case and sunglasses, left the building, and jumped in my car.

While driving home, I was thinking about what I was going to prepare for dinner. The last few nights I'd had leftovers. I was yearning for a fresh meal. I got home in about 30 minutes, my usual drive time to the second.

When I pulled up into the driveway, there stood Stanley, as usual, in his yard.

I stepped out of the car and said a quick hello before heading for the door. "Marc. Marc! Let me talk to you really quick, bruther." He rushed over to stand beside me on the walkway.

"Not now Stanley, I'm tired."

"Come on, bruther. I'll be quick, I promise. Okay? Okay! Hey, champ you've been real quiet lately. I haven't noticed any honey's popping up in the middle of the night. No honeys during the day. I hardly see you anymore! Is everything all right? I would kinda like another peek at that honey wearing the stuff."

I looked at Stanley. I really just wanted to go inside and get myself some dinner. But for some reason I find I don't have the heart to be harsh with his simple ass anymore. I sighed heavily. "What stuff are you talking about, Stanley?"

He grinned and looked around as if checking for other nosy neighbors then gave me a low waist two thumbs up. Stanley grabbed his jacket and then flashed his chest at me as if he were nude. "So you want to play charades? Is that it Stanley? Okay, 'flasher'! Did I get it right? Cause I'm tired and hungry and just want to go on inside the house and take a load off."

He slapped my shoulders and said, "Come on man, tell me about it! Don't leave me hanging on a string, bruther! That woman what was over here bout a month or so ago?" I gave him an 'I don't know what you are talking about' look.

"The one with the trench coat! You have to remember that morning Marc! Come on, goshdarnit!"

"Okay yeah I remember the trench coat diva. And?"

"Well, I happened to be walking out to get the newspaper when her and that tall drink of water left and she opened her coat and flashed me!" He yelled loudly, "Yeah Marc! Yeah, no shit bruther! I like her! She's got *fire!*"

Stanley looked towards his house just as the blinds inside his living room flipped shut. He tried to compose himself real quick.

I said, "Stanley get it together!" in a hush-hush voice. I couldn't believe it; Donna had flashed Stanley the morning she left with Shelia? I didn't know what to say. In an attempt to stall any further conversation, I told him, "Listen, you and I need to get together and when we do I'll fill you in on what really happened that morning, okay? But right now I really have to get inside."

Stanley grinned and turned to look at his house again. "Okay brother. Whew! Okay. Looking forward to it!" he said in a hush-hush voice. He flashed me a single thumb, a peculiar grin on his face. He then turned around and yelled, sprinting towards his house. "Yeah, bruther! Yeah!"

I could never understand why this Arkansas cracker was always in a rush to call a black man 'brother'. He did it with every black man that I'd seen him talk to and it used to irritate the shit out of me even though I'd usually bit my tongue. But once, several months back, before I realized how harmless Stanley actually was I came home upset from being stood up by Donna for a lunch date and I blasted him.

"I'm not your 'bruther', Stanley. My name is Marcus Haley, and I suggest you address me that way. If you can't, then I suggest you don't call me anything at all. What I mean is, don't get all up in my kool-aid before you know the flavor. And what *that* means is don't start kissing my ass before you know if I want it kissed or not. I am about business and money not ass kissing." It was harsh and Stanley's crest fallen look made me feel guilty even though he deserved it.

"I'm sorry. Didn't mean any harm bru- er, uh, Marcus Haley, honest!"

My anger at Stanley evaporated and I felt ashamed for speaking to him that way. "Look Stanley," I told him, "it's brotha, not *bruther*" I imitated his southern accent. "That's all I'm saying. If you are gonna call me brotha, just do it right." Stanley looked relieved. "Okay then, 'bruthor' he said in an attempt to mimic the flavor I'd given the word. Damn. Poor Stanley couldn't buy a clue. Since then, he'd obviously forgotten the lesson I'd given him in brother etiquette and reverted to his own variation of the word.

Stanley had walked into his house and I went into mine thinking, 'Shit! Now I'm gonna have to explain to that fool what really happened that day.' I knew, beyond a doubt that he wouldn't forget the invitation. Obviously, he wouldn't be getting the correct version but even a more watered down version of the story was more than I wanted to talk about with Stanley.

The house was quiet, as usual. Just the way I like it, normally. Stanley's short visit had put me in a weird place. Donna was crazy! Why in hell did she flash him her tits? All of a sudden, my quiet, usually comforting house was the last place I wanted to be. The walls closed in around me. I wanted to get away from the silence. I realized I needed to go out, maybe hit up a happy hour or two. I couldn't stay too late because I had to be up early to meet Tyler. Still, I was in the mood for some straight up soul and a tightly packed room of people getting their groove on. I flipped through my cd collection and found a real old school mix to get me further into the mood.

"Now this is the CUT!" I put it in the player and flipped threw the songs to find the track I wanted. Tony Toni Tone and DJ Quik came through the sound system.

"Well let's get down then!" I said to the empty house. As the music played, I danced up the stairs to change out of my suit. '*Come on lets get down lets get down lets get down!*' I cha-cha'd around the room. '*Now table one that's my folks, and table two, that's my folks. Every body knows my name.'*

I couldn't wait to get out there so I could put some of these moves to the test on the dance floor. I hadn't been to a club in a long while.

The song ended and Mint Condition came on. *'What kind of man would I be if I lived unfaithfully, and what kind of girl would you be if you did the same?* 'I turned on the shower and sat on the edge of the tub. This song took me back to the first time Donna and I got tangled up in the sheets. Damn. At the time, I was thinking it was a cool song to make love to. Hindsight being 20/20 I realized maybe she'd cried when this song came on not because she was so lost in emotion she couldn't control herself. Maybe Donna cried because she knew being with me was living unfaithfully to who she really was. Over and done with, I reminded myself and hopped in the shower.

When I got out, I heard the bumping beat of George Clinton's Atomic Dog. "Awwhshit!" You can't mess with me when that song is on. This song took me back to the days I was on line with the Ques. I moved to the music like I used to back in the day when the bruhs and I would put it down and win any step show we entered. Butt booty naked, I relived one of my most memorable moments from my college days. I took a step here and pulled out a silk shirt. A step there and I found pants to match. *Why must I be like that? Why should I chase the cat? Nothing but the dog in me '*. I was dressed and ready to hit the scene.

I turned the music off on my way out the front door. Maybe it was the moonlit night, the same as it had been a month ago that made me recall Sheila and her parting shot. She'd said things weren't over between us. I'd insisted they were. This must have been where Sheila was standing when she shouted out that we were definitely not done with our little talk.

She'd asked me why I was alone and when I told her she got all girly and weepy and demanded we finish our talk later. Thank God, she'd forgotten about it. She and Donna must have worked things out. Maybe they were planning to raise Sheila's love child together. Shenequa has two mommies and all that shit. I laughed to myself as I got in my ride and headed off to Bonita's. But Sheila's question came back to me during the short drive to Bonita's.

Why was I still alone? I turned the corner to pull into the parking lot of Bonita's spot. Sheila had asked me that question it seemed like a lifetime ago. I didn't really have a good answer then and I didn't now. Whatever! I didn't dwell on it too long because my stomach was growling. I had to get inside where there was some good music and most importantly, good food.

In Bonita's parking lot, I sat in the car for a few minutes, trying to find music on the dashboard to fit my mood. Nothing was working. I was dressed to get down but in a heart beat I decided I wasn't feeling up to a crowded, sweaty room with a bunch of buppies trying to find a way to feel as if they were still as young and hip as they were in the eighties. I put the car in reverse and pulled out of the parking stall.

I didn't punk out. I just didn't feel up to the pretentiousness required to get through one of Bonita's happy hours. "Here's my card. Call me if you want to 'network', or, 'Let's try to hook up and see if we can optimize our individual potential'. I left the uppity Negroes to their theatrics and drove back home. I pulled into the garage and opened the freezer I kept out there to grab some frozen gumbo.

I'd put 15.00 dollars towards a gumbo feast Sam, a friend of mine, had a week ago. Sam was the gumbo king. He would have a gumbo party, for $15.00, you could eat all the gumbo you wanted, and he sent you packing with a plastic bag full of gumbo. Back in the kitchen, I grabbed a beer out of the refrigerator as I waited for the gumbo to defrost. I took my beer upstairs and changed out of my happy hour clothes and into some kicking it around the pad threads. The quiet of the house was comforting once again.

The doorbell rang. I thought of Stanley immediately. I should have gone out like I'd originally planned. He was probably outside the door with a six-pack of brew and a waiting ear. I told him we'd talk some other time, meaning not today! I walked to the door and there he was, just as I'd thought, minus the beer.

"Hey Stanley, now is not a good time for our talk. I have a busy day tomorrow."

Stanley said, "Awhh Marc I am not here for that! We need a whole weekend to discuss that! I just forgot to tell you that the other woman who was here that day came by earlier. I was so caught up in talking about the flasher I forgot to mention it. Anyways, she rang the doorbell a few times then left. Just thought you'd want to know" He gave me the signature thumbs up and ran across our communal grass back to his house.

So Sheila had stopped by earlier today huh? Why, I wondered? She couldn't seriously think she and I had anything left to discuss. I walked back into the kitchen wondering what had prompted Sheila to show up on my doorstep again.

Oh well! She didn't leave a message on the door or my machine. I knew that if she'd gotten my address from Donna she'd also somehow gotten my phone number. Whatever reason she had to come calling must not have been important.

I'd changed out of my happy hour clothes into my robe and slippers. I grabbed the remote and flipped through the channels searching for something interesting to watch. Why in hell am I paying all this money for cable and there is never anything good on except for the occasional game?

I pulled my gumbo and beer closer to me on the TV tray and relaxed into the lazy boy. There was nothing on regular TV so I grabbed the DVD remote and began flipping through the stored movies in the player. I got to one of my favorites and clicked on the play button. The saxophone signaling the opening notes to 'Love Jones' came through the surround sound.

Nina had just ditched her man and met the dude who was about to recite poetry to her at the club with that sexy ass sister from Devil in a Blue Dress. I couldn't remember her name but I remembered that chick sucking in her breath when her and Denzel were getting their groove on and telling him, *'ooh, that's my SPOT!"*

Still thinking about the other movie with the sexy, big-breasted sister, I stopped Love Jones and started flipping to find the movie cause I wanted to hear big chest say that shit again. I found it and forwarded it to that specific part. *"Ooh, that's my SPOT!"* I backed it up a few seconds, *"ooh, that's my SPOT!"* I love a woman who isn't too shy to let you know you'd hit gold. "Hell yeah!" I said to the empty house, pulled the cell phone from the pocket of my robe, and started flipping through numbers. I haven't made a booty call in a long time but baby girl moaning that shit had me knowing tonight I needed a warm body up under me. I needed someone who would know that just because we got sweaty tonight I wasn't looking to start, or renew, a relationship. I'd just skipped past the a's, the b's, and the c's in my phone directory when the doorbell rang.

At first, I thought it was the movie. I'd just flicked past Danielle, the aesthetician-too clingy. Knock. Knock. Knock. Knock. Ding-dong. It wasn't part of the movie. Someone was at the door. Shit!

I paused the movie at the exact spot where baby girl was saying, "*ooh,*" and headed to the door. Thinking it might be Stanley again; I closed my eyes and took a deep breath. I exhaled as I opened the door, fed up with Stanley and just wanting to be left alone to find the perfect booty call. I opened the door and with my eyes closed, trying to show him how tired I was said, "Yes Stanley, what is it now?" I was already dressed for bed. He had to get the hint.

"Well hello to you too, handsome." Stanley all of a sudden sounded like Donna. I peeked out of one eye then popped them both open.

Just as I had been a month earlier when Donna had showed up on my door unexpectedly, I was struck speechless. She wasn't wearing a trench coat so I guess we weren't in for a repeat of her Jessica Rabbit routine.

"What brings you by without calling, D?" I stuck my head past her looking into the night to see if Donna had Sheila in tow. Nothing but darkness past her except the blinds of Stanley's house slit open wide enough for me to see a double pair of eyes glued to my doorstep.

"Marc, I know I fucked up, okay. I'm so sorry about that! I know I left you last month with a busted down door and my shit to clean up. I know that I didn't even call you to let you know I was alright when I knew you must have been worried about me with all that went down that day."

Donna thought I was worried about *her* after she and Sheila left that day? I was amazed at her ability to only think about herself. You can't count on much in life, but damn if you couldn't count on Donna to think the whole world revolved around her. The sun didn't shine until she opened her eyes to let her tell it.

"I just want to stay the night, Marc. One night. Tonight. Tonight, I just want to hold you and I want you to hold me back. Things have been a little rough for me this past month. I need someone who loves me unconditionally to just hold onto for a minute so I can try to get my mind straight and figure out what I'm going to do. I don't want to be alone tonight." She looked as if she'd been through a storm.

Can you say crossroads? I'd already skipped past Danielle's name and Donna was next on the list. I figured I'd quickly skip past her number to get to Felicia, the orthodontist. But Felicia wasn't a sure thing. I had before me someone whose spot I knew backwards and forwards. It wasn't a difficult decision to make.

I could feel that spot calling to me from the doorway. I knew Stanley and crew were watching from behind the blinds. I said quickly, "Come on in, D." She walked in and I closed the door behind her.

The part I left unsaid when I'd invited her in, 'Let's get naked, lick, kiss, and fuck each other into oblivion' was in my eyes.

I stood in the entranceway. Junior was stirring. Rising to the occasion. If, like last time, Donna asked if there was a gun in my pocket or was I just happy to see her, I'd take her right there in the foray.

Blood reached my brain just before it did my dick, which allowed me to really stop and think about Donna's request. After everything that had happened she thought all she needed to do was show up and I'd be putty in her hands? She may have had me sprung before but that was over the day she walked out of my life.

"This is bullshit Donna! You don't know what you want but we both know it's not me! You had me a year ago and you left me for a goddamn woman! If you need someone to *hold you* go find your girl if you can get her untangled from *Billy.*" My mouth, my mouth, my mouth! Always telling the truth when sometimes, it should just shut up. I knew good and well the warm body I wanted under me tonight was standing right before me.

"You son of a bitch! Who do you think you are talking to, Marc?" Donna cried. "I came to you looking for solace and you treat me like some junky looking to score?" She turned back towards the door to leave.

My desire to hit a spot had me blasting all my frustrations towards her. She deserved it, though, so I couldn't feel but so bad.

"Donna, stay. Stay. Okay? I don't know what you are getting so mad about. If anybody had reason to be mad, it's me. You know I could go on for days about the way you fucked me over."

Donna turned back to me with tears in her eyes. "Marc, you are so damn wrong! I have *never* come at you like this even when all your hoochies called at all hours of the night. I knew it was you and I, ride or die. You told me that shit yourself! What's wrong with you? I thought you loved me! I come to you with a simple request and you treat me like shit on your shoe?" Her tears spilled onto the carpet.

She was always good about guilting me into what she wanted. Tonight I wasn't having it.

"Look, you said you need someone who loves you to hold you but if you stay the night there's going to be a lot more than holding going on. I'm sorry I came at you foul but you know your ass has a lot to answer for considering how you played me last month. But even considering all that, yeah, you're right, I still love you. You and I go too far back. You want me to hold you? I want that and more. For *tonight*. I'm not trying to get back with you." The last thing I needed was her misunderstanding my intentions.

I'd put all my cards on the table. It was her turn to ante up or fold.

Donna reached out to hug me in acceptance of my terms. But I had to make my point clear before this went any further. "I don't want you thinking you can just turn to me when things get foul with you and your girl but, damn Donna, I can't think of anyone else I'd rather hold tonight than you!"

Without a word, Donna took my hand and we headed upstairs. Through the walls of the house, I could hear a distant, "Yeah brother! Yeah! WHEW!" How in hell could Stanley hear what had just taken place from behind my newly reinforced door? I'd have to pull his coat PDQ about making his spying so well known. Donna gave me a disgusted look. She'd obviously heard Stanley. "I wasn't the one who flashed him."

She had the good grace to look slightly ashamed. Then she grinned. "He was clocking me so hard I just wanted to do something to shock him, Marc." She said, laughing.

"Yeah you did that. I may have to move. He'll be sniffing around here after you for years to come."

When we got to my room, I told Donna to sit on the bed and take her shoes off. I went around with a fireplace lighter and lit the various candles placed around the room then clicked the lights off. Donna sat on the bed watching me. I lit the last candle sitting on the nightstand and sank to my knees in front of her.

I rubbed her calves with enough pressure to make it hurt a little but not hard enough to bruise her delicate caramel skin. Donna reached out and rubbed my head as I kissed her calf. I pulled her hand away and gently tossed it from me.

"No touching. You wanted to be held. You didn't say anything about holding me. Tonight, it's just me. You alright with that?" Donna moaned and dropped her body onto the bed in surrender. I massaged her thighs then moved on to her hips. "Turn over." I told her in a voice I didn't recognize as my own. The emotion I felt was a bit unexpected. It had been a long while since I'd touched Donna this way.

I stood up to allow her to get comfortable on the bed. Donna grabbed a pillow and placed her arms around it, laying face down while I slowly unzipped her jean skirt. "Lift up, baby." She adjusted her hips to allow me to pull the skirt off. I tossed it to the floor. Donna was wearing a black thong. The thin piece of material connecting the flimsy front of the thong, the back played peek-a-boo with my eyes. It disappeared around the area I most wanted to get at and re-appeared just under the small of her back.

Donna had gotten a tattoo in the small of her back since I'd last been with her. Between the sinewy muscle of her rib cage and the ass that made a brother want to fall down to his knees in worship, was a black fairy laying on its stomach with cheeks resting in its palms, staring at me as if to say, *'you've gotten this close, now what are you going to do with our lady here'?*

I stared at the fairy as if I were having a conversation with it. In my head, I told the fairy, 'I'm just trying to make her feel good, and I want her to forget what brought her here tonight.' In the darkness it seemed the fairy winked at me, implying it's blessing to my intentions. I sank to my knees again and kissed the fairy. My hands massaged Donna's gluts. Baby girl was even firmer than I remembered. She took her Pilates seriously. I flicked my tongue over the fairy then planted a full kiss over the image. I massaged Donna's ass muscles until she was writhing beneath me.

I reached into the nightstand and brought out a Magnum. I ripped it open with my teeth and sheathed myself.

Slowly, I brought the full weight of my body onto Donna's backside and slid slowly into her inviting warmth.

Donna arched her backside, giving me full access. She sucked in her breath as I took it to the next level. "Ooh Marc, damn baby". Donna moaned, rotating her hips in answer to my quest for her spot. If I kept at this pace, I was going to explode any minute.

"Turn over baby." Donna slowly flipped onto her side.

"You remember how I like it, eh?" She said in a sensual voice. Laying side by side, Donna put her leg over mine and we continued our rhythm. "Did you miss this, baby?" Donna breathlessly asked me.

My voice was heavy, "Yeah baby, I missed it. Did you miss this?" I asked with a wicked grin and wiggled inside of her.

Donna squealed then laughed huskily. "Even my toys don't wiggle that good baby!" She said with a huge grin. Then the smile left her face as she threw her head back and moaned, lost to the feeling. I rubbed my hands across her hips and reached further back, squeezing the firm mound of flesh and pulling her even closer, then maneuvered so she was under me.

We sweated, laughed, kissed, and touched for over an hour. When I felt the urge to release myself into the reservoir tip I'd switch positions or stand up suddenly and do some jumping jacks. Donna laughed.

I didn't want the night to end. As much as I'd insisted to Donna that this was a one night deal the moment I'd hit that pot of gold I was searching for and found platinum, I forgot all about everything I'd said.

Somehow, I'd also forgotten about Donna's impossible head of hair. She tried so hard to keep it straight but you could always see that hint of wave on humid days. Wanting to avoid chemicals Donna got her hair pressed every two weeks but would usually end up wearing a ponytail the year we were 'together' because every night we'd sweat that press out and her hair would turn back to whence it had come. Straight from mother Africa and which ever tribe of Indian her forefather or mother had gotten with. The result was wavy hair, which for some reason Donna didn't want to deal with.

Right now, her hair was soaked from our co-mingled sweat. Curling and waving and sticking up like a fro. I'd finally given into the urge to release every pent up emotion I'd held in check since we'd last been together like this. Donna had screamed out in release more times than I can count.

"I still love you, Marc," Donna whispered in a quiet, sleepy voice. I got up and went to the bathroom to toss the condom in the trash. I was sweaty and smelled of sex. Instead of jumping into the shower, I wanted to hang onto the scent of our liaison for a while longer. I crawled back into bed, snuggled up behind Donna, and drifted between the plains of fully awake and unconsciousness. She started to snore softly and damn if I didn't get choked up. I'd missed just hearing her breath next to me. I heard myself saying, " I love your funky ass too, baby."

"I heard that." Came a strange voice. Was that Donna? I was on the descent into the sleep of a satisfied man. From somewhere a long way away I heard faint music. The song turned into a video in my half dream and there was Tina Turner standing by a chain link fence. But she wasn't singing, she was talking to me! "I heard what you said Marc. But let me ask you, what does *love* have to do with it, *Marc*?" She asked me with that sexy, husky voice. "I don't know, Tina!" Was all I could think of to say. "Well you better figure it out brother." She told me, and then broke into her signature song, walking around the chain link fence just like in the video. I started grooving to the beat. 'Yeah! What does love have do with it?"

All of a sudden, I was wide-awake. I regretted being with Donna tonight, even as I snuggled closer to inhale the scent of her. I knew when I woke up tomorrow Donna would still be Donna. She'd still have the Sheila issue to deal with. For that matter, so would I. Somehow, I believed Sheila when she'd said things weren't over between us. It was too much to figure out right now. I drifted off again this time to a dreamless sleep.

I woke up at about 3 am in the morning wondering who the hell was straddling me. When it all came back to me, I lay there without moving. I didn't want to wake Donna up to begin what was sure to be an awkward morning. I realized in my first moments of clarity that much to my shame, I still wanted it all with Donna. How I could want that considering all the very good reasons I shouldn't was beyond me but I was never surer of anything in my life. What would I do about it was the question. I couldn't see myself going back to letting her call the shots and ruling the course and speed of our relationship. I wanted her all the time not when she was desperate and willing. Not with *her* dictating when we made love. I wanted to be the one she came home to. Not some other woman. Not Sheila. I was tired of being alone.

In between all the moaning and huffing last night Donna had told me she could never love any man the way she loves women but men, especially me, gave her pleasure she'd never experienced with a woman.

At the time, I took her words as a testament to my skills. Today, in the early hours before the sun rose, her words came back to me like a bad dream.

Lying there, smelling her, running my fingers through hair that had gone back way beyond a hot comb, with wet spots on the sheets as evidence of her having experienced many orgasms, I recalled a telephone conversations I'd had with her several months back about the men versus women issue. She'd told me that emotionally, a man could never fulfill her like a woman. Last night, from what she'd said in the heat of passion, thinking she was complimenting me, it was obvious she hadn't changed her mind.

The past year without her in my life flew before my eyes. Donna had been all about controlling how much time we spent together. That meant that we never saw each other anymore once she and Sheila hooked up. We'd been the second coming of Bonnie and Clyde, ride or die. True friends, even before we became a couple. After Sheila, I got a phone call here and there and Donna seemed to think that was enough to maintain what we'd had.

Laying there with her leg and arm over my thighs and stomach I recalled calling Donna and asking if she wanted to hang out. Go out. Anything. I just wanted to see her. She always had an excuse. There was one time I suggested we hook up and she actually said yes. She ended up leaving me hanging, sitting at a quiet table in the back of Bonita's place. She just never showed. She claimed, later, that something had come up at work. I forgave her, as always, but still we'd never managed to hook up prior to her showing up unannounced on my doorstep a month ago.

I'd had a dream not too long after Donna and I broke up. I still recall it with clarity. I was in a maze and I kept searching for Donna because I knew that the moment I found her I'd also find my way out of the maze. I heard her voice calling me, "I'm over here! Turn left then right. I'm right here, waiting for you!"

In the dream, I followed Donna's instructions and still couldn't find her. I finally found the way out on my own and realized the second I walked out of the shady maze into the blinding sunlight Donna had never even been in there with me. In the moment between the dream and consciousness, my own voice came to me. I'd wasted so much time looking for her so we could leave together and the whole time I was by myself.

I'd tried to describe the dream to Donna during one of our phone calls. She laughed it off by saying she'd been in the maze all along, I just hadn't followed the directions to her location correctly. I let it go and laughed it off with her but I knew that dream had meaning. It allowed me to place our relationship into proper perspective. I was the one searching for her; trying to be with her. She was the one who kept moving, trying to avoid the moment when we'd be face to face.

Another dream I'd recently had came to mind. I was walking down a one-way street. I was in a desperate hurry to get where I was going but it seemed like the longer I walked the further I got from my destination. I thought about turning around but when I looked back, I realized I'd come too far to turn around now. Only one car ever passed during my walk down that long quiet street. Donna was the driver. She pulled over, got out and to me for a while. She was telling about a book signing at the bookstore later and how excited she was to meet the famous author. I tried to convey to her that I needed a ride. She should take me with her and drop me off on her way to the bookstore. Somehow, I couldn't get the words right. She didn't understand what I was saying and kissed my cheek before jumping in the car, driving off, and leaving me all alone with a long walk still ahead of me.

A little more rejuvenated after spending time with Donna I continued my walk. Miles and miles later Donna pulled up along side me, got out, and began talking a mile a minute again. I still couldn't form the right words to make her understand I needed a ride. When I followed her to the car and tried to open the passenger door Donna reached out and locked it.

She mouthed, "No, no." And shook her head at me. She pulled away again and drove off into the sunset.

Recalling the dream now, I realized it was another metaphor for our relationship. Donna would contact me when she had a moment; check to make sure I was still there for her then leave me stranded the moment she'd gotten her assurance.

I decided at that moment that all that shit had to end right this minute. Either we'd be in this thing together for once or it was all over. I fell asleep confidant that in the morning I was going to turn this whole relationship around.

I never got the chance. We both slept through the damn alarm and didn't wake up until the sun was burning through the slits of the blinds. Donna ran around like a crazy person trying to shower, dress and get out of the house in time to make a mandatory meeting at the bookstore. "We need to talk, Donna!" I called to her on her dash downstairs.

"I'll call you later baby!" She shouted back and rushed out of the front door.

I WONDER WHY

I got to work later than usual but no one seemed to notice my tardiness. The place was humming. Something I'm usually happy to see. Today I didn't even notice. I stayed in my office and only gave a half-hearted attempt to pay attention to the items in front of me. In my head, I battled with Donna until she was forced to see things my way.

When it was time for me to leave and Donna still hadn't called, I figured I was going to have to track her down. I'd just closed my briefcase and was heading out the door when my private line rang. I leaned over the desk and checked the caller ID. "Woman, you better be glad you called me before I had to call you!" I said with a smile in my voice. The tension I'd felt all morning was suddenly released. She'd called just like she said she would.

"I told you I would, baby. What? You don't trust me?" Donna asked in a sexy teasing voice. My brain told me to continue the flirtatious mood. My mouth said, "No, actually I don't Donna."

Silence on the other end of the line for a long moment. "You're joking right?"

"Maybe." I told her. "Look, we've just got a lot to talk about, okay? Are you free tonight? I'll cook dinner."

"Oh you *trust* me to show up, eh?" Donna sarcastically replied. Any trace of sexy flirtation was gone from her voice.

"Look! I'm not trying to have this conversation over the phone!" I answered. "Are you free or not?" Now I was angry.

"Well what do you mean by *free?* I mean I'm not free to have dinner and hear all about how you don't trust me. I'm not *free* to have sex with you one minute then have you berating me for being a horrible person the next!" Donna hissed into the receiver. There must have been someone else in the room, otherwise, I knew, she'd be shouting at me.

Damn, this was going to be way harder than I'd imagined. "Look Donna, I didn't say I don't trust you! I said 'maybe' I don't. Whether I do or not depends on what you have to say about last night. So, are you *free* to come over for a bit of sustenance tonight so that we can discuss what, *if anything,* last night meant.

"You think it didn't *mean* anything to me? Is that what you are saying, Marc?" More hissing. "Do you *know* how long I stood outside your door getting up the nerve to knock? Do you know how much I've *missed* you in my life? Did it mean anything?" Donna was on a roll now. "Yeah, Negro! I'm free to discuss just what last night meant to me. You be ready! I'll be there at six!" She hung up the phone. She didn't slam it, which indicated to me she didn't want whoever may have witnessed her call that she was upset. But she was pissed. No doubt about it.

Damn. How in hell did she turn this around on me when I was supposed to be reading her? I sat down on the edge of the desk reeling. I'd been so happy she kept her word to call me but then I just couldn't stop my mouth from speaking exactly what was on my mind. I remembered so many other times this same scenario had played out.

I'd have legitimate complaints or questions and Donna would turn it around, get unreasonably upset and try to make me into the one with a problem for addressing the damn issue in the first place. In the past, while realizing her tactics, I'd usually back off. Just like I had when I asked Donna if she was attracted to women and she blew up at me.

Had I pressed the issue then I could have saved myself feeling like a fool when she finally admitted she was. But, like a fool, I let the matter lie, hoping to avoid a confrontation that would be the end of us. This time around, if there was going to be another time around, I wasn't about to allow that shit to work on me again.

I turned onto my street at 5:50 pm. Donna's car was in the driveway. She was on her mobile phone talking a mile a minute. Obviously, I couldn't hear what she was saying but she seemed pretty agitated. I clicked the garage door open to let her know I was coming. Donna ended her conversation pretty damn quick and put the phone away, looking over her shoulder in my direction. She obviously didn't want me to know anything about the angry conversation she'd just had. What the hell was that all about?

I pulled into the garage and got out. Donna got out of her car and met me at my car door. Neither one of us spoke as we entered the house through the garage entrance. I hit the wall-mounted remote and we both watched as the garage closed soundlessly on the world outside where we stood.

We were struck mute. I wanted to say so many things right at once but nothing sounded right. It's always awkward. Historically, after an argument between the two of us, neither one of us wanted to say the wrong thing to set it all off again.

But things had changed. I was too old to keep playing this game and didn't care if I was jumping back into hot water just by speaking my mind. I wanted the whole deal with Donna and I resolved before I put head to pillow tonight. I'd resolved earlier to get the pleasantries out of the way and dive right in to the deep end. But right now, I wanted to see if Donna had changed from her old ways. Was she going to just ignore the unpleasant conversation we had? If so, what would she say instead?

I waited her out. Instead of starting up where we'd left off on the phone I simply asked, "Are you hungry?"

"I could eat." Donna replied. I left her standing in the storage alcove next to the door leading to the garage and walked into the kitchen to pull out the roast I'd left marinating in the refrigerator several days before.

I put the dish in the oven, turned to open a bottle of white merlot, and poured myself a hefty portion. I took a swallow and let it register on me for a moment then addressed Donna, still standing by the garage door. "You want some wine?" She left her post, walked into the kitchen, pulled a wine goblet down from the hanging rack, and placed her glass in front of me without uttering a word.

I filled her goblet to the rim then went about preparing our meal. I pulled out asparagus and garlic, washed, and cut them up. Determined to make Donna be the one to break first, I casually asked if she wanted to watch TV while I finished the meal. She leaned against the counter and nursed her merlot without response. I asked again. "Huh? Oh, I'm sorry. No. No. I'm good right here. Some music would be good though."

"You know where all the CDs are. Hook it up!" I thought I was waiting her out but she was doing a pretty good job of waiting me out.

Determined to win this battle of wills I put the finishing touches on the asparagus salad as Donna made her way to the living room.

"I haven't heard this cut in a long time. Good music to talk to." Donna called out from the living room. Donna shared my love of music. I heard the first strains of an old favorite drift through the Bose speakers on the ceiling of the kitchen. D'Angelo's soprano tone came to me like he was standing in the kitchen. *I want some of your brown sugar.*

The moment the song came on, I looked over the bar into the living room at Donna and started bobbin my head; I couldn't help but smile. *When I first saw you baby, I wanted to die"*

Donna smiled back. "Ooh Marc, this was our song! Remember how we got down to this at the clubs?

I sang along with D'Angelo instead of responding. "I want some of yo brown shuga. Awh, Awhhhhh, Awwhhhhh." Donna lay on the couch where she'd had the epiphany that allowed us to be a couple for a short while.

I'd just about finished the dinner preparations. I put the asparagus in the refrigerator to cool. All thoughts of confronting Donna had vanished along with the last of the bottle of white merlot.

Donna lay on the couch, sipping from her glass as I continued our dinner preparations. Track after track, D'Angelo was taking us way back. We relived the memories in silence. I checked the oven. The roast's smell filled the air. My stomach growled. The song, "Lady" came on. Closing the oven door, I started stepping to the groove.

Donna appeared in the kitchen doorway, signaling her empty wine glass. I took the glass and placed it on the counter, then took her hand. We stepped to the music. I knew I should cut the dance short and say what had been on my mind since last night. I was sure Donna had some more angry words for me for that matter. But we held all the words at bay and just kept up the slow stepping to the smooth groove of D'Angelo. Towards the end of the song, I pulled Donna closer.

The song ended and we stood facing each other in silence. Finally, I pulled her fully into a bear hug. I was stalling. Why couldn't things just be simple?

The next track started and we stood locked in our embrace. We barely swayed as D'Angelo sang about his best friend and his wife. It felt so good to hold Donna like this again.

The buzzer on the oven sounded. Good thing it did. I released Donna, grabbed my glass of wine, and took a sip. I'd decided while holding her to just let things lie for right now. I wanted this evening to be special. When I finally sat Donna down to have that talk she might not be back in my life for a long while, if ever, if things didn't go my way. I was forestalling the inevitable.

Pretending as if we were still a couple and everything was cool, I asked Donna to go to the store and pick up a pie or something for dessert. A wicked grin spread on Donna's mouth. "Can I drive your car? Please?"

I protect my ride like I do my home. I'd never let Donna anywhere near the drivers seat in all the time we'd been together. Everything must change, I thought to myself. It's just a damn car. How can I get her to budge on her stance if I wasn't willing to compromise a little myself?

"Pl-" I began, but Donna interrupted, saying, "Please be careful, I know I know Marc you love your cars more than just about anything! I just want to drive one! You really gonna let me?"

"Yeah, yeah. Whatever. Just be careful, woman." I took the keys off the hook and tossed them to Donna. I didn't give her my workday ride; A Dodge Ram, hemi engine, custom tires and rims, and a slamming stereo.

I'd grabbed the keys to my Mercedes CL. I normally only took that baby out of the garage when arriving in style was of the utmost importance. Donna had been asking to drive it for years.

Donna's eye's sparkled as she fingered the keys to the Mercedes. Then, without another word, she rushed out the door. I heard the garage opening and closing. I had to work fast. I wanted to set up a candlelight and rose petal dinner for Donna.

From the sliding door in the living room I stepped into the backyard and walked quickly into the garden greenhouse; my passion, outside of work, cars, and Donna.

I kept a bag of fallen pedals from my carefully cultivated rose garden in a plastic bag in a small fridge in the greenhouse. I grabbed a handful and hurried back into the house, spreading the rose pedals over the hardwood floor where Donna would walk on her return.

Next, I grabbed some incense from the study and lit a few sticks in strategic points throughout the house. Somali Rose is the bomb! It's so hard to find that when I finally stumble across a brother selling some I buy out his entire stock.

Time passes faster than you want it too when trying to set up a surprise, I've noticed. I grabbed my phone and called the car.

I knew Donna would answer because the navigation system would announce who was calling. "Hey?" Donna answered on the first ring.

"It's just me. How far are you out?" I asked. Hoping I had a little more time to set up the house the way I wanted for her return. Also, I wanted to make sure my car was still intact.

"I'll be back in about seven minutes according to the navigation system in this baby. Marc, I love this car! Can I have it?" She giggled and hung up the phone.

I sat for a few seconds relishing the sound of her voice. Anticipating what was to come. Then I rushed around the room lighting candles. Finally, I placed the matching candleholders from a cupboard in the kitchen on the table. I lit those and sat back to admire the affects of the room.

I knew I shouldn't be setting up a seduction scene. I *knew* it. But I guess I wanted to stall the inevitable. Have one more night with Donna without demands, just one more night of gratification before reality came back into our relationship.

I set the table for two. I'd pulled out the kente cloth napkins and placemats. I'd just finished stuffing the last napkin into a wine glass when I heard the garage open. Quickly, I lit the candles on the table and brought out the food on serving platters.

With that done, I rushed out to the garage and grabbed the Albertson's pie from Donna. "Close your eyes." Donna giggled. She was always up for this kind of game. I walked her into the kitchen with my hand over her eyes and guided her into the dining room, setting the pie in the center of the table.

"Okay, open your eyes, now."

Donna slowly opened her eyes. "Oh my god! Marc! It's beautiful! Everything looks so good and the food smells great! You are a wonderful man Marc. a wonderful man. Donna leaned over to kiss me. I cleared my throat. I was about to start with the baby please stuff. I grabbed the pie and went to put it in the oven.

As the oven door closed shut, I turned to Donna. Now, maybe, with her relaxed and feeling pampered, I could approach the subject of her and I.

Her phone vibrated loudly from her purse on the table. The mood was broken.

"Do you need to make a call? You can use the study." I said, remembering her heated conversation from the driveway. Donna checked the number. "Nah. It's nothing important. I want you and I to enjoy this evening uninterrupted. I believe there was something you wanted to talk to me about," she said with a sly grin, and then went to wash her hands at the kitchen sink. We sat at the candlelit table together.

Trying to reclaim the mood, I blessed the food and poured the wine. Before I filled Donna's glass, her phone went off again.

"Turn it off." I suggested, hoping with everything in me that she would.

"I better take you up on that offer. I'll be right back." She grabbed her mobile phone and hurried off to the study.

I was ear hustling, I admit. I was damn curious to know who she was talking to in such a hushed voice. All I could hear was "uh, umm, well I don't know! Yes! But-right now?" in the same strained, whisper she'd used with me this afternoon. The study door closed behind her. Feeling like a stalker in my own damn home, I walked silently to the door of the study and put my ear to the door.

"Well, shit! I know. I know! Um okay…okay…okay! Bye!" Donna said. I rushed back to my spot at the table, pretending to enjoy my meal in her absence. "Everything alright?" I asked casually as Donna came into the kitchen with a false face.

"Marc, I'm sorry, but I have to leave. You've set all this up for me, now I have to go, and I feel so bad! It's just something came up at the bookstore and they need me to come straighten it out."

I looked at her for a long moment. "Donna, its okay. Go handle your business. I understand." I didn't really understand though. Her call hadn't sounded like a call from a frantic co-worker. I managed to control my mouth before I blurted out; *"I've loved you for a long damn time. I've waited for things to be right for you. It finally seemed like you were seeing things my way and now you want to leave because of some mysterious phone call? I know you aren't going to the bookstore but where ever you are rushing off to, stay there! Don't come around here anymore because I'm DONE!"*

Donna had already mentally moved on to her next assignation, otherwise, she'd have read the meaning of my silence from the intensity of the look I gave her. "I'll make it up to you, baby! I promise. Maybe if I get finished early I can come back? Would you like that?" Donna asked seductively. Instead of responding, I grabbed my glass of wine and headed upstairs. "Marc? I asked if I could come by after I'm done." She called after me. I moved up the stairs without a word. I don't know what I thought she would do but I heard her keys jangling then the front door closed.

I rushed back downstairs and grabbed the keys to my truck. I took a final gulp of wine and ran into the garage.

Following Donna's trail, I already had planned what I would tell her and Sheila when they hooked up. Both of them were full of shit. Donna had walked out on me for the last time and Sheila better not ever think about showing up on my doorstep again.

It had to be Shelia on the phone. I could tell because Donna was suddenly submissive and demure. I reasoned neither one of them could whoop my ass. Both of them were going to sit there and listen as I got all this stress off my chest. Then I'd walk away and leave them to their fucked up lives.

At the stoplight, I was three cars behind Donna's car. She had no idea I was clocking her. I followed her onto Rita Street. I thought she would turn left towards the house she shared with Sheila but to my surprise, she kept going. Donna's car turned down Second Street and continued for a few miles.

Okay. She wasn't heading home. They must have decided to meet somewhere else. Donna continued her drive with me still several cars behind her. She turned into a residential community. A left here, a right there, then Donna's car pulled into a brightly lit driveway.

I drove slowly past the house as Donna walked up to the door. There was a for sale sign two homes down. It looked deserted so I parked in the driveway. From that vantage point, I had a pretty good view of Donna and the doorway of the house where she rang the bell.

"What the hell am I doing?" I asked out loud. Spying on Donna? I don't even have the right. She's not my woman. I tried to talk myself into driving away. Fuck it. It's too late now. I'm already in the mix. Might as well sit back and observe.

Donna rang the bell again and then knocked on the door impatiently. A few seconds later the door opened. I had my binoculars out.

Some buster wearing hospital pants without the matching hospital shirt stood in the doorway. The way he carried himself, his entire presence shouted to the world, "I'm Ghetto and I love it!" I focused the lens as Mr. Ghetto leaned against the doorframe, fingering Donna's hair before tugging her by the same fingered strand of hair and pulled her into a sloppy kiss. My mouth dropped wide open.

It's a very good thing I didn't have my gun with me. I was filled with an intense hatred against the man touching Donna. Had it been Sheila, I could have understood. But she rushed out on me to hook up with some man I'd swear was knew in her life? Jealousy consumed me. I envisioned myself getting out of the car and rushing over to smash in this dude's face. Then I'd-I'd what? I'd do nothing, I knew. I heard my mother talking to me from back in the day when I'd been so hurt over Karen's betrayal. Donna was not worth another second of my time.

I pulled away from the curb and drove home slowly. I couldn't believe she had played me again! My pride kicked in as I retraced the route I'd came. The man in the doorway wasn't even handsome. He didn't have anything on me in that department. Based on the beat up 1989 Accord in the driveway-shit, based on the dump he lived in for that matter, he was no competition in the financial department. I had the man beat anyway you looked at it, except for the small fact that Donna left me to be with him.

I felt every bit of the fool I was. What the hell was I doing out here wasting my time following Donna's ass when she could ditch me for such an obviously trifling Negro? I was so glad I never approached the subject of us trying again.

Suddenly, I wasn't even angry at Donna or her no shirt having, hospital pants wearing, broke as a joke, reject of man anymore. Don't hate the player hate the game. At the stoplight, I bowed forward with a wave of my hand, conceding the game to the brother. He could keep his prize. Shit-I almost wanted to turn the truck around, go back, shake shirtless man's hand, and thank him for taking Donna off mine. Make no mistake; I still felt, betrayed, lead astray, *bamboozled* even! Still, I was relieved. I'm free! Suddenly, I burst out laughing. The driver stopped next to me at the light looked over at me in horror, as if I were crazy. When the light turned green, she pealed off, getting away from the madman in the Dodge Ram.

I turned the radio on to drown out my thoughts. I picked up KBLX this time of night usually so I gave it a shot. *Now why do you think Jack snuck down the hill? He needed love, love he couldn't get from Jill"* I shook my head to the groove. Ray Parker Jr. at his finest!

So many years lost! So many years had passed when I could have started something with someone new. I'd passed up on a lot of contenders thinking if I stayed single long enough I'd win the day and have Donna at my side for the long haul. The only rationalization I had for the years I'd wasted was that Donna had come to me right after I'd lost Melody.

Melody and I would have eventually married, had kids; had the love and laughter in our lives I'd always envisioned for myself; the kind of life my parents had. I knew this. Melody had gone and died on me before we'd had a chance to realize any of those things. I guess I'd never forgiven her for that. I'd been with other women; women who weren't Melody, in a way I knew she wouldn't have liked. Melody, who only wanted my happiness, damn sure wouldn't have wanted me to hang my hat on the chance that Donna would switch teams and, maybe, decide, I was the man on the opposite team she wanted and needed to be with.

But Melody was long since gone. In her absence, and I guess as a way to punish her for leaving me too soon, I found someone not even good enough for Melody to have considered a friend, and held on for dear life.

The deejay at KBLX seemed to be feeling my mood. The next track on the radio was a vintage Prince cut. *"Be glad that you are free! Free to change your mind. Be glad with what you had baby what you got. Be glad for what you got!* I finally got freedom from a 10 year long addiction.

USED TO LOVE U

I pulled into my driveway and pulled the truck into the garage. I got out and walked over to the remote next to the kitchen door. Before I had a chance to click the garage door closed, Stanley appeared on the driveway with a six-pack of Anchor Steam beer. I recalled Florida Evans breaking a crystal bowl when she'd heard the news that James was dead. 'Damn, damn, damn!" That's exactly how I felt at this moment. I wasn't ready to talk to Stanley.

"Hey bruther, what'dya think about you and me getting together Saturday and having that talk just like you said? I brought the brewskis. You can keep em chilled till then. I can't wait, man. I've been wanting to know your secret! You're gonna spill it all right? Buddy to buddy!" Stanley asked, throwing up his best imitation of thugs flashing a gang sign by giving me his two thumbs up.

Too tired to deal with the drama and ready to hit the sack I gave Stanley the middle finger. I turned to walk into the kitchen but turned back, in spite of myself, and noticed Stanley's face. At first, he showed surprise, then hurt. He lowered his head and headed back toward his house. Damn! Nothing that had happened tonight was Stanley's fault.

I yelled after him, "I'm just kidding, Stanley!" He turned back to me with such a hopeful glance I was ashamed at my rudeness. To replace the bird I'd just tossed him, I gave Stanley a single thumb up to let him know we were cool. Stanley hurried forward and gave me the beer before rushing back out.

"Saturday, then?" He asked. "Yeah brother! Can't wait! WHEW!"

I closed the garage door and walked in the house. The phone was ringing. I figured it would be Donna's ass so I took my time getting to it. "Speak!" I barked into the receiver.

"Hey! Hey. What's wrong? You okay?" Sheila's voice sounded into the receiver.

I cleared my throat. "Sheila? Let me guess. Donna gave you my number? Its not listed," I said to cover the shock I'd received that she had my home number. I definitely hadn't expected her to be on the other end of the line.

Sheila ignored my sarcastic reply. "Marc have you seen Donna?" Sheila continued, breaking into a sob as she mentioned Donna's name.

"Well, yeah. I mean no! Look girl, she stopped by earlier but now I don't know what she's getting into. She left out of here in a rush. " I told Sheila, reliving shirtless thug pulling Donna by the hair into a wet kiss.

Sheila was obviously trying to regain her composure before she spoke again. "Is she on her way here Marc? She was supposed to pick me up from work."

I was at a crossroads again twice in one night. I could ruin both of their nights or I could say I didn't know where Donna had gone.

I'd decided to cover for Donna but my mouth decided otherwise. "Look Sheila, Donna stopped by earlier but she left when she got a call and cut over to some nigga's house off Tangerine Street. Don't ask me how I know. But trust me, that's where she is right now."

"Oh my God! She's fucking around with *Billy*! Shelia screamed into the phone.

I could tell she was struggling to maintain control of herself. In a tightly controlled voice she said, "I…Marc, can you please come get me? I…um, look I know you don't owe me anything, okay. We ain't friends or anything but the thing is, I think I had a miscarriage!"

I reeled from the sudden turn in events. I sat heavily on the stool next to the wall phone. Sheila's new found composure left her. She blurted out, "I was at my desk and all of sudden I felt a gush of fluid. I rushed to the bathroom and there was all this blood! I'm pregnant! There shouldn't be that much blood right? But maybe I'm not anymore. Pregnant, I mean. And Donna's fucking Billy right now? I can't believe this shit!"

The irony of the situation was apparently lost to Sheila. I wasn't about to connect the dots for her, though. I'd already opened Pandora's box just by telling Sheila where Donna was. It boggled my mind that Sheila had just miscarried the baby she'd conceived with Billy while cheating on Donna and most likely, the very moment she was having the miscarriage Donna was undoubtedly having sex, cheating on Sheila, with the father of Sheila's miscarried child.

"Welcome to my world." Was all I said. Maybe it was insensitive of me but I couldn't help it. "Look Sheila, you probably need to get to a hospital. Fuck Donna right now. You need to see about your baby!"

"Marc, like I said, I know we don't know each other very well but right now you are the best I can do! There is no one else I can call without having to explain this whole mess. You already *know* everything. I'll go to the hospital tomorrow confirm what I already know but right now could you please just come pick me up? Otherwise I'm going straight to Billy's house and *kill* those two!"

Damn! "Okay, Shelia," I told her. "What's the address?" The address she gave me was way the hell over in Rocklin. It would be past eight before I got there. "Give me a about half an hour and I'll be there. Don't leave. Shelia?"

"What?" Came Sheila's muffled reply. It sounded like she was trying to hide the fact that she was crying.

"DO NOT LEAVE! Okay? I'm not going to drive all the way down there just to find you gone." Her crying eased up a little.

"Okay, I'm going to wait for you, Marc. I promise." She said, and hung up the phone.

Given that I'd just felt the same murderous rage Sheila had expressed, I could commiserate with her anger, and Donna wasn't even my girlfriend! We'd had sex last night but at this moment, I didn't even like her anymore. I didn't like Sheila much either but I didn't want her to catch a case behind Donna's cheating ass. Unlike me, Sheila might not stop at just imagining the violence she wanted to do. I had a brand new door and handy dandy crowbar under the bushes to prove Sheila let passion overrule her good judgment when it came to Donna.

I jumped in the Mercedes for mission: Rescue Sheila. I needed speed because I had a sinking feeling Sheila would wait only so long before thoughts of Donna and Billy together overcame her. I didn't want her to give up on waiting for me and rush over to Billy's tore up shack to carry out her threat. As I drove I flipped through my CDs. Only Pac fit my mood.

I never was one of those Negro's who blasted music through quiet neighborhoods so loud people could feel the bass through their front windows. Tonight though, I cranked the volume up high. Damn my neighbors. I didn't care what they thought of me at this point. Pac, the prophet, had some shit to say and it needed to be said loudly.

Somebody help me! Tell me where I go from here? Cause even thugs cry, but do the Lord care? I try to remember but it hurts! I'm walking through the cemetery talking to the dirt.

Whenever I reached a point where everything around me was out of control, I could always count on "thug-life" Pac. The brother new how to articulate pain, misery, and rage like no one else on the planet. For every negative emotion I had, I could listen to Pac shout out his frustration to the world so I wouldn't have to.

I rolled down the freeway, towards Sheila, feeling every word coming through the speakers. Speeding to the address I'd had the foresight to get the directions to from Map-Quest before I left, it came to me that I was trying to stop a double murder. I didn't *really* think Sheila would go through with it. Just the same, I called on the spirit of every ancestor that went into the making of me. I called on the spirit of Melody, whose body was laying in the dirt in a cemetery in San Diego. Finally, as I approached the address, I called on God to find Sheila and talk her into waiting for me.

I was at Shelia's job quicker than I'd thought possible. Thank God, I hadn't been pulled over for driving while black in too nice a ride. That shit had happened so often when I took the Mercedes out that I couldn't believe I'd forgotten the speed limit in my quest to reach Sheila in time.

I pulled into the driveway of her job just as Sheila burned rubber peeling out of her parking space. I swerved the Mercedes diagonally to block the small entrance/exit-way. "Thank you, God, Melody, ancestors!

Thank You!" I thought to myself. Immediately after giving thanks, my next thought was, "She better not be crazy enough to ram my car! I'd have to whoop her ass for real this time if Sheila so much as scratched my bumper. No little tap on the head this time. It was a pretty head and I'd hate to have to bop it again, but I would if she slammed into my car.

Sheila, playing chicken, revved her car and slammed on the gas. I got out of my car and leaned against the door. She stopped less than an inch before she hit my ride. "I told you not to leave! " I shouted. I was at the driver's door to Sheila's car in a second. "Didn't I say to stay put till I got here? Where do you think you where going? And I KNOW you weren't trying to push my car out of the way!"

In spite of my angry tirade, my heart was in my throat. For a second there, I'd actually thought she was going to ram into my car and continue towards her revenge. Sheila rolled down her window but wouldn't look at me. "I know, Marc, I know! But you took so long I thought maybe you weren't coming or had gotten lost or something. I wasn't going over to Billy's. I swear"

Good thing the parking lot was empty, save her car and mine. I didn't need any witness around if I had to force her into my car.

"Yeah that's why you were about to ram my baby with the 'Kill Bill' look in your eyes." Sheila looked at the ground. "Look, go put your car over there and we can get it later, okay." Shelia looked up at me with tears in her eyes. Where I'd remembered smooth skin, she now had bags under her eyes and white tearstains down her cheeks. Her mascara had run making her look like a depressed circus clown.

Meekly, Sheila reversed, pulled into a marked stall, and parked. I opened the door to help her out, placed my hand on her elbow, and guided her back to my still idling car.

"Damn Marc, I didn't know you were rolling like this, I thought you only drove that big ass truck." Sheila said, obviously trying for small talk as she settled her tall frame into the small seat.

I obliged her. "I'm not one to flaunt. This baby is just a little something, something I picked up last year to roll when I need to get somewhere in a hurry."

" MMM, very nice!" Sheila said. "Thanks." I asked where she'd like me to take her. "I don't care, Marc. I just need to not be alone right now."

That was the extent of our conversation. I couldn't very well drop Sheila off at the nearest Starbucks. She'd just hitch a ride and go back for her car. I didn't want to think what she'd do after that so I headed home. For the rest of the long ride we sat in silence. It popped in my head to say, "Come on! Lets go break em off, then!" But Sheila was definitely not in a playing mood. She'd just lost her baby and found out her girl was cheating on her with the same man she'd used to cheat on Donna.

Sheila gave no indication if she was more upset about the loss of the baby or Donna cheating with her baby's daddy. I'd had the foresight to switch Pac for some soothing music the moment Sheila sat down. "Fuck the world!" or "Hit em up!" was definitely off the menu. Instead, Laila Hathaway crooned as Joe Sample tickled the ivory. Sheila had just about fallen asleep when I pulled into my garage.

Even at this time of the evening, I could see Stanley in his yard with a rake but there didn't appear to be anything needing to be raked. It was such a thin cover. This was beneath even him. Pulling into the garage I made sure to click it closed from inside the car instead of from the door by the kitchen. Even so, I heard, "Yeah! Yeaaah Marc! Whehewww! Go bruther. Switch em up! That's right!"

Shelia sat straight up and looked around the quiet garage with wide eyes. "What was *that?*" I gave her the condensed version of the Stanley story and Sheila laughed quietly as she unfolded her long body from my low-slung car. I entered the kitchen behind her. Sheila inhaled deeply the second after walking into the house, the scent of my disastrous dinner with Donna still heavy in the air.

"Wow! I hope there's some food left. I haven't eaten in forever. And I wouldn't say no to a glass of that wine. I'm pretty sure I can have a drink now." Sheila said, indicating the bottle on the kitchen table as she passed through the kitchen into the hallway leading to the living room. "It smells so *good* in here!" I realized a fraction of a second too late I should have kept her in the kitchen.

Sheila walked into the dimly lit living room, noticed the rose petals strewn on the carpet, and stopped in her tracks. Slowly wheeling on her heels she turned back to the kitchen to stare at me with incredulous eyes. I leaned against the counter, anticipating what was coming.

Obviously going back over what I'd told her during our brief phone call, before I'd rushed off to her rescue, Sheila finally asked, "So Donna was here earlier, huh, Marc?"

I nodded. I'd already told her that much so there was no point in trying to change my story now.

Sheila eyed me. I knew if I didn't have the right answer to her next question there was going to be hell to pay. "What, *exactly*, did she stop by for? You've got this whole joint hooked up like some seduction scene. Candles on the table? Roses on the floor? A meal to die for? What the hell is going on with you and *Donna*, Marc? You told me Donna and you were just friends! That's what you told me, right?"

I did not need this drama, especially considering the fact that I'd already decided Donna and I were not even a scintilla of a possibility.

"It's not like you think, Sheila." I lied, kicking rose pedals out of the way as I lead her into the living room. "I just did this as a friendly gesture for Donna. She told me she was feeling unappreciated-at - uh, work. Nothing else was going on. I promise you! Just an old friend trying to make another old friend feel appreciated" I lied. I do NOT have feelings for Donna. That much was true; at least it was now.

"Look, I tried to give Donna's self esteem a boost but she found a better boost and her ass bounced out of here before we could even eat. That's all you see here."

Sheila cut threw my line of bull. "Marc, don't even try to lie. I know you're still in love with Donna, okay. No platonic friend would go out of his way to do all this," she said, indicating the rose petals. "But look, it's never gonna happen! Whatever fantasies you had about you and her making it together is all shit! I'm not even mad at you, now that I think about it. You are fighting a losing battle with Donna. Shit, I gave *my* best to be the one she would want to spend her life with. I *know* she was never satisfied with what you had to offer; otherwise, she'd have never gotten with me. She was obviously not satisfied with what I had to offer either, or she wouldn't be with Billy right now! I don't know how you handled it but when I got tired of trying to be the one for her and Billy walked back into my life I sort of just gave up. Not enough to really leave her but still, I guess I just stopped trying. How come you never did?"

I'd only tonight just figured out myself the reason I'd kept hope alive waiting for Donna and even though Sheila was willing to put all her cards on the table I wasn't ready to put mine down yet. Not with her and probably not with anyone. It was enough that I knew. Finally.

Sheila took my silence as proof that I still loved Donna. She tried again. "Marc, Donna is a free spirit. Apparently, Billy is too. But I couldn't keep up with Donna for nothing in this world. Neither could you, obviously. So here we are, the two of us, standing together due to the damage Donna has done, on a rose strewn carpet."

I guess that answered the question about which catastrophic event Sheila was most concerned. The baby she'd miscarried didn't enter into her monologue. Her speech might have been devastating to me if I had any lingering thoughts or hopes of Donna being mine.

"Marc," Sheila said, walking towards me to urgently clutch at my arm, "I heard the two of them on the phone one evening when he called for me. He pretended to be my cousin. That's what we'd decided to do if he called and Donna answered. I acted like I was asleep when she answered the phone, assuming Donna would tell him I wasn't available and hang up. But Donna and Billy talked and talked and talked as if I weren't in the room. I'm wondering now if both of them weren't playing me the whole time I thought I was playing her! The difference in the *quality* of the playing I did with a guilty conscious is that I was torn up about being with Billy again! For Donna, it just seems to me now that she was having fun at my expense, and, maybe yours too."

I was caught totally off guard but I was so glad I'd decided to go pick Sheila up. Every word coming out of her mouth confirmed the decision I'd made in the car driving away from Donna and Billy.

"Marc, I wasn't even supposed to be in town tonight. I was going to see my parents and Donna *claimed* she couldn't get out of work so I planned to go by myself. I'd planned to be gone for a week and get back this Sunday but I wanted to surprise her so I came home early. I just dropped by the job to check my messages before heading off to be with her. That's when I started bleeding. I tried to reach Donna but she didn't answer her phone. I tried all the other numbers I had for her but couldn't find her. That's when I called you!"

I just shook my head in disgust. I could not believe what I was hearing! Donna had played both Sheila and me. Why? How could she so trivialize the many years we'd been cool by pulling me into this crazy, mixed up drama? And what was so special about Billy that she pulled out of here so fast to go do with him what I'd thought we were about to do? Something wasn't adding up right. Whatever. I was just glad she'd done what she'd done because it lifted the fog from my eyes.

Instead of focusing on Donna's multi-layered betrayals I asked Sheila, "So, what are you going to do now, Sheila?"

"I don't know, Marc, I-." Before she finished her sentence, the phone rang. I checked the caller ID box. I got the next shock in the long night of shocking events. Donna was calling from her mobile phone.

Placing my finger to my lips, indicating to Sheila to stay quiet, I clicked the button for speakerphone. "Hello! And what can I do for you, Miss Donna?"

"Oh Marc I'm glad I was able to catch up with you. I tried earlier but I guess you were out. I just wanted to tell you again, how sorry I am about having to cut out so quickly when I stopped by. I had to help Shelia. She was going through some things and needed some girl time. She's better now."

I didn't respond so Donna continued, "*Also,* I wanted to know if I could come by to finish what we started earlier? Her voice, seductive but low, let me know Billy was somewhere on the premises. Her ass didn't even stop to consider the fact that I knew for a fact she wouldn't have added that last bit if Sheila was really in the room.

"Oh, uh, yeah!" I cleared my throat. "Thanks, Donna! Come on by," I winked at Sheila who plopped herself into a chair at the table and put her head in her hands. "Let's definitely finish up what *you* started, as long as Shelia is okay now and all."

Broke down Billy didn't make it happen for you, huh? I thought. Well, Donna *had* told me I was the only man who could get her off. My pride had to get a boost wherever it could at this point because most of it was shredded to pieces because of this whole ordeal.

Donna continued piling dirt onto her own grave. "Cool, I just need to run by my girlfriend's house on the way." Meaning she had to wash the scent of Billy off, before she came to me for what I guess she considered the bonus round. "I should be there in thirty minutes." She told me.

"Cool! Cool. Hey! Tell Shelia I said 'Hi' and I hope she feels better." Donna had the audacity to say softly to the non-existent Sheila beside her, "Shelia, Marc says he hopes you feel better." Both Shelia and I shook our heads in disbelief.

"Awhh, see? You two can maybe still be friends! Sheila said to say thanks Marc. She's sorry about the door. She expressly told me to tell you that you are one of the good guys."

"No problem," I told her. "Put her on the phone. I'll let her know in person that things are cool between us." Donna paused for a few seconds. "Sheila? You okay? She must have a sick stomach again. She just rushed off to the bathroom again. It's her pregnancy. I'll just make sure she's okay then I'm on my way, Okay?" Donna hung up.

Without a word, I warmed a plate of food in the microwave and placed it in front of Sheila. This was some shit beyond anything I'd believed Donna capable. Pretending to have a conversation with the person who was, at this very moment, sitting at my kitchen ready to eat the meal I'd prepared for Donna?

Shelia shook her head again in disbelief. "I'm so disgusted right now I couldn't possibly eat. " Sheila said, before diving into the food in front of her as if she hadn't eaten in days.

I walked to the cabinet over the stove and reached up for my top shelf liquor. Johnny Walker Blue was a requisite at this point. This was a two hundred and fifty dollar bottle. I normally only pull it down on special occasions or with special company. Tonight was very special for me. I was free!

I poured a shot for myself and slammed it back. It went down smooth. I poured another and let it glide down to my empty stomach. The effects were immediate. My body warmed instantly.

"Mmm! Now that's some good liquor, Shelia. I'd offer you some but I don't think you should have any booze until you know for sure that you aren't still pregnant"

Placing the bottle back on the shelf, I turned back and sat opposite Sheila. "Vhy do ju kee ee uh ver?" She asked, holding a hand up to cover her mouthful of food.

I smiled. "Johnny Blue isn't every-day drinking liquor just because you are in the mood for a drink, see? All bottles in that cabinet cost a hun or more."

Sheila took great efforts to chew and swallow the next mouthful she'd just taken before replying, "I can understand that, I guess. So what? You keep the raunchy stuff out for your friends in a wet bar somewhere, huh?"

She'd hit the nail pretty much on the head. "Nah, it's not exactly like that, Ms. Lady. It's just that I break the good stuff out only on special occasions. If you keep your good stuff out with the ordinary stuff somebody might get it twisted and assume they can pull it out just to watch a game or something."

Now that we'd discussed the psychology of where I stored my liquor I had something much more important to talk about. "So what are we going to do? Donna is on her way here and it's about to get crunk up in this mug, Ms. Lady. How do you want to play it? "

It was crazy but at this moment, Sheila had become an ally to me in a war against Donna. I was ready to set it off! I assumed Sheila would be down with my program but the woman kept surprising me. I thought she'd say, "Okay let me hide in the closet and come out kicking ass when she gets here!"

Instead, covering the last mouthful of food before swallowing heavily she said, "Marc, I gotta be out. It's been a really, *really,* messed up day and it can only get worse once Donna gets here. I'm sorry, but I'll leave you to deal with Donna so I can get home and pack my shit before she gets back. I know that sounds like a punk move but if you could do me this solid, I'll owe you forever. And really, as much as I feel like slapping the shit out of Donna I don't want to go to jail for not stopping with a slap. Can you take me home?"

I was taken aback by her response but impressed all the same. I got up to grab the keys off the hook where'd I'd left them less than a half hour ago. "I hear you, girl. Let's roll." I said, and headed into the garage.

From behind me Shelia asked, "Are you going to call her and tell her you'll be a few minutes late?"

"Hell no, if she comes by and I'm not here she can wait or she can leave. You only feel like slapping her, I feel like putting my foot up her ass. I don't want to go to jail either!"

We slid into the Benz and rolled down the driveway. Thankfully, Stanley had given up for the night and was nowhere to be seen. Or so I thought.

On the street, before heading toward the house Sheila shared with Donna, I glanced over to Stanley's home out of habit and damned if I couldn't see his two little beady eyes peering through the blinds. The man lived through me!

While driving, I tried for some small talk to drown out the awkward silence. "So what do you do out there in Rocklin, Sheila?"

She laid back on the headrest, "I handle accounts receivable for a mineral company."

Not much to go with there. I tried again. "So what do you like to do in your spare time? You know, between accounts receivable and rushing home to be with Donna, like you aren't going to do anymore, right?"

"I certainly won't be rushing home to Donna and as for the other, I don't know, Marc. I like to play tennis. I read books. I even like to write a little. That's about it."

Her responses didn't leave me with too much room for follow up questions. I didn't want to ask about what Sheila wrote about for fear it would get too deep. Switching up, I asked, "Shelia, do you want me to take you to your car instead of going home?"

"Nope, I most certainly do not!" She told me. "Just take me to the house Marc, I can get a ride to work in the morning from wherever I'll be staying."

Shelia obviously wasn't in the mood to talk anymore. Thankfully, I pulled up to her house a few minutes later and Shelia leaned over to kiss me on the cheek.

"Thanks Marc, you really 'are one of the good guys'. Don't ever change for anybody!"

If a dark skinned brother could blush, I would have at that moment. I'm not one for jumping all over compliments though, so I simply said, "Cool, and cool! I won't. You take care of yourself and make sure you go to the hospital before you do anything else tomorrow." Sheila gave me a sad smile and hopped out to head up the walk to her house. "Good luck with Donna!" She called as I drove away. Luck didn't even enter into it.

I flipped a U turn and headed back to my house. I drove down the quiet streets at 50 in a 25-mile zone. Damn a ticket. I had to get home and deal with Donna once and for all.

I turned the corner onto my street. Stanley's garage was open. He was sitting in a lawn chair sipping a beer. Donna was parked at the curb and got out of the car as she saw me approach.

Double shit! This was turning into a damn game. Tomorrow after work, I resolved to have a talk with Stanley about his spying and his crazy outbursts. No telling what his next reaction would be. Tonight he'd witnessed two women arriving, staying for a while, leaving, and the first one showing up again. He and Ramona must think I was the dog of the year, even though Stanley seemed cool with it, even happy for me.

Not even bothering with trying to block the next couple of minutes from Stanley's view, I parked in the driveway instead of pulling into the garage, got out and headed toward Donna, in a hurry to be done with her. On the way, in spite of myself, I cut my eyes in Stanley's direction. To my surprise, Stanley simply put one thumb high in the air as if he were at a concert holding a cigarette lighter but other than that kept his mouth shut. His silent gesture wasn't too off the hook. I had to give Stanley props for his silent tribute. He'd finally figured out less was more than enough.

Donna met me on the sidewalk in front of my house. I cut another glance over to Stanley. He was cheesing so hard I could see every tooth in his mouth.

Then out of nowhere he threw his head back and yelled, "Whew bruther, you've got a *habit*! Whew!"

Thankfully, Ramona poked her head out of the door. "Stanley! Get in here now! Now! Leave that man alone with his strumpets!"

Within seconds, Stanley folded his chair up, snuck a final thumbs up to me, hit the button on his own garage door and was gone from sight, dealing with his own woman and his own drama for once.

Donna's head jerked almost violently toward Stanley's house when his wife had called out. When Stanley was gone from site Donna demanded, "Who is that bitch calling a *strumpet*?"

Stanley's backward ass had probably made the mistake of telling Ramona Donna had flashed him. "First of all, don't you ever call Ramona a bitch again. She's old enough to be your mother so show some damn respect. Second, calm your ass down Donna. Do you even know what a strumpet is?"

"No!" Donna shouted. Now that was funny but I was too mad at her to laugh. "But I know from the way she said it, it can't be good. And who are the other *strumpets?*" Her eyes narrowed and she demanded, "Who was here earlier, Marc?"

As always, Donna attempted to turn the table and put me on the hot seat. It wasn't going down like that. "You ain't bit more worried about them two than I am. And you most certainly don't have the right to be worried about who does or does not get to come see me. Now get your ass in this house. We got some shit to deal with and it can't wait another second."

"Who the hell do you think you are talking to?" Donna said angrily. I ignored her comment, took her by the arm, and half dragged her into the house. Inside, Donna, the Gemini, showed another face yet again. "Damn! I didn't know you were into the man handling Marc. I like it! If I'd known that, maybe I would have told Sheila I couldn't go see about her right then. I see you want to play rough tonight, eh?"

Normally junior would have jumped a little at Donna's suggestive tone. I had nothing for her. Not even a slight one-eyed peep of interest. With my back against the front door and my arms folded across my chest, I stared at her. Now that she was here and this confrontation was actually, *finally,* about to happen I wanted to make sure I came strong, not just blurt out the first thing that came to mind. Donna could sense weakness like a lioness hunting for her next meal.

"Do you just want to stare at me or are we going to finish what we started? And by the way," Donna walked towards me and put her arms up to hug me, "Hi Marckie baby, how you doing?" I blocked the hug and walked into the living room, leaving her to trail behind me.

"How do you think I'm doing, Donna?" I plopped down on the couch.

Donna stood before me. "Okay, obviously you are a little miffed at me for leaving earlier. I'm back to make it all better, baby!" She tried to sit on my lap and I maneuvered so that she'd end up on the sofa cushion alone.

Instead of getting mad at my unresponsiveness, Donna kept trying. "Hey baby," she said, "what's wrong? I've apologized a hundred times. Come on now." She patted the cushion next to her.

My mouth couldn't wait for my brain to come up with the perfect words to fit my thoughts. Shit doesn't change. Mouth took control. I leaned closer to Donna, spoke in a voice full of hatred, and blasted her.

"Just who the *fuck* do you think you are, Donna? Huh? You walked out of here after you promised me we would talk through the situation last night. What it meant for the two of us. And why did you show up last night, huh? You claimed you just wanted to be held because you were feeling low. I guess Sheila strapping on some plastic isn't cutting it for you anymore. Is that it?"

Donna gasped and tried to cut me off but I wasn't finished. "Fine! The plastic is getting old. But you obviously had other places to go if you just wanted some real male dick so why keep coming over here? I let you in, treat you like a queen and then you leave *me*, the man whose been by your side through all your bullshit, to go fuck somebody who wasn't about shit! And now you have *gall* to try and play like everything is cool? Who the fuck do you think you are? Your shit ain't that good Donna."

Donna jumped up from the couch, eyes huge with rage. With disingenuous anger, she blazed back at me, "Wait just one goddamn minute, sir! This is bullshit. I told you Shelia needed me and even though she did me wrong, I still love her! I came to you last night because I needed to be with you but that doesn't change how I feel about Sheila. And you know good and *fucking* well, you would have done the same thing in my situation!"

"Oh is that right. Donna?" I was standing too at this point. "You think you know what I would do if had the choice between you and some scrub? You don't know shit about me, girl! If the situation were reversed I'd have stayed my ass where I was!"

Donna actually put her finger in my face, pointing at me as if I were a child she was scolding. "No you wouldn't have and don't you even try to deny it." She hissed at me. "If it was that *bitch,* Melody, who you've obviously never gotten over, you'd have left me in a damn second to make sure she was alright. I did the same thing and you've got the nerve to jump all over me, Mr. Big Shot!"

Time slowed down. The scene in my living room took on a surreal feeling. Did she just say what I thought she said? I stood quietly for a fraction of a second before the reality of Donna's words had a chance to register on my brain.

"Donna, don't *ever* call Melody out of her name again. Matter of fact, don't even speak her name again! You don't have enough class to even think what you and I had compares to what I had with Melody. Goddamn Bitch! And get your finger out of my face!" I grabbed her hand and threw it away from me. "Who do you think you are talking to? Obviously, you are still under the impression I believe your lying ass about going to see about Sheila when you left here. Just get out my house! Leave! Turn your ass around and get out of my face with all your lies! Get out!" I was shouting and my breath came out raggedly. I'd lost control the second Donna brought Melody's memory into play. Breathing heavily after my tirade, the surreal feeling lifted and I couldn't believe what I had just said to her. Apparently, neither could Donna.

She turned away stunned and the tears started flowing. Donna walked to the front door, turned back to me, and shook her head as if to clear it. "I don't know what has gotten into you, Marc." She said sadly through her crocodile tears. "All I did was go see about someone I care about in her time of need to make sure she was alright. I came straight back to you when I knew she was okay! I can't believe you would disrespect me so much for doing a decent thing!" Donna, the martyr, turned to leave.

"Donna, wait." I called out. She turned back, hope showing on her face. I walked slowly to stand in front of her. I took her hand from the doorknob and held it.

Quietly, I said, "I'm sorry about the name calling, okay? But stop with the lies already. All that shit you keep trying to make me believe is bullshit. You wanna know how I know its bullshit?"

Donna couldn't speak. She stood there staring with wide eyes while I continued, in the same tone, still holding her hand I said, "All that shit about your girl needing you being the reason you left was a lie. You and I both know it. Wanna know how I know?" Again, Donna didn't respond. Instead, she looked at the ground and tried to pull her hand away from mine. I held fast.

"I know this, Donna, because when you called *from Billy's* guess who was sitting here with me eating the meal you should have been enjoying?"

Donna's head shot up quickly. She didn't say a word but I could see the thoughts running through her head. "Yeah, that's right, baby girl. Sheila was hear and heard every word out of your mouth. So you know what? You can keep all your phony tears to yourself. That's right close your mouth." Donna stopped struggling to yank her hand out of my grasp and looked at me with defeat. Just for extra measure, to make sure she knew the full extent of her dirty dealing I asked, "And you want to guess how I know you were with Billy?"

Donna said, "Forget it, Marc. I'm leaving, okay? You don't ever have to worry about me again."

"Oh, no. Let's finish this. I know you were with Billy because I followed you when you left here." I told her.

Donna began again in earnest to pull away from my grasp. I clamped down. "That's right, I followed you and just like the man said in the song, your ass is cold busted. I finally know what you are all about and I don't want anything else to do with you."

I kissed her on the cheek for old time's sake and walked away. "Lock the door on your way out would you?"

"Marc," she tried.

"Just leave Donna!" I told her.

"Marc, please let me explain, I promise to tell the truth this time. I never meant to play you. You have got to know I wouldn't do you like that, if I could help it! Marc, there are things you don't know! You've got to believe me!"

I was on the verge of physically throwing Donna from my house when she ran towards me and grabbed my hand, sinking into a puddle of tears.

"Marc, I'm sorry. I'm sorry! I didn't mean to hurt you! I never meant for any of this to happen! You don't know what I've been through trying to do what I thought would help Sheila right after what you and I just shared. My God, Marc! Do you really think so little of me that you believe I could act like this if I didn't have a reason?"

With Donna groveling at my feet I felt myself starting to weaken but this shit had to stop. I'd had a feeling something was up besides her wanting to have sex with Sheila's man but the bottom line was, it didn't matter what those reasons were. The doormat was exactly where it belonged; lying at the front door, not on my back. I pulled Donna to her feet and walked her out the door.

I wasn't relishing Stanley's comments tomorrow because I knew he was watching from his house, as always. I turned the porch light off and walked into the kitchen, grabbed a bottle of wine and headed upstairs for the evening, hoping Donna would realize I was done and just go away forever.

The bell rang a few times but then Donna apparently gave up and went away. Silence! Finally! It was 12:45 am and I had to meet Tyler in less than five hours. I need sleep!

I refused to feel bad about Donna out there in the darkness. I took a few sips of wine before taking off my clothes and crawling into bed.

Donna must have known she had no one to go home to considering I'd just clued her into the fact that Sheila knew she had been with Billy. Whatever her reasons were, I didn't want to hear them and I was sure Sheila wouldn't either. And now her fall back guy, the one she always turned to when shit got too rough, was no longer available. I didn't care what her reasons were for doing what she'd done. I took a final sip of wine and laid my head on the pillow.

I was in the right. Donna was in the wrong. She was out of my life. End of story.

QUESTIONS

Beep, beep, beep, beep.

I woke up groggily. Damn! Why did I set the alarm for so early?

Last night came back to me in a rush. I was scheduled to meet Tyler at Wynona's Waffle House at 5 am so I had to get up and going. I spared a few thoughts for Donna; wondering what she'd done after she left here, but I didn't spend too much time dwelling on it.

From beneath my quilt, I could tell the room surrounding my warm nestling place was freezing.

Jumping out of bed quickly, knowing the cold would definitely wake me up; I went through my usual routine of turning up the heater; walking to the shower and turning it on. The fresh smell of coffee came at me from downstairs. If I could shake off the tiredness long enough to jump in the shower I'd be good to go.

By four O'clock, I'd showered, dressed, and run downstairs to grab my coffee. I needed to arrive at the restaurant before Tyler. That was one of my quirks I never bothered to question. Whenever I needed to meet with someone, I had to be there before they showed up.

Pulling into Wynona's at 4:30 am, I walked in, ordered the breakfast I knew Tyler always got when he came here because one of Tyler's many passions was the food he got from Wynona's. He always describes his meals in such detail I knew just what to get. Grits, eggs, home fries, sausage, and biscuits with Karo syrup. I'd have to ask him about that Karo sometime. That was a black folk thing I didn't know white folks were schooled to.

Tyler, being an early riser as well as one of those people who always arrive early, would be at Wynona's no later than 4:45, I knew. You can set your watch by the dude, which wasn't always a good thing. Just as I'd thought, right down to the second I'd predicted, in walked Tyler carrying an aluminum briefcase.

Tyler looked around the restaurant and I signaled him over to my table. "I can always count on you to beat me to the punch. I *knew* you would be here first even if I got here early." Tyler said as he took a seat.

"Damn, man! So you figured out my game just when I thought I'd figured yours out, eh?" An image of Donna floated before my eyes as I spoke. I shook my head clear. Tyler was speaking.

"Did you already order? How long have you been here? I figured you would be here early but I tried to beat you anyway." He chuckled.

I leaned back into the plastic chair. "Yep, already ordered the breakfast you always get from here." Tyler looked mildly surprised. "I notice what people are talking about at the office even when they think I don't, okay?" I laughed. "As for being here early, I keep a carefree life so getting up earlier than normal isn't a big deal" I said. That used to be the truth anyway.

Just as I was going to ask what Tyler had in the briefcase straight out of *Get Smart* the waitress brought our food. We spent a few minutes grubbing.

"I love these biscuits with the dark Karo!" Tyler exclaimed, sopping the last of his biscuit into the syrup. "I didn't even *know* about this stuff until my wife schooled me to it."

"Yeah, you're right, Tyler." I swallowed heavily and took another forkful of the potatoes. "This breakfast reminds me of my mom's cooking every Saturday morning when I was growing up!" I got nostalgic for home for a second. I'd have to drop by and see how she and pops were doing.

We'd practically inhaled our breakfast and sat back in our chairs, satisfied and rubbing our stomachs. It was time for business.

"So what's in the metal briefcase, Agent 86? Should I pull down the cone of silence so no one else can hear us? I'm surprised you don't have it chained to your wrist! You walked in hear looking like *Maxwell Smart*!"

Tyler laughed. "You need to keep better track of my expense sheet if you don't know what's in here, boss" he said, pulling the briefcase onto the tabletop.

I briefly recalled an expense claim for equipment I'd recently signed off for Tyler. Because it *was* Tyler's claim sheet, I hadn't bothered studying it too closely. I knew if he'd asked for it, it was okay.

Tyler opened his case. "Check this stuff out, boss-man." He said, sliding it towards me, "Now that's what I'm talking about! No wonder you crack cases so fast!" Inside the leather lined case was all manner of the most up to date in surveillance equipment; laser monitoring unit complete with tripod, fiber-optic cameras about the size of a credit card, micro room transmitters about the size of a deck of cards, something that looked like a high tech sports watch but was actually a digital camera. I picked up a listening device with a binocular mounting clip small enough to fit into the palm of my hand.

"This is that Super Ear I just read about in 'Spy' magazine right?" Tyler nodded and smiled. "I'll take that. And this one." I said, grabbing the Super Ear and a digital camera watch. "Man, I sure am glad you're on my team, Tyler. You don't *play,* do you man?"

"Not when it comes to work, boss. I'm the best you've got. I thought you knew!" He told me, thumping his chest."

I laughed. "Okay, you got me there, Tyler. I give props where props are due. But tell me then, chest thumper, why is this case so different from all the others? With all this equipment I can't understand why you couldn't nail this guy on the first day!"

"Like I told you yesterday, boss, this guy is just different." Tyler said, obviously embarrassed he'd had to bring in a second on the case. "I mean, he acts like he knows he's got a tail on him or something, you know? Or maybe I'm just slipping."

"Remember those instincts of mine I told you about?" I asked Tyler. He nodded. "Right now my instincts tell me you aren't slipping. I think you were right. Maybe this guy knows he's being tailed and is working extra hard to keep you off his trail. Or maybe, whatever he's doing is so foul he's already worked up elaborate means to cover his tracks. Whatever the case, you were right to ask for back up. That's not an indication of you slipping. It's just you are on your game enough to know we have to step the game up a notch to catch this guy. There's no shame in admitting you need help, Tyler. Damn man. You were on the job! You *know* sometimes you just need a partner riding shotgun for you to close the case. Now am I right or am I right?"

Tyler, looking humbled but ready to move on, replied. "You know what? You are the best boss I could ask for, Mr. Haley" Tyler said, with a sideways grin. "Let's go get this guy, yes?"

"*Yes!* And I've told you a million times; it's 'Marc', okay? Anybody that's been with me as long as you have should be able to use my first damn name, okay? You don't have to call me 'boss-man' or Mr. Haley. You Tyler" I thumped my chest, "Me just 'Marc'"

Tyler laughed. "Alright! Alright, I get it *Marc"* He said with a wry grin. "Lets do this then, shall we?" I nodded.

"Let me just get the check and we can be out." I told him.

"Hell no, *Marc!"* Tyler said. "This is my dime. I called you, you are working for me, right?" I nodded. "Okay, I hired you as back up and that means the meal is on me. My boss is cool like that. I'll just add this meal to my next expense account and it's all gravy baby!" Tyler said, as if I were an informant he'd just added to the payroll.

I laughed with him. "You must have a cool as hell boss! Pick up the check then, Mr. Wright."

We channeled our Nextel phones to be group talk and left Wynona's with full stomachs but a hunger to catch the sneaky bastard who'd eluded Tyler thus far.

On the way to our separate vehicles, Tyler and I drafted a plan to make sure every building Mr. Ivan entered was covered front and back.

The clock on my dashboard read 6:00 a.m. as I drove past the address listed on the file folder open on the passenger seat alongside the equipment I'd picked up from Tyler. The folder contained information Tyler had gotten from Invisible's wife as well as pictures of the house, Invisible himself, and a few of the wife. Tyler was right. For an older woman she was still remarkably attractive. Even so, when I held the photo of Invisible next to that of his wife it was hard to imagine the two as a couple. I couldn't place it yet, but something was definitely off. I'd marinate on it for a while and hope those instincts I'd just bragged to Tyler about kicked in.

The house was situated on a hill. I stopped four houses down and parked next to the curb on the opposite side of the street. At the same moment, Tyler drove past me and parked the rental car Id suggested he rent last night four houses down in the opposite direction from where I was situated. I'd told him to use the company credit card to rent a different car. In case Mr Invisible really was wise to being followed he wouldn't recognize the different vehicle and would, hopefully, believe the heat was off. I pulled the Nextel from my belt pouch and beeped Tyler.

"Hey, during your discussion with this guy's wife did she ever mention their age difference or why she hooked up with such a young cat?"

"I asked her about it. " Tyler said without further explanation.

"Well?" I prompted him.

"I got a call from my wife just as she was about to answer. I rushed her off the phone but I guess I forgot to get back to the question once I'd hung up."

I didn't say anything for a moment. Tyler *was* slipping; I hated to admit to myself. It would have been extremely helpful in cracking this case to understand how and why the two had initially hooked up. Maybe this guy had a pattern of befriending lonely old ladies hoping to find a sugar mama. If that was the case, maybe he was hitting the circuit again in search of any even richer woman. Whatever the case, the fact that Tyler had neglected to find out where she'd found the guy in the first place and this important piece of information made working on this case feel to me as if I were operating blind.

"If we don't catch him today make a note to call her back and ask where she met her husband, okay?" I finally said.

Tyler heard my unspoken rebuke loud and clear. "I'm sorry, Marc. I *knew* there was something I'd forgotten to ask Mrs. Ivan before she left. The call from my wife had me rattled and I just let the lady leave without asking her about it again because I was preoccupied with something my wife had said.I fucked up, man. Look, I'll call Mrs. Ivan after her husband leaves and set up a meeting tonight. Hopefully we'll catch this guy today and it won't be necessary to meet with her again without the goods she's looking for."

I couldn't be too mad at Tyler. I understood all too clearly, due to recent events, being too blindsided by events in your personal life to concentrate fully on your own work. Still, I'm sure I would have taken the time to get the full background info on such an important case in spite of all the drama I'd been dealing with myself lately.

"Yeah. Okay. Like you said, hopefully it won't be necessary but set it up just in case." Shaking my head, I clicked the phone closed and got comfortable in the seat of my truck.

According to the file, Invisible left the house anywhere between 6:30 and 8:00 each morning. Tyler had had the foresight to ask about Invisible's current occupation. Apparently, he drifted from job to job and was currently unemployed. Mrs. Ivan had told Tyler our mark left each morning to pound the pavement trying to find a job in the securities industry. By 8:45, there was still no movement from the house.

At 8:49 a slender woman, wearing sweat pants and sweat shirt, left the house and got into a beat up, older than dirt Dodge hatchback parked in the driveway and drove off. I couldn't get a clear look at her because she was moving too fast. I hadn't read anything about a maid or family member living in the house and thought again that Tyler hadn't done enough homework on this case.

At any rate, whoever the woman was who sped down the street happened to be she wasn't germane to the job we were being paid to do.

I hit Tyler up on the Nextel again. "What time does this guy normally leave again? According to your notes he should have been gone before that maid, or whoever she is, who, incidentally isn't mentioned in your narrative. What's up with that?"

Tyler ignored my pointed remark on his failure to document the occupants of the house.

"Marc, I told you it would be a long day back at Wynona's, remember. This guy comes and goes at all different times normally even though lately he's left at the times I noted. You want to follow the hatchback to see if Ivan meets up with her if he somehow manages to slip away from me again? I've never tried to follow her yet. Maybe that's the key?"

"No. He's not doing the maid. Don't ask me how I know. It's just the wrong trail to follow. I'm sure of that much."

Just as I'd finished speaking, the garage opened, and a metallic blue Navigator rolled down the driveway. "Tyler we have movement. Unless there's someone else in the house you forgot to report, that's got to be our boy! He's coming your way. You on it?"

Static came through the line but no response from Tyler

"Tyler! Answer me Damn it! Ole boy is moving! Where the hell are you?" I shouted into the phone.

Tyler voice finally came through. "Yes *boss*, I heard you the first time! There must have been a glitch on the phone. I told you a couple of times I'm on his tail."

"Well Damn Tyler, get your shit together! Which way is he going? Where should I intersect?" I barked into the phone. I couldn't really explain why I was suddenly so angry with Tyler.

Silence and mild static on the line was all I heard for a few seconds. Tyler's voice sounded through again. "Boss?" He asked tentatively."

"What!" Shouting into the receiver, I turned the truck around to follow Tyler following Ivan. "I mean, *what.* " I said more calmly.

"Who pissed in your corn flakes this morning? Are you *that* mad at me for forgetting to ask a question I can clear up with a 30 second phone call?"

At once, my mind went back to last night. I wasn't mad at Tyler, disappointed and concerned maybe. I was angry with Donna and misdirecting onto the very next person who made an error in judgment in my presence. And, in spite of myself, I couldn't shake the memory of Donna keeping vigil at my door for so long last night no matter how hard I tried to concentrate on the case at hand. There were so many similarities between what I was doing now, for money, to what I'd done last night, for love, or so I'd thought at the time.

I needed to get a grip on myself. "I'm sorry Tyler. I didn't mean to yell at you. I just wanted to know if you are clocking which street Ivan turned down. Do you think he spotted you? Which way is he going? I'll come from a different direction and he'll never know he's got two tails"

Tyler didn't answer right away. Then, out of nowhere, he said, "Was it good, Marc? Tell me about it. And before you go off again I've got him in clear view, okay? I may be slipping but not that much!"

"Yeah, when we get back to the office lets revisit that issue, eh?" I said.

"Yeah, I guess we should; there's some stuff I need to run by you anyway. But for real though, Marc, I've never known you to lose your cool over a case, whether you were sitting behind a desk or not! Is it a woman?"

I had to laugh in spite of my frustration. Tyler hit the nail on the head but I wasn't prepared to delve into the complexities of my relationship with Donna to what amounted to a hired hand. Tyler was good at his game, normally, and worked his ass off for me but that's all there was between us. I needed to be questioning his ass about his own woman seeing he'd neglected to garner very pertinent information from a HiCi client due to the urgent call from his wife.

"Where's he headed?" I asked Tyler, completely ignoring his attempt to pry into my personal life.

"Looks as if he's headed towards the Arden Mall." Tyler said, apparently giving up on his questions.

We followed Ivan to the mall and Tyler was several cars behind him. I'd passed them by to the next entrance and drove towards Ivan's car. I parked in an empty stall 10 cars down. Ivan got out of his car and headed inside. I beeped Tyler. "I'll track him inside, just in case he's seen you before, okay?"

He beeped back. "Okay, I've got his car in sight. If he somehow manages to get past you and back to his car I'll be on him."

"Not gonna happen." I told Tyler. "I'm out." I grabbed the digital camera/watch and strapped it to my wrist. I followed Ivan for about an hour inside the mall as he stopped at a shoe store and bought a pair of black pumps 13 pumps. The camera recorded his purchase. My hunch was right. I knew he wasn't doing the maid because there was no way that petite frame could support such large feet.

Next Ivan stopped at the candy store and bought about a pound of jellybeans. I got a picture of that transaction as well. It was probably irrelevant. The guy could have a nasty jellybean habit and was just satisfying his sweet tooth. But he could also be buying the candy for whomever he was going to meet.

Casually, without a care in the world, and obviously completely unaware I was following, Mr. Ivan walked into Barnes and Noble and scanned the shelves. I stationed myself at the front magazine stand and waited him out.

Obviously not finding what he was looking for he stepped to the information desk and accessed the computer. Satisfied that his book wasn't available Ivan walked out of the bookstore without a purchase. I let him leave without following and as soon as he turned the corner quickly went to the computer just before another customer got to it. "Sorry, this will be quick." I told the young girl. She turned away, "Oh my gaaawd! How rude!" The girl said and went off in search for another computer I assumed. I noted the book Ivan had been searching for. Interesting.

I rushed back out of the store and caught a glimpse of Mr. Ivan from behind as he entered Lane Bryant a few shops down from the bookstore. Thank goodness I hadn't lost him after I'd assured Tyler I wouldn't.

Either Mr. Ivan was cheating with a very tall woman with big feet or a very fat woman with big feet because Lane Bryant only sold clothes that started at size 14 according to the sign above the shop window.

Ivan went straight to the lingerie section, selected, and purchased a black lace bra that looked to be about a 40 D. I know bra sizes because I'm an avid student of breasts. Sue me.

Gathering all of his purchases, Mr. Ivan left the Arden Mall and stepped out of the glass doors back into the sunshine. I pulled the mobile phone from my belt and beeped Tyler. "He's coming your way."

"Got him." Tyler said. "I'll pull out just as he gets to his car and I'll post up by JC Penny and follow you this time. Let me know where you want me to meet up."

"10-4." I walked back to my car keeping a close eye on Mr. Ivan a few rows over. Tossing his packages into the back of the truck, he slammed the door, jumped into the driver's seat of the Escalade, and zoomed out. The candy must not be for him or he'd have kept it up front with him, I noted.

With only one car between Mr. Ivan and mine as he exited Arden Mall's parking lot, I was confident Ivan hadn't noticed his tail. Instead of getting on the freeway, as I thought he would, Ivan made a series of turns and finally pulled into the parking lot of a place called Luxury Suites. We were going to crack this case wide open today! "Yeah buddy, go get your freak on. Make sure to make it interesting for the watch here." I said aloud, patting the camera still strapped to my wrist.

Until this moment, I'd never known this place existed. Even though it was located in the busy Arden area the location was very secluded and off the beaten track of the other hotels in the area.

From what I could gather, Luxury Suites consisted of about 24 rental units intersected by what appeared to be about 3 conference rooms. I noted 17 cars in the parking lot. For this hour of day, I'd have expected the executives who would probably frequent this hotel to have long since gone on to be about the business of whatever they'd come to town for.

Mr. Ivan surprised me. Stopping at the back of his truck to place his purchases inside of a gym bag, instead of going straight to one of the hotel's rooms he went into one of the sliding glass doors I'd taken for a conference room.

Tyler hit me on the Nextel. "Okay, heads up Marc. This is where I lost Ivan two weeks ago."

"Got it. Why don't you park at the curb to the entrance and I'll park right beside big blue here." I told Tyler, pulling into the empty spot next to Ivan's Escalade. "How could you lose him here though?" There was only one way in and one way out to the Luxury Suites.

"Another thing I guess I forgot to mention in my notes." Tyler said sheepishly. "Two women got into Ivan's car and left. I was going to follow them but then I decided to stay and see who he left with, figuring that would lead me to the evidence I needed to close the case. I thought he'd figured out he was being tailed and sent the women out as a decoy."

"That's interesting." I told Tyler. Trying to process the new information Tyler had once again failed to note in his file. Suddenly, I remembered Ivan's purchases and the purchase he didn't make. "There's a bunch of other interesting things I found out while tailing Ivan at the mall."

"Like what?" Tyler asked. I got out walked into the lobby of the hotel. The desk clerks looked up at me expectantly but looked back down again as I settled myself into a lobby chair with a clear view of the conference room and Ivan's car.

"Like, he's buying clothes and shoes for a big woman. Also, he must not be used to doing big women because he was looking for the *Kama sutra* in the bookstore. That book has info and pictures on how to hit it from every possible scenario and position. Men with women, women with women, men with men-the whole nine. He's probably trying to find a way to do his new woman because he's never dealt with a chick either that big or that fat!"

Tyler laughed. "The woman who drove away his escalade was tall but she wasn't fat. Maybe she's the one? Damn! I should have followed *her!"* Tyler exclaimed. A second later he added, "How do you know so much about that book, boss man?" He finished with a knowing laugh.

"None of your business! " I laughed with him, feeling comfortable again. "Don't sweat not following the tall chick, Tyler, I have a feeling we'll end this whole thing before too much longer. We got ole boy covered both ways from Sunday. There is no way he's getting away today!" I told him.

Now that things with the case were looking up, I was in good spirits again. Donna was far behind me, as I'd resolved she'd be last night. I was in the field doing something active for my company for once in a great many years, instead of reviewing case files and expense reports. I resolved then and there to make it a habit to back up my investigators from time to time just to keep myself well honed.

For the next two and one half hours, I sat in the lobby, to the annoyance of staff behind the entrance desk, while Tyler sat in his rental car and complained at regular intervals.

He beeped me in the first hour, "I brought Prince's new CD to pump me up, and do you know this raggedy thing doesn't even have a CD player?"

"Tyler, I told you to rent a car. I didn't tell you it had to be an economy. You acted like the money was coming straight out of your pocket. Nobody told you to rent a bucket!" I told him with a laugh.

An hour later Tyler beeped again. "My legs are getting cramped! There is no damn room to stretch out in this thing!"

"Tyler! Again, you could have been sitting in any car they had available. Why didn't you get something more to your liking?"

"I was tying to save the company some money, Marc." Tyler responded.

"Look, as far as my *very* careful review of expenditures versus income is concerned you could have been sitting in a chauffer driven limo and I wouldn't have blinked at the cost. As a matter of fact, a limo would have been a better cover in this crowd." I told him as I eyed the Lexus's, BMW's, and Porches lining the parking lot.

Tyler hadn't beeped me to complain in a while and I was getting antsy sitting in the lobby waiting for Ivan's next move. I went back out to my car and pulled the Super Ear out from under the file folder, placing the listening device in my ear and setting the device to record. I should have done this as soon as he entered the room, I thought. Maybe I *am* getting rusty.

I held the device towards the conference room Mr. Ivan had entered. "And what happens here stay's here! Am I right gentlemen?" Muffled applause and muted affirmations were picked up through the device. Damn! Whatever kind of meeting Mr. Ivan had attended it was apparently over. There was so much conversation in the room now, so many male voices speaking at once, it was impossible to pick up a single conversation let alone single Ivan's voice out of the din.

At this moment, I knew Tyler and I weren't going to catch Mr. Ivan and a mystery woman sneaking off to one of the suites. I had to be ready to catch what was about to go down on camera because I knew I'd need all the proof I could to convince Mrs. Ivan that her husband was cheating with another man, or at least thinking about it.

"Tyler," I beeped him, "I'm going to reposition myself so that I can get a crowd shot. Right now, I'm parked right next to Ivan's car and if he is going to show his hand, he's not going to do it with someone sitting in the next car. Why don't you go into the lobby, bring your camera. There is a sofa close to the plate glass window and you can take pictures from inside without causing too much suspicion. I'll move my car right next to the entrance and take pictures from here. If he leaves then I'll be close enough to follow him out behind a few of the other cars without arousing suspicion and I'll beep you to let you know where to meet up with me."

"I got it boss." Tyler said.

I pulled out and drove to the side of the building parking alongside the red curb. From this distance I had a clear view of the entire parking lot and anyone looking in my direction would only be able to see the nose of my truck and, thanks to the tinted windows, nothing else. I got out, went around to the passenger seat, and hopped back into the truck.

Tyler casually strode past me without looking in my direction and entered the lobby. From the passenger side mirror, I could see him approach the desk and speak to the clerks, waving his hand in the direction of the sofa. The clerks nodded. Tyler smiled his thanks, walked to the sofa, and got comfortable. He rested his right ankle on top of his left knee then placed his arm in his lap with the camera facing the window in front of him. Tyler was set.

I positioned the watch/camera on the seal of the open window and held the Super Ear in the direction of the door to the meeting room. I pressed record then pause, just so it would be ready when Ivan came out, and put the listening device in my ear. My heart was beating fast and adrenaline was flowing through my veins like lava. I wished they'd had this kind of high tech stuff available when I'd first gotten into the game. I could have built the business up 10 times faster! But maybe I wouldn't appreciate success so much if it had come quickly due to technology instead of hard work and sacrifice.

I really wanted to get this cat on tape leaving the suites with his mystery *man*. He must still be a newbie at the homosexual lifestyle which was why, I thought, he'd been looking for the *Kama sutra* – to give him some creative ideas about how to have sex with men other than the obvious. "Ugh!" I said aloud and shaking my head at the thought.

To each his own I guess. Live and let live is my motto unless, of course, I have a client paying my company top dollar to find out how their partner was living to use in anyway they saw fit. And Mrs. Ivan was paying oodles of money for HiCi to find evidence of his affair. I was sure she'd be devastated to find not only was he cheating but also he was deceiving her on a dual level. Unfaithful *and* gay!

I felt bad for Mrs. Ivan. Last night I'd followed Donna and uncovered painful, if needed truth about her life. I was about to hand Mrs. Ivan some very painful truth about her young stud. The doors to the meeting room had not yet opened and I still couldn't make out any distinct conversation. I decided to call Xellron Inc., the software design company Mrs. Ivan had founded.

I got the number from the file folder. At least Tyler had remembered to include that in his notes. "Xellron, Inc. Tammy speaking."

"Hello may I speak with Mrs. Ivan? My name is Marc. I'm with HiCi."

The ditzy - no doubt blonde, receptionist on the other end of the line replied, "Hi Mike! How are you? She's been expecting your call! I think she's mad at you! But what was that about HiCi? You know I don't like sugary drinks!" She said with a giggle.

What the hell? First of all, how would Mike Ivan know his wife's secretary didn't like sugary drinks? Secondly what was she doing spilling her boss' personal business to a stranger on the line.

"Uh, yes. Hello? Let's try this again." I cleared my throat. "My name is Marc Haley, not Mike Ivan. I work for *Ms*. Ivan. Is she available?" Tammy drew in her breath sharply. "Ohmigosh! Sir, I'm so sorry! I *thought* you said Marc but then it sounded like *Mike*. I thought you were confused because Cerise told me Mike would be calling any second!" Calmly I said, "No, Tammy. I'm not confused. I've known what my name is practically my entire life."

"Me too!" She said excitedly as if she'd just discovered we had gone to the same high school or something. I waited for her to put me through to Mrs. Ivan. Tammy was silent but I could hear her breathing on the other end of the line. Where did Mrs. Ivan get this receptionist? Was she doing charity work for the 51-50 set or what? This was a perfect example of why I love Ashley so much. She was professional to a fault and would never, *ever* put me on front street the way Tammy had just put Mrs. Ivan out there. A prospective client would have hung up and Mrs. Ivan would never know her numbskull receptionist had lost her a potential account.

Still nothing from the Tammy, the receptionist from hell. "Tammy?" I enquired with patience.

"Yes?"

"IS MS. IVAN AVAILABLE?" I didn't want to shout but this woman was impossible. "Can I ask who is calling please?" She asked again.

"Yes. You most certainly can!" I used small words and a soft tone. This method sometimes soothes crazy people. "My name is Marc *Haley*." I said with resignation. *Haley*. H A L E Y! Do you have that?"

"Yes. I have that written down now. I really thought you meant Mike before, ya know."

I ignored her comment. "I'd like to speak with Mrs. Ivan. Can you please put me through?"

"Yes. Yes, of course. Um-" Tammy lowered her voice. "Could you please not mention this misunderstanding to Mrs. Ivan, Mr. Hexley? I'd sure appreciate it!"

"*Mr. Hexley* would never dream of mentioning our conversation to Mrs. Ivan." I told her. "Can you please see if she is available, Tammy? Thank you so much!"

Tammy didn't even pick up on my condescending tone. "Thank you Mr. Hexley! Tammy speaks of herself in third person too, sometimes! It's fun isn't it? I'll put you right through. And thanks again!"

There was silence on my end for a moment. I watched the doors waiting for Mr. Ivan to show himself ready to terminate the call in less than a second if he did, as Tammy made a few failed attempts at putting me through to Mrs. Ivan. I got voicemail for several staff of Xellron, Inc. I kept hitting zero for the receptionist. Each time Tammy came back on the line. "Xellron, Inc.! This is Tammy. How can I direct your call?" I'd had enough of waiting for Ivan to show himself and I'd had enough of Tammy.

"Tammy? Hi! This is Mr. Hex– I mean *Haley*. You put me through to the wrong number again. Must be a pretty complicated phone system you've got there. Please try to get me to *Mrs. Ivan* this time? It's important that I speak with her.

Tammy giggled. "You are *so* right! There are so many buttons to push! I'm sorry. Okay. Tammy is concentrating. 426. That's gotta be the right one. Thanks for being so patient, Mr. Hoxley!"

I sat in the seat of my truck stunned. People like Tammy could actually hold down a job at such a prestigious firm?

Another voice finally came on the line. A much more pleasant voice than ditzy Tammy said, "Hello Mr. Hoxley. This is Mrs. Ivan. How can I help you?"

"Actually the name is Haley as I told your receptionist repeatedly." I replied. Tammy's vacant voice sounded through again. "I thought he said Huxley! Sorry, Cerise!" she said, and disconnected from the line.

"Okay then, Mr. Haley is it the CEO of HiCi? What can I do for you? Or rather, what can you do for me? And, by the way, I have to apologize for my receptionist. I know she can be a bit distant at times."

"You've got that right! Where did you find her?" I replied.

"She's new and it's a very long, boring story. Suffice it to say I've taken her on suffrage and she won't be answering phones for me Xellron, Inc. I think I'll try moving her to the copy station. Anyway, I'm sure you didn't call to discuss my wayward receptionist. Do you have any information for me on the matter you were hired to procure?" Cerise Ivan asked.

Immediately, I forgot about Tammy, the poster child for "don't" with a circle and a X across her face as person to have answering phones for what everyone in the know considered a company poised to make the Fortune 500 list in a few years.

Mrs. Ivan's voice had me transfixed. She didn't sound like a sixty-ish year old woman. I was staring at her picture in the folder on the seat next to me. I couldn't believe the sultry voice I heard came from such an elder member of African American society. Her voice alone let me know Mrs. Ivan had it going on, older or not.

Why she was worried about Mike Ivan's pump buying, *Kama sutra* inquiring, homosexual meeting antics was a mystery to me. That voice could command any man in earshot to fall down at her feet in worship.

Again, I had to get a grip on myself. I shook the cobwebs clear. "I'm on the verge of procuring the items for which you hired me." I told her. "I just wanted to touch bases with you and maybe after you get off work we could get together and discuss the case."

That is *not* what I had planned to say. I'd planned to tell her what I'd seen so far and delicately but definitely tell her that Mike Ivan appeared to be living on the down low. That voice of hers had me planning a meeting just so I could reconcile the older Mrs. Ivan in the file picture to the young sexy as hell voice on the phone line.

"Let me check my schedule." I could hear pages being turned in front of Cerise Ivan. "That would be fine Mr. Haley. Where would you like to meet?"

Checking the address of Mrs. Ivan's company I said, "Maybe we could meet at Buck's Bar and Grill? That's close to your office, yes?"

"It is." She said. I will be there at 7:30 sharp. Please be punctual. I hate tardiness.

"If I get hung up, I'll call you. Your cell number is listed in the file." I told her, pressing end to disconnect the call after we'd said our good-byes.

Okay that was set. I figured we'd have a drink and I could explain to her, in person, the status of the case she'd hired me for, which was looking uglier by the second. What were those men doing in the meeting room that it was taking them so long to come out?

Glancing again at Cerise Ivan's picture I tried to reconcile the voice with the face staring back at me from the file folder. I focused with even greater urgency on the doors to the meeting room mentally willing the doors to open. I did *not* want to be late for my meeting. The case had vaguely intrigued me before I'd talked to her Ivan just due to the vast difference in age, ethnicity, and social status of Mr. and Mrs. Ivan. Now that I'd heard Mrs. Ivan's voice, I was doubly intrigued. Who was this woman? Her picture and now the sound of her voice on the phone had me picturing Dominique Devereaux – Diahann Carroll's character from the TV show Dynasty. I'd loved Diahann since I'd watched her as a little kid when she played Julia. The sooner Mike Ivan came out the sooner I could get evidence of his infidelity; the sooner to meet what appeared to be a real life version of my childhood crush.

Finally, the doors to the meeting room opened. I was disappointed to see only two very unattractive women leave through the double doors. Maybe the men had included "butch" lesbians in their meeting?

I zoomed in with the camera/watch. One of the women exiting the building was wearing a dress and the other was wearing slacks. I zoomed in with the tiny buttons on the little high tech spy device and got a close up peak at the legs of the one in the dress because I noticed a Greek letter tattoo on her calf. Being a Greek myself, I naturally zoomed in; trying to recognize which order this woman belonged to.

I beeped Tyler. "Are you getting these two chicks? Take pictures because I'm sure that meeting was full of men! What were these two ugly women doing in up in there?"

"I already got several pictures boss. Tyler responded. "Well," he said, "That's one for you and one for me, huh?" We both laughed. "From here I can't tell but did either one have a nice pair of tits or legs? Tell me there is *something* sexy about one of those ugly chicks because all I can see from here is tore up from the floor up!" I laughed so hard I almost hit my head on the steering wheel.

A thought struck me and I stopped laughing. The tattoo on the skirt-wearing chick jogged my memory. It was a Greek letter indicating, I thought, membership in a fraternity or sorority.

The Greek sororities I'd dealt with in the past had bright red, pink, green, and yellow colors in their emblems. The tattoo on this chick's leg was dark red and black which was the reason it caught my attention, I guess.

It seemed odd that the woman would have such a detailed Greek tattoo using such masculine colors. One of the symbols was a triangle, I could tell from the tiny image on the digital camera. The other symbol on the tattoo was an unmistakable Greek "K."

The two women walked hand in hand and stopped two cars away from Ivan's Escalade. I kept a close eye on them. The listening device now on record, I knew I'd be able to back it up and listen to their conversation later. I pulled the listening device from my ear and called HiCi. Ashley answered.

"Hello Marc. I recognized the number on the caller ID." She told me. "How are you? How is the case developing? Bet it feels good to be in the mix again, huh?"

"I'm good, Ashley. Yeah it does." I said impatiently. "But hey, I have a question for you though. Your sister – the one who drops in the office every so often is in one of the white Greek sororities, right?"

"Yeah, she is. And?" Ashley replied. I knew she was ready to take down whatever info I needed and get it ASAP. She could teach ditzy Tammy a thing or two.

"I need to make sure I'm not tripping. In the black sororities, I know what symbols mean. I need to be sure they mean the same thing for white

Greeks. Can you check with your sister and find which fraternity or sorority a triangle under a 'K' stands for?"

Without missing a beat Ashley answered, "I already know. That's Delta Kappa, sir. A fraternity."

Got him, I thought. In no hurry now I said, "Thanks, Ashley, you obviously know your Greek letters. Guess I don't need your sister after all."

"Well actually, Marc, the reason I know those symbols is *because* of my sister. Her boyfriend is a Delta Kappa. He has those symbols tattooed onto his calf."

"In that case, maybe you should contact your sister for me. Ashley, can you contact your sister ASAP and ask her to call her boyfriend and get as much info as she can from him about the organization without him giving up any trade secrets, which I know he won't anyway."

Ashley was on it in a heartbeat. My first hunch was correct. The two ugly women were cross dressers. I couldn't tell if one of them was Ivan because they were facing away from me. It didn't matter. If the Greek was Ivan, I had pictures of him in a dress holding hands with another man in a dress. With the tattoo and the location of the car in the photos from the digital camera, Mrs. Ivan would have enough to bury the guy but I planned to give her even more.

I didn't mention the matter to Tyler initially because I wanted to be sure about the facts before I talked to him again. The two men, dressed as women continued to talk by the car. By this time more men had joined them, some dressed as women, others in every manner of outfit from Armani to construction worker attire.

I didn't really care to listen to the conversation going on between the first two men, one of which I was certain now was Ivan, just due to his build and height. When the couple finally moved away from the car, my hunch proved correct as I noted the size thirteen black pumps he was sporting. I placed the earplug firmly in my ear again.

"It's not so bad anymore." Ivan said with a laugh. "She doesn't even want to have sex with me anymore and I let her think it was her idea! The bitch is so dumb, she hasn't got a clue!"

I chuckled to myself. That's what he thought, huh? I didn't even know Mrs. Ivan but I took it personal that this little white punk was dissing her like that to his faggot lover. I checked to make sure the device was still recording and pulled the plug from my ear, too disgusted to listen further.

Twenty minutes had passed and most of the men had left, some to the rooms at the on the grounds, others probably off to their jobs. Ivan, not having a job, had nowhere to be continued filling in his lover on his home situation.

I was getting impatient. Just as I'd grabbed my phone to call the office it rang. Ashley's name blinked in the display window.

"What do you have?" I asked by way of greeting.

"Hello to you too, Sir. I know you are impatient so I'll get right to it. Sorry it took me so long. I had to track my sister and her boyfriend down. They were at the movies and she didn't call back until the movie let out. Anyway, I got a chance to ask Dean, her boyfriend, about the tattoo and he said this was the first year they decided to introduce the idea of a tattoo to their members."

"Good. Good. What else do you have?" I asked impatiently.

"Well the part you'll find most interesting, I think, is that only the five founding chapter members were allowed to get them this year and they just got them last week in a special ceremony. Next year five more members are allowed to get them and so on and so on."

"Ashley, you are the abso-" She cut me off.

"But wait Marc! That's not the most interesting point!" She told me with in an exasperated rush.

"Excuse me! Please accept my apologies, Ms. Holmes. Please continue." I said with humor. Ashley was definitely pulling a Sherlock Holmes with all the info she was able to dig up.

"It's about time you recognized the skill!" We both laughed.

Ashley began talking super fast, as if she couldn't wait for me to hear the rest. "Okay, well if the tattoo you saw is the same as Dean's I already know who it belongs to!"

"Well don't keep me waiting Ashley! Who is it? And how can I be sure you're right?" As much as I wanted to believe she could hand me the name of Ivan's lover on a gift wrapped, silver platter the realist in me knew to take what she said with a grain of salt considering my best investigator had failed to come up with it, or anything else, now that I thought about it, on this case.

"Well! Okay so, like, Dean is one of the five founding members, okay?" Ashley always lapsed into valley speak when she got excited. You can take the girl out of the Galleria but you can't take the Galleria out of the girl.

She continued, "Another three live on the east coast, right? And I already told you those three were in town getting, like, ceremonial tattoos right? So just *last night* Dean took those three to the airport, okay? So, the only other founding member who lives here is Martin Everhart. He's got to be the one you saw with the tattoo unless one of the others doubled back after being dropped off at the airport, which Dean doesn't think likely - and before you start, 'No,' I didn't tell him anything about this case or why I wanted to know. He said all of this was public record."

I was amazed at what Ashley had been able to uncover in less than half an hour. She'd found the identity of Ivan's lover while Tyler had been on the case for over two weeks and had found absolutely nothing. Guess it was time to rethink who HiCi's best investigator really was.

"Boss?" Ashley asked.

"Yes?" I almost sang the word. All at once, I was in a fabulous mood.

"How you like me now?" Ashley asked with a snicker. The woman could pull a one liner to end all one-liners out of thin air!

I grinned from ear to ear. "Ashley Moe Dee, you are the bomb! You'll be, like, getting a nice little bonus for your work today, okay?" I said, imitating her speech habits a moment ago.

"I know I am!" She answered with a light laugh. "And you go right ahead and make fun of my upbringing, Mr. Haley. I'm not one to spread rumors so I won't mention that a certain CEO and very respectable member of society sometimes talks like he thinks he's Mos Def or something when *he* really gets going. I'm not one to talk, so you didn't here that from me!"

I laughed so hard I hit my head on the dashboard. "Woman, I am not going to mess with you. *I'm not worthy!* I must have been slipping because I forgot you know everything. My go to girl! Okay gotta run. I'll fill you in on the case later if Tyler doesn't beat me to it."

As I clicked off the line, I heard Ashley's parting shot, "Better *AX* somebody!" Ashley, of the alluring voice, enticing potential customers into the office to get a glimpse of her image, could just as easily turn the tables, snap her fingers in the air and twist her neck like she'd done it from birth.

I was laughing at the best thing that had happened to HiCi's antics (I knew she would never show that side of herself to clients) when I beeped

Tyler. As soon as he engaged the call, the smile left my face. The game was on.

"Let me tell you what I've learned." I proceeded to explain to Tyler what Ashley had relayed to me.

"You've got to be shitting me boss!" Tyler exclaimed. "So that was Ivan and his fudge partner leaving the last time I was here?"

"Yup! And come to think of it, why didn't you use any of that expensive equipment that day. You probably could have cracked the case then if you'd listened in to the meeting and gotten a clue as to what was going on inside."

Another large group of men exited the meeting room and Ivan and his guy/gal went to join them. Everyone was hugging everyone else. I turned my attention back to what Tyler was saying.

"I'd left the briefcase in my wife's car. I *tried* to call her and tell her to bring it to me but I couldn't reach her." Tyler said almost bitterly before he caught himself. "Anyways, I guess I was so focused on seeing a man leave with a woman I just missed what's now embarrassingly obvious. You are good Boss. Damn good!"

Mixed emotions crowded me. I was both proud of myself (and Ashley!) but at the same time, I was ready to rake Tyler over the coals. I knew I couldn't take him to task right now but I could still pat myself on the back for a job well done. First day out after many years of desk exile and I'd hit pay dirt!

Tyler continued giving me props and I soaked it all in, knowing he couldn't see me, brushed imaginary dirt off my shoulder and popped my collar, laughing silently at my own childish behavior.

But I was holding the phone in the same hand I'd popped my collar with, causing me to drop the phone mid-laugh. Trying to save the phone from hitting the floor of the car my elbow jerked and I knocked the camera and the phone to the floor. I reached down, searching with only my fingers along the floor board trying to find the phone, keeping my eye's trained on Ivan and crew but couldn't feel it. I had to look down and around the passenger seat and finally spotted the light from the phone underneath my seat. I reached under and extended my fingers, closing around the warm metal. I grabbed it. There was time to pick up the camera/watch, since Tyler was already filming from his end.

Straightening upright, I put the phone back to my ear. "Sorry about that. I dropped the phone." No response. "Tyler? You there?"

"Yeah." He said. "Yeah, I'm here. I was just getting a drink from the fountain."

I trained my eyes back on the crowd in front of the double doors. All silliness forgotten, I was back to business. "Okay, the next thing we have to do is figure out how to bring the curtain up on this ordeal. We'll follow Iv –" I stopped abruptly.

"Tyler, where is he? I can't see Ivan or his friend! Do you have them?" I asked frantically.

"*Sheeeeit*. No, no, no, no, no! The water fountain faces away from the window! I thought you had em boss or I would *never* have turned my back!"

I could not BELIEVE this! I dropped the phone into my lap, frantically scanning the crowd hoping I'd somehow overlooked the two tallest cross-dressed men. Nothing! They were gone.

A bible verse came to me from my Sunday school lessons as a kid. Pride goeth before a fall, Proverbs 16:18. I didn't understand the verse as a child, when Moms made me and my brothers go to Sunday school. But I certainly understood it now. One stupid, prideful action had caused me to lose Ivan.

I had to think very carefully about my next plan of action. "Okay Tyler, they're gone." I was speaking calmly again. "Obviously Ivan has to come back because his car is still in the lot so we have that on our side."

"Yeah." Tyler said. "He's probably tucked away in one of the rooms. No big! We wait him out right?"

"Right." I said.

So we waited. And we waited. Then we waited some more. At about 1:30 Ivan's truck was still in the lot, there was still no sign of him, and I was getting hungry.

In the downtime, I'd listened to the entire conversation between Ivan and Everhart. What I heard sickened me to the point of wanting to beat Ivan's ass. I knew Mrs. Ivan would kick him to the curb when she heard some of the things he'd said about her and having to be with a woman just to keep his meal ticket going.

Tyler beeped me. "Look, as long as the truck is still here I think one of us can leave. I'm starving! How bout I drive up to Super Burger and get us some Philly cheese-steaks?"

"I was just about to ask you about lunch, man." I said. The hotel doesn't have anything?"

"No, I just checked. The suites have kitchenettes but the hotel doesn't have a restaurant." He told me.

"Damn! I really would prefer to have both of us on the scene. Can you be there and back in less than 15 minutes? If anything gets too crazy I should be able to stay on top of him that long."

"I'll be back in ten. The lunch crowd is already gone." Tyler said. He left the lobby and walked back to his car, again without looking in my direction, just in case Ivan was watching him.

After about 15 minutes, my stomach growled, and still no word from Tyler, I started to get angry. Tyler should be back by now! Granted, there was still no movement other than the regular hustle and bustle of a hotel parking lot. Ivan's vehicle remained in its marked stall.

Tyler beeped me ten minutes after he'd said he'd be back. "What's up Tyler? Where the hell are you?"

"Marc. You are not going to believe this!" I was coming out of the burger joint and you know they have that triple X rated store and movie theatre across the boulevard, right?"

Groaning, I said, "Tyler, please tell me you did *not* go into the sex store when I need you on the scene here, man! I know you got some shit going on with your wife but Damn, Ty –" He didn't let me finish my tirade.

"Just listen for a second!" Tyler shouted on the line excitedly.

I pulled the phone from my ear and looked at it as if Tyler could see my expression. He obviously remembered to whom, exactly, he was talking to and altered his tone accordingly. With a much lower voice he continued, "I mean, Boss, just listen for a second and I'll explain, okay? Now, I want you too GUESS which two supposed women just left the movie theatre across from Super Burger. No! I can't even wait for you to guess! I've got Ivan and the man!"

Immediately I was in game form. "Leave the food and follow them!" Where are they going?" My stomach growled loudly. "On second thought take the food and follow them!" I'll eat it later."

"You'll have it in a second, Marc. They are on their way back to you as we speak."

I told Tyler to call me when they were five minutes from the hotel. I repositioned the camera and set it on record. Then I grabbed my gym bag, with the old school video camera, including the tri-fold from the back seat, sat and waited for Tyler to beep me again.

Thirteen minutes later Tyler informed me Ivan and company were five minutes away. I grabbed my gym bag, walked unhurriedly into the lobby, and approached the reception desk. I was happy to note the staff had obviously changed shifts. I didn't need anyone who'd seen me hanging around this morning wondering what I was still doing lurking about the hotel. "How can I help you sir?" said the kid behind the counter.

"I'm just looking for a room to rest these tired old bones," I told him in an imitation of Stanley's country accent. "It's been a long day and I can't wait to get some shut eye!"

"Well, we have a few choices available, lets see…" He checked his computer for available rooms as I stared out the window into the parking lot. Ivan and friend turned the corner and walked into the hotel lobby arm in arm. The clerk asked for my credit card and identification. I gave it to him and turned my back to the lobby doors as the two walked past me heading towards a room on the far end of the west wing. Martin impatiently slid his key card through the lock and the two hurried inside.

"Excuse me, uh, David." I said, checking his nametag. David, clearly bored to tears with his job stopped typing on the computer and looked up at me. "Yes?" He sighed.

"I reckon I'd prefer a room on the far east side facing that beautiful courtyard there." I motioned behind him to the lushly cultivated grounds, in the center of which was a gated swimming pool. "I'd like a second story room if you've got one." I added in my borrowed accent. I'd noted from just about any second story room on the east end of the hotel I could get a perfect view of Ivan and Martin's first story room on the west end.

"Whatever bro, let me start again." Bored David said as he clicked away at the computer console in front of him.

"Okay, I do have one room to your specifications. Its more expensive than most of the others because it has a double king instead of doubles." David could have been talking in his sleep for all the interest he showed.

"That will be fine. Thank you, David!" I walked out of the lobby and spotted Tyler standing by my car.

"Okay this is the plan." I said, and detailed for him how this was about to go down. I know I was supposed to be Tyler's back up but so far, he hadn't shown any initiative to take control of the situation. I'd have to talk to him about that later as well.

Back in the lobby, I got the room key-card from dead man standing, David, and walked up the staircase to my room. Although Ivan's room wasn't directly across from mine, the location still provided me a great view of their patio door.

Quickly positioning the camcorder inconspicuously to the left of the sliding glass door in my room towards Ivan's room I pressed record then pause. I then followed the same procedure with the Super Ear I'd tucked into my pocket before leaving the truck, I opened the sliding door to the balcony, settled into a chair watching the room below through a small slit in the curtain ready to wait out the sex session. The camera may not have been able to pick up any visual images yet but I could hear the rowdy sex session just fine through the listening device.

Just as I'd suspected, after about an hour, Ivan's door slid open. He was wearing the clothes he'd had on this morning when I'd tailed him and had the gym bag in his hand. I pressed the pause button again so the camera could pick up everything I was seeing. I figured Ivan would want to leave from the side gate of the courtyard instead of passing through the lobby again in his straight clothes.

Tyler needed to step up his game now. I needed him on the ready, set, go and there was no room for error.

Ivan turned back into the room for a moment and I could see frat boy laying in the tangled sheets, still wearing his wig but obviously nothing else. I'd taken the listening device from my ear so I didn't hear whatever Martin said but I got the gist of it as Ivan walked back toward the bed.

I beeped Tyler. "Invisible is just about on the move. Game time!" I said. Ivan bent down and kissed Martin for a long moment. It was obvious Martin was trying to persuade him to stay for a second act. Watching these two dudes kissing and carrying on in broad daylight I was so disgusted I wanted to stand on my balcony in full view and yell down, "Hey cut it out, damn it!"

Just barely managing to contain myself, I watched as Ivan finally disentangled himself from Martin, headed out the patio door, walked around the pool and out through the gate. I knew he'd have to pass my truck on his way to his own truck and wondered if he'd remember seeing it earlier in the day from the mall and put two and two together. At this point, it didn't matter. I had just about everything I needed to nail the lid shut on this case.

When I'd met up with Tyler at my car I'd told him to follow Ivan to the end of the world if necessary just stay on his tail. I knew the two wouldn't leave together and right now, I had an appointment with Martin Everheart. I grabbed the camera off the tri-pod to see the quality of the evidence. The two men kissing played back before my eyes. Wrong,

wrong, and wrong! I said to myself. I dropped the camera onto the bed, put the Super Ear in my pocket and walked out the door after grabbing an ice bucket, the iron from the shelf in the closet, and all the towels I could find.

Back downstairs with my armload of goodies, I walked across the lobby past David, who was so deeply involved in a Dungeons and Dragons magazine that he didn't even look up from the counter as I passed by. Poor David. Probably still lives at home with his Mommy, too. I managed a spare moment of sympathy for the hapless teen as I made my way to the west wing.

Knocking on the door, I called out in a cheery voice, "Room service!" There was no reply. I knew Martin was still inside. There was no way he could have dressed and left in the time it took me to get here.

"Someone requested an iron and fresh towels?" I called through the door once again. It was a weak lie but it apparently worked.

"One second, please!" I head the lock turn from inside and the door slowly opened. There stood Frat Boy, Martin Everheart, wrapped in a sheet, obviously ready to give me holy hell for disturbing his afterglow.

I pushed past him dropping my bundle to the floor as I did so and closed the door behind me.

Martin's eyes were huge as saucers. "What the hell do you thi…" he sputtered, but I cut him off.

Pushing him backwards with jabs to his shoulder until he stumbled onto the bed I punctuated each jab with, "Sit (jab) your ass down (jab) on the bed Frat boy (jab)."

Martin was sitting on the bed now looking at me in fear and confusion as I walked to the sliding door and closed the curtain.

"What's going on here? I'll call the police! I'll scream!"

"You mean like you screamed about an hour ago when Ivan's dick was up your ass?"

Martin gasped and held his hand to his mouth in shock. "How do you know...?"

Cutting him off mid-sentence I barked, "You and I need to talk! Let's start with, how long have you been fucking Cerise Ivan's husband?" As I said these words I was picturing Diahann Carroll, as Julia, receiving the same news Mrs. Ivan was going to receive tonight. Her imagined response made me angrier still.

Martin's white, privileged, I figured, ignorant ass, had never confronted a black man on a mission before. I knew he thought he could turn the situation around to his advantage by pulling on his Mr. Charlie coat. "Who the hell are you? And what are you doing barging into my room! Get your *black* ass out of here now! I'm calling 911" He hiss/lisped at me and reached out desperately for the phone on the nightstand beside the bed.

Awhh! See? Now why did he have to go and get racial on me? I'd kept all *my* prejudicial thoughts to myself. Martin was obviously under the misguided delusion that his threats could somehow cause me to rethink my course of action. I watched in amusement mingled with disgust and hatred as he finally managed to untangle his arms from the sheets he'd wrapped himself in to reach for the phone. He was able to dial a 9 before I calmly walked over to the jack next to the window and yanked it from the wall.

As I jerked the cord from the wall I said, "Man, don't make me have to beat your ass in this itty bitty room! What? Your man couldn't have gotten you a suite on the second floor? Think of it Martin. It would be so ugly. The press and everything, you know?"

I walked back towards him holding the evidence of the dead line in my hand. "Just think of it! 'Prominent member of society found naked and beaten, wearing a woman's wig in a hotel room in secluded area. Description of suspect: a black male between 20 and 50, over six feet tall with a shaved head.' They'd never find me, *Martin,* meanwhile, you and everything you've been up to will be plastered all over the Sac Bee. The story would probably get picked up by one of those 'odd but true' websites. Next thing know you'll have the AP or Reuters on your ass. Do you really want that? What would your family think? What would your fraternity make of this?"

Crying in earnest now, Martin, dropped the now dead phone receiver into his lap and, looking up at me with tears streaming from his eyes began, "Look, I don't know what you want but my wallet is…".

"Shut the hell up, Frat Boy! I'm not after your chump change man.' I need information. And you, Martin, or should I say, Martina, are going to give me every last detail I need."

Martin couldn't ignore the threat in my voice. I could actually see him visualizing the headline I'd described. All at once, he turned into the bitch he actually was. "I didn't have anything going on with Mike. I was straight! He pursued me!"

At these words, I started to pull the listening device from my pocket.

Martin, bitch that he was, began to cry in earnest. "Mister black man, please don't shoot me! My wallets over there." He jerked his head towards the dresser on the other side of the room. "Take the money. There's a lot in there! Mike left me a few thousand before he left!"

"Where did he get the money from Martin? Huh? We both know Mike Ivan hasn't got a pot to piss in nor a window to throw it out of unless his *wife* gives him say so. We are both agreed on that aren't we Fool!' I spat at him as if he were the court jester who'd displeased the king. "Shut up and listen!" In a quiet, calm voice I told him, "I am with an investigative service. You see this mike?" I pulled the Super Ear from my pocket. Martin let loose a stream of yellow liquid either in relief that I wasn't packing a gun or that he just couldn't contain it any longer.

I looked upon Martin's soiled visage with disdain. "I've been watching you for months! I finally found the evidence the brotherhood hired me for and you give me piss?"

Everhart whimpered and reached behind him to grab and cuddle a pillow. I continued. "You come here and meet with Ivan, by the way, he's married, you know? Yeah I guess you already know that, don't you? But he's fucking around *with you.* Now what should I do with this information I've just gathered?" I sat in the chair closest to the door and pretended to think long and hard while Martin continued sobbing into his pillow.

"I've got it!" I stood up suddenly, causing Martin to jump backwards onto the bed. "If I just send the tape recording of everything that went down here today to Ivan's wife and your frat everyone who needs to know *will* know about all your activities."

Martin Everhart looked up at me with tears in his pleading eyes. I could see I had his undivided attention. "Please sir, whatever your name is." Martin gushed out with his peculiar lisp. "It would ruin me if this got out. I beg of you! Please don't send it to my fraternal organization! I'll do *anything* you ask! Just please, don't send the tape."

I'm sure Martin imagined I'd demand a much more physical payment for my silence which he'd be all too pleased to oblige.

During the next 30 minutes, Mr. And Mrs. Everhart's boy must finally have realized there was no short cut to getting what he wanted from me. Martin tried to entice and cajole but ultimately realized he was dealing with someone who couldn't be swayed by his 'charms' and there was no way out except to answer all my questions.

Martin finally told me all about his and Mike Ivan's encounters, blaming seduction, pursuit, and culmination of their homosexual love affair on Mike Ivan's Svengali-like dominance. He even threw in his predecessor's, some of Ivan's other lovers before him, for good measure. Guess Mike wasn't new at this homosexual thing after all. That mistake was the first and only one I'd made so far about this case.

"You've been very informative. Very helpful." I told Martin, still wrapped in his shroud of shame, exhausted and drenched from sweat in his sheet.

"Break off the relationship with Ivan before it blows up in your face." I instructed. "As you must know your frat is paying top dollar to ferret out 'undesirables' and since you've convinced me that your relationship with Ivan was a one time deal I'll cut you some slack. I do have a heart you know? I don't know how you thought you'd go undetected once they determined homosexuals weren't welcome in the fold but they won't hear it from me that you've been engaged in any activity unworthy of your frat."

Martin sat in awe as he listened to my demands then once again pleaded his case not to expose his behavior. "Sir, I am the president of that fraternity and my grandfather founded the organization. My father was the president when he attended college. I wasn't aware they were looking to expel any members with alternative orientations but I'd pay any price not to be exposed! I am supposed to be following in their footsteps! Exposure of Mike's influence on me would ruin not only me, but my father and grandfather's legacy as well since they'd be connected with me! That would ruin the organization and I can't let that happen!"

I assured frat boy the information would remain buried as long as he broke off with Ivan. "I swear it's over as of right this very minute!" Martin sobbed.

"Make sure that it is." I said as I walked out the door, leaving Martin crying on his bed. I went back to my room, gathered my equipment, and checked out of my room. Back to the reception desk, I handed David a hundred dollar bill. I dropped the southern accent and said, "No information about me to anyone, David, alright? He winked and hit a few buttons on the computer and just like that, I never existed in the system. As an afterthought, I handed him my business card since I was looking to hire more staff anyway. "Very industrious of you David. If you ever want to move out of the hotel receptionist trade and make more than minimum wage come see me about a job." I handed him my business card and turned to leave.

"Cool!" David said behind me.

I knew the hundred might not be enough insurance if Martin Everhart put on his suit and came to the desk demanding answers and offering more than a hundred to get it. I'm no fool. Just because the information about me appeared to have been erased there are ways to bring it back up. But I could tell David was bored to tears knew he was throwing his young life away sitting behind the desk of the hotel lobby. Plus I knew the information contained on my card about confidential investigations would excite the dungeons and dragons player's wasted intellect and imagination. He could put some of those skills to use once he learned the ropes, no doubt. I got into my truck and headed out the driveway, positive David wouldn't give out any information about me if he knew he could leave his dreary job behind and move into a much more interesting line of work.

Beeping Tyler to find out his location he told me he was parked back at Ivan's house. I gave Tyler the full account of what had taken place with Martin in the last hour. "We have everything we need man. You can go home to your wife, buy her dinner on me."

Tyler said, "Boss, you are alright with me. I'm going to take you up on your offer but first I'll go back to the office and get started on the paperwork to close this thing up."

I said, "Tyler, the paperwork can wait till morning. How often do I offer to pay for dinner? You better jump on that offer before I change my mind!"

Tyler chuckled and said, "You are right about that boss man! Alright, Tyler out" and he clicked off the line.

IGNITION

It was almost 6:45 as I drove home to shower and change out of my surveillance clothes before meeting with Mrs. Ivan. She would probably be going straight to the bar and grill from work and dressed professionally. I pulled into my driveway and waited for the garage to open spotting Stanley in his yard with a shovel digging, a little hole. After pulling in, instead of heading straight inside and closing the garage behind me I got out and walked back out to where Stanley now stood on my driveway.

"Big man, how's it going? I'm looking forward to us hanging out. Hey, any ponies coming to the stable this week?"

I shook my head. "It's like this Stanley; I don't *do* 'ponies' but if you have to make my company some sort of horse, lets go with stallions, eh?" Why did I even go there?

Stanley grabbed his shovel from the side of the house where he laid it when he'd come over. He put it between his legs and started riding it! Almost at the top of his lungs Stanley yelled, "Yeah bruther, whew! Go boy. You ride them stallions! Yeah bruther ride em till the cows come home!" as he galloped back to his yard. Clearly, Stanley was out of control.

I left him to his antics and rushed inside the house and up the stairs to shave, shower, and slip into some evening casual slacks, shirt, and tie.

I looked in the mirror. I wasn't feeling the image I presented to myself. It wasn't me. What was I trying to do looking like a square? I stripped back down and slid on some silk thigh briefs, reaching down to rearrange the boys because the silk causes them to slide in uncomfortable positions sometimes. I splashed a little Blue Water on all the right spots to accent the smell of soap on my now clean and refreshed body.

The Blue Water permeated the room. I put on my fawn colored Armani suit with a gold shirt and a sable and gold pin stripped tie. I looked into the mirror again and was finally satisfied. Oh yeah everything is tight and all right. I was looking good, I knew. Something about getting dressed up made me feel as if I were on top of the world. I looked myself over in the mirror one last time before leaving, winked, smiled, and licked my lips like I was LL. "Watch out now!" I said to my mirror image as I headed out to get the Benz.

Stanley was still out in his yard when I walked out my front door. "Hot damn bruther, you look like a GQ model! How much did the suit cost? Marc, Marc, let me get a good look at you, bruther you look good! It must be *happening* tonight! "Yeah bruther. Whew!"

I just waved to him and continued down the walk when Ramona called out, "Stanley! Quiet down with all that noise! Leave the poor man alone so he can try again without all your foolishness!"

Now what was that supposed to mean? I understood now how Donna felt when Ramona had called her a strumpet. Exactly what was Stanley telling his wife about his encounters in front of my house anyway?

I pulled the truck into the garage and backed the Benz down the driveway. As I pulled into the street, I briefly glanced back at Stanley's house. He was standing in the middle of his yard with his arms straight in the air with his thumbs pointed up. I had to laugh. Some things just never change. I could never figure out what situations caused Stanley to give me the single or double thumbs up. Maybe it depended on the level of kinkiness he thought I was about to get into. Or maybe I got two thumbs up for the quality of the woman I was seeing?

Why I was spending even a little bit of time contemplating Stanley's eccentric behavior was beyond me. I was finally on my way to meet the enigmatic woman with the sexy voice I knew only from a picture and the scanty background information Tyler had listed about her. Worse, I was about to give her possibly the worst news she'd ever received.

Thirty minutes before I was scheduled to meet Mrs. Ivan, I pulled into the parking lot at Bucks Bar and Grill. Sitting in the car listening to KBLX, I looked around the parking lot, noting it was quickly filling with cars even at such an early hour. Even without a marquee to announce visiting artists, word of mouth spread quickly in Sac-town. Obviously, somebody big was performing tonight.

As I got out of the car, I noted a big black bus pull up on the opposite side of Bucks. I probably should have called Buck to see if he had a live act scheduled before I set up a meeting here. The Grill was a well-known spot for musical artists to try out a new sound or just to keep their chops honed for the bigger venues in San Francisco or Oakland. If the owner of the bus turned out to be somebody like Morris Day or some other funky type act, I'd probably have to move our meeting to another, more refined location. I couldn't imagine the image I had of Mrs. Ivan grooving to *Oak*

Tree or enjoying a crowd of thirty something black folks screaming "AWK!" and flapping their arms while doing the bird.

I hurried inside to find a seat. At Bucks, with a big-ticket artist scheduled to perform, I knew if I waited any later to go inside the only place left available to sit and talk would be the bar. I couldn't envision shouting out the delicate information I had to give Mrs. Ivan amidst the crush of bodies surrounding the crowded bar. In any case, whenever possible, I like to sit face to face and discuss business. I walked to the club entrance just as a line began to form. I could hear the artist tuning up inside and was completely shocked to hear the music playing. I couldn't believe my ears. Him? Here? Naw, it couldn't be. I mean I know the lot is full, and Buck did not allow impersonators, but still, a popular artist and music producer at my neighborhood bar and grill? I had to see this for myself!

As I hurriedly made my way through the line, I spotted Big G working security at the door. We made eye contact and he gave a quick wink, grabbed the mic on his lapel, said a few words, and gave a slight head motion indicating the entertainer's door entrance. I winked back. Big G knew his quick recognition and action was worth a fifty spot.

I approached the entertainer's entrance and Bonita, with her big-ass Cleopatra Jones looking afro opened the door and gave me her signature gap toothed smile. "Marc! Why didn't you tell me you were coming? I'd have saved you a better table than the one I can offer you now."

I grabbed Bonita and pulled her off her feet in a bear hug just to hear her girlish giggle. Twirling Bonita with more than a little effort, I told her, "It was a last minute thing. If I'd known who was going to be here, I'd definitely have let you know I'd be in the house! Plus, normally, *a certain hostess* I know normally would have pulled my coat to let me know this brother was on!"

"Put me down you caveman!" She rewarded my efforts with a laugh that belonged to a much younger woman. Good thing she'd told me to put her down. Bonita weighed in excess of 300 pounds. Bonita caught her breath and said. "And anyway Negro, *a certain hostess* DID call your house two or three times! You never answered even though I left two messages! What? You don't return call's now Mr. Big-shot?" She laughed and I smiled along with her joke even though my thoughts quickly went back to the last time I'd heard someone call me that.

In spite of the bad taste the memory of Donna and my last meeting left in my mouth, I still found myself ready to do the damn thing. Meet Mrs. Ivan and deliver the information she'd hired my firm to obtain. Afterwards I fully expected to get my groove on because I knew the club would be full of ladies tonight!

Bonita told me she'd gotten me as close to the stage as possible considering she didn't know I was coming. This is the very reason why I love Sacramento so much! Newcomers can't appreciate the close-knit black community because they are on the outside looking in. I'd grown up here, my people know and love me, and I, in return love, and appreciate the hell out of my people.

Bonita lead me to my table. I was within spittle flinging distance of D Angelo as he sat at the piano still warming up. I might not appreciate the closeness of his position as much as a woman might but still I appreciated Bonita's efforts.

D'Angelo stopped playing suddenly and jerked his head toward the bar, indicating he wanted to speak to Buck, who leaned against the vinyl watching his moneymaker warm up. As Buck made his way to the stage, he passed by my table. I cleared my throat as he passed and Buck glanced in my direction. Recognizing me, he stopped for a moment in pursuit of pampering his star.

"Good to see you, Marcus." He said quietly.

I nodded. "I didn't know you had it like that!" I said with a slight motion of my head towards D'Angelo as he sat waiting for Buck to join him onstage.

"Well you know, a brother still gotta be able to pull a rabbit out of the hat every now and then. That's my *word*." I grinned at Buck. He finished just about every sentence he uttered with 'that's my word'. You can take the boy out of Oakland but you can't take Oakland out of the boy.

"Handle your business bruh!" I told him. Buck gave me a 'thought you knew' look, gave me a quick wink and nod, and walked up the short flight of stairs to see to D'Angelo's needs. The man himself, still waiting for Buck to see to him caught my eye and threw me a nod just as Buck left my table. I threw him a double nod.

No words had been exchanged between D'Angelo and I yet I knew he meant to convey to me, "What up black man? Good to have you here." My double nod to D'Angelo was an acknowledgement of his fame and a "good to have you here" tossed into the mix. It's hard to explain the dynamics of a blackman's communication style to those who aren't a part of it.

Bonita sashayed through the crowd to ask what I wanted to drink. "Well beautiful, I have a client arriving soon so I'll hold off on ordering until she arrives. Can you keep an eye out for and direct her to this table when she arrives? She's around 65 years old, black shoulder length hair, probably wearing a business suit. She's a very elegant, professional woman. Also, can you give this to Big G?" I slipped her a fifty-dollar bill, and another twenty for her services.

She smiled and stuffed the twenty into her ample cleavage. "Thank you, baby. Marc, I will definitely keep an eye out for her, thank you." She winked at me and walked away.

I sat back in the chair and got comfortable. Scanning the crowd, my eyes lit upon a woman leaning against the bar. She was absolutely breathtaking! Standing at about 5'4"she was dwarfed by the taller men and women surrounding her. She would have been easy to miss in the crowd except she was exceptionally stunning. With deep chocolate skin the color of a Hershey Bar, she wore a fitted white dress that clung to her body like a second skin. Her hair slung over one shoulder to reveal the long line of her neck, and her eyes (those eyes!) never wavered from the stage. This had to be D Angelo's woman because he was gazing in her direction as well. Guess he wanted everyone to know she was with him.

I had to stop myself from staring. I was not about to mess with the big brother standing in the corner. He made Big G look like Urkel. I'm not a little man myself but I imagined if I went over to talk to the beautiful lady in white D'Angelo would forget all about our positive nodding and send his man to chuck me out the back door. The brother looked like the Incredible Hulk and it looked to me that he was a little angry he hadn't yet had the opportunity to hurt anyone yet.

When I finally tore my gaze away from the lady in white I realized D'Angelo and me weren't the only ones staring towards the end of the bar. Glancing around the room, I noted every man in the room stealing glances in her direction. Brother's were whispering to each other and slyly staring at her. I couldn't keep my eyes off her for long though, so I stole another glance. A huge hand grabbed my shoulder from behind me. "Oh shit!" I thought. "The jig is up! D'Angelo is going to have every man tossed out of the room just to keep all eyes off his woman."

Sure enough, I looked back, and there stood Mr. Hulk, standing at about 6-8, 390 pounds, and dressed in black leather from his hat to his boots. Hulk was packing heat, I could tell, but the gun, which he'd tucked into a side holster, looked really small pressed up against his big frame. Now why would a brotha this big need a gun? More importantly, Buck allowed the bodyguard to carry a weapon inside the club?

Things were not looking good for me. I was about to stand up and cause a big enough scene so that Hulk here would have no choice but to walk away leaving me in peace. "Don't look too hard brother." He jerked his head towards the lady in white. "We all see her." My famous mouth failed me. I said. "Oh I wont. Thanks. But that's very nice. Very nice." I don't even know what I meant by that. Hulk laughed and walked away. That was one huge, leather wearing Negro.

The current crisis averted, I continued to scan the room for Mrs. Ivan. The MC walked up to the microphone and introduced D Angelo to wild applause. I listened to his smooth style as he mesmerized the ladies in attendance. From the corner of my eye, in spite of big brother's warning, I kept track of the lady in white as well. The other brothers must have gotten the same warning I'd had because no one approached her. This was good for me because even though D'Angelo's bodyguard had initially startled me into incoherence, I was determined that if Mrs. Ivan didn't show I was going to, at the very least, say hello to the beautiful young woman.

It was 8:30 now. Mrs. Ivan was obviously not going to show. She'd probably seen all the cars in the lot, heard the neo-soul coming from inside, and decided she'd rather wait for a more suitable time to discuss business. I could kick myself for suggesting Bucks but I'd been thinking about her in suggesting we meet somewhere close to her work.

Bonita made her way back to me. "I haven't seen hide or hair of your client, sweetie. I'm sorry." She said. "That's okay Bonita." I told her. "I've been scanning the crowd too. I think I've been stood up!"

"Well let me get you something to drink at least. I know there must be something else you can get into tonight since your client didn't show." Bonita winked at me and I laughed.

"Don't mind if I do Ms. Bonita. Now that I know she's not going to show, I can hang for a minute and make the most of this outfit. Huh? What do you think?" I preened and fingered my goatee for Bonita and she rewarded me with another of her giggles.

"You are too crazy, Marc. Should I bring you the usual?"

"You know how I like it Bonita. Bring it on!" Now that I didn't have to worry about Mrs. Ivan, for the first time since I'd arrived, I relaxed and got into the groove my man D Angelo was putting down. A few minutes later Bonita brought me a Long Island Iced Tea. I reached for my wallet but she looked at me with a 'what the hell do you think you are doing nigga' look. I could only nod my thanks as she rushed off to attend to other guests. My eyes strayed once again to D Angelo's girl. She starred at him as if he were the only man in the room. The man obviously had her where he wanted her. Must be nice!

D'Angelo played the opening chords to *lady* and the crowd went wild again. In the midst of the music and noise from the crowd, I slipped into my own little deep space. I closed my eyes and felt the music reverberating through me, thinking about the kind of love it would take for a man to write a song like this for his woman.

What must it be like to have a woman as in tune with me as the lady at the bar was with the man on the stage? She was moving to each chord that came off the piano, caught every lyric as it drifted from his mouth and pulled it close to her, claiming the words as her own. D'Angelo was doing what he enjoyed most; playing his music to an adoring crowd and his adoring woman and she was there in his corner, vibing with him.

I wanted a woman who could feel me when I couldn't feel myself. I wanted a woman who could hear me when no one else could. Was it too much to ask to find a woman whose every touch left me yearning for another? A woman who could see me, as me, and only simple old me? Someone who could ignore what is on the outside for others to see, but to really see the inner me. The child at play, and the man at heart. I would want her spare thoughts to be spent on me, as mine would be on her. I would want the air she exhaled to be the air I inhaled and vice versa. I wanted her dreams to find my dreams as our minds ran away throughout the night. I would want her touch to be more stimulating than any drug known to man. I would want her to call my name and feel my ears tingle from the beauty of her voice. I wanted total love. My thoughts turned to Melody and what could have been. Had she been alive today, would she have been the one to fulfill all my wants?

D Angelo was almost finished with his final song for the evening. I checked around the room once more for Mrs. Ivan to no avail. The final chord of the last song evaporated into the crowded room and thunderous applause ensued. D'Angelo stood and bowed at the accolades of the crowd, then snuck out the entertainer's door. The bodyguard then stepped in front of the door to ensure no one followed. Buck's DJ took to turntables and started spinning. Couples hit the floor and I stood up to stretch and take one final look around for Mrs. Ivan even though I knew it was fruitless. We'd agreed to meet at 7:30 and it was now a little past nine.

D Angelo's woman was still hanging in the bar area. I'd assumed she would have followed him out the entertainer's door the moment he left the stage. The fact that she was still here seemed to me an act of providence I wasn't about to let slip past me.

I strolled over to the bodyguard who'd scared the shit out of me earlier. "A lover's spat? What's up with the lady in white? How come she didn't leave with D'Angelo?"

The big man laughed. "That's not his woman. Who told you that? Far as I know, him and Angie Stone are still hanging tuff.

I was shocked! "Brother-man, I'm pretty sure you asked me what I was looking at when you caught me checking ms. thing over there. If she's not D'Angelo's woman who the hell is she?"

Big man smiled. "I told ya don't look too hard. I was just commenting on her beauty and how you were staring. I had to check a couple of other brothers too. It's my job to make sure nothing and no one detracts from my man's performance. And believe me, if that were D Angelo's woman, I would have crushed your shoulder instead of just putting my hand down."

Putting his hand down? I'd thought the dude was going to break my shoulder in his grasp and he described it as 'putting my hand down'? If brother-man ever got tired of running after his star, I definitely had use for him at HiCi.

"If that's not his girl you're guarding what the hell am I doing here talking to you?" I asked the big man. He laughed. "I wondered when you'd figure that shit out. Handle your business brother. But check it. Tell her I said if you aren't man enough to satisfy then she can always call on the Bone Crusher."

"Now why in the hell would that fine lady I'm about to step to want to be associated with someone who calls himself the 'Bone Crusher?' She'll probably take that shit literally!"

He laughed and handed me his card before walking away. In a parting shot, Bone Crusher tossed over his shoulder, "Just tell her what I said man. We both know she's going to knock you out the box just like she's done with every other brother who stepped to her tonight. If you can't get it done, Bone Crusher can. Don't hate on the player man. Just let her know what I said, alright?"

Amused as all hell, I nodded to Bone Crusher as he followed D'Angelo out the back door.

It was time for me to make my move. If she shot me down, at least I'd have introduced myself and given it a shot. Nothing ventured, nothing gained. I'm not one of those men afraid to approach a beautiful woman. I've never understood what the fear thing is all about but I've witnessed confidant, successful men revert to shy little boys when faced with the prospect of stepping to a woman as lovely as the one at the bar. I'm not like that, because I know there are only two possible answers if I ask a beautiful woman to go out. She's either going to say yes or no. If the answer is yes then we can move on from there. If the answer is no, then at least I didn't let the opportunity slip past me. A negative response isn't going to destroy my world or insult my manhood. A 'no' response will just let me know I'm not the flavor she prefers.

I walked to the bar and ordered two top shelf glasses of wine, red and white. As I stood waiting for the bartender to bring my drinks, I noticed one or two rookies approach my target and try to spark up a conversation. I was close enough now to know that she politely greeted them but just as politely turned them away with a smile.

The bartender placed two very full goblets of wine on the counter. I paid the man and left another generous tip before starting my descent down the runway. I could see that her radar intercepted my flight half way through my landing. She smiled as I approached but I stopped several yards away from where she was standing. Instead of speaking, I just stared into her large, beautiful brown eyes then raised each goblet as if to toast her presence. She still hadn't uttered a word but I noticed that her eyes strayed to the glass of white wine. I took this as an invitation to introduce myself so I closed the distance between us proffering the white wine.

"Good evening. My name is Marcus. I've wanted to introduce myself to you all evening. Her voice sounded almost familiar to me as she said, "Good evening Marcus, thank you for the wine. I'm Cerise."

What a coincidence! I was supposed to meet Ms. Cerise Ivan here tonight. I was mighty thankful that she'd decided to skip the meeting, otherwise, I probably never would have met the Cerise now in front of me. My heart was beating almost out of control. I don't normally have such a physical reaction to someone I've just met but for some reason this woman set off every bell and whistle inside of me.

"Cerise is a lovely name. Do you mind if I take this seat and join you for a moment while we share our wine? Cerise looked at me in silence for a moment and I thought I was about to be sent away, hat in hand, as she had all the other brothers who'd approached her this evening.

Instead she said, "The seat is open and since you did buy me a glass of wine, why not. I haven't had anything to drink at all this evening because I've been waiting for someone and I wanted to keep my mind clear. I doubt that he'll show up now based on his track record but I've got to tell you that if he does I'll have to cut our first meeting short."

I liked the fact that she'd called our encounter "our first meeting'. This let me know she was open to the possibility of a second.

Trying to keep the ear-to-ear grin I was feeling from showing on my face I said, "How unfortunate *for him* that he hasn't arrived to apologize for being even one minute late. I'll apologize for him. I'm sorry I kept you waiting Cerise."

She smiled. "Do you always apologize for other's lateness?"

With utmost sincerity I said, "No, not at all. But since the other brother left you hanging I apologize for the fact he left you here waiting for someone who didn't have the sense to know what a fool he was for leaving you alone tonight."

Cerise raised her glass to me. "Wow, that was pretty quick thinking, Marcus. And you looked so sincere when you said it!" Before taking a sip of the white wine, Cerise swirled the liquid in a small circular motion as she placed the glass near her nostrils. Obviously, this woman appreciated good wine. I was very happy I'd had the foresight to order from the top shelf.

"Well Marcus, you are certainly saying all the right things this evening. You must be very good at picking up women in bars, yes?" Slowly and deliberately Cerise took a small sip of wine and held it in her mouth for a moment to savor its flavor before swallowing, eyeing me the entire time.

"Cerise I know I might seem like just another brother looking to hook up for the night but can we get real for a moment?" She gave a tentative nod and settled back. I continued, "First of all, I don't know if you are married or otherwise connected, but I did notice that you aren't wearing any rings so this gives me hope." Cerise started to respond but I quickly forged ahead in case she was trying to tell me she *was* either married or connected. If she was, I didn't want to know.

"Cerise, I've gotta tell you, I've been checking you out from the moment you strolled up to this bar. And I'm not by any means bragging but let me tell you, I've dated plenty of beautiful women before; so it's not solely your looks that have attracted me so much. I can't lay my finger on what it is about you that has me so mesmerized but I *can* say there is absolutely no word in the dictionary, thesaurus, or encyclopedia that can describe how I am feeling this very moment, just looking into your eyes."

Cerise didn't respond. Leaning against the bar she eyed me with a questioning look, as though she wondered if what I was saying was truthful or just another creative line to go along with all the pick up lines she'd heard this evening, probably heard all her life!

My last words to her hung in the air as we stared at each other. Finally, she said, "I am not sure if I should be flattered or nervous! You've known me less than 10 minutes and you've got my heart doing somersaults! What are you trying to do Marcus?"

"Look Cerise, there's no need for cardiac gymnastics, okay. I'm not some player trying to string you along. I'm just a brother who is very happy to make your acquaintance. But hey, you know what? Right now I've got a very urgent desire for something and I'd love for you to join me in indulging it.

Cerise looked at me as if I were crazy. "I thought you just said you weren't trying to string me along? How are you going to change tracks so quickly?"

I laughed. "You have no trust do you? I assure you Cerise, I'm not talking about what you think I'm talking about! Shame on you! I just wanted to get some food since I missed dinner. Do you think you can keep your dirty thoughts to yourself long enough to join me? I noticed you haven't eaten anything since you came in either." I smiled wickedly and Cerise laughed..

"You are bad! I see I'm going to watch out for you. Yeah I'm so hungry right now I'm surprised you didn't hear my stomach growling." She said.

"I did. I was just too much of a gentleman to mention it sounded like you had a lion hidden somewhere on you."

Cerise gathered her things and we moved back to my table by the stage. Bonita rushed over and asked if what she could bring us. I motioned her to come closer to me so Cerise couldn't hear what I told Bonita. Bonita took the order and, promising the order would be right up sashayed to the kitchen. Cerise tried to glare at me but ended up giving me an intriguing smile. "So you are so mysterious that even ordering food is a secret? And by the way, why didn't you let me order for myself?"

I stood up to take my jacket off, roll my sleeves up, and loosen my tie, staring into Cerise's eyes the whole time. "Gotta work on those trust issues, woman. I'm not trying to be mysterious, Ms. Cerise. I think you will *like* what I ordered for the both of us, plus I figured even as hungry as you are you'd probably order something nice and polite, like a salad. I wanted to be sure you had a good dose of protein so I ordered something a bit more substantial."

Cerise put her head down and laughed softly. "You are the cocky one aren't you?"

I didn't laugh. "Not cocky. Not even a little bit arrogant. But I'm not shy either Ms. Cerise. Am I being too forward?"

"Not at all. And if you aren't shy why haven't you asked me to dance, huh? Or are you too young to remember that this is the *cut* from back in the day?"

I stood up and reached for her hand. "Oh I remember the cut, I just figured since you have to be barely 21 that you probably didn't know anything about it."

We moved to the dance floor and swayed to *There'll never be a greater love* - one of Switch's most memorable slow jams. As I held Cerise close to me, her perfume took hold of my senses as we moved together slowly. We swayed back and forth to the music until the DJ threw on R. Kelly's step song. Cerise effortlessly kept pace as we shifted gears. She was so beautiful and her hands were soft and tiny. I felt like I was dancing with an angel who came down to earth just to be with me tonight.

The music wasn't so loud that we'd have to shout to each other to be heard, so Cerise and I talked through that song and the next, and the next. I found out she loves movies. Not just the current ones, but what she called "real" movies from back in the 30's 40's and 50's. She likes to travel abroad but hasn't found much time to do it since her work keeps her so busy. She loves music so much she has her own theme song, she told me, but she adamantly refused to tell me what it was though. She told me her favorite artists were Ella Fitzgerald, Lauren Hill, Floetry, Kenny Lattimore, Joe, and Tupac, and Nat King Cole. MMPH. Gotta love that! Also, to my surprise I found out she, like me, is a Blaxploitation movie buff. I didn't believe her. "Woman, you aren't old enough to know anything about those movies. You were probably just a itty bitty baby in the 70's" I told her.

"Please, I'm probably just as old, if not older than you!" I gave her a doubtful look. "Ah, you don't believe me I see. Go ahead test me." I racked my brain for something to trip her up and came upon a gem. "Way down in the jungle deep…" I was sure Cerise would have no clue what I was talking about. She stopped dancing and stood with her hands on her hips.

"The lion stepped on the signifying monkey's feet." Cerise said, snapped her fingers in the air, twirled around, and headed back to the table. She looked over her shoulder and laughed at me, as I stood staring after her in amazement. "Are you coming or do I have to finish the whole poem?" I finally followed. Damn I was enjoying myself! Ladies and Gentlemen, we have a winner!

"Do you believe me now?" Cerise laughingly asked. I reached the table and pulled the chair out for Cerise before sitting opposite her.

"Oh I believe you alright. So here's what I was thinking: when we get married, you should dress up as Cleopatra Jones, and I'll be Dolomite. What do you think?" Cerise had just taken a sip of water but when I said that she nearly choked.

Finally managing to gulp down the water without it spurting out, she said, "You are *too* crazy! I nearly spit water all over you. Bet you wouldn't have thought that was funny, huh?"

"Can't hold your water? I'll have to remember that." I said, with a wink.

The smile left Cerise's face and she looked at me with quizzical eyes, as if I were a complicated mathematical theory she was trying to figure out.

"Hmm, what's *that* look all about?" I asked.

"I was about to ask you pretty much the same thing, Mark. What's this all about? I am having the best time I've had in a really long time and I don't even know you! For some reason, I find myself completely comfortable and relaxed with you. Am I crazy? Are you feeling it too?" Cerise asked.

"Nah." I said. "Not at all." We both laughed because we both knew I was lying through my teeth. "Truth Cerise? I feel so comfortable with you right now I feel like I've known you for years."

Before either she or I could comment further, Bonita arrived with our order, a large platter of hot wings and a cold pitcher of beer. Cerise looked at me like I was crazy. "Who is that for? I know that can't be what you ordered for us," she said.

"Well, let me ask you this: do you like beer?" She nodded. "And do you like hot wings?" She nodded again. "Well then what's the problem?" I asked.

"Uh, my dress for one thing. Plus I don't know you well enough to pig out like this on our first da..., I mean, I usually don't eat like this unless I'm in a sports bar or something."

I looked into her eyes with and with mock sternness told her, "Cerise. You can't be afraid to lick your fingers and get a little dirty. Sometimes its okay to loosen up." I hit the nail on the head.

Cerise rolled up her sleeves, grabbed a napkin, looked me back in the eyes, and said, "I'm not scared Marcus. I was trying to be polite. But since you've thrown down a challenge like that, lets do this! But what are you going to eat?" Cerise asked, as she pulled the platter in front of her. Laughing, I pulled it back towards the center and we continued to talk and laugh as we demolished the chicken and beer.

When we'd finally finished eating and sat sipping on our beer, I asked Cerise to tell me about the fool who stood her up tonight. "What kind of man doesn't show up when he has a woman like *you* waiting for him, if you don't mind me asking?"

The mood at the table changed perceptibly as Cerise took a drink from her beer mug and hesitated. "Okay, it's a really long, sad story but bottom line is I've never met him so I don't know what kind of man he is."

I waited for more, but suddenly, Cerise was not very chatty. "So it was a blind date?" I probed for more information.

"No," she replied. I remained silent waiting for Cerise to continue. Finally she blurted out, "It wasn't a date, it was a, uh, business meeting. I never met the man because my mother went to the initial consultation for me since I was out of town on business but wanted to set things up with him quickly. I don't even know what the man looks like but my mother told me he's white and his name is Tyler and from our phone conversation today I know his last name is Haley. The meeting was a last minute thing so I didn't even think, until I got here, to ask how I was supposed to recognize him but figured I'd approach every unattached white male to see if he was my contact. No one fitting that description showed up tonight. I would have left but since D'Angelo was here…" Cerise's voice trailed off as she watched my expression turn from interest, to concern, to bewilderment.

I couldn't believe what Cerise was telling me. I didn't want to believe what she was telling me! This can't be happening. "What is it Marcus?" Cerise asked me, her face now mirroring my bewilderment.

I closed my eyes, took a deep breath, and asked, "Do you or your mother own a company by the name of Xellron, Inc.?"

Cerise was just about to take a sip of beer but set the mug down and looked me dead in the eyes. The playfulness was gone from her face and voice. "I didn't tell you the name of my company. Who told you that?"

I reached across the table and extended my hand, which Cerise shook out of habit as she continued to stare me down. "I guess we haven't been properly introduced. My name is Marcus *Haley*. And you, I believe, are the same Cerise Ivan I spoke with earlier this afternoon. I thought I was speaking with your mother and its she I thought I'd be meeting tonight. I thought she had stood me up as well."

Cerise was dumbfounded. "I can't believe this! *You* own HiCi?" She sputtered.

"I'm not sure how I should take that remark. Yes, I'm the owner of HiCi. Tyler is, or was, a top investigator of mine."

We were both silent for a moment. For my part, I was disheartened that the woman whose company I'd so enjoyed over the last couple of hours was none other than the client who'd hired me to tail her husband. I don't know how Tyler got it so fouled up! Surely, the elder Cerise would have mentioned to him that she was hiring the firm for her daughter and not herself. Then again, Tyler had overlooked more than a few very important details when he'd done the background research.

Cerise nursed her beer and remained lost in her own thoughts. I had no way of knowing what kind of spin she was putting on the events of this evening. To break the silence and bring her back to the present I said, "I knew there was something familiar about you but I just couldn't place it. I should have recognized your voice."

When she looked up at me, she suddenly looked very sad, and very lost. Finally, she said, "Forgive me, Mr. Haley Marcus. I guess I'm still in a bit of shock. All night I've been grateful that Tyler hadn't shown up because it gave me a chance to meet a wonderfully entertaining and handsome man. But now that I know you've handled the messy business you were hired for, I'm not sure how to react. I'm afraid I'm a little out of my element at the moment. You'll have to forgive me." She said with a rueful smile. The woman had more than just a touch of class. This had to be even more awkward for her than it was for me and she'd handled it with honesty and grace.

"Well this is definitely a first for me as well Cerise. And I know you must be feeling awkward with the situation. We have much to discuss regarding the 'messy business' you hired my company for but I'd like to propose something."

"Another proposal so soon?" Cerise joked softly.

"Yes. But this time it's a very serious proposal. First, let me be completely honest with you. I'm so into you right now I don't care about all the messiness we have to discuss later. I'll call you tomorrow to set up a proper business meeting and we can go over all the information that has been gathered to date then. Tonight, I'd like to propose that we finish the evening as we started it enjoying each other's company. For just tonight lets just pretend that you are Cerise, I am Marcus, and we don't have last names. What do you say?"

I knew I was way out of line. This was my client! But damn! You just don't meet a woman like Cerise every day of the week. I'd found her, no matter what the circumstances and I was willing to say whatever I had to spend just a little more personal time with her before we got down to business. I fully expected her to politely refuse, gather her things, and go. To my pleasant surprise, Cerise moved the hair away from her face where it had fallen when she'd suddenly found the table so fascinating. When she looked at me there was a smile on her lips to match the one in her eyes.

"You're on, Marcus. If *you* can pretend that the last 20 minutes never happened, just for tonight, mind you, then I can too. I really have enjoyed our time together tonight."

As soon as the words left her mouth, I immediately jumped back to the conversation from earlier so that she wouldn't have a chance to rethink her decision. "So what if you know the Dolomite poem. That's not that big a deal. I should have given you something more difficult."

Cerise, obviously glad to be back in familiar terrain, leaned back in her chair and crossed those sexy legs of hers. "Shoot your best shot Haley, uh, wait, I don't know your last name yet, do I? Shoot your best shot, Marcus." She said and laughed as I put my hand to my chin in 'thinker' mode trying to come up with something from a Blaxploitaion film that would stump her.

Bonita saved me. I saw her approaching out of the corner of my eye and said to Cerise, "Okay so what about the line that goes…Ah…Bonita is here. I guess I'll have to save that one for later." From the look Cerise gave me, she knew exactly what I was about and had the nerve to laugh at me!

"Marc honey, why haven't you introduced me to your beautiful young woman?

Cerise smiled, murmuring gracefully, "Thank you."

Bonita turned to Cerise and told her, "Don't thank me child. Thank your Momma and Daddy. I ain't had nothing to do with it!" Cerise and I laughed but Bonita turned back to me and waited expectantly.

"Cerise it is of great pleasure to introduce to you the woman that ruined me for all other women and is the heart and soul of this place, Ms. Bonita. Ms. Bonita, Cerise." I'd stood up to make the introductions and when I finished, I gave them both a courtly bow.

Bonita smacked me playfully on the top of my head. "Boy you better quit showing out." She said with a voice she meant to be stern but was instead, filled with indulgence. She turned to Cerise again, "Hello dear, it is so nice to meet you! You come back and see us anytime, with or without this thespian, you hear?" Cerise smiled and nodded her thanks once again.

Bonita turned to me once again, put her hands on her hip, and said, "Marcus Haley, it's about damn time! I haven't seen you smile so much nor *show out* like your doing right now in years." She'd caught me as I gestured to Cerise with my hand, head, and eyes that Ms. Bonita drank a lot so Cerise shouldn't pay any attention to what Bonita said. I earned another playful rap on my head for that one.

Ms. Bonita walked away switching that big ole' booty, mumbling to herself, "That boy ain't got a bit of sense" and shaking her head as her whole body moved in silent laughter.

Physically I shifted my attention back on Cerise, but Bonita's words had given me pause. Had it really been that long since I'd come to Bucks in such a good mood? Considering the women I'd been dealing with up until very recently, I guess it had been a very long time indeed.

I looked over at Cerise who was still smiling at Bonita's retreating back. I shook off the unhappy memories and said, "I was trying to tell you that woman is a hopeless drunk. Do NOT, under any circumstance, believe a word she says." Cerise laughed at me.

"Negro please. That woman is saner than you and I put together. I'm going to have to come back here and get to know her better." Cerise said.

"Now what would you want to do that for?" I asked. "You don't want to encourage her. She might tell you all kinds of lies about me."

"Or she might just tell me about you. Is that what you are so concerned about Mr. Thespian?" Cerise said with a light laugh. I gave her a wide-eyed innocent look and quickly changed the subject.

The DJ was preparing for the younger crowd now coming through the doors and starting to mix up the R&B and neo soul with the crunk sound, I was trying my damnedest to appreciate but just couldn't get into. I wanted the evening to last and couldn't imagine sexy, sensual, graceful, and classy as all hell, Cerise being happy to spend the rest of the evening on a crowded, sweaty dance floor dancing to "music" punctuated with "YEAH! and "OKAY!" while being instructed to shake her tail feathers or put her back into it. I wanted to find a decent way to ask Cerise to my pad without it seeming like I was inviting her over to view my "etchings."

"Cerise, I noticed you were really into D Angelo tonight. You were so into his music I thought you were his woman."

Cerise smiled, "Marcus, let me tell you how I feel about D Angelo, from one music lover to another. As he was playing, I wasn't even listening to the melody but just the lyrics of his song. What woman hasn't wanted her man to feel that way about her? You're my lady? Come on! It's every woman's dream that her man will feel that way about her. Was I supposed to look at the piano or the floor or something? Or would you have preferred that I was looking at you when he sang words that touched my soul?"

"Duh! You should have either looked at me or the floor but not ever at D'Angelo like he was the key to your hearts desire."

"I didn't know you were interested in my heart's desire. That's good information to hold on to. Anyway, how would you know where I was staring?" Cerise challenged me.

"I might have spotted you out of the corner of my eye but was trying to play it cool. I might have been listening to D'Angelo's words but been seeing your face. Did that notion ever factor into what you were thinking? Now that's what I'm talking about!" I was almost at a loss for words. I said *almost*.

"Well I am not complaining. Also, did I mention I have D Angelo's *lyrics,* along with his music at home? Care to join me? We can listen to some more of that 'soul touching' music without Lil John yelling at us."

Cerise stopped cold and looked at her watch. "What are you about, Marcus? I mean, don't get me wrong, I've had a very nice time getting to know you but are you really asking me to your house and I just met you today?"

I said, "Yep. What's the problem?" Cerise looked a bit surprised at my response, as though she expected me to retract my offer in the face of her direct questioning. Instead, I grabbed a spoon off the table, gave it a twirl in my fingers, and then sang into it. "Come on and go with me, Cerise. Come on over to my place." My timing was uncanny because just then the DJ played Nelly and Jahiem's latest version of the song. I put the spoon down and gestured towards the speakers. "It's meant to be woman. Even the DJ is trying to get you to see reason."

She grinned, and when she did, I knew I had her. "You know, that's' is one of my favorite songs. I even like this new version. You sure know how to charm a woman Marcus. What did you do, slip the DJ a bill or two to get him to play the song when you picked up the spoon?"

I winked at her. "That, my dear, is something you will never know." I said with a smile.

"Okay, Marcus, you win. I'll come over for a bit, it's still early. I'm not going to stay for very long though, just in case you have any other tricks up your sleeve you'll have to use them on someone else. I'm not the one to get busy with a man I just met, no matter how charming and persuasive he can be."

"What a suspicious mind you have, young lady. All I want to do is listen to some music and continue getting to know you. Is that wrong?"

Cerise looked as though she was struggling with herself but finally admitted, "No, Marcus, there's nothing wrong with that."

I pulled a quick roll, slide, shake, and button maneuver. I rolled my sleeves down, slid my suit jacket on, did a quick Harlem shake so the boys down low could rearrange themselves, and buttoned up the suit jacket. As I set a tip on the table Cerise asked, "Marcus, you don't live on the other side of the world do you? I can't be driving for an hour to listen to music then have to drive another hour just to get back home."

"No baby, I'm about 10 minutes or so from here. You ready?" She nodded. "Okay so all you have to do is just follow me and you can't get lost. I am driving a black Benz and the *On-Star* number is easy to remember, in case we get separated. Its 777-9312." I gave my best Morris Day impersonation.

Cerise looked pained. "I've noticed you are very charming and entertaining, Marcus. But maybe Morris Day is just not your forte?" She said and laughed.

"What are you talking about? I fingered my goatee, a la Morris, and gave a *Waa Haa!* Still in Morris mode, I told her, "The only *difference* from my number and the one in my song, was the last *digit baby*. Now follow me home. I want some *perfection!*"

Cerise laughed so hard she snorted. When she'd regained her composure, she sighed and said, "I haven't had this much fun in a long time, Marcus. Thank you. Home Morris!"

I bowed slightly and took her elbow to guide her through the crowded dance floor and out to the parking lot, happy that my night with Cerise wasn't over yet. Tomorrow we could be Mr. Haley and Mrs. Ivan. For now, we could still be Marcus and Cerise. We walked outside and I escorted her to her Lincoln Navigator, the same one I'd tailed this morning.

STAY FOR A WHILE

As Cerise got into her SUV I started to close the door but I stopped short when she said, "Don't drive too fast okay? I wouldn't want to lose you."

Adrenaline rushed through me in reaction to her softly spoken request. I wanted to take double meaning from her words but decided I'd better take them at face value. "Not possible. Call me in 30 seconds. That way we can stay connected and there won't be any chance of losing each other," I said with meaning. Cerise nodded in understanding and I closed the door. Walking the short distance to my car, I got in just as the *On Star* system beeped to let me know I had messages. I started to push the button to replay the messages and the phone rang. It was Cerise. "Hello beautiful, let's roll."

Cerise followed me home as we discussed everything under the sun except what might really happen when we got to my house. Five minutes into our drive, Cerise and I pulled up to a light not too far from the house. I glanced in my rear view mirror and told Cerise, "See? There was no need to think we'd lose each other. You are so close I can read your lips."

She replied, "Well if you can read my lips, tell me what I'm saying." She pressed the mute button on her mobile phone. Her mouth moved sensuously and my adrenaline kicked into overdrive even though I couldn't make out the words.

"Good one, Cerise. Obviously, I can't *actually* read your lips. What did you say? Don't hold out on me woman, cause the way your mouth was moving I'd swear you were talking dirty to me."

Cerise laughed and said, "Not gonna tell you. That's what you get for claiming to do something you can't. Matter of fact, as further punishment I'm going to hang up right now. I'll call you back in a sec." She said, then disconnected from the line before I could reply.

The light changed and I drove on, grinning. We drove for a few more minutes and I saw from the rearview mirror Cerise was renewing her lipstick. Another stoplight slowed my progress towards home. My eyes rolled at the thought that she'd soon be placing those freshly varnished lips against mine. Coming out of my vision of heaven, my eyes rested for a moment on the car to my right. It was Stanley! Just as he was about to look in my direction I played it off as if I didn't notice him, pretended instead to be reading a CD case. The light then turned green and Stanley took off driving well past the speed limit. What the hell is that about?

I started to race him out of curiosity but Cerise was following so I slowed down. The phone beeped and it was Cerise.

"Sorry about that Marcus, I just wanted to freshen up a bit. Did you miss me?" I was too distracted by Stanley's odd behavior to give her a properly flirtatious answer. Instead, I mumbled something as we turned the corner to my block.

As I pulled into my driveway there stood Stanley in his yard, rake in hand. What the hell was he doing? I couldn't believe it! I pulled into the garage as Cerise drove up the street and made a U turn. I guess she wanted to leave the way she came so she wouldn't get confused later. I opened the garage, parked, and hopped out of the car to greet Cerise.

As I made my way to the sidewalk, Stanley said, "Hey bruther.... long time no see? How ya been?" I gave him a quizzical look and replied, "I'm fine. *You* okay?"

Stanley stood there smiling with that damn grin, "Oh yeah bruther, just getting this yard together, you know? I try to keep it looking in tip-top shape. I've been out here two hours straight!" This nut was too funny for words. He can't believe that I didn't see him at the stoplight only moments ago!

Stanley, raking grass that didn't need raking, looked up and said, "I see the stable is open tonight bruther. A little early isn't it? Its only Thursday bruther! What prairie were you hunting on? Whew!"

Cerise was parallel parking next to the curb. To cut Stanley short I said, "Hey, hey, Stanley, watch it now. This one is special. Do *NOT* do anything to mess this up!" Stanley stood there grinning for a second as if he wanted to say something. I stared at him, in silent encouragement for him to behave himself and to get all of his questions and foolishness out before Cerise walked over towards us.

Stanley, never one to understand finesse, yelled out, "Whewww, heewwwwww bruther! Yeah!" Before turning and running into his open garage, clicking it closed behind him.

Cerise looked at me as she slowly got out of the car. "Marcus, what was that all about?"

I smiled and said, "He's just a little juiced about me telling him I'd decided to go ahead and help him with some of his renovations." Cerise took me at my word and as we walked to the door, out of habit, I turned around to look at Stanley's house.

Why, oh why did I turn to look? Cerise turned also. Not only Stanley, but Ramona as well, were spying at us through the open blinds of their living room window. She was in a corner peeking around one side and Stanley was in the other corner, noticing me notice them, Stanley put one thumb up and then pulled back from the blinds quickly. Ramona put a thumb up as Stanley disappeared. Two separate damn thumbs, one from him and now he had her doing the thumb thing as well?

Cerise and I both heard Stanley yell, "Whew bruther, yeah!"

Cerise looked a bit concerned. "I don't think I even want to ask what that was all about."

I decided to move up my meeting with Stanley. I needed to get together with him sooner rather than later. Beyond that thought all my senses were honed on Cerise.

I opened the door and said, "Welcome to my paradise away from all the madness." Cerise made appreciative noises as I showed her the house. As we passed the living room again, I grabbed the stereo remote and scanned until I reached one of my favorite CD's.

Before the music even began, Cerise reached out, took the remote from me, and pressed the stop button before handing it back. I gave an enquiring look and Cerise sighed deeply.

"Hey that was a pretty deep sigh. I thought we were going to leave tomorrow to handle itself, and enjoy what's left of the evening. Why don't I pour you a glass of wine to help you relax a little? I want you to feel comfortable in my home."

Cerise followed me into the kitchen and said to my back, "It's not that I don't feel comfortable or relaxed Marcus. Its that I feel too much so." I turned around to face her as she continued. "I just have this feeling you are about to turn on some wonderful love making music, and we'll be all rosy from the wine. One thing will lead to another and you and I will be upstairs in bed before the evening is over. You have to know I can't allow that to happen, Marcus. It's not going down like that. I'm sorry if that's what you think I came here to do."

I smiled at Cerise with understanding. The lady had class. "Hold on. You and I both agreed that we'd listen to more D'Angelo and just get to know each other, right?" Cerise looked as if she wanted to protest but nodded in agreement. "I'm a little surprised you somehow managed to change what we both agreed to do into me planning a big seduction scene. Have you no faith, little one? Yeah I was about to play some slow sexy music but I wouldn't necessarily call it 'knocking boots' music. If you want to call it lovemaking music that's fine, but not the kind of lovemaking you have in mind. This music makes love to your *mind*."

I held the remote out to Cerise. "Take it. Press play. You'll see what I'm talking about." Cerise took the remote, directed it towards the living room stereo, and barely grazed the play button before saying, "Wait. Wait. I told you Marcus I...."

I interrupted her, "Just a moment lady. You are going to play this music! Just hold on for a second." I took the remote back and adjusted it so that not only the living room speakers but also all the speakers in the many corners hidden throughout the house would be on as well. I handed the remote back to her. "I want to make sure you are surrounded by this mental lovemaking music." Cerise rolled her eyes as if I'd just said the corniest line ever but she finally hit the play button.

As the piano solo began Cerise rolled her eyes again, but this time I could tell, she did so not because she doubted my intentions but because the music was so beautiful. The lone trumpet overtook the sounds of the piano as Cerise handed the remote back to me and smiled as *How are things in Glocca Morra,* played on. I knew this particular piece would overcome Cerise's doubts. It was, to me, Wynton Marsalis' finest masterpiece of his musical career. Without a single vocal lyric the music spoke to love found, love lost, then found again.

Cerise stood before me with her eyes closed as if this music were just what she needed. I guided her into a chair and made sure she was comfortable, before selecting a bottle of wine from the cabinet.

I walked back to Cerise and said, "Don't open your eyes, I am handing you a glass of wine. It's nice and light. I think you'll enjoy it." Cerise felt for the glass, eye's still closed, and her fingers lightly grasped the stem of the wine glass. "Sit here and relax for a while. I need to turn the sprinklers off in the backyard. I'll be back in a flash."

Cerise gently guided the glass to her mouth; eyes still closed as she absorbed Wynton's mental foreplay, took a sip of the wine, and smiled. "Take your time." She murmured. I went to the refrigerator and grabbed a few containers of fruit with watermelon, cantaloupe, peach, grapes, mango, honeydew melon, banana, apple, and kiwi. I looked over my shoulder at Cerise as I placed all the items on the counter and she was still lost to the music. I walked quietly out of the kitchen, into the living room, slid the door open, and walked down the dark path to my greenhouse.

Inside the greenhouse, I kept a large assortment of exotic plants - cymbidium orchids, dwarf gardenias, birds of paradise, and two datura meteloides double cream. They filled the evening air with their fragrance through the open vents. Inside I kept my summer lamp oil suitcase, which held, of course, my oils but also abalone shells I'd collected throughout the years. Removing 20 shells, I quickly filled them with oil, placed them in the sand along the pathway to the greenhouse, and set them alight.

Knowing I had about one minute left of Wynton's serenade, I walked back in the greenhouse and moved a few plants off a table and pulled the two director chairs inside close together.

Silently, I crept back to the kitchen through the living room door to grab the fruit containers off the counter. Cerise was still lost to the music so I was able to creep back silently to the greenhouse, where I poured two more glasses of wine, then rinsed my hands off in the makeshift fountain. Finally, I flipped a switch on the wall of the greenhouse and the music from inside the house now filled the greenhouse. I'd set a few speakers in the greenhouse because I enjoyed listening to jazz as I cultivated.

Wynton's serenade ended. From my vantage point, I could see Cerise looking around. Not finding me in the house, Cerise walked to the open sliding glass door as the first strains to Joe Sample's accompaniment of Lailah Hathaway's *I'm not in love* began. She looked outside, saw me in the greenhouse, and the smile she gave was illuminated even more so from the oil filled shells dotting the walkway.

That smile was worth all my furtive efforts. Cerise slowly followed the pathway towards the greenhouse and admired the candlelit garden along the way, sniffing deeply as she inhaled the scent of the burning fragrant oils. Slowly, she opened the door to the greenhouse and stood staring at me shaking her head in amazement.

Smiling, I told her, "Come on in. Come in here woman." Cerise walked towards me gesturing to the gardens outside as well as the entire greenhouse. "This is all so beautiful, Marcus." She said.

"Thank you, lady. But you have to know there is no flower in this entire greenhouse that matches your beauty, Cerise."

Grabbing a slice of watermelon, I took a bite as Cerise moved closer to me to see what else I had in the containers. She and I were now face to face. I stood there taking deep breaths trying to keep my body and actions under control, willing all the adrenaline to redirect its energies away from its current destination.

I hadn't planned to seduce Cerise in the greenhouse, I just wanted to show her how much I appreciated her being her and had pulled out all the stops. In hindsight, now that she was in front of me with the music softly playing and the pathway glowing from the burning oils, I realized this could easily get me in trouble with her. I needed to regroup and get my thoughts together fast.

"Are you going to share the fruit or is it all for you?" Cerise asked playfully. All my good intentions left me in an instant. I took another piece of watermelon and slowly held it next to Cerise's mouth. She took a small bite. "That's very tasty. What else do you have for me?"

I told Cerise to close her eyes. She took a deep breath and eyed me suspiciously for a second before complying. "Lets play a game, You down?"

Cerise gave a short nod. "Okay, lets play your game, Marcus. Lets see what kind of man you are."

I was pretty sure I knew exactly what she meant and resolved not to make her regret the decision to come home with me tonight. But she'd agreed to play so it was all good, as long as I didn't take the game too far. I grabbed the other barstool guided Cerise to sit in front of me. "Okay Cerise, before you say anything, just listen for a moment…this little game requires that you do not speak or open your eyes. I promise not to do anything to you that I wouldn't want done to me." She seemed to relax after I reassured her that I wouldn't play any tricks. I could see she was peeking but that was okay.

Cerise said, "Before we begin I just want you to know that I'm not good at playing games unless I cheat, which I plan to do. Also, I'm leaving at exactly 1130. My girl Bernadette is expecting my call *from my car* or she will probably show up here with the rescue squad."

"Oh, so your crew is gonna roll up on a brother if I don't get Cinderella to her pumpkin chariot by the appointed time, eh?" I asked.

"That's right!" Cerise said with a large grin. It suddenly made since to me why Cerise had been so gung-ho to come to my place but the second she walked in started asking about my intentions. She had obviously called this Bernadette during the drive over to let her know where she was going. I actually admired her for doing so. In this day and age, it's smart not to take chances.

"Cerise, I'd never do anything to hurt you. I know you don't know that now but one thing you will learn about me is I am a very patient man. Keep your guard up as long as you feel you need to it doesn't bother me one bit." I told her. She nodded her appreciation. "But just so you know, when you walked in here, you were the perfect image of peace. The light from moon and seashells lit up your smile and it warmed me up. For a moment, I almost thought I was dreaming. You are too good to be true and the last thing I want to do is take that peaceful presence from you."

Cerise sighed and opened her eyes again, directing her intense gaze directly at me. "Hmmm, those are pretty deep words, Mr. Marcus. You don't even *know* me. Is this how you greet all your female friends?"

I'd wondered how long it would take Cerise to ask that question. She'd be naive not to. "Well, actually I don't invite many people over. Also, I've never greeted any guest in this particular way. I wanted to do something I've never done before for some reason. Maybe you just inspire me." I told her truthfully.

"Again, very nice words. But Marcus, do you think I'm going to sleep with you tonight? Because you know…"

I interrupted. "I said whoa with all that remember? I thought I was the game show host? I'll answer that question for you after the game now hush woman!"

"Okay," Cerise said and closed her eyes for a moment only to quickly open them again. "I was just have to say this, man. I know we agreed not to talk about this until tomorrow but given the way things are going between us I think we kind of have to."

Whatever she had to say was obviously weighing heavily on her mind because Cerise looked at me with so much intensity. Her body was tensed and her hands clutched the bar stool so hard her knuckles had to be cramping up. "Go ahead Cerise, what is it you want to tell me?"

She hesitated a moment and looked as though she were choosing her words very carefully. "Okay, I don't even know what you found out during your stake out today but I can guess its pretty deep or you would have told me right away there was nothing to worry about and probably would have never invited me here, am I right?" The woman was sharp as well as beautiful. I nodded to concede her point. "Okay, well I am not going to say the outside activities I suspected about Mike didn't worry me but…" Cerise's voice trailed off.

"Go ahead, you were worried about Ivan and what?" I prompted her.

She shook her head as if to clear it before saying, "You know what? Never mind about that. Suffice it to say, I'm just glad I hired you."

"That was not what you wanted to say. Talk to me Cerise. Don't be shy." I encouraged her.

As if unable to hold back the flow of words any longer Cerise blurted out, "This was no damn marriage in the first place! It was just an *arrangement*. I married him because I was stupid and felt sorry for him. I didn't realize it at first but that's the truth of my marriage. He was broke but he's an artist and was trying to support himself. I didn't care about money but now I see that's all he *did* care about. He doesn't give a damn about me. At first, it was okay but almost from the very start, I noticed there was something off about Mike. If I were to sleep with you tonight and not go home until morning he wouldn't care or even ask where I'd been." Cerise stood up now and started pacing in the walkway between the plants and the counter where I sat. She was just heating up.

"And the kicker, the absolute ultimate *kicker* is that in spite of what I've suspected I haven't been out there doing anything because I took that vow to be faithful and even though I realized right after I said those words in front of the minister they were a mistake, I tried to live up to them! Marcus, I know some people consider me to be a beautiful woman. I get hit on all the time! And do you know what? Even though I knew my marriage was doomed from the beginning and I wished I hadn't done it, it messes with your head to know your husband doesn't want you in that way. That's crazy right? I mean I don't even *want* him to touch me. But still, in my heart, I just don't want what I suspect to be true. I couldn't be that terrible a judge of character could I?"

Mentioning that Cerise had hired that ditzy receptionist was out of the question but I could see now why she was so conflicted and why she didn't trust her judgment when it came to me.

Cerise continued her pacing. Talking now, as if she were just figuring all this out for the first time. "And I shouldn't even care what he's doing because I wanted out anyway, right?" She didn't wait for my answer. "I should just be glad he's given me enough evidence to get him out of my life without having to suffer a huge financial lose. But to *know* that the bastard *used* me for my money so he could live some kind of rich and famous lifestyle when the whole time he's been sleeping with other men is just too much!"

The shock I felt on hearing these words caused my jaw to drop for a moment.

"So you knew all along?" I asked quietly.

Cerise walked back to the chair and plopped into it completely spent. "I didn't know. I suspected. You've just confirmed it for me." She was silent for a moment but then said quietly, "I want whatever you have on him delivered to my office as soon as possible Marcus. I need this nightmare to be over." Cerise looked as if she were about to cry out of frustration. She looked so sad, so lost.

"Cerise, in the morning you will have all the visual and audio evidence you need to get rid of this guy and he won't have a single resource to demand any financial settlement from you." Through teary eyes, Cerise looked at me gratefully and gave me a small smile. She seemed unsure what to say next now that she'd spilled her guts.

"Well... now that we don't have to have our business meeting in the morning lets just move on as Marcus Haley, unattached bachelor, and Cerise Ivan, soon to be unattached, beautiful woman." I told her, trying to bring a smile to her face.

It worked briefly but then Cerise got lost in her thoughts again. Quietly she asked, "What is it you really want from me Marcus? Why did you bring me here knowing all that you do about me and my messy life?"

I pulled her chair closer to mine and learned over to whisper in her ear. "Hush, no more about Mike, okay? I don't care about him and I don't care about your messy situation. I've had messy situations a time or two in my life as well. The trick is knowing when to cut your losses and move on."

Cerise reached out to give me a quick hug and a peck on the cheek. Now that she'd said everything that had weighed so heavily on her before she was almost back to being the same playful, flirtatious woman I'd met only hours ago. "Are you trying to be my knight in shining armor? You trying to rescue me Mr. Haley?" Cerise asked with a Scarlet O'Hara southern accent.

"I told you to hush. Let me finish." I told her.

Cerise smiled and folded her hands on her lap. "I'm sorry. Go ahead." She said.

"Look Cerise, I understand that things are weird for you right now. I *completely* understand the pain you are going through because you were betrayed by someone you knew was no good for you to begin with. But you *have* to be quiet now because we were playing a game and if you keep talking then you are cheating because you're not suppose to be talking. Remember?"

Cerise smiled and saluted but said nothing. "Okay, now that we have thoroughly discussed all other relevant matters I'm going to serve you some fruit if I may. While serving you I am going to say a few things about this evening we've shared together. If I say something you disagree with, then shake your head but *do not* speak. If you agree with what I say then nod."

Cerise settled back on her stool and closed her eyes again, signaling she was ready to begin. "Are you ready?" I asked. "Ye…" Cerise began but I interrupted, "You really are a cheater aren't you? Just nod. No speaking, remember?" Cerise nodded and I slowly placed several pieces of fruit to her mouth. Cerise bit into each piece of fruit, shaking her head after some and nodding vigorously after others.

"Okay Cerise, even though we only met hours ago there is something going on between us, would you agree?" Cerise's head was motionless for a second and I thought she was going to shake it but after a few seconds, she nodded instead. "Right. Then, I suspect that it will take several months to free yourself from your husband. Don't get sad on me again." I said quickly as Cerise frowned. "I only bring that up to ask my next question." The frown left her face as I placed a small slice of kiwi to her lips, which she licked first and then bit into.

"Do you want me to disappear as suddenly as I appeared so that you can deal with your divorce without distraction?" I asked, placing a slice of honeydew to her lips. Without hesitation this time, Cerise took a bite of the melon and shook her head. "Is that no to the fruit?" I asked. Cerise shook her head. I smiled. "Should I keep giving you fruit to taste or can I kiss you now?" Cerise opened her lovely eyes and stared into mine as she nodded.

Luther Vandross came through the speakers. My all time favorite cut from him. *If Only for One Night* played and Cerise placed her finger gently over my lips to and said, "Just let me hear the first verse."

Cerise seemed to be in a different mood than any I'd previously witnessed during our short but eventful acquaintance. Luther crooned in the background as Cerise removed her fingers from my lips and slipped her arms around my shoulders. Softly, she said, "You said something about a kiss?"

I didn't need any further invitation. Pulling Cerise more closely to me, my lips found hers. For the next several moments, we explored each other as if it this was the moment we'd been waiting for all night. For me, it was. Luther's song ended and another began as we kissed.

Finally pulling myself away from her with a mischievous glint in my eyes, I grabbed a slice of honeydew melon and slowly slid it along her neck and jaw line. Following the trail of liquid the melon left behind, I gently licked and kissed the juice away.

Cerise reached down and took a bite of the melon still in my hand and said, "Marcus you are a little kinky I think!"

"You disapprove?" I asked with a sheepish grin.

"Oh hell no!" Cerise replied immediately.

Cerise reached up for another kiss but I pulled back. "Control yourself woman." She laughed. "Time for my final question." I said. Cerise rolled her eyes and looked as if she'd rather continue what we started than answer any more questions."Cerise, you asked me earlier did I think you were going to sleep with me tonight. Well the answer to your question is yes, I think you are."

Her mouth jaw dropped and her eyes opened wide. "Marcus, as fun as the last few minutes have been what kind of women do you take me to be? I mean, no matter how good of a connection we seem to have, I just can't meet a man and go to bed with him the same night and…"

Before she could protest further I pulled Cerise close to me again so that she could feel the effect she was having on me. "Okay that wasn't my final question. Do you think I'm playing a game Cerise? Do you think I'm just out for a piece of ass? Or do you trust me when I say that I want more than just a one night stand?"

Cerise looked into my eyes and said, "Yes Marcus, I believe you." She groaned as she ground her body into mine before pulling back again. "I believe that you've been entirely honest with me tonight but I really don't like how fast this is all moving. I just can't go out like this Marcus. It's too soon!"

"Woman, you are going to learn to trust me if it's the last thing I do." I said. "Let me clarify what I meant about sleeping with you." Cerise sat on her barstool with her arms folded ready to shoot holes in whatever I said, I knew. I pressed on nonetheless. "Cerise, you asked me if I thought you were going to sleep with me tonight. I said yes but did you want me to tell you a lie? If two people are vibing like us and in tune with each other why wait a few days for the inevitable just so you can say you didn't do me on the first night you met me? Does a few days really make a difference? I'm not going anywhere. Tonight will be the first night of many as far as I'm concerned and you know it too."

Cerise and I laughed and she didn't deny what I said. "I know you can't put a time limit or date on when you are going to make love to someone for the first time Marcus. If the mood is right and the feelings are registering off the chart than anything can happen. But for me, I can't just jump straight in the sack with someone because we vibe. All the pieces of the puzzle have to be in place for me to be ready to go there. And as much as I want you to take me right here on the greenhouse floor, it's just too soon and not only that, but Bernadette will be expecting my call at any moment."

"So this not sleeping with me is more about saving face to your friend and less about the time frame for what we both know is going to happen?" I asked. Cerise stammered around for a response but I moved on.

"Let me ask you this then. If this weren't the first night but the second or maybe the third or fourth, would you think enough time had passed so that I could take care of that body of yours and you could take care of mine?" My need to feel Cerise beneath me was becoming urgent and in spite of my resolve to let her leave at 11:30 as she insisted, I was pulling out all stops to get her to stay.

Cerise nodded 'yes', then shook her head 'no', and then shook it again vigorously as if to clear her confused thoughts. This woman had obviously gone through too much for one night. I felt guilty for the pressure I was applying.

"So you want to stay but at the same time you have to say you can't. You know what? I can dig that. I know you want to me as much as I want you but your mind is telling you to go and I have to respect that." Cerise looked relieved and disappointed at the same time. To save her any further confusion I pointed towards the clock hanging above the greenhouse door. It was 11:23

Cerise sighed and groaned at the same time. "Thank you for understanding, Marcus. I don't really understand what I'm doing myself. You really are a knight in shining armor aren't you?" She walked towards me, pressed her body against mine, and said, "You aren't going to take advantage of my weakness and convince me to stay?" She sounded almost hopeful but I knew when to leave well enough alone.

I pulled her more firmly to me again, feeling her soft body mold itself into mine and took advantage of my last few minutes with her. Between kissing and caressing each other, I asked Cerise what it would take for her to be happy. At first, she appeared not to have heard me, as she was currently busy placing her tongue lightly around the contour of my ear.

She finally stepped back, breathing heavily and said, "Can I get back to you with that question? My head is full right now and I want to truly know what will make me happy but not just will make me happy tonight. No 'off the top of my head' random list that is meaningless. But be warned, Mr. Haley. You asked and I'm going to have an answer for you the next time we meet." I nodded quickly resumed taking in as much of her as I could as the Isley Brothers, *Between the sheets* came through the speakers.

At 11:29, I pulled Cerise away from me. Gruffly I told her, "I'm not a knight, Cerise, even though I'm trying to be noble. I'm not going to pressure you to stay. I know you told your friend you would leave here at 11:30 and I'm going to make sure that you do. But make no mistake, the next time I have you in my arms I will have all of you and you will have all of me. Right now, you have to leave before I change my mind and go caveman on you."

"Another kiss for the road?" Cerise asked. Before the words left her mouth, I pulled her to me again and kissed her with an intensity I never even knew I possessed. Gliding the tip of my tongue over her fruit sweetened lips before plunging in to ravage her mouth a final time before I let her go, I think I bit her tongue at one point.

I definitely had to get her out of here before I lost all control. Managing to untangle myself from Cerise, who was now clinging to me as if she wanted to beg me to let her stay, I escorted her to her car outside.

With both of us too lost in lust to say anything, we walked to her car in silence. Before Cerise climbed into her car, I gave her another quick kiss and closed the door. Cerise started the engine and shifted the gears into reverse as if on automatic pilot. I tapped on the window and she rolled it down.

"Don't forget to call Bernadette." I told her. She smiled, gave a quick wink, and reversed out of the driveway and into the night. I walked back into the house feeling like I was on cloud nine. I was sexually frustrated as all hell, but still I was flying high.

I grabbed my glass of wine and headed out back to put out the burning seashells. I grabbed the bowl of fruit, locked up the greenhouse, and headed back up the garden path. I could hear another Isley Brothers song playing. They sang about hearing footsteps in the dark and I sang right along with them, ready to go to sleep and dream about Cerise.

I turned off all the lights downstairs and was about to head upstairs when the doorbell rang. Thinking it was Cerise coming to beg *me* to let *her* stay, I flung the door open wide with a huge grin on my face. To my surprise, Sheila was standing on my doorstep.

LOVE THE ONE YOU'RE WITH

"What the hell? Sheila! What brings you to my neck of the woods? You and Donna at it again or is she here too?" I left her standing at the front door and walked back to the kitchen, calling over my shoulder, "Come on in, unless you came all the way over just to stand on the doormat."

Shelia came in and closed the door. I'd tried to play it off and not look at the outfit she had on by walking away but since Cerise had already left my hormones screaming, I couldn't help but notice. Sheila was dressed for the hunt.

She called from the doorway, "Well actually I just happened to be heading home from Baker's Place and thought I'd stop by. I know it's late. I hope you don't mind. I bought a book and had some coffee but now I have the jitters. I guess I had one espresso shot too many."

In the kitchen, I grabbed the rest of the wine left over from earlier and poured two more glasses. While doing this, I was thinking Sheila should definitely not be here. Not after I'd shown such exceptional self-restraint with Cerise, and knowing for a fact that Sheila wanted a piece of me.

In an attempt to keep things on a friendly and conversational level between the two of us, even though I wished with all I had in me that I hadn't opened the door in the first place, I said, "I know Baker's Place. They make excellent coffee."

Lame, lame, lame! They make excellent coffee? My small talk needed some work. I mean, yeah, Baker's Place was a locally owned and operated black bookstore and coffeehouse where you could listen to a variety of music while browsing the shelves or just sit and relax. The atmosphere is comfy and the employees welcome you with arms wide open. Somehow, I didn't think Sheila had come to my place to discuss the amenities provided by Baker's Place. Nevertheless, I stayed on that train of thought.

"So what book did you buy?" Shelia sat at the kitchen table and thanked me for the glass of wine I placed in front of her. "The caffeine leaves me with the jitters and hopefully the wine will mellow me out just a bit."

Thankfully, Sheila didn't notice my jitters as she noticed, obviously for the first time, the art I had displayed on the walls of my kitchen. When she didn't reply I asked, "Sure. Did I miss the book title?"

She smiled, "I'm sorry, it's the coffee. My reaction time is not what it should be. The book, yeah. Um, he's a new author on the circuit. His style is just captivating. I mean you start reading and don't want to put the book down. He writes with such a strong manly voice that it could put some women off, but there is something about the story that makes you keep reading. It's *Every Goodbye Ain't Gone* by Aaron Sam. You should read it."

I remembered hearing from Ashley that Baker's Place was hosting a book signing with Aaron Sam a week or so ago. This was a comfortable, safe topic to discuss.

"I drove by when he was here and there were quit a few people attending his signing. He kind of came out of the blue and caused a real stir with his first novel, right?" Sheila replied, "Yes that's him."

Sheila sipped on her wine and an awkward silence fell. To fill the void I said, "I didn't know you were into the arts." But even as I said that it made sense that she would be. Art was one of Donna's passions as well. Donna had shown me how to take a deeper look at paintings and photographs for what the artist was trying to convey.

Shelia stood up and walked up to an original on my kitchen wall. "I recognize the Gordon Park work here," she gestured toward a smaller framed piece I'd placed close to the Park's photo, "but who is *this* painting by?"

I smiled and said, "A personal favorite of mine, that one. She's an artist from San Diego not many people have heard of yet. Her name is Regina Denise; she's doing things with a paintbrush I've never seen before. Regina's style is unique, I get a new version of a story each time I look at her work."

Shelia stood in front of one of Regina's paintings for a minute. "I can see what you are saying. It's beautiful." I poured myself another glass of wine.

Shelia, out of nowhere asked, "Marc what's up with you and Donna? I know you care about her and she cares about you, but is that the extent of it?"

"I wrote a song about it, ya wanna hear it?" We both laughed. By now we'd moved into the living room and I grabbed the remote and said, "listen to this song, it will sum up our relationship on that level." Teddy Pendegrass' deep bass came through the speakers. *"Looking back over the years, I guess I've shedded some tears...told myself time and time again this time I'm gonna win, but another fight, things ain't right, I guess I'm losing again. It takes a fool to lose twice and start all over again. I think I better let it go. It looks like another love T.K.O."*

Shelia looked as if she understood exactly what the song meant to me with regard to Donna and I. Her expression told me that my TKO with Donna mirrored her own experience. Slowly, she placed her wine glass on the table and walked to within inches of me. I didn't step away. Sheila reached up to place her hand around my neck. I went with it. No doubt. We stepped to the music for a moment in slow motion.

"Awhh shit! I see you know a little something something bout stepping Midwest style, huh?" I said, as Shelia took a slow dip and came back on point.

"I can step with the best of em. I took lessons!" I laughed as Teddy played. Testing her stepping skills, I changed it up a bit into a more difficult step that required two people to really be in sync. Sheila was right on the money.

"Alright girl, I see I can't mess with you. You are a stepper O.G. if ever there was one." I gave her the credit she deserved. The song ended on a step that had Shelia and I standing so close I could taste the fumes from the wine on her breath.

"What's the next song? This is fun!" I didn't have to answer because just then the next smooth track began.

Shelia said, "Okay, follow *me* this time." I took another quick sip of wine, smiled, and did a quick tilt of the head as if to 'say lets do this', and Brandy's latest cut kicked in. *"The more they talk about our love"* played as Shelia's stepping moves brought her closer and closer until we were pressed against one another in our groove. The perfume she was wearing had my animal instincts in full gear. I whispered as we stepped, "Hmm, what is that you're wearing?"

Shelia didn't answer but kept her hips in motion in a teasing manner almost like a bully on the schoolyard. I felt like saying, "stop it!" but the words wouldn't come.

Finally Sheila whispered, "I'm wearing "*Hypnotic*, you like?"

"I like. Yes. It's nice and seductive. Not too strong, not too soft."

Shelia stepped away in time to the beat, grabbed her glass of wine, took a sip, and said, "Well maybe you should get a little closer and take nice, deep, slow, breaths so you can be hypnotized. Maybe it'll put you in a trance. They say it calms the savage beast." She said as she stepped her way back to me. We both smiled as we continued to move to the music.

"So you want to hypnotize me huh?" I said. "Now why would you want to do that I wonder?" Sheila stopped dancing and tilted her head up at me, giving me a crooked smile, her teeth lightly biting her bottom lip.

"So it's like that, Sheila?" I set my glass of wine down on the table. I might hate myself in the morning but hell, we were two consenting adults, she was here, and I was ready, thanks to Cerise.

I grabbed Sheila and slowly dipped her in time to the music, bringing her back up to run my fingers through her hair before pulling her closer. Anticipation brought a low growl from the back of my throat.

"MMM, Very animalistic of you Mufasa. I like a man who growls…lets see if I can make you roar."

Shelia reached out and started unbuttoning my shirt slowly, pulling the tails from my pants and pulled it from my shoulders. I wasn't used to being the one seduced. Normally I like to be the one to charm, seduce, hunt – but there was definitely something to be said for letting the woman take the initiative. "Do you know what you are doing woman?" I asked. "Play with fire and you might get burned."

"I know exactly what I'm doing. I'm doing what I've wanted to do since that day in your kitchen." Sheila said. That worried me a bit. Before this went any further, I had to make sure Sheila knew what the deal was. "So what is this all about, Sheila? You gave up women after you and Donna split?"

Sheila leaned in close and whispered in my ear, "Actually Donna and I are back together…does that bother you? Or does it…excite you?" Sheila reached down and rubbed at my hardness through the fabric of my pants. I grabbed her hand away and held it away from me.

"Let's get something straight right now. Unless I got the two of you in my bed the thought of you being with her doesn't excite me. And since Donna is your girl again, even after all that shit she pulled and all that smack you were talking, I assume you want to have sex with me as revenge for her sleeping with your Billy boy? How am I doing so far?"

"Well if I am looking for revenge only you and I would know I'd gotten it, unless you plan on telling her. I certainly have no intention of telling. I think you are scared of me." Sheila was obviously trying to taunt me into ending the conversation and jumping her bones. I was fully prepared to do it, I just didn't need or want any backlash from the crazy lesbian/bi or whatever the hell they were duo.

"Okay straight up Sheila, what's your deal? You came over here for sex or are you gonna pull the 'I just want to be held' deal at the last minute? I'm not in a holding kind of mood so you better know what you are getting into." Instead of backing away or even responding Sheila slowly pulled her sweater over her head, dropped it on the floor, unsnapped the front loading red lace bra and let it fall to the floor as well. "Still think I just want to be held?"

Shelia's breasts were so perfect they seemed almost fake. Of course, now, at the point of no return, I had found out for myself. I pulled her roughly to me, crushing her soft body to my chest. Shelia reached down and unzipped my pants. They fell to the floor. Gently grabbing a handful of Sheila's hair, I pulled her head back to reveal the lines of her neck. I reached down and ran my tongue lightly behind her ear before gently biting the back of her neck. Sheila's moan told me I'd found one of her magic spots.

Sheila continued to massage me but it was time to move things forward. I took her hand and placed it inside my underwear. She didn't hesitate for a moment but took my shaft in her palm and stroked me so expertly you'd never believe she could be into women too.

"Take em off Sheila." I ordered. She didn't need to ask what I meant. Sheila unbuttoned her pants and let them join the pile already there. The red G String looked like it was on fire. I took a moment to admire my new playground before hooking a finger in the string on her hip and tugging it so hard both strings snapped and I held the tiny fabric in my hand. I dropped those to the floor as well and ran my hand over her silky mound, teasing her with my fingers causing Sheila to gasp and grab hold of my shoulders.

Breathlessly she said, "Just so you know Marcus, I'm not here looking to make you my man." My finger entered her and I massaged her from the inside. Sheila closed her eyes tight and held her breath for a moment before expelling it in a rush. "Ah…I just want you to know that all I want from you is this right here, some good old fashioned fucking. No strings."

I walked her to the couch and laid her down running my tongue across her nipples. Struggling to finish her speech Sheila continued breathlessly, "I don't want to hear you love me, you hope we can keep this going, or anything like that. Okay? You are just going to be a piece of ass for me. That's it. AHHH!"

I brought my face so close to Sheila's face that she was blurry. My voice was quiet but intense, "Some ass will be had tonight Sheila, but it won't be mine. You'll have your one night stand and your revenge, but I don't believe you really only want it to be a one time thing. But that's all I want so as long as you know that's all it *can* be I say you need to shut up now because I got some things in mind for your mouth that don't involve a lot of talking."

Shelia reached her hand between us to close her fingers around me. "Oh you think so? Well I see you got something to work with at least," she said with appreciation. I grabbed my glass of wine and took a sip. I pulled Sheila off the couch and reversed our positions so that now I was lying on the couch and she was kneeling in front of me. Slowly Sheila took me into her mouth and worked me over so well I knew I'd have nothing left for later rounds if I didn't stop her now. I ran my hands through her hair and said, "I think we need refills," then jumped up and walked quickly into the kitchen with both our glasses. In the kitchen, Sheila stood by the island and waited for me to refill our glasses. When I'd finished she walked seductively towards me, put her arm around my neck and drew me closer for a kiss. I shifted my head and her mouth met the hollow of my throat. She sucked on my neck so hard and so long, I knew I wouldn't be wearing collarless shirts for a few days.

I picked Shelia up and sat her on the island. She wrapped her arms around my neck and her legs around my waist. I thrust almost violently against Sheila and the heat from her body surrounded me. It felt as if I had stepped from the cold into a warm Jacuzzi. Stimulating chills shot through my body and I had to take deep breaths to keep it together. During the next half hour, Shelia and I put the island to excellent use. We'd take a small break, take a sip of wine, and change positions before going at it again like animals. No kissing, no sweet words, just grunting and moaning and sweat. This was obviously what we both needed right now. Two hours later we'd moved from the island to the floor, from the floor to the table, from the table back to the couch and finally from the couch to my bed. Shelia and I fell asleep with her head on my chest.

I woke up at 6:30 am and the first thought to come to mind was when I could see Cerise again. Then last night came back to me. Obviously, Sheila had left. I rolled to my side and noticed a note on my nightstand. "Thank you for a fun evening, it was fabulous. You were right about one thing. I'm sure you can figure out what that is. Sheila."

I tossed the note aside and didn't give her another thought except to wish that last night I'd had Cerise in my arms instead of Sheila. Why don't I get some of the good breaks? But it was all good because last night had been *all* good as long as Sheila didn't flip out and turn into a groupie.

I hadn't heard from Donna since the night I'd left her standing on my doorstep so long ago so she was on my mind for a moment. I couldn't believe she and Sheila were back together! While driving to work, I decided to call her because my birthday was next month and although I'd decided never to talk to her again, for as long as we'd known each other we would get together on our birthdays and have lunch. I was in a mending fences kind of mood. Maybe because I'd just had a sex-fest with Donna's girlfriend the previous night. At any rate, I felt like all scores had been settled and I actually kind of missed my ace. I left a message on her cell phone telling her to call or email me soon.

In the office that morning, everyone was in a good mood. Payday has a way of putting a smile on people's faces, especially considering how much overtime several of the investigators had worked.

Before reaching my office door Tyler approached me. "Boss the paperwork is done for the Ivan case. It was great working with you. Let me know if you need anything else from me." I told Tyler there was another case on my desk that I wanted him to initiate. He followed me in and I handed him the file. I hadn't had a chance to review it Ashley had said it seemed to be a big money case based on her initial assessment. I told Tyler to look it over and let me know if he needed anything. Somewhere between the end of the case yesterday and having him in my office this morning I'd decided to give Tyler another chance before I took him to task for the sloppy work he did on the Ivan case. I'd monitor him closely this time around though.

I closed the door behind Tyler and called Cerise's office. "Hi this is Marcus is Cerise available?"

The secretary was just as ditsy as yesterday. "Oh no, Milton she's not available now, she'll be out the next (3) days. Sir would you like to speak with someone else?" Where in the hell did she get Milton from Marcus?

"No. Thank you. Can you transfer me to her voicemail?" Thankfully, she got it right on the first try. "Okay sir, here you go and have a wonderful day!" After the beep, I started to speak but then hung up without leaving a message. What was the point if she was going to be out for three days? It was sure nice to hear her voice on the message. I leaned back in my chair debating whether call her home. I didn't want to appear too anxious considering how we'd left things last night. Then again, why shouldn't I call her at home? Her case was finished and I still had plenty of information to give her so it would be a business call.

I grabbed the file Tyler had left and scrolled down to her home telephone number. The phone rang several times and finally someone answered. It was obviously Mike. I couldn't believe he was even still there! Ivan spoke briskly into the receiver, "Yes?" For a moment, I thought about hanging up but reconsidered quickly. "Hello. Hi is Mrs. Ivan available?"

"Yes she is available. May I ask who's calling?"

Without thinking I replied, "No you may not."

Ivan hung up on me. I hit re-dial and when Mike answered in the same brusque manner I politely asked again, "May I speak with Mrs. Ivan?"

He replied, "I know you heard me the first time but I'll repeat it just in case you can't hear. *Whom* may I ask is calling?"

I tried to stay calm. After all, I'd called this man's home asking to speak with his wife. He didn't know what I knew so I guess he had every right to demand to know who I was. In a professional manner this time I said, "Yes. I'm a contract employee of Mrs. Ivan. May I speak with her please?" That damn fool hung up on me again. This time, I got angry. He better be glad we were on the phone rather than in person or I'd teach his rude ass a thing or two. I called back and before he could say a word I managed a cheerful, "Hello, may I speak with Mrs. Ivan, sir?"

Mike replied in a haughty tone, "Yes you may once you tell me exactly who you are because I'm the man of this house and I don't remember hiring any contract employees without a name."

The man was coming foul but he was blocking me from my goal so I struggled to keep the conversation professional. I wasn't going to allow him to come sideways again. Nonetheless, before I could say anything he continued, "Did you hear me or are your ears too clogged with dirt to hear properly? Who are you and what business do you have with my wife?"

That fake Ivy League demeanor might have served Mike well with everyone else but it was time to let him know he wasn't talking to no punk. "First and foremost, if you disrespect me one more time, I'll make sure I handle you when I see you. I can't believe you are trying to play the role of the 'man of the house' when in reality you are just another woman in residence. And for your information, my *name* is Marcus Haley with HiCi. Maybe you've heard of my work?"

From the sharp intake of breath on the other line, I could tell Mike now knew exactly who I was. "How dare you call my house? How dare you start peeking into my life and telling my wife lies! You goddamn nigger!" When he said 'nigger' his voice was muffled and he spoke in a whisper as if he didn't want the word to travel any further than where he stood. In the same muffled whisper, he said it again. "That's right I said it! Yeah you heard me and I'll say it again every time you try to call my house. If you know what is good for you nigger, you'd better just stay away from us."

I was stunned to the point of speechlessness. Its one thing to respectfully say what you feel and another to think that you can say whatever you want. I have never let a man disrespect me and not be knocked out or corrected. I couldn't start raising my voice or yelling into the phone without my staff hearing the conversation. The speechlessness lasted about a half a second and I totally lost all pretense of professionalism.

Calmly I told Mike, "Your wife needs a real man not some wanna be woman. Don't try to con me into thinking you are a real man cause I know for a fact you like to get from other men you sorry ass cross dressing bitch. Do you know I will whoop your ass for calling me out of my name? Now put Cerise on the goddamn phone before I get in my car and drive over there."

Some people just don't know when to quit. "Oh, so I guess you think you are a real man?"

"Don't ask me. Ask Cerise. She knows." Mike gasped into the phone but didn't respond. Damn! Why did I go there? I couldn't believe he had gotten me so angry I'd just compromised Cerise, but I couldn't do anything about it now.

Mike struggled to speak and then seemed to get distracted. He covered the mouthpiece on the phone but I could still hear him say, "Oh okay, okay, I don't...." and then the phone banged onto the floor. Cerise's unmistakable voice came over the line and I could hear the two of them arguing. This crybaby was telling Cerise everything I had just said.

I couldn't believe I'd let the fool get me that pissed off. In all my years running HiCi, I've never been anything but professional. Obviously, my feelings are all mixed up in this case. Shame on me.

I could hear Mike whining. "What's going on Cerise? First you come at me with a bunch of lies about being with men and then I find out you've got the hots for some investigator dude. You wonder why I'm distant! It's because of you and this guy Cerise. You think I didn't know what was going on with you two!" He talked for a few more minutes but I couldn't make out what he said.

Cerise actually laughed but not the same pleasant one from last evening. "Pretty good Mike. That was a hell of a Hail Mary you threw but Marcus is not my 'investigator dude'. He is a professional and he was investigating your sorry ass. Try another excuse because that one isn't working." It was quiet for a second and then a door slammed. Cerise picked up the phone. I had a good idea what was coming next.

"Marcus, this is Cerise. Exactly what in the hell is going on? Are you both done comparing dick sizes? Why would you tell my husband that you and I were at a hotel the other night? If you said that it was strictly wishful thinking, this is all business honey and don't forget that."

Struggling for calm I said, "Cerise, I didn't say anything about a hotel, I only said…"

She interrupted, "Just stop Marcus, lets keep it professional. I have enough drama in my life right now without throwing you into the mix." Cerise continued her rant and I let her get it all out.

When she was finished I said, "Cerise, your husband is lying to you. He was being incredibly rude and disrespectful and I couldn't go out like that."

Mike's voice came through the background. He was yelling out of control like a crack head needing a fix. Cerise drew a deep breath. "Marcus, I'll talk to you later, this is not how I want us to handle business. By the way, if you have any further business to discuss with me, try my cell-phone." The line went dead.

"Damn," I whispered to my empty office as I banged the phone back into the receiver. I took a couple of deep breaths trying to bottle up my frustration.

Why didn't I call on the cell-phone? Why did I let Mike's pansy ass get me so upset? I'd really just wanted to hear Cerise's voice and recapture that feeling I'd had with her last night. To find out Mike was still there after she had proof of his secret life was a shock but still no excuse for my behavior.

Tripping out like this over a woman I'd just met was definitely not my M.O. and I'd never tried to come between husband and wife no matter how attracted to her I was. What was it about Cerise that made me lose my senses like this? Sitting at my desk, I got more and more pissed at myself for what had just gone down. I grabbed the pencil holder and threw it across the room. "FUCK!" I shouted.

Several people rushed through the door to make sure I was okay. "I'm fine people, just had to let off a little steam. Get back to work. I'm okay." Tyler stayed in my office and closed the door after everyone had left.

"Tyler, go ahead and holster your gun, there's no intruder to shoot. I told you, I'm fine." Tyler holstered his gun and took a seat. I had to laugh. "Every senior investigator here is licensed to carry a gun, why in the world were you the only one to come in here with yours drawn?" Tyler looked at me and then around the room as if double-checking no one else was present.

"Boss, I've worked with you since you opened this place and I've never heard you yell out like that before. I thought someone had burst in through the back and had you in a tight spot. Seeing that isn't the case, what the hell is going on?"

I gave Tyler a lame excuse about losing some money in the stock market. He seemed to believe me and headed for the door mumbling something I couldn't make out.

"Hey, what's all that about Tyler?"

He replied, "Nothing boss, I was just saying that's why I don't invest my money in that junk, I'll take my little pocket change from my CDs and call it a day."

Before he closed the door behind him I called to him, "Good to see you had my back if I needed it. Thanks man." Tyler smiled and just walked out of the office.

I stood up, took a deep breath, walked over to where the pencil's lay scattered and gathered them up. I told myself I'd let Tyler handle all dealings with Cerise from now on. It was for the best.

That's what I'd decided but the second I sat back at my desk I picked up the phone and dialed Cerise's cell-phone number. I called at least seven times and left four messages but she never picked up. I didn't want to sound desperate but for some reason I needed to hear her voice. I called a local florist and had a dozen roses delivered to her job. I figured this would be a safe way to apologize without causing any more problems.

I sat at my desk the rest of the day alternately berating myself for my behavior both on the phone and then afterwards, and trying to figure out what to say to Cerise should she allow me to apologize. Thank God, it was Friday. I needed the quiet sanctuary of my home to help me relax for a couple of days.

BREAK UP TO MAKE UP

That weekend and the next few weeks passed by without incident. I hung out with Kevin every now and then, played some basketball, went to visit my mom. I even went to church with her a few times but being a 'BMW' as Sheila had called me, every single woman, from 20 to 80 it seemed, decided to set their sights on me. I stopped going to church with Mom but thought about finding a little congregation somewhere without so many desperate single women looking for a 'God fearing husband'.

Although everything was calm again and I was feeling rejuvenated I had to struggle to stay in that good frame of mind. I hadn't heard from Donna even though I'd left her a couple more messages. Cerise never responded to my apology flowers. I'd decided it was best to leave well enough alone and let her deal with her drama without my interference.

On my way home from the office that Friday evening I realized my birthday was Monday. I kept telling myself turning 35 alone didn't bother me. It became my mantra. But just in case someone had something planned for me, before heading home I'd checked my email, cell-phone, and the answering machine at home. No messages.

On the drive home, I had to admit I was disappointed that I hadn't heard from Donna and was still obsessing about Cerise at the same time. One woman I shared a ton of history with and the other I'd fallen for in less than 48 hours.

I like to feel as if I was in control of my own destiny so I had to admit the decisions I'd made with regard to women had gotten me where I was today, about to turn 35 alone. The year had been full of drama and bullshit I'd helped create. Messing around with crazy ass Sheila was proof positive that I had been out of control. I put on some BB King, cranked up the volume, and let him wail. The music was perfect for what was going on in my head.

I pulled into the drive way and Stanley was walking away from my porch. BB had me mellow by the time I got out of the car and I smiled in his direction. "Hey Stanley what's up?"

Stanley grinned, "Bruther, a woman came to your door a couple of minutes ago, looked around real sneaky like then, set this box down."

He had my interest. I looked at the box as Stanley continued his story. "After she walked back around the corner, I came over here to make sure she wasn't leaving nothing dangerous. I'm watching your house like a chicken hawk!"

I wasn't about to say 'thank you' for that but I took the package from him. It was a square shoebox in brown paper wrapping. I put it to my ear and shook it looking at Stanley. "You think it's a bomb?"

Stanley's crazy ass hollered, "Holy shit bruther, what are you doing?" and dove into the bushes.

I laughed so hard I couldn't stand up straight. "Stanley get up, there is not a bomb in this box, especially if a woman walked up here and dropped it off on the porch."

Stanley sat there near the bush as he contemplated what I had just said, "Bruther, as many ponies that are loose in your stable you can't say one way or another. Whew!" Stanley stood up and wiped the dirt from his clothes.

I don't know what came over me but I heard myself saying, "Stanley come on in. I still have that Anchor Steam in the fridge. Lets have a beer and talk."

As soon as I said it, Stanley yelled, "Whew Hew! Bruther, its finally time? Is it time for me to walk on your ranch and see where you brand them ponies. Yeah bruther! Whew! Let me go tell my Romie, whew bruther yeah!" Stanley ran across the grass into his house.

I decided to break out the good stuff for Stanley because he's been a good, if annoying, neighbor. I grabbed a stack of short ribs out of the freezer and put some beers on ice. Since not even Kevin or my family had called, I figured I'd kick it with Stanley and call it a birthday celebration, a nice, quiet, reflective celebration. I grabbed the brown box and sat down at the kitchen table. It was very light, almost as if nothing were inside. I pulled the wrapping off and opened the box. Inside there was a card from Ashley.

"Happy Birthday boss, I hope you party like hell over the weekend because Monday I need to talk to you about a job reference." I took a deep breath and sighed. Damn!

I couldn't understand why my secretary was thinking about leaving HiCi. I hoped it wasn't because of money because she knows I'll match anyone's offer she had. Hell, I'd throw another 15% on top of that just to keep her.

Reconciling myself to spend my Friday night with Stanley the thumb man, I put the ribs on the grill and grabbed a beer. I was in a good place now. I had planned on taking a rare day off on Monday but now I'd go in and convince Ashley she had no business trying to leave HiCi. Everything else I just shut out of my mind. I planned to listen to some good jazz and have a meal with my neighbor.

Stanley sure wasn't wasting anytime. Less than 15 minutes since I'd left him he rang the bell. I opened the door to find Stanley standing there wearing a robe over his pajamas and carrying an overnight bag.

"Okay, well you made it right on time. Come on in. I just put some ribs on the grill and the beer is cold in the freezer. You're not planning to stay the night are you? What's with the overnight bag?"

Stanley laughed and said, "Hell nah bruther, I'm not a pony! This here bag has cigars, glasses, and a bottle of talking whiskey. Bruther, my father gave it to me. I have two shots a year and I'm gonna share one with you."

"Ah…very nice Stanley. Thank you."

Stanley made himself comfortable at my kitchen table. "Damn bruther, I love the arrangements, looks like you have the stable situated just like a cowboy is suppose to have his ranch…whew!"

We talked, ate, smoked cigars, and sipped on whiskey for almost five hours. Stanley told me about his childhood, how he met his wife, the prejudice they'd encountered in the south and how hard it was to adjust to 'big city life'. He also talked about his kids and how bored he was now that he was retired. I suggested he take a little job somewhere just so that he wouldn't have so much time on his hands. He'd also have less time to spy on me, but I didn't tell him that.

Feeling mellow, I shared more than I should have but it wasn't like Stanley was in my social circles so it was all good. We sat in comfortable silence sipping the last of our whiskey when the doorbell rang.

Stanley looked at me with a grin, "What do you say cowboy? Can I get it?"

He was so damned eager and I was feeling the whiskey. "Hell yeah bruther, answer the door."

Stanley tilted his head to the side and squinted one eye as if he couldn't see me properly with both of them open. "You serious Marcus?"

"Yup! Hey, maybe its one of my ponies, as you call them. Guide her into the stable for me, eh?" The liquor had me talking crazy.

Stanley jumped up, tied his robe, and grabbed his glass of whiskey. Before rushing to the door, he flashed a quick thumbs up. "Whew! I get to greet the pony!"

Of course, I was going to follow behind him at a distance because I didn't want anyone getting the wrong idea with Stanley in his robe. Stanley opened the door and there stood Ramona, his wife, dressed in black leather from head to toe. "Stanley, I think its time for you to come home now."

She smiled at me as innocently as if she were greeting me at the supermarket wearing jeans and a sweatshirt, waved, and walked away. Stanley looked back at me and pointed his head in Ramona's direction as if to show me he had a top-notch pony in his stable too. I gave him a thumbs up and Stanley's eyes rolled back as he dramatically clutched his heart in delight at my gesture. Stanley took his shot to the head and galloped out the door. Before closing it behind him, Stanley turned back to me. "Bruther, it's been a pleasure, whewee! I'll see ya tomorrow to pick up my things."

Stanley was the only visitor I had the entire weekend. I didn't call Cerise or Donna and was glad Sheila hadn't called me. I had some good rest and watched a few good movies. I woke up Sunday morning feeling refreshed. I went out to run some errands, came home, and relaxed. I fell asleep that night listening to the soothing sound of Dave Koz's smooth saxophone.

I woke up Monday morning before the alarm went off. I walked downstairs and grabbed a cup of coffee and a bagel. I planned on taking my time getting to work today because technically I wasn't suppose to go in but I wanted to speak with Ashley and see what I could do to keep her working for me.

The phone rang several times while I was in the shower but I wasn't going to jump out to answer it. While getting dressed, I hit the button on the machine to see who had called. All my family members were calling to wish me a happy birthday. I couldn't help but smile. Some people will never miss your birthday, your parents, people you donate money to, and family members who may owe you something for a past favor. I planned on going by my parents later so they could ask me, right on schedule, as usual, "Hey boy, where are our grandkids? You know it's not good for man to be alone."

I grabbed my black Armani suit, gold fitting silk shirt, black socks, and black boxers. I put my clothes on the bed because before getting dressed I had to make sure the head was freshly shaved, nails trimmed, and teeth sparkling. I cleaned up, grabbed the Drakkar cologne, and splashed it over my body. I grabbed the remote and turned on some "Just in Case" by Jaheim. That is a smooth ass groove no doubt.

I finished getting dressed and jumped in the Benz heading to the office. I called the office and Tyler answered the phone. "HiCi. Can I help… Oh, what's up boss? Just saw your number on the caller ID."

"What are you doing answering the phone?"

Tyler laughed. "Ashley ran to the ladies room real quick and asked to forward the calls to me. I knew you were going to check in at some point but why are you calling so early? You are supposed to be enjoying your day off." I told Tyler I had some business with Ashley and would be in and out, hopefully in 30 minutes or so.

I pulled into the parking lot and I could see my people were on the ball because the lot was full. I walked in the door and heard nearly had a heart attack.

"Surprise! Happy Birthday Marcus!!!"

I couldn't believe it! Including the office staff just about everyone I knew was here. Wynona, Buck, Kevin, my brothers, mom and dad…everyone. I even noticed Stanley and Ramona standing at the back of the crowd. I was so moved I couldn't speak. Never in my thirty five years had anyone thrown me a surprise party.

I walked around the room shaking hands, kissing cheeks, and getting claps on the back. "Happy birthday, man!" Kevin grabbed my shoulder from behind. "Dawg, how in the world did you keep quiet about all this? You know you can't keep a secret to save your life."

Kevin laughed. "Ole girl only told me about this last night. She apologized for the short notice but said she was worried if she'd told me sooner I'd have spilled the beans." He pulled me away from the larger gathering. "So what's up with you two? I thought that thing was deader than dead?"

Laughing, I asked him, "What? I haven't ever had anything going on with her. Are you crazy?"

Kevin looked around the room and started nodding. He said quietly, "Oh, I'm hip. Don't wanna let the hired help know your getting your freak on with the wild woman huh?"

"What in the world? Look man, Ashley and I don't…you know what? Never mind. Let me go over there and thank her. We playing ball on Wednesday?" Kevin nodded.

"Hey, Ashley wasn't the one." I stopped and turned back.

"Wasn't the one *what*?" I asked. Kevin grinned and mimicked me, "*You know what? Never mind.* Go thank Ashley" he said, and walked away laughing.

I stopped to talk to several more people, including Stanley and Ramona, who were so happy to have been invited they were grinning ear to ear. I kissed Ramona on the cheek, shook Stanley's hand, and thanked them for coming.

Finally, I was able to make my way across the room to where Ashley was sitting, laying back in the cut, and observing the party with a smile. She'd had the perfect plan for getting me here on my birthday! How did she even know how to contact all these folks? When I reached her, I took her hand and bowed. "Thank you. Thank you for everything. This whole thing is amazing, Ash. I don't know how you pulled it all off."

Ashley looked puzzled. "Well I know I'm amazing boss, but I can't take credit for someone else's work. All I did was supply the names of some of your business associates, and come up with the excuse to get you here this morning. The person who set it all up is in your office."

Kevin's laughter a few moments ago made sense now. He knew who had set all this up. So did Ashley and everyone else. It was my turn to find out. I thanked Ashley again and with my heart beating a mile a minute, I walked to the office.

I opened the door and there was Donna sitting on my desk. She was even more beautiful than I remembered. I walked over to give her a hug. "So *you* are responsible for all this? I'd just wanted to have lunch with you and you arranged all this? Thank you. I assumed you forgot."

Donna just returned my hug and whispered, "Marcus, I could never forget your birthday. I just wanted you to be surprised." I was touched beyond belief. This kind of thing was way out of character for her.

Donna gave me a small peck on the lips and walked towards the door. "I'll see you at your house in one hour. Is your spare key where you always keep it?" I had totally forgotten about that key. I'd asked Donna to hide it for a guy who was putting in my floor back when we were dating.

"Yes the key is still there, probably buried under some leaves. You'll have to really look for it. What is the next surprise?"

Donna blew me a kiss. "Don't be late for breakfast" she said, and winked. I walked with her back into the office area and mingled for a while longer. About 40 minutes later Donna called out, "Marcus, again, happy birthday! Now I have to go before I get fired! I'll talk to you later. Have a great day."

I wasn't about to spoil it. My family, along with everyone else except the employees had gradually drifted out. I looked around at my hard-working employees and said, "Unless you all have something pressing or an appointment, take the day off! You don't have to go home but you've got to get the hell out of here. Go enjoy yourselves." Everyone except Tyler scattered to their offices and cubicles to gather their things before I changed my mind.

I jumped in the car and sat there for a few seconds before driving off, not knowing whether to cry or laugh. I have never had someone take the time to plan a birthday for me. I have set up some nice gatherings for a few people but it had never happened for me. The one time I thought it was going to happen, I ran into the apartment complex because I heard the music and to my surprise, no one was there. It was the apartment adjacent to mine.

Donna actually came through for me. I still had issues with her, obviously, but I could put those aside for the day. Things were definitely looking better for the prospect of a renewed friendship. It was so damn good to see her again after so long. I could definitely take those issues up some other time because today was my day. Donna had parked in the driveway so I parked next to the curb in front of Stanley's house.

Before I could put the car in park, Stanley stepped from behind his weeping willow tree. "Whew bruther, she's in there, and I don't know how she did it. Yeah bruther, hot damn she's looking better than a prairie flower in the spring."

I laughed, "How did you get back here, change, and take your post so quick?" Stanley just grinned, gave me a thumbs up, and went back behind his tree.

As I walked to the front door, Stanley, as if he couldn't resist himself, hollered out, "Hot damn bruther the stable is open for business early…wheewwwww!"

"Stanley I told you the other night you've got to chill on the…" I stopped. Stanley must have ran into his house after his parting shot because he was nowhere to be seen.

I walked in the house and I could smell bacon, eggs, toast, and pancakes. Donna never used to cook for me! As I walked towards the kitchen, I said, "Now this is what birthdays are all about!" Donna was standing near the stove buttering some toast. She was wearing one of my long sleeve white button-down shirts and that was it! "Well damn, I need to have birthdays more than once a year if I get this type of treatment."

Donna winked and replied, "Well this is your 35th birthday and I wanted it to be special." I didn't want to talk about Sheila. I didn't care that this was going nowhere. At this moment, I was just glad she was here.

Without another word, I crossed the distance between us and the jones shot a lightening bolt through my body! I ran my hands up under the shirt gently touching her thighs, hips, and along her waist. Her skin was soft as if she had just stepped out of a tub of buttermilk. I brought my hands down from her waist and up through her hair. As I ran my fingers through her hair, I gently scratched her scalp as I pulled her close to me and just looked into her eyes. Donna was smiling and making appreciative noises, purring low in her throat.

"Umm hmmm, I like this a lot. I didn't realize how much I missed it," She murmured.

I bit down on my lip because it was difficult to keep from just tearing my clothes off and taking Donna where we stood. She loosened one button on my shirt and kissed the hollow of my throat. I started rubbing and lightly scratching Donna's back almost as if we were already in the bed making love. I picked Donna up and set her on the island countertop, resting my head on her chest. We hugged without speaking while I continued to scratch her back and run my fingers through her hair. Stepping back slightly I stared into Donna's eyes. I took half of a step back so I could see her face. It's crazy stimulating when you can communicate with someone without even saying a word.

I stepped behind Donna, jumped up on the island, and wrapped my legs around Donna's waist as I pulled her close to me. Deeply inhaling her Somali Rose oil scented skin, I held up her hair so I could give attention to the part of her neck that gets no love. I know that's one of Donna's sweet spots. When my lips touched that smooth skin goose bumps appeared momentarily but were replaced almost immediately with a flush on her skin that traveled well below and above the spot I was attending to. Donna shivered and I whispered in her ear, "Hmm, so now how should we end this celebration?"

Donna surprised the hell out of me when she responded, "Who say's it has to end?"

I didn't want to ruin what was turning into a great day having discussions like that. I wasn't even trying to follow up that line of questioning. The question came out of the blue because there was no alcohol involved and as far as I knew there were no arguments between she and Shelia, otherwise I'm sure Donna would have been far more agitated and upset than she was now. Instead of responding, I ran my hands along the outside of her thighs.

"Not many people can render me speechless Donna. I just hope you and I are on the same page. I was probably thinking one thing and you the other."

"Marc, I love you, I really do, and I'm so sorry for all the things I've done to hurt you. You have definitely been the constant in my life. I would like to see what could possibly be very soon."

My first thought was that we'd already tried what could possibly be and she'd turned away from the possibilities with me to explore the possibilities with Sheila. I didn't voice my thoughts because I was in a good mood and didn't want to spoil what was about to happen.

Donna jumped off the island turned around and gave me a kiss that tasted so sweet my heart actually skipped a beat. I started to unbutton the shirt Donna was wearing but she interrupted me.

"Eat first, *this* is not going anywhere," she smacked her own ass and walked towards the refrigerator. "We have all morning, afternoon, and evening for that."

What about after that, is what I wanted to ask but didn't. After our last argument and what I'd done with Sheila, which I had no doubt Donna knew about, I couldn't believe what I was hearing. Just for today, I decided to ride it out and see what Donna was up to without a dissenting word. I'd keep my guard up though. It was good to know the time limit she'd set. I could pace myself.

I jumped down, grabbed my plate, Donna dished the food onto my plate and we sat down at the table talking about what had been going on in our lives since we'd last seen each other, both of us carefully avoiding the topic of our last meeting.

Donna finished eating before me, got up and said she was going upstairs. I rose to join her.

"No. You stay here. I'll call you when its time for you to, um, *come"* *Donna* grinned wickedly, winked, then ran upstairs. Seconds later the sound of water running in my bathroom upstairs filled the quiet house. I finished my breakfast and went into the living room.

Lying on the couch waiting to be summoned, I refused to think about what was about to happen and what it might mean. I was content to accept Donna's gift of herself for my birthday and let the rest sort itself out later.

After a few minutes Donna called down, "Marc! Don't make me wait too long." For some reason I couldn't explain, I took my time getting off the couch. My eyes closed, I imagined what was coming. I was happy to have Donna back in my house and waiting for me upstairs but…but…

"Marc!" Donna almost screeched. I laughed quietly to myself, heaved up, flicked the CD player on to random play, and walked towards the stairs.

As I went upstairs, New Editions latest hit, *Last time* began playing. Donna was sitting on the edge of the tub wearing my robe as I entered the bathroom. Just the sight of her like this brought out the freak in me and Donna knew this.

"What took you so long? I've been waiting for you to come up and undress me," Donna said with a husky voice.

Crossing the short distance between us, I gently slid the robe off and drank in the sight of her standing there in my shirt. Donna smiled, "Don't look so serious Marc, I won't bite, unless you ask very nicely."

I grabbed at the shirttail and with a snap of my wrists, the buttons went flying everywhere. Donna stood naked before me and I pulled her to me. Reaching between her naked body and my fully clothed one, Donna slowly peeled each piece of clothing from me.

We were both naked and I wanted to move in for the attack but before I attacked I asked, "We have all day and night, right? I mean, that *is* what you told me."

"I'm yours Marc, for however long you want me." Donna replied with lust heavy in her voice.

With those words, I felt no need to attack right away. Gently, I assisted Donna into the bubble filled tub. We sat there for a long while just luxuriating in the warmth or the moment before washing each other.

Again, we talked and whispered tones only of the here and now and not about tomorrow or yesterday. With all that wasn't being said, I must say, it couldn't get any better than this.

The bubble bath we soaked in was a leftover from the time Donna had lived with me. It must have been somewhere in the back of a cabinet somewhere but Donna had managed to ferret it out. I'd bought the Imani as a gift to her long ago and she'd left it here when she took everything else that belonged to her the night she'd moved out.

We stepped out from the large oval tub and dried each other off before Donna walked to the bed and lay on her stomach. I applied the towel to her backside to make sure there wasn't one drop of water remaining.

"Marcus what happened to us?" Donna asked.

My eyes roamed the backside of her body as I applied the towel to Donna's calves and feet. "Well Donna, I guess my mo-jo was just too good for you and you had to go over to the other side because you couldn't control yourself with me"

We both laughed. "Actually Donna, lets not worry about the past, it'll always be there. I don't care about what happened then, I'm more interested in the future, better yet, this exact moment, and your delicious body."

Donna smiled up at me for a second. "You're right! Let's just enjoy your birthday. I'm sure things will work out for us this time."

Dropping the towel on the floor, I walked over to the cabinet, grabbed some fragrant body oil she'd also left behind and began rubbing and massaging it all over Donna.

I ran my fingers through her hair as I kissed along Donna's spine. I touched every vertebra in her back with my tongue. I could feel the heat from her body as it called my name! 'Marc, Marc, it's yours just come get it!' The oils allowed our bodies to slide back and forth nice and easy.

As our bodies delighted in the pleasure of the motion, the oil from her body began to cover my body.

Donna turned over and I poured more oil into my hand and massaged it along the front of her arms, stomach, breasts, and legs. Up and down my hands went, spreading oil and massaging at the same time. Gently I began making love to her breast with my tongue, a kiss here, and a kiss there. A nibble and a pinch. A pinch and a kiss. A kiss and a long sensual suck. Donna closed her eyes and moaned, writhing from my administrations. It's amazing what a tongue can do to a lonely kitten. I could hear it purring saying, "Marc get down here!" My tongue lightly traced, "not yet" across her stomach. She closed her eyes and I could see that she was on fire! I kissed her stomach and my tongue followed the fine trail of soft hair to the love below. "Here kitty, kitty," I called softly as my tongue dipped and played in her fountain until she couldn't take it anymore. Donna grabbed my ears and the oil allowed me to enter her in one smooth hard thrust. We delighted in the pleasure of the rhythm we created and it felt as if we hadn't spent any time apart. Our bodies were so in tune with each other, she knew where to touch and kiss to speed me up or slow me down, and I knew exactly what she needed to take her over the edge.

Much later, with Donna snoring softly at my side, I was so dehydrated I climbed out of bed and headed downstairs to get some water. I looked outside at the setting sun hardly believing the sun was going down. Donna and I had been making love for hours. I stood at the window drinking my water thinking about how good it felt. We fit together so well it just didn't make sense that we couldn't make things work outside of bed.

I looked in the freezer to see what I could make for dinner tonight before realizing I really wasn't in the mood to cook. Maybe we should hit the town tonight. I could hear the shower running and decided to go upstairs and join Donna.

Steam from the shower clouded the bathroom and I could see Donna through the clear shower door, moving her body to the music and singing along with Joe.

"It's nice and hot in here I see," I said to Donna.

She replied, "You should see how hot it is in here. Come join me, unless ya scared."

"Scared? Please this house will catch on fire if I step in there. That's how hot I am!"

"Well call the fire department and get in here! Burn me up baby."

Stepping into the shower, Donna moved under the showerhead to make room for me as the water ran through her hair and down her body. I switched places with her and pulled her close to me. The water hit me in the shoulders and neck with Donna's head on my chest. I poured some conditioner into my hands and began massaging it into Donna's hair.

"Damn Marc you must be ready for round 7. That feels so good!"

"Seven is my lucky number." I grabbed the body soap and starting with her shoulders worked up a good lather, making my way to her back, that soft round ass, and rubbed the back of her legs. I was starting to get excited so I turned Donna around and took a step backwards allowing the water to rinse her off.

I stepped back and said, "Close your eyes its time to rinse the conditioner out." I ran my fingers through her hair ensuring all the conditioner was out. When her hair was free from conditioner I told her, "Now, get out!" We both laughed. Donna knew I was getting excited because it was starting to show. "Don't worry baby, I'm gonna take care of that in a sec."

I laughed as she stepped out of the shower, so I washed myself, rinsed off, and jumped out. Grabbing a towel to dry off I peeked into the bedroom. Donna was naked on the bed rubbing lotion over her body. I walked over to Donna. Dropping the towel I said, "Hit me up before I turn into an ash monster?" I turned around, shook my ass in her face, and gave her a lap dance. We burst out laughing as Donna smacked me on the butt with some lotion and rubbed it in.

I turned around and lay on top of her as I stretched her arms out holding her wrists. I gave her a kiss, traced the side of her neck with my tongue, and ran my fingers through her wet hair. Donna's body began to writhe beneath me so quickly I had to jump up or we'd never get out of the house tonight.

"Lets get dressed and go get something to eat. I hear your stomach growling. We will finish this later. "

She smiled, "Yeah, let me eat and get some more energy but I tell you what, you could have played the part of the Energizer Bunny with all that juice you've got."

Donna and I finished getting dressed side by side in front of the wall of closet mirrors. We were looking good except for Donna's hair. I sat on the bed as she finished up working a miracle, somehow managing to arrange her curly wet hair into something that complimented her face.

KC and Jo-Jo were putting it down as I walked downstairs, poured two glasses of white Merlot, and returned to watch her finish her makeup. I handed Donna her glass and stood close behind her so our bodies could touch. Our eyes met in the mirror.

"Thank you, Marc," she said, taking the wine glass from me and motioned her head towards the mirror. "We make a cute couple, don't you think?"

"We sure did make a good looking couple. You are just now figuring that out?" She laughed, but I continued, "Well let's have a good look. Hmm, you could be a few inches taller." We both laughed. "Nah, I'm teasing.

On the way downstairs, we decided to head out of town to a secluded restaurant about 35 minutes away. The city, Mountain House, had just become official in the year 2003 and a lot of people didn't even know it existed.

I peeked out of the blinds in the living room and sure enough, Stanley was outside sitting in a lounge chair in his driveway with a beer. I helped Donna put on her coat and said, "I don't have to tell you about Stanley. He's outside."

She started laughing, "I flashed him once Marc. He'll remember me, no doubt." We laughed.

"Okay, go get in my car and I'll entertain him for a minute or two and then we gotta split."

We walked out the door and I turned to lock it as Donna headed to the car calling out a hello to Stanley. He got up as I hit the remote to unlock the car doors. I don't know what she did after saying hi but Stanley was smiling and doing the cabbage patch.

Donna sat in the passenger seat and closed the door. Stanley met me on my walkway and I had to ask, "What was that? A dance?"

Stanley replied, "Oh yeah bruther, I've been practicing. If Terrell Owens can do it, so can I! Whew!" and started the dance again. "Damn bruther…first she flashes me and just now she licked her lips with that gloss shining everywhere…" He began howling like a wolf! "OOOWWWW!"

His front door opened and Ramona yelled, "Stanley get in here!"

I smiled as he gave me a thumb up and softly said, "Yeah bruther, yeah…whew!" before turning and calling out, "I'm on my way sugar plum." He turned back, winked, and gave me one more thumb as I walked to the car and got in. Donna traced her lips and we both laughed.

We had a wonderful time on the drive and over dinner. Donna and I ordered a scrumptious filet mignon served with rice pilaf, vegetables, and a bottle of wine as we discussed her family, mine, business, and everything else under the sun except Sheila.

This is what I missed about the two of us hanging out. When she wasn't doing dirt Donna was just fun to be around. As I poured the last of the wine Donna raised her glass and said, "I'd like to make a toast to you on your 35th birthday, and to the future."

Our glasses tapped and we drank the toast, before walking outside on the patio with our glasses of wine, and looked into the sky. The stars were very bright tonight so I pointed out the big and little dipper and tried to remember the different star systems from my childhood. We finished our wine in silence, admiring the beauty of the night.

Back inside the restaurant Donna paid the tab and said, "Marc I'm ready to go get a big banana split for dessert. I know the perfect place in San Francisco if you are up for the drive."

We jumped in the car and headed to San Francisco. The music was blaring and we sung all the cuts at the top of our lungs. We arrived at Nu-Nu's Ice Creamery and had a huge banana split. Donna and I fed one another scoop after scoop. After we devoured the banana split, I held one cherry in the air and raised an eyebrow at Donna. Slowly but surely, our lips met at the cherry and I allowed her to take it in her mouth. As she chewed on her cherry, I grabbed the final cherry and dropped it in my mouth. A few seconds later, I stuck my tongue out and the stem was tied in a knot.

Donna nodded and laughed, "Ah, now I see why fireworks and flashes of fire spark up when you use that thing."

I bowed, "Nothing but the best for milady." Donna smiled, blew me a kiss, and strangely enough started blushing.

All day and night I'd avoided the comments she'd made about the two of us making it work this time. Donna had been the woman of my dreams and I thought I'd love her forever. She'd eluded me for years in regards to a relationship and now she was acting like putty in my hands. We'd spent the day making wild, passionate love and I had very high hopes that the remainder of the evening would be used to do the same.

The day and evening had been excellent so far but for some reason my soul wasn't satisfied. In spite of the constant hints Donna had tossed out, I knew more than likely she'd be out of my life for good if things didn't work out between us again. I didn't want that. I didn't even know, for certain, that I wanted to try again. Cerise's image came to mind and I shook my head to block out the memory of her. It was no use even thinking about her.

We held hands and walked around the Wharf. San Francisco is beautiful at night. Walking along Pier 39, Donna and I stopped at the docks near the restaurants and stared out into the ocean. I opened my jacket and stood behind Donna as she snuggled up close to me. I could feel the heat from her body against mine.

"Thank you so much for such a wonderful birthday Donna. I'm glad I had the wonderful opportunity to share it with you. Just like old times, eh?"

Donna replied softly, "Marc you are one of a kind. If I lost you, you could never be replaced. I'm happy to have known you for such a long time. You indeed, are a woman's dream, my best male friend, and a wonderful lover. I don't want this to ever end." We held hands as we walked back to the car to head home.

As we drove back, Donna had her hand on my lap. Absentmindedly she began rubbing my thighs, stomach, chest, and ran her hand across the smooth skin on top of my clean-shaven head. She and I talked about our last 10 years together and the good times we've shared. Fool that I can be sometimes, in spite of myself, I found myself contemplating the possibility of getting together again for more than just a day, depending of course, on what Donna had to say about what was going on with her and Sheila.

As I slowly tried to introduce meaningful discussion to expand on the hints Donna had been dropping, she managed to change the subject, slipping, sliding, and dodging my questions. Now that I wanted to talk about us, Donna kept the conversation revolving around our most adventurous love-making episodes.

"Marc, do you remember coming over to my house and us walking to the park around the corner from my house. We made love on the slide at the park at midnight. I was all for it and you were nervous as hell, you kept saying, '*what if someone sees us or kids come out to the park*' and I stripped naked on the slide and you said, '*to hell with the kids*' and we put a dent in the slide from rocking so hard?"

I remembered the episode and cracked up laughing because there were definitely not going to be any kids at the park at 12 in the morning and if there were they were probably doing the same thing Donna and I were. Donna, exhibitionist that she was, wanted to make love in the park under the moonlight and all I could think of was would my booty be on the front page of the paper. In retrospect, I just now realized that after that night a freakier side of me came out that I didn't know existed.

Donna's ploy had worked again. She'd taken my mind off what I'd been trying to discuss and had me strolling down memory lane. I pulled the car over and parked at a coffee shop.

"This is bullshit Donna, first you keep talking about how you want to be with me forever and then you pull every trick in the book to avoid discussing how we can make it work. I'd given up on us being together but you've indicated repeatedly today that you wanted me to be thinking in that direction. Now that I want to discuss it, you are trying to avoid it. What the hell is up?"

Donna knew things were getting deep, "Oh Marc, that is so unfair baby I'm not..."

"What's up with all this Donna? Are we just going to be birthday booty calls for each other or..." I trailed off, unable to continue. I was too confused to form any rational thought. Why was I pushing this? Her reluctance to talk about it already let me know I'd be better off saying thanks for the birthday fuck and being done with it.

"I see we aren't going to finish this until I make a decision huh?" Donna said quietly.

"Well, since you were the one to make the suggestion in the first place, *thank you!*"

Donna sat quietly for a long moment before responding. "Marcus I'm going to tell you something okay? Please, I don't want you to say shit until

I'm done though. Please? It hurts to tell you this and I've never told anyone else. A tear fell from her eye and ran slowly down her cheek.

"First and foremost you are not a booty call. I would never use you like that. It's not about sex with you and I thought you knew. Every time we've been together whether we got naked or not, I'd leave confused more than ever. I'd be so twisted. We could make love and it would be unlike anything I've ever experienced before with a man or a woman."

"You've told me this before. Tell me something I don't know, why don't you?" I almost hissed at her.

All of a sudden, Donna was angry. "You wanna know why I can't stand men?"

I didn't know she couldn't stand men but nodded yes.

"The reason is when I was fourteen I caught my uncle jacking off while watching me take a shower." I had the good sense not to interrupt, as Donna seemed to be reliving the moment. "The bathroom was huge almost half the size of a normal bedroom. Matter of fact, it was a converted bedroom to an extra large bathroom. I think one of the residents who lived there before us was handicapped but I'm losing my point." She paused, smoothed her hair, and took a deep sigh.

"Anyway, my uncle would *baby-sit* for my parents when they went away and my uncle would sneak in, hide in the closet and do his thing. I couldn't say anything to my mom or dad because I didn't think they'd believe me and everyone loved uncle Chester. He meant the world to them. I knew what he was doing and would try everything I could think of to take a shower in peace but he always found a way to be in there and not get caught. He'd watch me, do his business, and leave after a couple of minutes. I was so humiliated. But what could I do?"

"Did Chester ever…" I started to ask. Donna interrupted me. "No he never did. If he would have ever walked towards me, I would have screamed at the top of my lungs and shit would have really hit the fan. I locked the door repeatedly, but he always managed to get in. I can't believe he was so stupid not to realize that there was a small mirror near the closet. From the shower the mirror reflected the closet where he did his thing. It sickened me to watch him twice pull out his pecker and jack off. Usually he'd be far enough in the closet to where I could barely see him but those two times stick in my mind like a bad dream. I was scared to shower and when you are the only child there's no one you can ask to talk to you while you shower. I asked my mom not to let him baby-sit or not to go away for the night but it never worked. I finally got smart enough to put a chair against the doorknob and it finally stopped."

"From the time I was 14 I hated boys and men and their veiny, ugly peckers. Men were just yuck. I didn't mind them as friends, but anything else was just a turn off. I tried to work past it and even had a fling or two with boys in my high-school class but after they got what they wanted from me, I was no longer interested in them. Then you and I met. I know you remember how I reacted when you first hugged me."

"Yes I do. You drove off talking like I was the best man you ever met but acted like trying to get close just so I could get some. But Donna, we were friends for years before we even made love. That should have shown you something baby."

Donna laughed. "But, my point is, it wasn't you Marc. Even after we made love, I couldn't shake my hatred of that male *thing* and I knew I must be gay. But then after Sheila and I had been together for a while I felt so strange. I would sometimes ask myself 'what am I doing with a woman'? And every time I was with her, I remembered how good it felt to be held by you, and, I don't know, it's just very complicated.

Donna was in a full, all out, cry mode now. She stuttered as she sobbed, "Why can't you just accept me the way I am? I accept you for who you are. Why can't things just stay the same?"

"Accept you? That's all I have ever done! Do you think its normal for a man to have a woman in his bed with a T-shirt and panties on and not be excited? Or to watch you step out of the shower naked, and rub yourself down and just pretend like nothing excites me? Or what about the bullshit stunt you pulled with Sheila's ex? And yet here we are, we've spent the day together and you didn't seem to mind my *veiny thing* at all. I am not accepting of you? You of all people can't possibly believe I don't accept you for who you are!

Donna continued to sob as I said more, "I'm 35 now, and I needed some stable shit in my life. I have waited for you for too long Donna. I really believe it's too late for us but I guess I just hate to think my wait was in vain, that I wasted so many years. Now I'm going to ask again and I don't want bullshit this time. I want you to look in my eyes and tell me what its gonna be. Is it sex only or will we possibly have a relationship?"

I became very nervous for some reason. Now that I'd put it to her like that I was almost terrified at the thought that she might acquiesce and decide to give it a shot. Again, the image of Cerise danced before my eyes and I blinked rapidly to shut it out. Focusing on the matter at hand, I told myself not to trip. I was pissed off at this point. She didn't answer so I started the car and Donna grabbed my hand as I placed it on the stick to put the car in gear. I could see that she was hurting. Tears fell freely from her eyes.

I sighed, "Donna I'll always be here for you. We've been through too much together for me not to be. Now lets get home, I'm tired."

Donna smiled through her tears and rubbed the back of my neck. She leaned over, kissed me on the cheek, and whispered in my ear, "You aren't too tired for me are you?"

I looked glanced over at crazy, complicated as hell Donna. "I'm pissed but I'm not crazy!"

We both laughed softly like folks do after arguing. The ride home was quiet after that exchange. We listened to music and I contemplated my next move. Was I just going to let it be like it was before? Donna showing up and the two of us sexing like crazy until the next time she showed? I didn't want that but I also wasn't about to pass up the rest of the night with her. We arrived at my house at 1:30 in the morning. I parked in front of Stanley's house because Donna's car was still in the driveway.

As we stepped out of the car, I looked towards Stanley's house, which, thankfully, was silent and dark for once.

The house was cooler than normal because I had left the sliding glass door open. As Donna and I took our coats off, she appeared to be looking for her keys. I asked, "Are you staying the night or going home?"

Donna grabbed her keys and smiled, "Relax baby, I'm not running out on you tonight. I plan on cuddling up and holding you until the sun comes up. I just want to grab my overnight bag out of the car."

I ran upstairs and started the shower so I could be nice and fresh. I changed the sheets from today's earlier escapade. Donna walked in, dropped her overnight bag on the bed, and began taking her clothes off to get into the shower. I stood there just fascinated, almost as if it were my first time seeing her naked

Donna turned her back to me as she unsnapped her bra. I said, "whatcha turning around for? I've seen those lovely twins before!"

Donna turned around, ran towards me, jumped up placing her legs around me, and started kissing me. I loved this crazy shit about her. I held Donna around her waist and walked backwards until we fell to the bed.

"Marc, I love you and that's all I have to say about the matter. Now lets get these clothes off so we can shower and make some angry love."

As she slowly removed my clothes, she gently began kissing my neck, chest, stomach, and making her way down. "Errrrrrdddddd" she yelled, "Double D's."

Laying on the bed anticipating her mouth on me, I was caught by surprise. My eyes flew open and looked at Donna quizzically. What in the hell did double d mean and why did she make the sound of screeching tires?

"Dirty dick!" Donna shouted then ran and jumped in the shower with me chasing. I knew I wasn't dirty but the girl can be crazy sometimes. I went with it.

"How you gonna call me dirty dick?"

She laughed, "Well it rhymes kinda and sweaty dick doesn't." I couldn't help but laugh at her crazy ass ways. We hadn't had such a great time together in years. I walked to the closet and grabbed the plastic miniature footstool. I normally use it to tie my shoes but it was about to serve a different purpose.

I set the footstool down outside of the shower and grabbed a glass of cold water. I stood up on the footstool as she showered with her eyes closed and poured the cold water directly on her back. What in the hell was I thinking!

Donna screamed and grappled around, pulling the shower rod down in her frantic scrambling. When the rod went down, I tried to save it from falling and fell into the shower myself. I almost broke my neck! I wouldn't be able to explain it to anyone had I hurt myself.

"Damn you Marc! What are you doing!" We laughed and laughed. I was lying in the shower naked on my ass and she was standing there not knowing whether to be pissed as she kept laughing.

"Marc are you crazy, you could have given me a heart-attack!"

"I'm sorry baby, I had to get you back for calling my dick dirty." I couldn't stop laughing. I almost broke my ass doing a damn prank.

I grabbed the footstool and sat down in the shower as the water ran down on me. Donna smacked me on the top of the head, "Marc you are a damn crazy man. You could have hurt yourself. My hair is all wet now and I just did it earlier!"

"Your hair would still be dry if you hadn't pulled down the rod I was leaning on." Donna and I couldn't stop laughing as the water ran down on us.

The position of our bodies gave me sudden inspiration and I pulled Donna closer to me so that her thighs were at my eye level. I wasn't laughing anymore.

Donna grabbed the conditioner and began massaging it into her scalp. As she continued to work the conditioner into her hair, I grabbed the loofa from the floor of the shower and managed to pick up the soap after a few unsuccessful attempts, and washed her body while balancing myself on the stool. Playtime was over as I washed Donna's feet, calves, thighs, and her carefully cultivated garden.

"Marc you are off the hook! How are you gonna be sitting down there laughing your naked ass off one second then studying my ankles like they hold the key to the universe the next? I'm not complaining though, the way you are touching me is nice."

I tried to look up at Donna, but the water splashed into my face, obscuring my vision of her.

"I wouldn't be down here studying your ankles, and thighs by the way, if you hadn't wigged out on me."

Instead of answering Donna gyrated her hips so that her middle was directly in my face inviting me to take a taste but with the water from the shower hitting me in the face I could barely breathe, let alone taste. I tried a couple of times but with the steady downpour from the shower, I felt as if I were about to drown. I gave up for the moment, laid my forehead against her pelvic bone, and just continued washing Donna's lower half as she rubbed my head.

Anyone viewing us from outside our shower bubble would have thought Donna and I were crazy but somewhere in the back of my head I knew this was one of those crazy moments that would flash before my eyes with my last breath. I wanted it to last a bit longer.

"Donna reach back there and turn the knob to the right, the water is getting cold."

Donna reached back and contrary to what I'd said she turned the knob to the left. The cold water rushed into the faucet and down on us. Donna squealed at a decibel loud enough to shatter my eardrums.

"Marc! Marc! It's too cold. Why'd you tell me to turn it right?" she yelled, and climbed onto my shoulders in a futile attempt to escape the cold water.

Clumsily, I reached behind Donna and turned the faucet to the right bringing a relieving stream of hot water back down on us. We were both laughing again, close to tears.

"I meant my right, Donna! What the hell?"

"Oh my goodness, I should have known that. I've used this shower a thousand times. I'm so sorry! Are you okay?"

Laughing, I said, "Well damn, where were you going? How ya gonna climb on top of me? I think I got some rug burn on my shoulders."

"Marc you did that on purpose! You told me the left."

"I said turn it to the right. I figured you'd know which right I meant since you've used this shower 'a thousand times' like you said. You can't blame this one on me!"

The water continued to flow, now nice and hot. Donna grabbed my head and held it against her stomach as we laughed. But being that close to the kitty caused the laughter to leave me in a heartbeat.

I kissed Donna's stomach as I rubbed her calves and thighs. Donna lifted up a toned calf and placed it on the footstool beneath me for better footing.

"Now Marcus, you've been a bad boy today," Donna said, pointing a finger at me. "Let me think how you can make up for it." My hands massaged her thighs as she spoke but out of nowhere Donna grabbed my head and pushed my face into the garden I'd tried to get at earlier.

Donna started laughing almost hysterically and I almost bit my lip off because I wasn't expecting that move! Well I was but not in the shower.

I couldn't let her have the upper hand on me. She was still laughing as my face was pressed against her but I was about to turn the tables. I reached higher and rubbed the curve of her hips just as my tongue plunged into her and teased her to the point that I felt the explosion that rocked her body. As the water continued to run down my neck and shoulders, Donna massaged my head and moaned in delight as I managed to sample what she offered without drowning in the downpour.

My tongue brought Donna to another explosive climax before she pulled me up from the footstool. I leaned her against the wall of the shower and Donna quickly picked up the condom I'd placed on the edge of the tub and applied it, before we joined together, as nature meant, and we experienced explosion after explosion until the water was lukewarm again.

"We have to stop before one of us collapse's!" I told Donna, out of breath after we'd finished 'showering'.

We dried each other off and then walked over to the bed and flopped down on it. I looked at the clock. It was 2:45am. I set the clock for 5:00am but before I could even say goodnight Donna was snoring.

ALMOST DOESN'T COUNT

The alarm clock went off at 5:00am and it seemed like I had just closed my eyes. Why didn't I take the day off? I rolled over to turn off the clock and Donna didn't even budge an inch. I jumped up to start my routine as quietly as possible so as not to disturb Donna's sleep. The 'shower episode' as I would always call it from last night forward, must have really knocked her out because she lay in the same position as she'd furled into last night. I finished getting dressed and Donna hadn't budged. I reset the alarm for 7:00am because I knew she didn't have to be at work until 8:30am.

I scribbled a note asking her to give me a call on her way in so I could call the alarm company and have them activate my alarm via satellite. I drove to work and sipped on my coffee as I listened to the sports station.

"Good morning everyone," I called to the office staff as I entered the building, "Did you all have a good day off?" Everyone cheered. "Good because I did too!"

David, my newest junior associate had joined the firm a couple of weeks ago. He'd transformed from a dungeons and dragons geek and showed promise, just like I knew he would. This morning he had jokes. He called out, "Hey boss, why do you have red blood shot eyes this morning? And what's up with the funny walk?" Everyone laughed.

"See? This is why I don't give ya'll days off! You all need to work overtime tonight to make up for yesterday." They booed me as I walked into my office.

Tyler walked in right behind me. From the look on his face, he obviously had something heavy on his mind. "If it's okay with you I need to not work that overtime tonight boss."

"Tyler, everyone out there knew I was joking. What's up? You look like hell."

Tyler gave a halfhearted attempt at laughing. "Yeah. Yeah, I knew you were joking. But the thing is, we need to talk. Do you have a few minutes?"

"Of course Tyler, come on in and close the door behind you. So what's up, everything okay?" I hit Ashley up on the intercom to tell her to hold my calls.

"Well it's kind of hard to ask you this because....well.... never mind boss, I'm fine." Tyler stood up and started to walk out.

"Hey Tyler, have a seat. Come on, let's talk. You pounced on me the second I got in here so I know something is up. Do you need money? More time off maybe? Something's going on with you Tyler. I wasn't going to talk to you about this right away but you've been slipping buddy. You're work on that Ivan case was sloppy as all hell. You want to tell me what's going on?

Tyler slumped heavily in the seat across from my desk. "It's not about money or time off boss, Marcus."

"I'm listening" I told him.

Tyler struggled for words before finally saying, "It's just the other night I came home, and I could have sworn someone was leaving from the back as I came through the front. Damn Mar- boss, this line of work can play tricks on you. It's a shitty thing to be doing surveillance on people to catch them cheating but now I need someone to...well I think watch my house."

I couldn't believe what Tyler was telling me but I kept my face expressionless. I waited for him to say more but he sat there nearly in tears and didn't say anything else for a minute. I looked at him enquiringly but Tyler turned his head down to study the creases in his pants.

"Okay Tyler, enough with the bullshit. How are you gonna drop something like that on me and then clam up? This is me man! Don't play me like that Tyler!"

Tyler raised his head slowly to look at me with tears in his eyes, drew a deep breath and said quietly, "I'm not playing, Marcus, I'm dead serious."

"Okay so what's up? Jasmine and you have been together since before I've known you. What is she doing differently to make you suspect her now? You've given her everything she could possibly want and now you think she's having an affair? Are you just going on a hunch? Because if you are then, damn Tyler, you of all people should know there are real signs that you should look for before starting an investigation."

Tyler looked at me dead in the eye and said, "You had a hunch a few weeks back with the Ivan case that hit pay dirt. Do you remember that? You can't grant me the same benefit of the doubt?"

"I remember it man. But look, I've wanted to talk to you about your performance for awhile and kept putting it off but now it seems like I can't avoid it. You've been slipping man. Your instincts are off and you screwed up royally on that Ivan case. You want me to trust this hunch of yours based on what? Prior to the Ivan case, I'd have said lets do it but now, I have to wonder if you even know what to look for in a cheating spouse. Do you feel as strongly about your hunch as I did about mine?"

Tyler nodded resolutely. "If my instincts have been off, and I'm not denying that, its because I've been so distracted with what I suspect is going on at home. I know what I know Marcus. I just need to prove it."

"Well if you feel that strongly in light of what I just said, I guess *maybe* we have to act on it."

"Thank you boss, I knew I was right to come to you about this. I need your help again and if I'm wrong then you can throw it up in my face, fire me even! But boss, I've got a strong feeling I'm not wrong about this one. Jasmine is cheating on me, I just *know* it."

"Okay, one last time before I jump into this with you Tyler, I've known you and your woman for years now. I am not sure we are going about this the right way."

Tyler fixed his gaze on me in a way I'd never seen before. "Boss, I've been here for you since day *one*. I worked for *free* when you needed. I was here for you when you couldn't even pay for the pens and pencils. Did you forget that loyalty I gave you? On the strength of your hunch that you'd turn a one-man operation into a profitable business, I signed on and have been with you from the start. I need something from you now! I'm just asking you to help me out this one time and, on the strength of like I said, if I am wrong about Jasmine I won't ever come at you like this again."

Tyler went there huh? He knew what he'd just said would be the quickest way to get me to agree with whatever he had planned. I owed him and he knew it. I'd tried to pay him later for the two months he'd worked for me for free and he'd told me not to worry about it. Now I knew why he'd said that. He wanted something over me. I was stuck.

I pointed at Tyler, "You know you're ass is wrong as all hell for bringing that shit up when you know perfectly well I tried to make good on those two months. But you also know good and damn well that I take care of all my debts so when I do this with you we are square and you can't ever throw that at me again!" I was almost shouting.

Tyler nodded, "Right! I'd never have gone there if it wasn't so important, Marcus. You have to believe me. You do this with me and we are even, completely squared."

Tyler got up, shook my hand, and murmured another quick thanks before walking out and closing the door behind him. I was completely conflicted because Tyler was a good man and I did want to help him but from what I knew of Jasmine, she was a decent woman who didn't deserve the indignity of a surveillance team trailing her every move.

I had a feeling Tyler's hunch was way off base but due to that damn debt I owed him, I planned to help satisfy his curiosity.

After Tyler left, I checked my answering machine. Eleven calls! Seven were business related but the other 4 were personal. My mother called to say 'I love you and why haven't you been over for dinner lately?' There was an unintelligible message from Shelia, which I didn't plan on returning. My masseuse called to confirm an appointment. Lastly, there was a message from Cerise!

Tyler and his request and the night I'd spent with Donna flew from my thoughts as I listened to Cerise ask if we could meet at Buck's after work today for a few drinks. It had been so long since I'd dared to hope that Cerise would even give me the time of day! I couldn't call her back right away for fear of sounding too anxious so I spent the next few hours reviewing new files and contacting prospective clients to set up their initial assessments.

A few hours after I'd heard Cerise asking to see me I called Donna's mobile phone, partly out of guilt at my anxiousness to call Cerise back just to hear her voice, and partly to see if Donna had simply forgotten to call me to let me know it was cool to activate the alarm system at my house.

Donna knew it was me before she answered.

"Hi Marc, what's up honey? How are you doing?"

"Hey Donna, how are *you*? You know you were supposed to *call* me when you left so I could activate the alarm this morning. Did you make it to work on time?"

Donna didn't answer right away. I assumed she must have been dealing with a customer but then I heard a female voice giggling in the background. It was too intimate a giggle to be a customer.

"Uh hello? Donna? Are you there?"

"Oh I'm sorry Marc, I forgot wh-," Donna started to say and then she giggled.

The other end of the line muffled as Donna obviously covered the phone with her hand and tried to prevent me from hearing what was being said on her end of the phone line.

"Donna, I'll catch up with you later. I need to call the alarm company and set the alarm." Without argument Donna said, "Okay!" and hung up the phone. What the hell? I never got a chance to ask if she'd made it to work on time. I called back to make sure she wasn't still at my house, though with all the giggling I doubted it because Donna may be a lot of things but she wasn't crazy enough to have company at my place.

I dialed her number again and Shelia's ass answered the phone. "Hello Marc did you have a nice evening last...."

Donna grabbed the telephone, "Hi Marc don't pay her any attention. She is just acting stupid. She and I are sitting here having lunch." I could hear Shelia in the background giggling like a kid on the playground.

"Donna listen, I don't have time to play games with you or Shelia. I'll talk to you some other time. Did you get the rest of your stuff from my house when you left? Cause if you didn't I'll be dropping it off to you. Thank you for a nice birthday party and last night was great. Lets not repeat it."

I sat there for a second waiting for a response but the phone was muffled and I heard, "Mmmmm, Mmmmmmm." Apparently, her hand must have slipped off the phone during their make out session while I was fussing.

Disgusted, I hung the phone up, called my alarm company, then started reviewing a new case. A few minutes later Ashley called. "Sir, I have Donna on the other line would you like to take it."

"Tell her I'm gone for the day. Thank you." It was best that I didn't get back on the phone with her because it would have been on like hot buttered popcorn. How in the world could Donna justify what she was doing right now with Sheila with how she'd been with me yesterday, and last night? I'd been so sure I was over her after the Billy incident but I'd forgotten that sometimes Donna can be so fun to be around, I found myself slipping yesterday and forgetting how dirty she could be. That would never happen again.

Donna probably waited until my birthday to show up because she knew I'd actually want to see her then, then she'd rushed out of my bed straight back into Sheila's. The surprise office party was nice and I appreciated the effort but it looks like they thought I was a toy they could pass back and forth between them now.

The last of any doubts I'd had about Donna were gone forever after that phone call. Instead of being sad about that, I was actually more relieved and resolved than I was after seeing her with Billy. She was never going to change. I couldn't even be mad. She didn't do anything to me I didn't willingly allow her to. Clarity is a beautiful thing. I'd done my best, even given it one last shot, and it hadn't worked.

Often in stressful situations, I imagined I could still talk to Melody. I imagined what she'd say if she could see me right now. I'm sure she would say, '*Its about time you let her go Marcus Haley! And its time to let me go too, baby. Move on with your life-in the right direction this time.*'

I knew she was looking down on me from her place in heaven, wondering what happened to the man she used to know. Wondering why I'd spent so much time pining after someone who was obviously so flawed she'd never be able to have a normal, monogamous relationship with anyone, man or woman. Now those flaws I'd worked so hard to rid myself, which allowed me to have such a wonderful relationship with Melody, had come back with a vengeance after she died.

Melody would want nothing less for me than that I find someone who would be able to replace her, and provide the life-long love and laughter I'd wanted since I was a kid in school. I knew she would have hated that I chose Donna as that woman when I knew, in my heart, there was no way I could ever make her mine.

That really, was the truth of the matter. *I knew* I could never make things work with Donna and that was the very reason I'd held on to her for so long. If I continued on my quest for the unattainable I'd never have to reach the point where I would have to finally admit to myself that I might not ever have what I'd found with Melody again. Or worse, maybe I *would*. Then Melody would really be gone, with no one else left in this world to mourn her. It seemed so disloyal to really search for and possibly find the kind of love that could ease Melody out of my heart at last.

Let me go. I know that's what Melody would tell me. I'd wanted so much to spend my life with Melody, and realizing I was finally ready to move past what I'd shared with her brought tears to my eyes and hurt my heart. It was time, though. I knew it was because my stomach jumped every time I even thought about Cerise, and now she wanted to see me. Whether it was business or she wanted to build on what we'd started so long ago, I knew it was time to prove to Melody and myself I could still be the man I was before she died. It was time to move forward without Melody and Donna and I intended to do just that.

For the rest of the day, I pondered, what Cerise could want to discuss with me and tried not to get myself too geeked up at the thought of seeing her again. I'd given up hope that there could be anything between the two of us. Even though I'd gotten Cerise the evidence against Mike Ivan she was looking, for I'd taken a serious wrong turn when I let Mike goad me into alpha male behavior. To keep my mind from her I dissected two files and assigned them to investigators. At 5:15pm, I grabbed the phone and called Cerise on her cell-phone.

"Hello Marcus, how are you? Do you have time for a drink or will I be holding up the bar alone?"

She was being friendly so I tried for the same tone as well. In my best Jamaican accent I said, "Wus a beautiful gurl like you doing drinking early in da week, eh? And why would a Yankee like me allow you to drink alone? I'll meet you at the spot, and ya...don't be late ere?"

Cerise laughed, "I'll see you there in one hour," and hung up.

I called Bucks Bar and Grill and asked to speak with Buck or Bonita. Bonita picked up the phone. "Who dis?" Bonita barked into the phone.

"Hey there sexy lady who broke my heart. How are you doing this evening? I just wanted to tell you I miss you and I'll be there in a bit."

"Shut up, boy," Bonita cackled at me. "I'm old enough to be yo momma's youngest sister and I don't have time for none of your foolishness. You never call unless you want something so what is it this time?"

Laughing, I asked, "Beautiful B, is there anyone in the house tonight? What's going on at the grill?" I was hoping that Buck had a little something on the under as he does from time to time.

"Nah sweetie it's quiet around here. The DJ is not working tonight and we don't have any special guests. The only people here are playing pool or darts and listening to the jukebox. Quiet as it is you know you are always welcome. You coming through this way?"

Damn, it was going to be a jukebox night. I'd wanted something special like the night D'Angelo had played.

"Okay Bonita, I'll be there in an hour. Later."

Bonita started to say something, " Wai...." I clicked the phone off before she could finish. Damn! I didn't mean to hang up. I think Bonita was about to say something but I missed it. Hopefully, she was going to tell me that she'd have my wings and beer ready and would save me a good table. I'd catch up with her at the door.

Ready to leave the office, I gathered my glasses, cell-phone, and CD's to put in my briefcase I noticed there was one light still on in the office. It was obviously Tyler because he was the only one who stayed late.

I walked over to the window to shut my blinds and turn off the fungshui waterfall just as a hand landed forcefully on my shoulder. I turned around quickly with my fist balled up ready to knock somebody's ass out.

"Whoa, whoa, whoa boss, what's that all about?" It was Tyler of course. For a second the silent office had me thinking somebody else had crept in to attack me. Dirty living will do that to you. Sheila and her boxer get up came to mind when that hand touched my shoulder.

"Damn Tyler, don't be sneaking around. I knew you were here but I didn't hear you walk in. Shit you startled me!"

Tyler apologized but didn't seem very sorry to me. He was too anxious to discuss what we'd talked about earlier.

"Sorry boss, hey lets set that surveillance up for Thursday night. I'm telling Jasmine I need to go to Monterey to follow a lead. We can talk about the rest tomorrow."

I still wasn't feeling it but I said, "Okay, lets definitely talk and be on the same page tomorrow and fool.... don't be sneaking up and grabbing me. You are liable to get knocked out."

Tyler and I both laughed because we both knew he'd done that on purpose and caught me off guard with that one. I told Tyler to set the alarm and I'd see him in the morning.

On the way to Bucks Bar and Grill, I hit the flashing button on the on-star system. Two messages. "Hi Marc, this is Donna...I'm sorry for what happened earlier today. I had one long island too many. Call me." I hit the re-dial button.

"Hello Marc baby, how are you?" She sounded as if nothing had happened earlier today.

"Donna, when did you start having Long Islands in the morning? Look, never mind. In order for us to keep our friendship over the long haul, we are going to have to keep it strictly platonic from here on out. I can't keep playing with you and Shelia. I know you know what happened between us awhile back. You two are attached at the hip and that's cool. I know where I stand. What you did for me for my birthday was incredibly nice and it was good to have one more time with you but it's over. I'm moving on Donna. No more uninvited company from you. If I call you and you want to come through cool but other than that don't just show up at my spot."

"But…" Donna tried to interrupt. I cut her off. "Call me if you need me for anything other than sex." She tried to interrupt again but I didn't give her the chance. "Donna, hush with the bullshit and understand what I'm telling you. If we are going to play, it will be on my terms not yours. Strike one, two, and strike three. You can't just get up and bat again. If this is going to be a booty call thing, I'm going to be in charge of when it goes down like that. Now, you know if shit hits the fan, I'm there for you. Call me, other than that I'll call you."

The line was quiet for so long I wondered if Donna had hung up while I was talking. Then, quietly she said, "Yes, you're right Marc. I am sorry about everything. I'll talk to you later" and hung up the phone.

COME AS YOU ARE

Pulling into Bucks nearly empty parking lot, I spotted Cerise's ride. She must have just arrived herself since the automatic headlights still hadn't shut off yet.

Bonita was standing at the front door, "Hey baby! How ya doing? That pretty lady you brought last time is here at the table in the corner." I bent to give Bonita a kiss and she popped me lightly on my head.

"Damn Bonita, I've told you, you can't just bonk me on the head to carry me to your cave. Behave yourself!"

"Little boy, please…you can't handle this! Now hush, I was trying to tell you earlier I have tickets to Drayby's Day Spa. The problem is they need to be used today. They're yours for $40.00 a piece if you want them"

"Bonita now you see why I love you so much. But how you gonna charge your man $80.00?"

"Honey don't give me that hang dog look. You know those tickets are $75.00 a piece. Give me my money before I knock you out!"

I pulled out a $100.00 bill and handed it to Bonita, she walked away, tucking the money into the cleavage of her ample chest. "Thank you sugar!" she called over her shoulder.

I glanced around the Bar and spotted Cerise exactly where Bonita told me she was sitting. We made eye contact. I smiled with genuine pleasure to be seeing her again. I almost felt like I'd been holding my breath and now seeing her sitting there waiting for me I could finally exhale. I still didn't know what she wanted to see me about so I tried not to get too far ahead of myself and mess things up like the last time I'd seen her.

"I hope I'm not too late" I said as I took a seat across from Cerise. "You are looking beautiful as ever. Thank you for the invite."

"Hello Marcus, according to my watch you are exactly 4 minutes late. Had it been one more minute, I might have had to cut you." We both laughed.

"Damn Cerise, you are looking nice today. That suit you are wearing, well I should say the suit is wearing you well."

She smiled, "Thank you Marcus, you don't look to shabby yourself. Nice tie with the shirt." I smiled as I looked at my watch,

"Thank you. Hey did you order anything yet?"

"Well I guess it wouldn't matter since you are peaking at your watch. Do you have another appointment?

"Oh no baby it's not like that, you have my undivided attention this evening for as long as you want."

"Good, I'd hate to have to handle this all alone. It's just to much to deal with by myself."

I gave her a puzzled look. "What's going on? What do you need my help with?

Cerise laughed and I was even more confused. Then I got it. Bonita approached the table with hot wings and a pitcher of beer. Cerise said, "Wow...relax Marcus, don't take life so serious. What did you think I was talking about" she batted her eyes innocently and we both laughed.

"Good one, good one. How could I have forgotten I have to watch out for you? I see you like to keep people on their toes."

Cerise and I made small talk as we enjoyed the hot wings, beer, and music that was playing while sitting at the table. I slipped the tickets for the day spa in my left sleeve. I looked at Cerise and started laughing. "What's so funny? Is something on my face?" Cerise asked.

I replied, "Yup! " and I pointed at a big gob of hot sauce on her left cheek.

Cerise wiped her face with the napkin. "Did I get it?"

She had but I played it off and laughed, "Nope."

She wiped again. "Did I get it now?"

I said "Nope."

She was about to get up and head to the bathroom and I said, "Here, let me get it." She leaned over so I could wipe her face and I took my napkin, slid the tickets to the day spa in the napkin, and wiped her face. I handed her the napkin and said, "Look at all that hot sauce."

Cerise looked for the hot-sauce on at the napkin, turned it over, and finally opened it up as the tickets fell to the table. 'Bam!'

She looked at the tickets and raised an eyebrow quizzically in my direction. "Lets go! The spa is open until 11 tonight."

"I can't do that Marcus."

I looked at her with a wing in my mouth and mumbled, "Why not? I didn't say lets go to a room in the hotel. It's a day spa."

She laughed. "You just don't give up do you?"

I finished sucking on my bone before replying, "Well, why should I? It's just a massage and I'm not doing it. It won't take more than a couple of hours. We can talk as they give us a massage. I'll even drive. Its only 20 minutes away. You can leave your car here. You scared?"

She smiled and took a deep breath, "Okay Marcus. Okay. Let's do it."

Before she changed her mind I dropped two twenties on the table for the tab, grabbed a hot wing for the road, and said, "Lets go scaredy cat!"

We both laughed as we walked towards the door and Bonita held it open until we exited. Bonita mouthed to me "be good" and winked.

As we walked to the car, I worked that hot wing down to the marrow. Cerise started laughing and replied, "Did we eat the same hot wings Marcus? Look at that bone, its perfectly clean!" I laughed as we got in the car, rolled down the window, and threw out the chicken bone. I looked at the on star button to see if it was blinking and it was all-good, no blinking lights meant no messages.

"Marcus you are a litter bug, you threw that bone out in the parking lot."

"No I'm not, what you don't understand is that a lonely and hungry dog with no friends will be wondering around and appreciate the fact that I tossed the bone."

She laughed and replied, "Please Marcus if dogs could talk, the dog that finds that bone would pick it up and look around and say, 'damn who's cheating! There's nothing on the bone.'" I started laughing because it was true, if a dog found my bone the only thing he could do with it is bury it.

As we drove to Drayby's Cerise and I had discussed plays, music, and we even discussed her current situation with the husband. I was happy to hear they were in the process of divorcing but even with all the evidence against him, Mike was still making Cerise's life hell. Discussing the situation was obviously working Cerise up into a ball of anxiety. I stopped her and said, "Listen we are going to have a good evening, we can discuss Mike some other time, okay? You are obviously in need of some pampering so this spa treatment is right on the money huh?"

She smiled and visibly relaxed. "I agree." I parked the car and noticed Cerise looking around the lot.

I asked, "Are you looking for somebody?"

She replied, "No, I've just never been here before and I just try to be familiar with my surroundings."

I stepped out of the car and walked around to open the door and help Cerise out of the car. We checked in at the counter and the receptionist asked, "Will you two be together or separate?"

"Together, thank you." I could see that Cerise was perplexed by my comment and what 'together' meant and how it related to us. I told her that we'd share a room together away from the public and she'd have her own tub.

The receptionist handed us a towel, robe, two pairs of shorts, and two bottles of ice water. "Men to the left and women to the right. When you are done changing, please walk down to the Oasis Room. Your masseuses will be waiting for you both." I walked in, changed into my robe, and locked up my belongings. I sat in the waiting area for 5 minutes and Cerise still hadn't come out. Then I spotted her peeking around the corner looking nervous. When she saw me, she walked quickly over to me clutching at her robe.

"Sorry it took so long, I had to pin my hair up and do some women things."

"No problems, lets go do this. Don't worry I'll be in the same room with you." In the Oasis Room, there was a man and woman waiting who escorted us to individual tables facing one another.

The woman greeted us; "Please take off your robes and lay face down on the tables so we can begin your massage. Go ahead and set your water on the stands. Sir you want a deep tissue and the Ms. a European massage correct?"

I replied, "Yes that is correct."

I stood there for a second looking at Cerise and she said with a nervous giggle, "Get face down on that table or I am not taking this robe off."

"I'm not trying to stare at you. I have this nice lady here waiting to rub me down, I was just making sure you were okay."

She smiled and replied, "Yeah okay, whatever. Get on that table so we can begin."

The woman masseuse smiled and took my arm leading me to the table. I dropped my robe and stretched out on the table, placing my face down in the hole. As soon as I did this, the woman and man switched positions. Apparently, he was my masseuse. Oh well, I wasn't here for the woman. I was here for the massage. This big fella was digging into my muscles so deep, I was about to tell him to stop, he was digging deep into my back muscles and I could feel the tension loosening up as he continued. A few seconds later, I could hear Cerise breathing deeply almost as if she were about to go to sleep. The next 20 minutes was perfect. The man and woman had switched so we could get two different types of massage and for 10 minutes they massaged away all our aches and pains. I could tell they were about to take a break because they stopped to drink some water.

I looked up and said, "Hey, are you okay Cerise?"

"Yes I'm okay. A bit embarrassed, but okay."

"Why are you embarrassed?"

She said, "I didn't know you were going to drop your robe right in front of me. Where are the shorts they provided?"

I laughed. "Why would I wear shorts for a massage? I'm not embarrassed but I see you seem to be."

She replied, "Marcus, you are crazy, my booty is too big to be just out there."

I couldn't help but to laugh out loud. Then out of nowhere the big woman smacked me on the ass with her bare hand and said, "Quiet down buddy. This isn't a bar." What in the hell was that all about? I couldn't believe it and I didn't know whether to laugh or be quiet. I stayed quiet as long as I could.

For the next 30 seconds, I tried my best to keep from busting out laughing. This was one of those situations where you are supposed to be quiet, then someone does or says something funny, and you try to hold in the laugh but it only gets worse! I couldn't help it and I started laughing. Cerise looked up at me.

SMACK! She smacked me again! "I said pipe down buddy!" Cerise started laughing uncontrollably! I couldn't do anything but laugh. The two masseuses walked out of the room.

After we stopped laughing, I said, "Cerise did you see that? She must really like smacking my ass!"

Cerise tried to catch her breath. "She told you to quit talking. I guess she meant business," she said with a muffled giggle.

Once we settled down, I said, "So, what cha think so far?" She answered, "It's okay. The string in these shorts isn't the best. As he massaged my lower back his hand kept slipping almost touching my ass." I told Cerise that he wasn't trying to feel her ass and to relax.

"Marcus this is fun. I was a bit uncomfortable at first but I like it."

I was still stuck on the ass smacking so I said to Cerise, "What was she thinking smacking me on the ass like I was a regular in this place? You can't go around smacking customers on the ass can you? There has to be a rule about that don't you think? Do you think she was drinking?"

Cerise was cracking up again. The big fella came back in and said, "Okay you two, we will be back in 20 minutes. Go ahead and drink some water, relax, and please don't get up. We'll be back to get you in the mud in a bit."

As they exited the room, I sat up and looked over at Cerise. "Can I come lay on your table with you? Or maybe I should just come lay on top of you and finish the massage for him." Why in the world do I always have to say exactly what I'm thinking?

Cerise lay there for a second and I thought she was about to blast me but she said, "Don't even try it Marcus, stay on your table or I'll call smack ass lady back in to deal with you."

We started laughing as I laid back on the table to relax. Give me an inch...I said, "My massage would feel better, you know this right?"

"You think so, huh? This massage would be a really hard act to follow."

"Yep, I know so."

Cerise took a deep breath. "This is wonderful. I am so relaxed right now. I should have had this massage thing years ago! I don't know about the mud though. He did say mud right? I don't do mud, it will find its way into places it doesn't belong and who knows if the mud is clean."

I reassured her that the mud was clean mud. "The temperature of the mud and the chemicals kill any germs that could get on your skin."

"Yuck, that's not very reassuring Marcus." Just the thought of hundreds of people using the mud before us...ugh" Cerise shuddered. "And the things they could do in the mud. Oh no I'm not doing it."

"I can understand your reservations," I said. "But that's why I don't mind coming here. They've developed a way to pump in fresh dirt and hot water for each client. That's why it costs so much. We will get to see how they do it in a bit."

"Well I better see fresh dirt turned into mud or else I'm not taking a dip. Who knows what lurks in used mud. Some kind of used mud lurking...thing!"

I laughed at Cerise. For someone so beautiful and successful she was obviously not used to being pampered. We lay in comfortable silence for a few minutes but the question that had been burning in my head since I'd gotten her first message finally had to be asked.

"So are you going to tell me why you wanted to see me tonight?"

"Mmm, I was wondering when you would get around to asking that question." I waited for her to say more. She didn't.

"And..." I prompted her.

"And it's an excellent question, Marcus. As questions go yours is very good. Very, uh...timely?" Again, she left it at that.

"So you aren't going to tell me then?" I asked.

"Nope!" Cerise said cheerily.

I pondered pushing the issue for a moment but decided the important thing was that she *had* called and appeared to be happy to be in my company. I decided to leave well enough alone.

"So what can you tell me then? Maybe about how you managed to find a broke Tom Cruise look alike?"

"Oh you have jokes huh Marcus? Sounds like sour grapes to me. I mean, yeah, Mike is still at the house until he can arrange alternate living arrangements, but we are in the process of divorcing. We haven't slept in the same bedroom for ages. I'm sure your notes told you that. But even with all that, it sounds like you are jealous of Mike even with all you know about him, and even though you know I'm divorcing him."

"I'll let you think I'm jealous if it's going to allow you and I to have dinner later this week. But for real, how did it happen? A woman like you ending up with a closet tinker-bell?"

"I am not sure I want to get into this conversation Marcus. But let me ask you something. Why do you feel you can ask me about my personal life?" Cerise said with frost in her voice. I don't scare that easily.

"Well," I said, "There isn't too much I don't know about you already my dear. Your mom gave us quite a lot of info on you during the initial case assessment. I have 10 questions I initially ask and those questions pretty much give all the details we need to know about a person before we decide whether or not to take their case."

"This is not the time nor place for this discussion either Marcus. I'm not discussing my personal life in a room full of strangers."

"The lady has secrets. Okay I can respect that," I told her. "But there's nobody in here but you and I. Plus, in a few minutes, we'll be alone again in the mud baths. You want to see me but you won't tell me why. You won't talk about how you ended up with the man I helped you divorce. You know what Cerise?" She inclined her head up from the table to look at me.

"What?" She asked quietly.

"It's all good baby girl. If you are worried or scared or unsure that's cool, don't even worry about it. I was just trying to get to know you a little better."

Cerise took a deep breath, exhaled, and said, "Lets finish this conversation in the mud room or wherever we are alone next."

The two masseuses walked into the room and told us it was time for our mud bath. The big fella placed my robe over me and said, "Okay, you both can sit up slowly and don't rush to get off the table. Take a few seconds after you sit up, drink some water, and when you are ready, exit to your left and go into room 2MB."

Cerise and I sat up for a few minutes staring at each other drinking water. Cerise seemed to still be a bit embarrassed.

"Marcus," she said softly, "What are we doing? Why am I here with you almost naked? I barely know you!"

"What's wrong with being naked with Marcus?" That got a laugh out of her but I could see she was actually waiting for me to answer her question. I said, "Look Cerise, we aren't in a hotel, we are in a spa. It's you and me relaxing as friends. I am assuming you at least want a friendship with me since you asked to see me, and it doesn't appear you want to talk about business. The night you came to my house was no different. As much as I wanted you to stay... it was probably a good idea that you left. Do you want to be my friend? Am I at least right about that?"

Cerise's face lit up with a beautiful smile. "Yes, Marcus I would like that very much. I just don't want there to be any misunderstandings between us, considering the near nakedness and all."

"I'm sure there will be no misunderstandings about where you and I stand," I told her. "Now that you've set me straight on us, lets head over to the mud so we can finish talking."

Cerise replied, "Marcus, it's not about setting you straight. I just don't want the lines of communication between us to ever be unclear. If you have something to say, say it and I want you to know I don't bite my tongue with my friends."

I stood up, headed towards the door, and said under my breath just loud enough so she could hear, "I'll bite your tongue, you wont have to worry about biting it."

Cerise said, "Did I hear what I think I heard Marcus? You are freaky!"

Holding the door open for Cerise I managed an innocent look. "What? What? I didn't even say anything and you are calling me names? Not nice!"

Cerise looked a bit confused. "What did you say Marcus?"

"I only said, 'Fine, don't bite your tongue," I told her.

She laughed, "Yeah right!" she said as we headed into room 2MB.

We watched as the tubs were flushed, cleaned, and re-filled. I looked at Cerise and said, "Satisfied there aren't any 'used mud lurking things' in there?"

She smiled and said, "Yes I don't have a problem with it now. The mud is fresh." She said it like the little lady from Poltergeist who announced, '*This house is clean!*'

Cerise had layers. I was enjoying her company immensely. "Sir, Ma'am, your mud bath is ready. Go ahead and get in and we will come back in 10 minutes to make sure that you are comfortable. If for some reason the mud is too hot just press the call button over the tub and we'll come in and adjust it."

Cerise walked over to the door and grabbed an extra towel as big fella left the room. She was going to make sure I didn't see her body. As she headed behind the changing curtain she said, "Marcus you are going to have to turn your head when I get ready to get in the mud and no peeking."

I laughed and replied "Okay."

As Cerise grabbed a towel and headed back towards the tubs, I turned my back, dropped my robe, and shook my butt at Cerise before stepping into my tub. I looked over my shoulder and Cerise's mouth was wide open. She tried to play it off like she wasn't looking but she'd taken a quick peek. I caught her eye and she turned her head and started laughing.

"Marcus, you are crazy! Oh my goodness! How can you just drop your robe and shake your bare ass at a woman you barely know! You need counseling Marcus! No, you need Jesus kid." We both laughed.

"It was very easy, I just dropped it. Wanna see how I did it again?" I teased.

"No!" Cerise held up a hand. Just turn your head or close your eyes or something." I did as she asked and when she said I could open them, Cerise was buried up to her neck in the mud.

I knew things were about to get interesting because I was about to start asking my questions that I didn't get answers to earlier but she beat me to the punch.

Cerise said, "This mud feels weird. It's different. Now how exactly is this supposed to help me?"

"Well the mud is supposed to pull out all the impurities in your skin I think," I said.

Cerise was moving around trying to get comfortable and finally said, "Okay, now I'm comfortable. Marcus before we start talking about my life lets talk more about you. I'll answer any questions you have of me if you answer my questions of you first."

Why do women want to go first when the question game is played? I think its because they get all the information they want from you then start dodging the questions you ask of them. Nevertheless, I went with it. "Okay what's question number one? And you only get four. Agreed?"

"Agreed." Cerise relaxed in the aromatic mud as she thought of a good question. "Okay question number one. Tell me about yourself Marcus. Where were you born, education, employment history and family?"

I said, "Nope. That's cheating. You asked four questions rolled into one."

She grinned at me. "You caught that huh? But I'll tell you what, let me have this one and the rest will be sweet and simple. Girl scouts honor." She raised a muddy hand out and gave the Girl Scout salute.

I sighed heavily and began, "Okay I was born in a small town along the Mississippi River so I guess that makes me a southern boy. My parents moved to California when I was 5 years old. I have two brothers and a buddy who is like a brother to me. I am the middle child. My oldest brother's name is Jeremy and he's the entrepreneur of the family, there isn't anything he can't buy or sell. Next in line would be me. After me, there is my younger brother Johnny. He's in real-estate. My brothers and I live within 45 minutes of each other and our parents and it's nice for family gatherings. I haven't seen them much this past year." As I said it, I realized that I missed my family even though they were close. I resolved to visit them more often.

Cerise smiled. "Sounds like you have a really nice family. Okay continue."

"Okay, lets see education. Well I have a bachelor's degree in public administration and I am a thesis away from a Master's Degree in

Education. I do not have any kids but if the right person comes along, I hope that will change. I'll put in an order for five or six depending on her hips."

We both laughed. Cerise asked incredulously "Five or six? You gotta be kidding me Marcus. There must be a new male birth canal because there is no woman going to put out 5 or 6 rock heads like yours for you. You better start buying pets and treating them like kids."

I laughed along with her. She was calling me names. That meant she liked me. I was feeling more and more good about this. "Why wouldn't a woman want to have five kids for her king? Do I need to stand up in this mud to show you why a woman will do anything I ask her to?"

Cerise replied quickly, "No don't do that, thank you very much! Marcus. You are crazy. You obviously think very highly of your, uh, *abilities.* Okay whatever you say, some woman will have five kids for you."

"You know I'm just playing with you woman." But I mumbled under my breath with a devilish grin, "Couldn't you handle it?" Cerise gave me the 'Negro please' look.

I held up two fingers signaling that I could settle for two kids. She replied, "That's more like it!" I'm not sure, but I think something important just happened here.

I wanted to finish this line of questioning so I could pry into her life too, so I finished. "Last but not least, work. Well I started my company a few years ago and prior to that I worked for the Sheriff department for 7 years."

Cerise interrupted, "Tell me more about your time with the Sheriff's Department. I have a few friends who are officers. They didn't have nice things to say about the department."

I grimaced because I wasn't surprised by any stories she probably was told. I continued on, "Well, I began my career as a deputy and I was on the fast track for promotions, or so it initially seemed. Once I reached the level of sergeant, my upward mobility came to a halt.

I worked my ass off and was responsible for training new employees and sergeants supervising investigators. I worked homicide, gangs, narcotics, you name it. I became the best at what I did. I became familiar with all the divisions and what was going on within them. It got to be that I was the 'go to' person when it came to investigations. I received kudos from my peers and superiors."

Cerise asked, "So why did you leave?"

I tried to figure out how not to drag out my answer. "Well, I would often hear from my superiors how invaluable a employee I was to the department. However, when it came time for promotions, the guys, or more often, women, who were getting the promotions were the same people I'd trained. The final straw was when an airhead with no aptitude for the job got promoted over me. At that point, I made up my mind it was time to leave. The ironic part of it all Cerise is, once I turned in my resignation they offered me a Lt position. I wasn't satisfied with the bone they threw at me. The assignment was in a deadbeat unit and I'd still be responsible for training. I deserved better treatment. So I declined and decided to do my own thing."

I glanced over to see if Cerise was bored with my story. She didn't appear to be.

"Wow Marcus. I'm sorry to hear that but it doesn't surprise me. It was obviously a good move because I know you are making way more than the Sheriff himself." I smiled and stuck my tongue out at her. We sat back in the mud and the next two questions were fairly simple. She asked about the type of food I liked, my hobbies, and pets. Then came question number four. "Marcus what turns you off in a relationship?"

She dropped a bomb on me no doubt. I sat there for a second thinking about an answer to the question. I didn't even have to think before I responded. "Well, I could go on and on about my turn-offs, being a lesbian is at the top of the list by the way, but other than that it's a woman who plays a role to get next to me."

Cerise looked confused. "Can you elaborate on that point?"

I didn't want to open up a can of worms that I wasn't ready to deal with so I said, "Well in some instances, and I am not putting all women in this category, but when a man and woman first meet, the woman is polite, nice, but sometimes what you see isn't what you get. She's wearing a mask. Then over time, as she gets comfortable, the mask comes off and you ask yourself who is this woman? This is not the woman I started dating. *Big* turn off!"

Cerise actually giggled a little. "Yeah I know a little something about people wearing masks. You are right about that. So, go ahead and finish. I am sorry for interrupting."

I said, "Oh I don't mind you asking questions because I want to be clear about what I'm saying."

She nodded in understanding that I was giving her own words back to her. I wasn't playing tit for tat. I just needed her to know that just as she didn't want to be misunderstood, I didn't either.

I continued on, "I also don't like when a woman does the, 'I'm down, yes, yes, oh I agree, we are on the same page,' and the 'we are alike in a lot of ways' thing. If a woman doesn't like something, she should just say it. Why even go through all the I do's when they really are I don'ts?"

"I agree," Cerise said with a smirk and we both burst out laughing. "Okay, go ahead and finish."

"Another big thing that really turns me off in a relationship is a woman who doesn't know when it's the right time to argue or correct her man. The time for correcting or disagreeing is not in front of his buddies or in public places. I don't believe there is any situation or comment that can't wait until later and if it must be said, he needs to be pulled to the side. Walk up to that man and say, 'Honey can you come outside with me for a second? I wanna give you a kiss and talk to you.' Then let him have it but not in front of the boys."

Cerise said, "Well doesn't the same go for a woman?"

"Yes, the same goes for a woman. Of course," I said. "Out of respect and love for their relationship, I would expect a man to do the same for his woman. If her friends are visiting and she snaps at him, I expect him to bite his tongue. Or, if during a conversation amongst a group of friends, she happens to disagree with him on a subject that he knows she normally wouldn't disagree with him on, I expect him to bite his tongue! A man should bite his tongue just as he would want his wife to do in the same situation. Now I do expect him to give her that look."

"What look?" Cerise asked.

"The look that conveys 'you'll pay for that comment in the bed tonight!'"

Cerise said, "Well if that's the case she should mess up more often."

I almost choked on the water I was drinking because the comment caught me off guard. Well, well, well little miss shy can be a little freaky herself huh?

Cerise asked, "Well are you speaking from experience or is this all hypothetical?"

"Just bits and pieces are my experiences and then some are things I've watched occur in lives of people I know," I told her.

"Did you think to butt in and comment when you noticed these irritating things?" she asked.

I replied, "As a rule, I don't get involved in the personal affairs of my friends unless I'm invited in. I let them know up front that I don't like giving advice because some people can't handle the truth of the matter."

"Interesting. Very interesting Marcus," Cerise responded coyly.

I thought this was a good stopping point for my questioning session plus I was tired of sitting in the mud. I said to Cerise, "Hey why don't you ring the bell so we can move on to the next phase."

"Oh is it getting too hot for you?" Cerise asked.

I know a double entendre when I run into one, but I didn't bite. "No we can finish once we get in the other tub," I replied.

Cerise rang the bell and the big masseuse walked in and asked, "Are you ready to get out?"

She replied, "Yes we are." He grabbed the curtain, pulling it between Cerise and I. Cerise winked and said, "I'll talk to you in a bit."

The female masseuse walked over to the empty tub on my side of the curtain, turned the water on full force, and poured a small jar of solution in the water. I assumed the same procedure was going on behind Cerise's half of the curtain.

"What's that you're pouring in the water?" I asked.

She replied, "It's ginseng oil, and shea butter soap. They help energize you and moisturize your skin while you bathe. The water in the tubs will shut off automatically. If it's too hot ring the bell and one of us will come back in and adjust it. Sir, make sure you shower before getting in the tub," and left the room.

I stepped out of the tub of mud and walked over to the shower. The mud was everywhere. I turned the water on full blast grabbed, flung, and rubbed the mud off my body. I stood in the water until the water was no longer brown running into the drain. I called over to Cerise while she was showering and asked how things were going with her.

"I'm very busy," she called over the curtain. "Leave me alone! This damn mud is everywhere!"

Laughing, I pulled on the shorts I'd been given and sat down in the relaxingly warm water. "Awhh…this is perfect Cerise" I called out. "Hey, come on now you should be done by now. My turn to put you on the grill! Finish up, call the guy and tell him to open the curtain."

Cerise replied, "Oh hush Marcus this was your crazy idea! I don't know why in the hell I decided to join you in sitting in some funky ass mud. I have mud between…never mind, its everywhere!! I'll be there in a second and for the record don't play a million questions, you only get four!"

I replied, "you get a little dirty and get feisty and what do you mean four questions only? You asked me a gazillion questions back in the mud baths!"

Cerise said, "Marcus, I know I only asked you four questions. The other ones were only redirects or clarifications, not questions. The first one may have been long but that's the bonus question the person who goes first gets to ask."

"Oh, I get it! You just make this shit up as you go along to keep the upper hand, right?" I asked.

"Yup!" Cerise called out. I had to admire the nerve of her. At least she told me when she was cheating.

Cerise finished her shower, got in her tub, and rang the bell. Biggie Masseuse came back to open the curtain and left without a word.

This was an interesting evening. I had been smacked on the ass by the masseuse, spilled my guts to Cerise, and my skin was now pruned to maximum prune-isity. I could see that Cerise was getting restless so I asked, "Hey do you mind if we soak for ten and then get out of here? My body can't soak up anymore mud or water."

Cerise replied, "That sounds like a good idea to me! I thought you'd never ask. Where are we going afterwards? I mean if you have somewhere to go or someone to meet that's cool. I am sort of hungry though. The beer and chicken we had earlier aren't cutting it anymore."

"I don't have any plans. I told you, you have my undivided attention tonight. I am glad you mentioned getting a bite to eat. I was going to head home and make myself a huge breakfast if you had to go home."

Cerise asked, "Why would you eat breakfast this late at night?"
I gave Cerise the Negro please look. "You absolutely cannot tell me that you haven't had breakfast food during lunch or dinner."

She replied, "No I haven't. I eat breakfast foods during breakfast, lunch foods during lunch, and dinner foods during dinner hours. Doesn't everyone?"

I shook my head sadly. "Awhh Cerise, you don't know what you are missing. But okay, what do you have a taste for right now?"

"Well, at this point, I just want to eat before I get sick." Cerise said weakly. To prove her point her stomach growled so loudly I could hear it from under the water.

"You are just like my sister in law. She gets nauseous if she doesn't eat something every three hours.

She replied, "Yeah I can't miss any meals Marcus, so feed me before I turn into a vampire and bite you and turn you into a vampire too."

"Sounds good to me!" I told her. "Get your bite on home-girl. But I need to warn you, you'll get sprung off my blood and keep coming back for more."

"Is that ri…?" she started to ask.

"That's right. That's a fact jack." I came back before she'd even finished her question.

I felt like I was in high school for a moment. I don't know why I thought about New Edition and their song "Candy Girl." I stood up in the tub and started singing the song and doing the dance moves from the video. Cerise sat in her tub cracking up. The conversation and feel of the moment took me! In all my years, I don't ever remember feeling this way before. I was with Cerise and I felt perfectly comfortable just being crazy ole Marcus from around the way.

Cerise laughed as I finished my New Edition review. "Okay fool, I'm so glad you got that out of your system. It is out right? Because I have to eat now. Get out of the tub, go dry off, and let's go!"

What a perfect opportunity. "Well candy girl, I haven't even gotten to ask my four questions yet so why don't we head to my house and I'll cook breakfast. You down or would you rather eat at Denny's?"

Without thinking about her response, for a change, Cerise responded, "Okay. I definitely don't do Denny's so lets go to your place. I want to stop and get my car on the way if that's okay?"

I said, "Well of course its okay because when I'm done eating I'm going to sleep! I wasn't planning on driving you back to your car, you'd have to crash in the spare room or walk or call a cab or something."

Cerise laughed. "Walk? Marcus you are out of your mind. I know you didn't say walk!" We both laughed because she knew I was just kidding. "And that comment about staying the night, I already told you I don't get down like that Marcus." Cerise told me. "Plus, if I did ride to your house in the Benz, that's what I would be driving home or to my car."

I laughed so hard I accidentally snorted. Cerise called over the curtain that the masseuse had once again pulled closed. "So what are you trying to say with *that* laugh? Are you trying to convey to me that I couldn't drive your car if I needed to?

"That's right," I said. "You couldn't drive my car. My car is my other woman until the real woman comes along!"

"Well maybe I'm....never mind...that's why I need my own car so I wont be depending on you to drive me later. But I hope your woman keeps you warm on a cold night."

I wasn't about to let her off the hook. "Finish what you originally started to say chicken butt," I told her. Cerise let out a surprised squeal at the name I'd called her. "What's the matter? You scared to be *clear in your communications* with me?"

"Marcus?" Cerise said my name so sweetly I knew she had something sour to add. "You like reggae? " I told her I did. You know a group called Third World?" Again, I told her I did. "Good! Cause ya playing me too close brotha. Back the hell off. What are you thinking? Scared of who? You? I don't think so."

Deciding to let her continue thinking that for the moment I finished drying off and told Cerise to meet me in the lobby. I knew if I stayed in the room, I'd pull that curtain back. I walked out to the lobby and waited for Cerise to finish getting dressed. The receptionist walked over and handed me a coupon for 15% off on our next visit.

A few seconds later Cerise came around the corner and said, "Okay, lets go see what us got to eat!" in her best Shug Avery imitation.

We jumped in the Benz and headed back to Buck's to pick up her car. As we were driving, I asked Cerise, "You sure you don't want to go home and get a change of clothes?"

"If I go home right now it won't be to get a change of clothes but go to bed all that *energizing* ginseng has left me feeling like rubber. I'm tired."

I replied, "Okay, the only reason I ask is because its….never mind. Let's go get your car."

Cerise said, "Oh now you are the scaredy cat afraid to finish his statements."

I didn't answer for a long moment but at a stoplight, I looked at her and leaned over so close our noses almost touched. "I am no cat baby. Better realize that real quick." I growled softly in her ear. "Now, I was saying the only reason I asked about clothes is because after you eat one of my meals, you'll want to lay down and let that food digest. You'll be too full to drive. It's mmm, mmm good like that!"

Cerise laughed as I pulled away from the light and continued with the drive. I asked, "What's so funny Dracula?"

"You are Marcus," she replied. "Look at you trying to get me in the sack! By the way, I don't have that gene that causes me to go to sleep after eating a hearty meal."

I couldn't believe she went there with the sack comment. I said, "Oh so you think this is a ploy to get you in my room? Please, when you are ready, you'll climb up there willingly with arms open wide."

We both started laughing as we neared Bucks. Just outside the parking lot Cerise asked, "Marcus, its early in the week. You sure you'll be able to get up for work? I don't want to keep you out late and you get in trouble."

Giving Cerise a crazy look I asked, "Get in trouble with who? I'm the boss and you're the boss. Maybe you are asking yourself that question? I don't want you to go home and get into a fight. I mean I know you told me you are divorcing Mike but you also said he is still living there until he can find someplace else."

She replied, "Please, he comes and goes as he pleases. I haven't seen him in two day as it is."

We pulled up to Bucks. "Good, now that we have that straight, let's meet at my house so we can eat."

I parked next to Cerise's car, she walked around to my door, and I rolled my window down. "Let me guess. You forgot how to get to my house?" I said.

She replied, "No I didn't forget how to get to your house. Marcus." Cerise said, then leaned in, and kissed me on the cheek. "Thank you for the evening. You have no idea how nice it's been for me. But let's keep it nice, huh?" I'll meet you at your house in 20 minutes." With that, Cerise walked to her car, unlocked her door, and got in. I backed up and headed to the pad.

As I drove home, I went through the contents of my refrigerator in my mind. I figured I had everything I needed. I was planning on making a breakfast that would lay us both out.

I took a shorter but more complicated route home than the one I'd taken the first night Cerise had followed me home. I wanted to rush in and clean up a bit. Checking my rear view mirror I noticed Cerise's car following closely behind. I didn't even know when she'd managed to get behind me when I thought she was in front of me. Some investigator I was!

I turned on to my street and Stanley was outside putting up a bug zapper. Why? Why at 11:00pm at night did he have to put a bug zapper up?

I pulled up and hit the garage door opener. Cerise parked in the driveway directly behind me. I stepped out of the car and hurried over to Cerise as she stepped out of her car.

I said, "Could you just stay in the car for a second? I just need to holler at my neighbor for a few minutes. I'll be done in a minute."

Cerise gave me a weird look but nodded. "Okay," she said. "I need to make some calls anyway." She got back in the car and closed the door.

I turned towards Stanley's house and sure enough, he was heading my way with a brown paper bag in his hand. I said, "Hey neighbor. How ya doing tonight?"

Stanley tossed the bag to me unexpectedly. I caught it out of reflex but stared at him like he was crazy. "What's this?" I looked Stanley up and down for tossing the bag at me like that. What was the fool wearing? I forgot to be mad and menacing because Stanley was just too funny for words sometimes.

"Stanley, you do know Pac is dead, right? Plus he'd been out of jail a long time before he died." Stanley had on a "Free 2pac" t-shirt and overalls with the bib hanging from his waist.

"Hey brotha! I see you like my gear. I was checking out the swap meet with the wife and thought about you so I grabbed us matching shirts. Whew! Check it out homie."

Damn! A day at the swap meet had done more for teaching Stanley the lingo than the two years I'd spent trying to school him.

I opened the bag up. He wasn't kidding. It was my own XXL "Free 2Pac" t-shirt. "Wow Stanley, vintage Pac. You are the m..." before I could finish my sentence Stanley interrupted.

"Who's that fly honey brotha? Whew! Is that my girl?" He was trying to see past me into Cerise's car. I grabbed his arm and pulled him a few yards away to make sure Cerise couldn't hear our conversation.

"Stanley, *your* girl is in your crib I assume." I inclined my head towards Cerise. "*That's* the winner I was telling you about before. Remember when I told you don't mess this up?" Stanley nodded. "Well you didn't mess it up for me. I did. Now I got her back over here and I'm gonna try to get it right this time so I need you to chill. She's skittish. Don't want her to bolt, you know?"

"Oh!" Stanley said so loudly his voice echoed through the quiet street.

I put my finger to my lips and held my hands down low. "Chill Stanley!" I said quietly.

"Oh," he said again but toned it down a bit. "Yeah brotha, I feel you. I tell you what my n...," My eyebrows flew to my hairline and Stanley quickly changed it up. "I tell you what homie, you keep em coming till ya find the right one kid....keep em coming! But good luck with her."

He was just about to walk away and I thought I was home free. Damn if Cerise didn't choose that moment to step out of the car. "Sorry, Marcus, I need to use the little girls room" she said.

Stanley got a look at her and completely lost it, "Whewwwwwwwww, Hewwwww! Hot damn you are as beautiful as a Georgia peach!" He started walking towards Cerise but I stepped in front of him to block his path.

Cerise smiled politely but I noticed she was shifting her weight from leg to leg. "Hello Stanley. Marcus has told me a lot of nice things about you" she lied.

That was all it took. "Yeah bruther, she knows my name!" He held his hand up for a high five. I left him hanging but Stanley didn't seem to notice. "Whew! She's the one bruther...she's the one! Wheeewwwee!" he shouted before inclining his head to Cerise and dashing back across his lawn and into his house.

I'd had such hope for him since he'd gotten the lingo down and all, but he was getting worse, not better. Cerise and I were laughing so hard we were both in tears as we turned to walk in my house. We stopped as Stanley and Ramona stepped outside their door.

Stanley pointed to Cerise. Even from the distance, we could hear him say, "She's the one Homie."

To my surprise, I heard Ramona say, "Yeah? Whew! I approve. Much classier than the others." I tried to muscle Cerise into the garage but she'd apparently forgotten how badly she had to pee. She stayed rooted to the spot watching Stanley and Ramona watch us.

They both put their hands out in front of them but instead of flashing Stanley's signature thumbs they held up both index fingers and both thumbs, which I was completely lost to figure out. "Whew!" Ramona hollered, and they both turned back into their house.

I didn't say a word as Cerise and I walked in the house. I knew the question was coming but I'd wait to hear the question before I rushed to explain the unexplainable.

I clicked the wall mounted garage door opener to close and we stepped into the kitchen. Cerise wasn't nearly as mad as I expected her to be. In an amused tone Cerise asked, "Okay Marcus, what was that all about? And what was that with the 'touchdown' hand signal?"

I laughed and said, "Apparently you know more about what it was all about than I did because I didn't get the double L hand signals until you just said that."

Cerise said, "Come on Marcus, maybe you didn't get the touch down signal but he was practically drooling over you and I. Share Marcus, what's the deal? Why does your neighbor act like that? It made me feel weird the way he stared at me."

I went for the simple route and told Cerise that Stanley was a good neighbor but was really just a rural southerner trapped in the city. Those types are apt to pay more attention to their neighbor's coming's and going's than us westerners.

Cerise thought about that for a second and then replied, "Oh, I get it. You have several women here at your house on a regular basis. That's why they kept putting the emphasis on 'she's' when they were talking about me. Is that it Marcus?"

I closed the kitchen door and thought fast. "Let me rephrase it then. Stanley and his wife met in Arkansas. They didn't get a warm reception from the residents there due to a white man being with a black woman so they moved to California. It was her idea because she has family down in Southern California. So really, what you have is two southern folks trapped in the city based on their love for one another. He and I hung out a few weeks ago and he broke it all down for me. He misses all the things southern boys do such as hunting and eating everything that crawls, and keeping up with the neighbors."

"Think about it. Had you met Stanley in a grocery store, you would think he walked right off the set of a Andy Griffith Show! You wouldn't believe he was married to a black woman by listening to his southern drawl. But they've been together for 15 years and that's cool. So, he's good to her is actually pretty harmless, and that makes him okay with me. He's..."

Cerise could obviously smell a snow job when she heard one. She cut me off. "That's so sweet! But why does he hang out waiting for you?"

I answered honestly this time. "Hell if I know. All I do know is each night he hangs out and greets me when I get home. Sometimes he waits up late into the night waiting to speak. Strange? Yes. The *whew hewwwing* and *yeah bruthas*....At first I was a bit worried about my man but then I realized he's good people. Sometimes he's over enthusiastic but Stanley is good with me and you can take my word for it that he and Ramona didn't mean any disrespect to you."

"Okay Marcus, I'm going to take you at your word on this one and not assume I'm just another one of your ladies of the night visiting."

"Okay. Good. I can deal with that," I told her. Changing the subject as quickly as possible, I said, "Now, do you want the television remote or stereo remote?"

"I'd like to watch a movie while you cook. Do you have any DVD's? Well actually, I better not watch anything because after I eat I'm going to have to leave" she told me.

"Black folk!" I responded. "Always' eating then running. Our people don't have that home training anymore." Cerise grabbed at her chest like she was stricken with pain at my comment. Then she stuck her tongue out at me.

"I've got a real live soon to be Fortune 500 ghetto fabulous queen up in here I see" I said. "Look Cerise, it won hurt to start a movie and then finish it when you come back will it?"

Cerise gave me a seductive smile. "What makes you think I'll be back?" I looked her in the eye and said, "Because you are here now."

"Yeah whatever. That doesn't mean anything. I want an answer!" Cerise said trying to appear cool but she lost the battle. "Marcus I gotta pee! Where's the bathroom?" I laughed at her predicament and pointed the way. Cerise rushed off to relieve herself and I started pulling out the breakfast food.

When she emerged from the first floor quarter bath, she started right in again. "That's much better. Now, what makes you think I'll be back?"

I thought about returning her 'playing me too close' comment but opted instead to just be honest since this seemed to be an important issue to Cerise. "Well, give me one reason why you wouldn't return?" I asked and waited. Cerise didn't respond so I went on, "I haven't asked anything of you except your company. I'm not trying get into your pants and I've let you set the tone for our friendship. Plus, you called me, remember?" I played my trump card and stuck my head in the refrigerator to look for the eggs so Cerise couldn't see the huge smile on my face.

Apparently, she'd gotten a satisfying answer so she let the subject drop and walked into the living room to scan my movie collection. "What do you know about this movie?" she asked. I stuck my head around the door and saw she was holding up *Love Jones*.

"Come on now, you think you got a lock on that one? That's just about every black person's favorite movie "I told her.

Cerise popped the cover open and inserted the movie into the player. "Really? I thought it was just me!" She laughed. "Well I don't want to start something that'll have me here all night so I'll just watch this one, it's not that long."

The delicious aroma of breakfast cooking filled the house and I hollered out, "Cerise, do you like grits?"

She called back, "Not tonight I don't."

I laughed. "Good, I didn't make any for you anyway." I heard a faint, "Forget you." From the living room and smiled to myself as I finished the breakfast preparations.

Twenty minutes later I called Cerise in, told her she could take her tray of food into the living room. Her plate was filled with pancakes, strips of bacon, sausage, scrambled eggs, and two pieces of toast.

"Whew Hew!" Cerise imitated Stanley, and I fell out laughing as she continued, "who did you think you were feeding? There is no way I can eat all of this"

"Try" I told her, and went to the fridge for the orange juice. "But Marcus, this is way too much food" she said again.

"Look Cerise, you said you were hungry so I put a lot of food on your plate but I'm not going to force feed it to you!" I said with a smile. "Just eat what you can and I'll finish it off. How's that?"

"Okay. Thanks. Everything looks and smells really good" Cerise carried her tray into the living room and I followed with my tray. She ate and watched the movie, peeked at me, ate some more, peeked at me again, for almost twenty minutes.

Why was she so damn nervous? I was starting to get offended so I asked, "Cerise, what's up? You keep peeking over here at me like I'm about to attack you or something."

Cerise appeared genuinely shocked by my comment. "What? No, no Marcus. It's just that I can't believe you made this. If I hadn't seen you in the kitchen preparing it I would have thought you got it catered or something," she replied, "Everything was excellent! What did you put in those eggs? And these pancakes are so light and fluffy! I didn't think I could eat it all but, damn, do you have anymore back in the kitchen?"

I laughed out loud. I knew I made the type of breakfast that would cause you to lick your fingers. I replied, "There's more if you like, but I can't tell you what's in the eggs. My mom would kill me. I can tell you the bacon and sausage are both free range and from corn fed animals. That's why it tastes so good."

Cerise replied, "Oh I'm going to find out how to make the eggs if I have to call your mother and ask her myself."

"Umph!" I said. "Like that?"

Cerise smiled and said, "Yup. Just like that. Just you watch and see." We both laughed. I looked over at Cerise a few minutes later and her plate was bare except for the one sausage.

I said, "Um, Cerise, I thought…" Cerise interrupted. "Hush Marcus. I know I said I wasn't going to eat it all but the eggs and cakes were delicious. Plus its really rude to comment on how much food a woman eats," she said with a huge grin.

I took our trays with the empty plates into the kitchen and ran the water to get them ready for the dishwasher.

Cerise called out, "Want me to get that?"

"Nah, go ahead and relax. The movie will be over in a bit," I told her. I started cleaning the kitchen, and saw Cerise put her feet up and recline on the sofa chair. I put the dishes in the dishwasher and wiped down the counters. Cerise was so into the movie she stopped talking to me. I swept the kitchen and when I turned to ask Cerise if she wanted anything else, I noticed she had dozed off. I thought about grabbing a pot and banging on it scaring the hell out of her. I laughed at the idea but couldn't bring myself to do it. It was close to 1:00 in the morning and I wasn't about to wake her up to drive home.

I grabbed a comforter out of the closet and placed it over her as she slept. I turned the TV off and headed upstairs but left the kitchen light on in case she woke up and couldn't remember where she was in the dark. I thought again to wake her but she was snoring like a grizzly bear and obviously needed some rest. Upstairs I put on a pair of pajama's to be polite, just in case Cerise wandered in. I didn't want her to get the wrong idea.

DON'T BE AFRAID

The sound of a bell woke me up. I lay quiet for a moment but didn't hear it again. Shit was I dreaming? Flimsy traces of my dream floated back to me. I was having a party. Loud music, lots of people, plenty of food and alcohol, I couldn't remember much else about it though. I flipped over to look at the clock. It was 5:00 a.m. I jumped up and went to the bathroom then it hit me. Cerise was downstairs last night! I wondered if she was still here.

I grabbed my robe, walked halfway downstairs, and peeked around my blind spot. She was gone. I knew I'd hear it from her once I called her because I didn't wake her up but she'd obviously needed the rest and I wasn't going to apologize for letting her get some uninterrupted sleep.

The aroma of freshly brewed coffee filled the house. I definitely needed a couple of cups to get me going this morning. I showered and started to get dressed in a rush so I could head downstairs to read the paper with my coffee. I grabbed the remote for the CD player and hit scramble because I didn't care what played. I just needed some music and not the daily dose of news.

In my dream, I remembered hearing Jaheim's song playing and just like that, it was the first song on the CD player. I cranked the volume up a notch because Jaheim knew how to bring it, no doubt. I sang along with the CD. *"Just in case I don't make it home tonight, let me make love to you for the last time."* Yeah Jaheim was bringing it this morning. I finished getting dressed and headed downstairs looking and feeling good. My head was clean, goatee trimmed, cologne had me smelling good, and the gray three piece suit would make heads turn if I happened upon a happy hour after work or managed to twist Cerise's arm into going out with me again tonight.

I bounced downstairs to the beat of Jaheim singing to his lover. In the kitchen, I said good morning to Cerise and went to pour myself a cup of coffee. Wait. Huh? I backtracked to where Cerise sat at the table sipping a mug of coffee as if she sipped coffee in the same spot every morning.

"Let me try that again," I said. "Good morning beautiful!" I couldn't suppress the huge grin that spread across my entire face the second I realized she was still here.

Cerise had changed clothes. "Did you go home and change then come back?" I asked. Before she could answer I said, "Not that I'd mind if you did. Its quite a pleasant surprise to find you back here so early."

Cerise yawned and stretched like a cat in the warm sun. "I didn't go home. I keep an extra outfit in my car and changed this morning right before I answered your door." When I woke up on your couch my first thought was to come up there and throw a pot of cold water on your ass for letting me fall sleep. I don't like sleeping away from home."

Shit! I stayed calm and asked, "What did Stanley want?" I asked, trying to pry without just outright asking who showed up. Cerise didn't reply as she sat there at the counter. I walked over to the adjacent counter and poured myself a cup of coffee. I glanced to see if she was staring at me in disgust but she was looking out the window.

I said, "Cerise the reason I didn't wake you up was because you fell asleep so fast and started snoring I just figured you were too tired to drive home. Sorry Stanley woke you up so early what did he want?"

Cerise replied, "It wasn't Stanley it was a woman named Donna. I wasn't going to answer it but she just kept ringing it." Damn, Damn, Damn.

"Hmm, what did she say?" I tried to act disinterested.

Cerise looked at me and said, "Well first, you look very handsome this morning Marcus. Second, I had to give your *early bird girl* a piece of my mind this morning."

"What do you mean my early bird girl? Donna is a friend who sometimes shows up without calling."

Cerise said, "Tell me something I don't know. I woke up around 3 a.m., and went out to the car to grab my bag and briefcase. I needed to make sure I didn't have anything scheduled first thing this morning. Well, after I showered and checked my planner the doorbell rang. I wasn't going to answer it Marcus but she wouldn't stop ringing the doorbell. It could have been an emergency or maybe it was an emergency booty call. So, I opened the door and she stood there looking me up and down like I was a red headed stepchild."

As Cerise was telling me what took place, I didn't know whether to laugh or try to keep a straight face. Instead, I walked over to the refrigerator, buried myself inside claiming to be looking for the orange juice, and mouthed to myself, "Ain't that some shit! Cerise took Donna on?" I closed the refrigerator door not realizing I still had a huge smile on my face.

"What are you cheesing so hard about?" The caffeine must have kicked in right about that time because all of a sudden Cerise became agitated. "Is something funny Marcus? Maybe I missed the punch line?" She asked with a catch in her voice.

I could tell that all kinds of thoughts were going through her head about who Donna was and why she was at my door so early. I said, "Its nothing, it's just that Donna and I go way back. I wish I could have seen the look on her face when you answered the door. She never thought in a million years that a woman finer than her would answer my door."

Cerise said, "Marcus you pick em weird, don't you? So, what's the real deal with the trench coat bandit? Is she an ex? If it's none of my business or if I'm too personal than say so."

"No she isn't an Ex. She could have been had she given a brotha some play but she didn't. I don't have anything to hide from you. If I did you surely wouldn't have been allowed to stay the night at my pad."

"Desperate times call for desperate measures I guess," she said.

I was becoming a bit annoyed at Cerise's attitude but I gave her the benefit of the doubt, assuming she wasn't a morning person or maybe her sleep hadn't been as restful as I'd assumed. In any case, I calmly said, "I'm not sure what you mean by that."

Cerise quickly replied, "Marcus, your *friend* was dressed as if she had just climbed out of bed. Plus, her man must have kicked her ass because she had a black eye and huge scratches across her face."

I was startled by the news but not entirely surprised. I'd known it was just a matter of time before Sheila and Donna veered off into the land of domestic violence. They were both crazy as hell and both had volatile tempers.

Not wanting to get into a detailed conversation about my relationship with Donna and the person who had given her a black eye I kept it simple. "Her 'significant other' must have bopped her upside the head," I told Cerise. "I knew it was coming. I'll check on her later."

Cerise crinkled her face. "She must have a real fool for a boyfriend," she said. "Anyway, your girl stood there looking at me like I was crazy. I asked if I could help her and she stuttered and stumbled all over her words asking where you were."

I waited for Cerise to continue but she seemed content to leave it at that. "So? What did you tell her?" I finally had to ask.

"I told her that you were upstairs sleeping and to check back later then I closed the door. She didn't look real happy when I closed the door on her. Almost like she was in shock. Should I have let her in?" Cerise asked now that she knew there was no possibility of allowing Donna to come in.

Conflicted, I was upset with Cerise for even answering my door and also with Donna since I'd just told her last night not to pop up unexpectedly. But I'd also told her that I'd be here for her if she needed me. She showed up because she did and got turned away by some woman she must have known was new in my life. And Cerise seemed to be getting some sort of enjoyment at the misfortune that had befallen Donna and from turning her away. Maybe I'd been wrong about her? The last thing I needed in my life was another bitchy female.

I wanted to tell Cerise if she was ever over in the future not to answer my door but the words wouldn't come. Prying further Cerise said, "You and she must have something going on because she stood there stuttering and now you are at a loss for words. There's no need for you to clam up baby," she said. "We are just friends. Go ahead tell me the real deal. I'm not your woman. Are you sure you are just friends with her?"

I'd had enough. "Look Cerise, I'm not sure where all this is coming from," I told her. "I don't like your attitude and I don't like the fact you apparently think it's funny that one of my friends got beat up." Cerise had the good sense to look ashamed, but I wasn't finished. "I told you she's not an ex. And if she was my woman she wouldn't have needed to ring the bell, she could have walked right on in. And, yeah, you're right. You aren't my woman and you never will be if this is the way you always act."

"Fine by me!" Cerise huffed.

"Fine by me too!" I said right back to her.

We were at a stand off and I wasn't backing down. Cerise was quiet for a moment but when she spoke again, the bitchiness was still in her voice. "Who's decision was it to break up, hers or yours?"

At this point, she was really playing me too close. I figured I'd better leave before we had more words and ruined even the possibility of friendship between us. "Look Cerise, I need to get into the office early so maybe we can continue this discussion later?"

Still coming way too strong Cerise said, "Didn't you tell me last night since we both own our companies we have nothing but time. Don't start looking at your watch now!"

Sighing heavily, I knew I was at a crossroads. I'm a private man. I don't like to discuss my personal life with anyone. I could kick Cerise out and avoid this conversation but last night I'd thought Cerise might become a part of my personal life and I had to admit her behavior this morning sounded more jealous than bitchy. If she was jealous, she probably felt threatened by Donna and behaved badly out of instinct. She'd marked her territory and the more I thought about it the less angry I was. I wanted to be her territory. Plus, I knew a little about acting crazy when provoked by jealousy so I decided to cut her some slack.

"You are right Cerise," I told her. "There's no need to rush off I just really hadn't anticipated having to have this discussion with you so soon. But you seem to be threatened by what happened here today and I don't want you to feel that way. I'm gonna give you the straight up deal."

"I'm not your woman so I don't feel threatened but yes, please, give me the straight dope" Cerise said, and sat back in the chair with her arms folded. I felt like telling her to shut up and leaving her ass in the kitchen and going to work like I'd planned but I didn't go there. Had she been Donna or Shelia, I would have let her have it! She wasn't like either of those trifling women though, at least I hoped not. She was the woman I'd met at Bucks and who'd captivated my thoughts ever since. So, who was the real woman? The one I'd met then or the catty woman sitting stubbornly at my kitchen table like she wanted to kick my ass for lying to her. I guess there was only one way to find out.

Before I could even get a word out Cerise popped up out of her chair and gathered her planner from the table. "Marcus, you don't even know me. What we have is just the very beginning of a friendship and I've obviously thrown salt in a game you've been playing a lot longer than you've been playing m...." She couldn't complete what she'd been about to say. "Never mind. I'm out of here!"

Can you say irrational? I watched as Cerise grabbed her overnight bag from the floor. She stomped to the door and I thought how sad it was that I'd been so wrong about her. I followed behind her to lock up after she left but Cerise paused, with her hand on the doorknob, took a deep breath, and turned around with fierce eyes.

"You have nothing to say, mister?" I had nothing to say. "So you're just going to let me walk out?" Her voice cracked when she spoke. She was obviously on the verge of tears.

I still didn't say anything because I hadn't done a damn thing wrong. What was I supposed to say? I was done with bending over backwards for women just so they wouldn't leave. She wanted to go…she could damn well go.

I remained silent and Cerise walked out the door and closed it quietly behind her. At least she didn't slam it and wake the neighborhood. Guess it just wasn't meant to be. I had a silent word with God and asked if maybe he could give me a sign next time around so I didn't go getting my hopes up over someone I wasn't meant to be with. Shaking my head, I reached out to lock the door and Cerise walked back in, stomped into the kitchen, grabbed her keys from the counter without looking at me, and headed back to the front door. The man upstairs acted fast! I couldn't let her leave like this.

Calmly stepping in front of her, I blocked her path. "So this is how you operate? You ask me out, I treat you with nothing but respect but at the first sign of smoke you run for the door?"

Cerise attempted to walk around me and I stepped in front of her again. "Marcus, I don't have time to play games with you." Her voice was shaking and I could tell she was only moments away from breaking down completely.

"I'm not playing, I'm deadly serious," I said.

Cerise tried to speak calmly. "Look, we had a good evening but I should have woken up in my own bed not on your couch!" A tear made its way from the corner of her eye and slid down her cheek. "This isn't how friends are suppose to hang out," she said as she angrily brushed the tear from her face. "And friends don't go crazy just because a woman comes to the door. I don't know what I'm doing Marcus, I should just go."

She made to leave again but I stepped in front of her. "So would it have been better if you'd woken up in bed next to me? Would you have been nicer to Donna then?"

Cerise laughed and sent a tiny spray of snot into the room. Embarrassed, she pulled a tissue from her jacket pocket and wiped her nose.

"No that wouldn't have been better Marcus," she said softly, studying her shoes. "I know I don't have the right to jam you up. I thought I was cool with just being friends but when I saw that woman so early this morning I wanted her to get the hell out of here and far away from you without really even knowing why."

I asked, "Now that you've had a little time to think about it do you know why now?"

Still looking at the floor, Cerise said, "It's crazy but in spite of what I said last night, I think we have something worth examining here. But I can't afford to be caught up in any drama with anyone because of my divorce. So I was confused and rude and belligerent and a total bitch this morning," she took a deep breath, dragged her eyes from the floor, and looked directly into mine. "And I'm sorry. I obviously cannot handle this friendship right now. I like you Marcus. I've had more fun with you the two times we've been together than I've had in years. But obviously, I can't do this.

I took the bag and briefcase from Cerise's hands and set them on the floor. Gently taking both her wrists in my hands, I stared into her eyes. "Now, let me see if I have this right. You can't do this?" I asked and placed a light kiss on her forehead.

Shakily Cerise replied, "Yes."

I stepped closer. "And since you can't do 'this', that means I won't be able to do this?" I asked as I wrapped my arms around Cerise's shoulders. She was shaking.

Cerise escaped my embrace and went to stand by the kitchen sink. I crossed the distance between us slowly and Cerise held her hand out to stop me from hugging her again. "Marcus," she said with uncertainty in her voice. "I'm serious. I can't do this…can I?"

Placing my hands on her shoulders I turned Cerise gently around so that her back was to me. I rubbed her shoulders as we stared out the kitchen window. I said, "So then what I'm doing now would be out of the question. Is that right?" I moved her hair to the side and lightly kissed her neck.

Cerise gave a jerky nod but didn't move away then shuddered as if she'd gotten a sudden chill. "That is definitely out of the question Marcus" she said quietly then relaxed her body against mine

I placed my cheek on the top of her head and inhaled her scent. "Hmm, okay, what about this?" I asked, as I placed my hands in her hair and massaged her scalp firmly yet gently.

Cerise moaned deep in her throat. "That's not acceptable either. Don't we have to go to work?"

In answer, I bent down and kissed the same spot on Cerise's neck as I gently pulled and played with her hair. Placing light kisses along the line of her jaw and chin; I gently turned her back around to face me and kissed her soft lips briefly. "Is this a felony?" I asked, quickly dipping down to kiss her chest through the opening of her shirt.

Cerise's breath caught in her throat but she managed to say, "Oh yes, that's punishable by death." She shook her head as if to clear it. "Marcus this isn't who I am. Technically, I'm still married and I shouldn't be doing this with you! There's just something about you that breaks my defenses down. And, uh…I have an appointment in two hours so even if I wanted something to happen here it couldn't."

"An appointment, huh? Well you won't be late, I just need to find out what I won't be able to do with you once you leave," I told her.

Maneuvering Cerise so that the palms of her hands were flat against the refrigerator I reached around Cerise's waist and fiddled with her belt until it slid off her waist. As I did so Cerise rested her head against the refrigerator and said with passion in her voice, "You are past the friendship zone Marcus. Penalty on the field."

Slowly, I unzipped her skirt and it fell to the floor in a pool at her ankles. Cerise looked incredible in black fishnet panties. She looked down at her skirt and looked back up at me. Stepping out of her skirt, she turned to face me. "This is what I was talking about. We cannot do this." With each word, she took a step toward me. Cerise stared in my eyes for a long moment and then launched herself at me.

She kissed me as if I was her first passionate kiss and I returned the favor. Within seconds, we were both almost naked.

Cerise, breathing heavily said, "Its 7:15 and I have a prospective client to meet at 9:00. I can't be late to that appointment. I am serious Marcus."

I replied, "I only need 3 minutes. I'll be done then!"

"WHAT!" Cerise shrieked. "In that case I'll just leave now." She made a fake effort to pick up her clothes but I grabbed her wrists, pulled her to me, and nibbled on her ear. Cerise chuckled softly and flipped the script by trying to walk me backwards towards the couch in the living room, placing her hand over my mouth to keep me from saying anything.

The last of her reservations appeared to have flown away. I kissed the palm of her hand and ran my tongue across her fingers. Cerise was panting

"Oh my. That's….Mmm that's nice."

I turned Cerise around and began kissing her back and spine as we slowly made our way to the couch. I grabbed the comforter and practically dragged Cerise back into the kitchen where I knocked anything on the table to the floor and spread the blanket on the table.

A surprised look spread across Cerise's face. "You are kidding right?"

"Please woman, I'm not giving you none. We are going to take a nap on the table though!" I said, and held my hand out for her to join me.

Cerise laughed as she took my hand and I lifted her so that she was sitting on the table. I knew this caught her off guard because she probably thought I was going to lay her on the table and jump up there with her. I don't think so. Nope, too generic, not exciting enough, and I had other plans. I walked over to the other edge of the table and rolled the blanket to create a make shift pillow. I whispered in her ear "go ahead lay back and relax."

She did so without hesitating but said. "Marcus you messed up. Where are you going to lie? It can't be on top of me because the table is too hard and there definitely isn't enough room on either side. Nice try but poor planning."

We both laughed but I wasn't laughing at her comment. I was laughing because she had no clue where I was going with this. As she relaxed back on the table, I stood between her legs and bent to kiss her for a long moment. My hands gave her breasts loving attention until her nipples were as hard as diamonds. I placed my mouth where my hands had been and savored the feel of Cerise's smooth skin on my tongue. Kissing her navel and the smooth skin beneath, I slowly made my way lower and placed both knees on the floor before enjoying the best and most memorable meal I've ever had at that table.

I explored Cerise until she moaned and writhed beneath me. She let out a squeal and her entire body tensed, shuddered, and relaxed. I continued my exploration going for number two but she reached down for my hand and placed it on her breast then she gently tugged on my ears until we were eye level. I understood. Slowly we became one being as I entered her. I felt like I'd died and gone to paradise. Her warm soft love surrounded me and as if she were welcoming me home after being away for too long. We rocked to an ageless rhythm for what seemed an eternity.

I was trying to be gentle because I knew it had been a long time for her but timid little Cerise shocked the hell out of me when she moaned, "Tell me its good Marcus," she looked in my eyes and gave me a wicked, sensuous grin. "Is it good to you?"

"Uhhhhh, shit!" I practically growled. "Keep talking like that and you are going to feel exactly how good it is to me."

"Is it good Marcus? Do you feel what I'm feeling?" Cerise panted. I would never have taken Cerise for someone to talk dirty during sex but her questions and playful laughter caused me to lose my damn mind. I drove into her with an intensity I didn't even know I had. Cerise raised her back from the table, clung to me for dear life, and matched me with an intensity of her own I couldn't believe.

An hour later, thoroughly exhausted, I grabbed Cerise's hand, pulled the blanket from the table and went into the living room to lay it on the couch. I laid on top of it and pulled Cerise down so that she was laying with her head on my chest.

In a voice filled with wonder Cerise said, "I have no words for what you have just done to my body. I'm still tingling all over."

"I know what you mean, baby. I feel the same way. My knees are like jelly," I told her and kissed the top of her head.

She looked up with unsure eyes. "So you were there with me? You felt that incredible feeling too?" She asked.

"It was okay," I said, and shrugged my shoulders. "Okay!" Cerise pretended to be outraged. "If it was just okay why were you grunting like a wild boar? Grrrrrrr."

I laughed so hard I almost knocked her to the floor. That caused her to laugh and we both rearranged ourselves, and settled back down, chuckling softly.

Cerise grew still in my arms and I knew the moment had turned serious. "Marcus, this doesn't change anything you know. I mean, I slipped up, I am human for God's sake, and it's been a very long time for me. But it was only a slip up. Nothing more." Not exactly the words I'd expected to hear from Cerise after such an incredible experience in the kitchen.

"So that was the first and last time? Is that what you are trying to tell me?" I asked. "If you want to think that to make yourself feel better about your 'slip up' that's fine by me," I told her.

The sexy temptress was gone. In her place was the woman who'd built a Fortune 1000 company and she was downplaying her interest in what had happened to gain the upper hand. Cerise didn't fool me for a second as she said, "It was pretty good, Marcus." 'Pretty good!' What happened to "that incredible feeling" she'd expressed only minutes ago?

I raised my eyebrow, settled my head back on my raised arm, let Cerise go through the motions of trying to downplay it now that the initial glow had worn off. "So it was pretty good, huh?" I said with amusement in my voice.

Cerise continued, "Yes, pretty damn good. And you're probably the best lover I've ever had, even though that's an appallingly short list. But nothing's changed. I don't think I can have this relationship with you now. So, don't fall in love. We are still just friends." She stood up, grabbed her clothes, and headed to the shower.

I rolled my eyes and mimicked Cerise. "Marcus this doesn't change anything. We are still just friends."

"What kind of gansta shit are you trying to pull? I don't think so." I told her retreating back. She stuck her tongue out at me and went into the bathroom, closing the door behind her.

The clock on the mantel above the fireplace told me it was 8:15. I wanted to be at work in forty-five minutes and Cerise had an appointment in an hour. I snuggled into the couch for another 2 minutes thinking about her comments. 'Pretty good...*probably* the best I've had?'

Ah hell no, she was going eat those words. I walked into the steamy bathroom and said, "If that water gets any hotter you'll need some burn cream."

Cerise replied, "Oh I love a hot shower, gets me refreshed and feeling good! Marcus what time is it?"

"Don't worry about that, you have time," I replied as I walked over to the linen closet and grabbed her a clean wash cloth. I stuck my head around the shower curtain to hand it to her but she was using the same one she'd used when she woke up this morning. She saw me peeking and tried to be indignant. "Marcus, I'm trying to shower!"

"I just finished tasting that fruit and now you wanna play the shy role?" Cerise clicked her tongue at me and turned towards the spray of water again. I pulled the curtain open and got in the shower with her. The water hit me on my shoulders as I took Cerise's arm, turning her around to face me. "Marcus, I can't.." she began, but I kissed her to shut her up then bent to kiss and massage her breasts. Cerise moaned, "Marcus I need to be finishing up not starting it up again."

I ignored her and pressed Cerise up against the wall, kissing her and licking the trickles of water on her face. I grabbed the bar of soap she was using and began washing her body. Once she was completely covered in soap, I backed up against the adjacent wall and watched the water rinse her body. Damn she was something spectacular! As I stood there watching her rinse off I asked, "So you'll be back tonight right?"

"What for? I already got what I wanted!" Cerise responded with a huge grin.

"No you didn't. You put a band aide over a major cut baby. Around 6 or 7 tonight that body will be craving just a little bit more. If you don't start acting nice I might not give it what it needs," I said with a small grin of my own.

As Cerise stepped out of the shower and dried off she said, "Well the only way you'll know if you are as good as you obviously think you are is if I come back tonight huh?"

"I'll see you tonight," I told her and finished my shower as Cerise gathered her belongings and left the room.

Upstairs in my bedroom Cerise and I finished getting dressed. Cerise gave me a kiss and headed to the front door. She stopped at the door and looked back at me. "Thanks for hooking me up. See you around?" and blew me another kiss.

Turning from the mirror where I was straightening my tie, I let her think she'd won. I smiled and said, "Cool, see ya round." Cerise closed my bedroom door and I heard her feet on the stairs. A few seconds later I heard the front door close. Guess I'd know if I was right about her, if I'd read the sign from above correctly, in a few hours. Until then, I wasn't going to worry about it.

ALL MY LIFE
(I've prayed for someone like you)

I grabbed all my belongings, headed downstairs and out the front door. As I locked the door I talked out loud to myself, "You are the man, Marcus Haley. Who is the man? You are the man!"

I felt like dancing! Cerise may have left here thinking she had the upper hand and that things were back on a platonic level. I knew better. Baby girl was going to spend more than a few more times on that table, the couch, and my bed. I turned around to head to my car and there was Stanley. For once, I wasn't even slightly annoyed at his presence. I was happy as hell and didn't care who knew.

"You did it brotha, Wheweee! I saw her leaving with a huge smile on her face," Stanley shouted from across the yard. He arranged his hands in the 'touchdown' signal he and Ramona had used last night.

I shook my head at him, trying to play it cool. "What are you talking about?" I asked trying to keep the smile from my voice and face but failing.

Stanley called out, "Bruther you kept that pony in the stable all damn night. Sweeeeet! I knew Ramie and me couldn't have been wrong! Ewwww Weeeee, gitty up! Bruther…That sexy, southern bell looking hottie was here all night. I knew she was the one bruther! Did you stick it to her?"

I looked at Stanley hopping around looking as excited as a puppy. I gave him my best Johnny Witherspoon "*bang, bang, bang*" impression, and told Stanley, "I blew her back out!"

Stanley yelled "Awhh hell! Yeah! Hell yeah! Cocka doodle goddamn do bruther! Cocka doodle doo! Whew!"

Just as he got going Ramona opened the door, looked around, saw Stanley and me, and asked, "What the hell is going on out here?"

Stanley called to his wife, "Told ya last night's girl was the one! She stayed all night and left here grinning!" Ramona looked pleased with the news Stanley had just given her and flashed me a solo thumbs up. Stanley looked at her incredulously, and she grudgingly raised her other thumb in their signature two thumbs up salute.

Ramona grinned at me and called out to Stanley, "Leave that man alone and let him go to work!"

I wiggled my eyebrows at Stanley when I saw the sexy get up Ramona was wearing. "*You* go blow a back out. I gotta get to work. I'll talk to you later." I jumped in the Dodge and looked over at Stanley. He gave me two thumbs up and rushed into his house.

I backed out of the driveway in the Ram, and grabbed the cell-phone from the dash box and called the office. Ashley answered the phone with that voice that had all my male clients drooling. "Hello sir, how are you?"

I replied, "Hello Ashley, how're things at the office?"

She answered, "The only person to call in was Tyler. He told me to tell you to check your voice mail as soon as you came to work."

"Okay,' I replied, "Anything else?"

Ashley responded, "No that's it sir."

"Okay, thank you Ashley, now can you please transfer me to my desk."

Ashley replied, "Yes sir," and forwarded me to my desk phone.

I listened to several inconsequential voicemails before I reached Tyler's urgent message. "Hello Boss, this is Tyler. I'm sitting on my house today. I know I told you tomorrow but I think her visitor is coming by today. I overheard a telephone call. Call me when you get in please." I called Tyler on his cell-phone to find out what was going on.

"Hello this is Tyler, How can I help you?" I wondered why he was being so formal.

I said, "It's me Marcus. What's the deal Tyler?"

Tyler said, "Hey boss, sorry I didn't recognize your number. Let me tell you what's going on. Before I do, will you be able to join me today?"

"Yes but it would have been nice if you would have called me before I left the house so I wouldn't be dressed in business attire," I told him.

He replied, "Sorry boss. Okay, here's the deal. Yesterday, I told baby that I was going to hit some golf balls today. She knows that I'm usually gone for a few hours once I get out on the course. I unlocked the window downstairs in our study and drove around the block. I walked back to the house, climbed through the window, and sat there for almost thirty minutes before I heard anything. Then the phone rang and my wife answered. "She'd taken the phone in the hall across from the study I heard her say to be here by 11:00."

I tried to reign him in. "Tyler what if you are wrong here? And before you start with the 'I've been here for you' speech just answer that question. What if you are wrong bruh?"

Tyler was silent for a second and seemed to actually be considering my question. Finally, he said, "I'm not wrong on this boss. If you heard some of the stuff I heard her saying on the phone you'd know I am doing the right thing."

I said, "Okay, I need to change and then I'll take point once I get there." Tyler started to argue with me but I cut him off. "Look Tyler, your woman is no dummy. She knows what you do for a living. You don't think she'd recognize your car parked down the street? Come on now, you know the rules of the game. We cool?"

Tyler responded, "Boss, I've got the point, don't worry about it." I could here the anger in his voice. I reiterated, "Tyler I have point once I get there. Let me tell you something, just because it's your woman doesn't mean I'll compromise my skills! If we are going to do this shit we are going to do it right. Do you understand me? I don't like it, but I have your back. So again, you know I need to take point, right? Don't take this situation any different than if you were working it for the company. Okay?"

Tyler paused for a second and said, "You are right boss. That's why I asked you to help me, because I can't see anything clear right now."

I replied, "I know. It's all good. I'll see you in 35 minutes and don't make a move until I get there. We straight?"

Tyler replied, "Okay, we are straight."

I picked up the pace on the freeway to the office so I could change and get to Tyler's house as soon as possible.

I walked into the office and told Ashley that I would be assisting Tyler and she could reach either of us on the cell-phones. I changed clothes, jumped back in the truck, and headed to Tyler's house. It took about an hour to get there and I called him on the cell-phone to let him know I was on my way. On the way, I stopped and grabbed a couple of breakfast burritos from La Mia's Mexican Restaurant. As I headed down the freeway, I thought about Cerise. Baby girl was complicated but I think I had her figured out. I was pretty confidant I'd see here again tonight.

Thinking about Cerise had me on autopilot. I looked around and realized I'd driven at least five miles the wrong way. I shook my head to clear my thoughts. So much for "my skills" I'd told Tyler about. I backtracked and headed for Tyler's house again when my mobile phone vibrated. I checked to see who was calling but the number was blocked.

"This is Marcus. Hello?" The phone was silent so I hung up. I looked at my phone to see if I was getting any service and I wasn't. I waited until I had signal strength, scrolled down to Cerise's work number, and called.

"Hello, Xellron Inc. How can I help you?" The dingy secretary answered but she seemed less scattered this morning. "Hi may I speak to Mrs. Ivan?"

She responded, "Mrs. Ivan is in a meeting right now. Can I take a message?" I said no and hung the phone up.

I'd hoped the blocked call had been from Cerise but it obviously couldn't have been since she wouldn't be calling from a meeting. The phone started vibrating again. "Hello this is Marcus. How can I help you?" Silence. I looked at my phone again and I had service so I said "Hello?" I started to hang the phone up and then I heard,

"Hello Marc. This is Donna. What's going on?"

I shouldn't have answered the phone. I said, "Hey Donna what's up? Everything is everything on my end."

She replied, "What's going on Marc? I come by and you have a woman answer your door? You didn't mention her the last time we spoke did you? You spent your birthday with me and never once said you were seeing someone else?"

I listened to her with a big ass grin on my face then said, "I didn't know I was suppose to report to you."

The phone was quiet for a while then she replied, "Well Marcus, I...I...I didn't say you had to report to me. But out of courtesy to our friendship you could have men...."

I interrupted her, "Out of courtesy? You of all people don't get to lecture me on the *courtesy to our friendship!* You know what? I'm not even going there with you. I gotta go." I went to hang up the phone but I heard her say, "Wait...wait!" I put the phone back to my ear.

"What?"

"You are right Marcus, I shouldn't have come at you like that."

I said, "You're damn straight Donna cause you had me and left me for the wolves. So there will be no sympathy shit jumping off."

The phone was quiet. Donna then said, "Can we just be the friends we've grown to be? I would hate to lose you as a friend."

I thought about that for a second and replied, "Of course, now I gotta go. I'll be talking to you later, I'm sure," and hung up the phone. I grabbed my CD container and searched through it looking for something to put in the stereo. I didn't want to sit there in silence thinking about what just happened. The phone began vibrating again.

My first thought was to ignore it but Donna would call all day and night until she had got her point across. I took a deep breath and said, "What do you want now?"

The other end of the phone was silent for a second. I said, "Speak up! What is it now?" Then softly came the voice I most wanted to hear.

"Uh hello, Marcus this is Cerise did I reach you at a bad time?"

Timing, timing, timing! I said, "Oh hello beautiful, sorry about that. I didn't know it was you."

She replied, "That's okay. I just wanted to let you know that I had several messages from my soon to be ex-husband this morning. He's packed up everything he wanted from the house and left. He told me that he went into our account and took $400,000 but left everything else for me! I didn't believe him at first but he said he hired a lawyer who drafted up the paperwork. I am so happy!"

I said, "That's wonderful but do me a favor, call a locksmith have them change the locks today, and do not go to your house alone. Okay?"

"Yes." Cerise replied.

"Cerise, I'm serious. Do not go to your house alone. Call me when the attorney stops by. I want to make sure he isn't tripping."

She said, "I understand. I'll call the locksmith right now. Maybe later when I get off you and I can go by my house if it's okay with you?"

I said, "Good idea. I'd love to go with you to your house. Call me. Right now I have to go because I'm at my surveillance spot."

She replied, "Okay, and by the way you were right. My body didn't wait until 6 or 7. I'd like some more sir," she said with a British accent like the boy from Oliver Twist. "Do you have anymore sexual healing potion left or did I use it all up this morning?"

"I sure do. I'll make sure the potion has the right ingredients. Gotta go. Talk to ya later." I told her.

"Bye Marcus," she said and hung up. I wasn't feeling what Cerise had told me about Mike just bowing out like that but if it were true, then my day was getting better and better!

I exited the freeway and called Tyler, "Hey T, what's up I'm exiting I-5 now. Where are you posted?"

He replied, "I'm on Jerry St. When you get here, I'll brief you and you can take point. I'm 6 houses east of the target, parked behind a motor home. Boss...thank you."

"Okay, I see the Winnebago. Go ahead and head around the corner and park on Gerome Ave. Now brief me on what's going on and why we are here today." Tyler proceeded to explain how he overheard her making plans for an 11 o'clock lunch and never mentioned it to him. We sat on the house for awhile and at 10:30, she left the house. I trailed Tyler's woman and she drove to a pizza place where she met a few girlfriends and had lunch. They stayed at the restaurant for three hours talking and laughing. It didn't look like she planned to sneak out to meet some mystery man. I called Tyler and told him so.

"Boss, we can break it off. I'm supposed to meet her at Ageless Beauty Store in about an hour to give her some money."

I told Tyler to meet me in the parking lot at the gas station. When he pulled up I asked, "Tyler are you sure about this? I think you are paranoid."

He replied, "Boss, I am not tripping. I am serious. There is something going on. I don't know what it is but she's sneaking out on me. Do me a favor; let's try one more time? If we strike out again, I'll leave it alone. I swear." Tyler had a concerned and desperate look on his face. I agreed to help him again.

We went to lunch and then headed our separate ways. It was 4:30 when we parted and I called Cerise as soon as I got back in the truck. "Hello I'm surprised you answered your phone. I was about to leave you a message. What time are we heading to your house?"

She replied, "Hello, Marcus sorry I didn't call you back with that information. I was in and out of meetings all day. More great news for me! I was able to convince an Executive Director of a conservator company to let us come in and set up their network system."

I was excited for her. "Great sweetie! I am happy to hear the news."

Cerise lowered her voice. "Marcus, the deal was worth $450,000 and that was just to set up the systems!" Damn! Baby girl was playing in the big leagues with that deal. "Okay," she continued in the same hushed tone, "Wanna hear some better news? The attorney that I was telling you about came by and I signed all the paperwork for the divorce and settlement."

I replied, "That's great but I still want to come by with you. Did you call the locksmith?"

She replied, "Okay, and yes I did what you said and the locksmith changed all the locks in the house. I even had the alarm company go out and reset the codes. Marcus I am so happy! It seems all this good stuff just happened the second I swallowed my pride, broke down and called you."

"Ah, the truth comes out at last!" I said, "Well I am happy for you Cerise. You deserve happiness and I just hope I am there to share a piece of it with you."

"I wouldn't have it any other way," She said, "I'll see you in a few?"

"Yup," I said, and hung up.

We met at her office. Seeing her brought to me again, how happy I was things had turned out well after such a bad start this morning. She was everything I wanted. Beautiful, smart, sexy, independent, and into me. What more could a man want?

We arrived at Cerise's house and the garage was open. We both walked in and I asked Cerise if anything was missing. "Well I guess he took all the tools which is weird because I work with the tools, he never touched them. Not a problem though! It's a small price to pay for my freedom. Um, let's see, the container with the wedding china, and his weight set. That's all."

Cerise and I walked in the house and noted he had taken only what he'd listed on the letter from the lawyer. There was a note on the counter and Cerise walked to pick it up. I held back to give her privacy but she motioned me over. "As you told me this morning, you tasted the fruit. I have nothing to hide from you Marcus."

The note read, "Dear Cerise, I am sorry things didn't work out for you and I. I've struggled with my addiction to men all my life and I guess this time I really have to figure out which way I'm going to go." As if he didn't already know, I thought to myself. The note continued, "The attorney should have contacted you today regarding the settlement and divorce. I wish you the best and I hope you and that black bastard of an investigator work out. I am happy and out of your life for good. Signed, Your Ex."

Cerise read the letter, balled it up, and threw it in the garbage. We spent the next 3 hours re-doing the pin numbers for the alarm system just in case Mike had gotten the new numbers from the alarm company, checking to make sure all the locks had been changed, and making calls leaving messages to make sure Mike had been removed from all their joint accounts. When that was done I held Cerise against me and asked softly, "So do you want to spend your first real night as a free woman alone here or are you coming back to stay with me like you should?" I smacked her on the butt and ran into the living room.

Cerise gave chase and I turned around as she jumped into my arms. She asked, "Do you want me to stay the night or are you just after my fruit? Scratch that. I don't care what the answer it. I'm staying the night."

"Excellent. Pack up a bag I want to hurry up with the boring sex so I can wake up with you in my arms."

"Boring sex, huh?" Cerise asked. I yawned, and stretched my arms. "So boring I'm dying to get you home. Hurry up woman!"

She smiled and headed towards the stairs. "I'm going to pack something nice to wear for you tonight."

I yawned again. "Just make sure it has easy access baby" and winked as she stuck her tongue out at me. While Cerise was upstairs, out of the blue, I wondered what my mother would think of her. I hadn't taken anyone to her house in awhile. The last time I did, moms had her clown suit on and gave me a piece of her mind for bringing home a woman she considered unworthy of me.

It was a few years ago, but it was fresh in my mind and every so often, my brothers will crack a joke about it. I sat there thinking about how moms grilled me about Roxanne. I met Roxanne at a library. She told me she worked for a law firm as a paralegal and she was cool to talk and hang out with. That was nothing compared to what I had with Cerise and hoped to have again tonight but we were two different peas in a pod and I guess that's what I liked about her. Plus, she was "poppin the most", her body was perfect. We had hung out a couple of months before she met the family. I went to visit her one-day in Berkeley and we ended up driving back to my place. The plan was to spend breakfast and brunch with her in Berkeley. Then we'd head back to Sacramento for lunch and Dinner.

I didn't mind driving because at the time, I had a convertible mustang and the drive was nice. On the way back to Sacramento, my mother had called and said, "Come over for dinner. Your brothers are here and I made dinner. I've been calling you all day. Where have you been?"

I explained to mom I was visiting a friend in the Bay Area and was on my way back home.

She replied, "Good… We'll see you in a bit."

I explained to her that I had Roxanne with me and I'd have to bring her. I knew mom didn't like my brothers or me just bringing women over for her to meet but she pretty much demanded I come over. I told moms that I'd catch them on the next round because I had this new chick with me but she insisted that I bring Roxanne with me to dinner, as long as I came.

Mom's specific words were, "Child, just bring her with you to dinner. I guess I can deal with this one. But I tell you son just find one and be content."

I told her, "Okay, but we can't stay long."

To this day, I don't know what the hell I was thinking about. Roxanne and I arrived at my parent's house and the moment Roxanne stepped out of the car it was as if the blindfold I'd kept across my eyes in all my dealings with her was finally lifted. Once I came around the car to open the door for Roxanne, my mouth dropped wide open. Why hadn't I noticed Roxanne was wearing a white see through shirt with a black bra, white stretch pants with a black G-sting, and had enough gold on to loan two necklaces to everyone in the G-Unit?

As I opened the door, Roxanne said, "Thank you, my nigga," stepped out and grabbed her stretch pants up to pull over her black G String that was showing above her pants. I stood there looking and feeling stuck. I couldn't say what I wanted to which was, "Who are you? I don't believe we've met." Roxanne reached in her purse, pulled out some very greasy looking lip-gloss, and applied it.

I looked at her pierced stomach, beat up toenails, pierced tongue, and three-inch fingernails, and wanted to get back in the car and drive the hell away from my parent's house. But I couldn't turn back now because it would be wrong. Roxanne and I were just friends, I reasoned as I rang the doorbell. I wasn't committed to her but it had been moms who had demanded that I bring her along.

As we waited for someone to open the door Roxanne said, "Dis is guen be fun!. I'm kinda nervous dough'

It was too late to give her a grammar lesson. My mother was going to kill me for bringing this woman here, even though she'd insisted!

I took one last glance at Roxanne as she adjusted her breasts so that they wouldn't stick out so much. My dad opened the door with mom quickly approaching behind him. Pops grinned like a fool and said, "Hell son! I mean hello son. And who is the lovely lady? Mmm!"

I thought, "What the hell is Mmm? Keep your drool off my girl!" I said instead, "Dad this is Roxanne. Roxanne this is my pops."

Roxanne said, "What up pops? How ya feeling and hanging today? You cool?"

Pops was happy to reply, "I'm good…I'm good. You two come on in."

As Roxanne and I walked in Dad cut me off, trying to follow the booty. My mom stopped Roxanne and I.

"Hello son" she said as she walked right past Roxanne and gave me a hug.

I said, "Mom this is Roxanne. Roxanne this is my moms."

I watched my mother play the role and say "Hello, welcome to our home. Make yourself comfortable baby. Go ahead and head into the living room." Roxanne went into the living room and moms gave me the meanest look in the universe and smacked me in the head as I walked by. She was not putting on the show for me that she had for the rest of the family. I tried not to take her dislike of Roxanne so personal, since it was she who ordered me to bring Roxanne home.

When I walked into the living room Jeremy whispered, "What up bruh? Let's roll to the bathroom to wash our hands." He then gave the nod to dad and Johnny to do the same. My two brothers, dad, and I headed to the restroom to get cleaned up.

The first thing pops said after he closed the door was, "Damn boy where did you find a woman with all that ass?" I looked at him like, you've gotta be kidding me!

Then my brothers chipped in with their bullshit. "Marcus damn, couldn't you buy her an outfit that fits and I can't see through? Marcus, did you pay for the tits? Marcus, juicy got you crazy?" Oh, it was on. I was the brunt of jokes for the next 6 months.

My dad said, "Son on a serious note, you know your mother doesn't like to see women dressed inappropriately. You know *I* don't mind but your mother is a bit more old fashioned."

Johnny chipped in, "Pops you just like looking at her tits."

We all laughed while I tried to explain, "Dad I told moms we were heading to my house! She insisted that we come over."

He said, "I know why you were heading to your house. Humph to handle that huh?" I laughed along with my brothers. We finished up in the bathroom and everyone was cordial to Roxanne for the rest of the evening, even moms, and Roxanne said she had a good time at the house. Although Roxanne was different, she was good people.

I would have kicked it with her longer but she lied to my family and I don't like liars, no matter what the reason. While we were eating dinner, moms had asked Roxanne what she did for a living.

Roxanne replied, "I manage a bank. I count the money in the vault for customers." Of all the job descriptions and duties, she said she counts the money in the vault at a bank for customers? Later we laughed our asses off about it and it was obviously different than what she told me she did. Later I found out that Roxanne's husband was in jail for running prostitutes and she was handling the girls until he was released on parole. I think she and I had lunch once after that but I couldn't get down like that with the prostitutes and pimps. To this day Moms pops me in the head every time she thinks about it.

When Cerise came downstairs, we jumped in our separate vehicles, and headed to my house. When we pulled up, I looked to see if Stanley was outside and didn't see him. This was the first time in I can't remember how long that he wasn't outside spying on my comings and goings. I rushed Cerise inside just so that I could have this one time without his comments or interruptions.

On the way to my house, we'd stopped at the waffle house to get something to bring home. We sat down in the kitchen to eat our breakfast just as the doorbell rang. I ignored it and the bell rang again. Cerise asked, "Aren't you going to answer the door? Or do you have something to hide?"

I gave her a *yeah right* look, said "humph" as I got up and headed for the door. The truth was I just didn't want any interruptions on my time with Cerise but I wasn't going to swell her head up by telling her that. I opened the door and Stanley was standing at my doorstep.

"Hey bruther, how ya doing?" He leaned to the left and I mimicked his movement. "Whew!" he said with a smile, "Nice! Uh, bruther do you have any music I can borrow for the night. Whew just one CD will do. I got a ton of music but I'm looking for something different than the Garth Brooks type stuff I usually listen to. I want something that's more, uh, ya know bruther, Whew!"

For the first time ever I had a chance to embarrass Stanley the way he was always embarrassing me. I could have taken the high road and cut him a break but where's the fun in that? Loudly I said, "Oh you want some love making music?"

Stanley put his fingers to his lips and said, "Shh, bruther!" he whispered, "Whew! Can we keep this low?" He again leaned over and tried to peek around me and I mimicked his actions, continuing to block his view. I smiled at Stanley as he brought his attention back to me. "Whew!" he shook his head as if he'd just remember why he'd come to my door. "So can you help me out? My fire is starting to go out and I need to get back."

Now I knew why he wasn't outside spying when I'd arrived home. He was inside hooking up Ramona for a change! "I got something for you," I told him, "You can keep it too. It'll get you back up and have her smoking like a chimney. Hold on, I'll be right back." I left a crack in the door and headed to the living room to grab Stanley a CD. I quickly searched through my burnt CD's and grabbed a copy of the one that said, "Get Naked Music" I'd bought from someone in a parking lot. I came back around the corner and I couldn't believe what I saw. Stanley had his damn head in the door trying to see into the kitchen. It reminded me of a puppy I once had. I would work with the puppy trying to train it to sit until I told it to get up. I'd walk away and the puppy would stay sitting until I was out of sight, then it would look around and slowly get up. The moment I would come around the corner the puppy would sit down as if it had been sitting there since I left. That's what Stanley reminded me of that instant because once he saw me although he didn't immediately rush to pull his head out of the door, he backed away slowly with his eyes closed, as if he couldn't see me, I couldn't see him, and he pulled the door back to the same position I'd left it in.

My man was a riot and a half. I chuckled as I opened the door and said, "Did you see what you were looking for?"

Stanley replied, "I wasn't looking around. The door opened and I tried to close it shut bruther…I did see her though…Whew she's hot like a Louisiana Hot Link!! Whew."

I handed Stanley the CD and said, "This will work. It'll make you sweat like a hog in the summer heat." His metaphors were starting to rub off on me.

Stanley's eyes grew round. Even more excited and agitated than usual, he said, :Sweet Bruther. Sweet… Damn, I'm ready! Bye." Stanley turned and hurried back to his house. I turned around and Cerise was standing there laughing so hard she had tears in her eyes.

She said, "Marcus you are a nut!"

We took our plates to the living room to eat and I told Cerise I was going to pamper her tonight.

"Pamper me? Hmmm what do you mean pamper me? Or are you talking about the type of pampering I received this morning?"

I smiled and replied, "Let me break it down for you. I will....never mind...you'll have to just experience it and if you don't feel completely spoiled and pampered then you can spank me."

Cerise laughed. "You might like that and not do a good job just so you can get spanked!"

"True, true," I said. We laughed and joked around a bit more while finishing dinner. "Okay," I said to Cerise, took her plate, and pulled her to her feet, "Head upstairs and change into your robe. Don't worry about wearing anything under it. Just come back downstairs. But give me about 10 minutes to prepare."

Cerise headed upstairs and I went into the downstairs guestroom and started the bath water for her. As the water ran, I poured in some aroma therapy bubble bath, turned on the stereo and put in a CD that played the sound of babbling brooks and ocean waves. I lit a few candles and turned off the light so the shadows danced on the walls, grabbed a few fluffy towels, and placed them on the sink for her to dry off when she finished soaking.

In the kitchen, I uncorked and poured two glass of Champagne and called for Cerise. I dimmed all the lights in the house for the perfect ambience. Cerise walked down in her bare feet. I looked up at her and my heart stopped. All I can say is she looked radiant. Her hair was pinned up and the electric blue silk robe she wore made her look sexier than ever. I handed her a glass of champagne and escorted her to the bathroom. She walked to the bathroom; looked in, and reached up to kiss me for a long moment.

I told her to call me once she got comfortable so I could come scrub her back. She smiled and said, "Oh, you aren't going to join me?"

I shook my head. "This is pamper Cerise night," I told her and gave her a light push. "Go on, let yourself be pampered, okay?"

She had a huge smile on her face when she said, "Okay, I'll call when I'm ready for you!" I walked into the living room sat down in the lazy boy chair and reclined.

Cerise soaked for 15 minutes before she called me, "Marcus can you come here please?" I grabbed the bottle of Champagne and headed to the bathroom. Cerise looked completely relaxed surrounded by suds. "Can you pour me another glass of Champagne?"

I smiled as I pulled the bottle from behind my back and poured her a glass. She said, "Oh you are on top of it!" I winked and went back to my lazy boy. The sound of the flowing river made its way into the living room and relaxed me as much as it probably was helping Cerise relax. This was nice. It was a cool CD. I guess I'd just never taken the time to listen to it.

I fell asleep for a few moments but woke up immediately when I heard Cerise call, "Marcus, I'm ready for you." I opened the door and saw Cerise deeply inhaling the scent of the aroma therapy bubble bath with her eyes closed.

When she opened them I said, "You look like you belong in a picture on my bedroom wall."

She smiled and said, "Are you getting in?"

I sat on the edge of the tub and replied, "Nope, its all about you right now. Hand me the wash cloth and soap." I began washing Cerise's back and neck. As the warm water ran down her frame, she closed her eyes enjoying the moment.

"Mmm Marcus, this is very nice!" I washed her legs, feet, and even between her toes. I wanted it all clean just in case I went there! Grabbing one of the towels I'd laid out, I held it up for Cerise. She stood up, and I began drying her off.

"I might get used to this type of treatment," she said.

"We'll see if you feel that way when you get my bill," I laughed and Cerise lightly hit me on the arm. I handed the towel to Cerise so she could finish drying off. "I'll meet you upstairs okay?" I told her, "I need another five minutes and then you can head up." I walked out of the bathroom and ran to try to find some self-heating massage oil I knew I had somewhere in my bathroom.

Five minutes on the dot Cerise came upstairs and I told her to lay face down on the bed. She removed the clip from her hair, it fell to her back.

I said, "Pin it back up baby we aren't finished yet," I told her. Cerise lay on the bed and laid the towel across her lower half. I grabbed the remote and played a CD containing the best slow jams of the century, I turned off the light and closed the door. It was dark but I knew where to go and what to do. I removed the towel, poured some oil into my hands, rubbed it to warm it up, and then began massaging Cerise.

"MMM that feels wonderful, Marcus." She said.

As I continued to give her a massage, Cerise moaned softly as I worked on rubbing the kinks out of her shoulders. I continued to pour oil and massage until I worked up a sweat. I finished massaging Cerise and slapped her ass lightly to let her know I was done. She pulled me down to kiss me and I was ready for some action!

"Can I get a little more pampering?" Cerise whispered.

"Cerise, you hussy! What do you mean?" I raised my eyebrows in mock surprise.

,"If you need instructions I guess you are not as smart as I thought you were" Cerise giggled.

"Oh ask your body when I'm finished did I need instructions." I said. Quickly disposing of my clothes, I joined Cerise on the bed, and this time it was Cerise sweating from the hour-long workout.

I must have dozed off because when I woke up Cerise was sitting in a chair at the bathroom sink. She was braiding her hair and humming an unfamiliar tune. I lay on the bed just admiring her and thinking how delicious it felt to wake up after such an intense lovemaking session and see Cerise with a smile on her face. I was ready to do it again!

"Hey, you ready for round two, sexy?"

"Oh you are awake! I tried to get a light nap but I must have put it on you brotha cause you were snoring like Captain ca ca Caveeeee Man!" Cerise said. We both cracked up and I threw a pillow at her.

"Get over here and give me a kiss with your crazy butt!" Cerise strolled over to me, leaned over, and gave me a kiss, rubbing my chest as she did. I love to have my chest rubbed. I said, "Mmm you smell like me," I said with a grin, "Ready to absorb my scent again?"

"I'm hungry. You worked all that dinner right out of my system. I want to go get some cheesecake Marcus. Do you mind?" She laughed and said.

It was only 8:45pm "Cool let's go." I said. I jumped up and pretended to be grabbing for my pants and underwear.

"Marcus, you gotta be kidding me?" Cerise said. I knew what she was about to say but I went with it.

"What?" I replied.

"Get in there and wash your funky balls man!" She said.

We both laughed as I threw another pillow at her. "I was just playing with you baby," I said, as I jumped in the shower, washed up quickly, and got dressed.

As Cerise and I headed downstairs, I said, "Lets take the Benz and lets see if we can leave without Stanley noticing us."

"Are you serious?" Cerise asked, "Is he really watching you that much?"

I said, "Oh yeah, Stanley seems to know when I'm leaving and when I return. So lets go through the garage. Maybe he only notices when I'm walking out the front door." We walked into the garage and sat down in the Benz. I leaned over, kissed Cerise, and said; "Now that was delicious."

She smiled and said, "Oh you like? Ready for round two?"

I smiled and said, "Oh yeah when we get back from getting dessert I'll be ready for that other dessert no doubt." Cerise looked at me in surprise.

"Wow Marcus, you are like the energizer bunny aren't you? You just keep going and going! Or is it all talk?"

I smiled at Cerise and said, "Oh, you'll find out soon enough whether it's all talk."

Just as I was about to turn the key, Cerise grabbed my hand and said "Hey I know how we can ditch Stanley. Are you down?"

I said, "Okay lets see what ya got. It won't work. Just fyi."

Cerise said, "We shall see."

Cerise hopped out of the car, stood on the car door's ledge, and pulled the little red handle that disconnected the garage from the opener. After Cerise pulled the lever releasing the garage from the mechanical device, she walked over to the garage door and flicked the light switch to the off position.

"What in the world are you doing?" I asked.

"Relax big boy, I wont break anything. Or are you afraid of the dark?" she said.

I replied, "Scared of the dark? Please, its dark when I'm down there between your soft and sexy legs! You don't ask if its too dark then did ya?" I got her back for the funky balls comment with that one.

She smiled and said, "Hmmm maybe you need to get back down there right now smarty pants."

I laughed and told her, "Nope...no more for you tonight. I see I'm going to have to ration out my stuff, you are so greedy!" We cracked up as Cerise left the garage and walked into the house.

Cerise was gone for about 5 minutes. She was taking this seriously! I turned on the radio and waited for her to return and when she did, she walked up to my drivers-side window. I rolled the window down and said, "Yes how can I help you?"

She said, "Okay, I'm going to open the garage. Do not start the car until we roll it out of the garage and onto the driveway. I'll jump in once you start the car. Just don't start it until I put the garage down."

I started laughing and replied, "Okay, but its not going to work."

"Marcus, don't be jealous cause you couldn't figure it out. So just go with it." she said. Cerise opened the garage and I placed my foot outside the door and began pushing the car backwards while she pushed from the front. The car rolled out of the garage and Cerise closed the garage and jumped inside. I looked all around for Stanley but he was nowhere to be seen. Ain't this something!

"Okay, lets go!" Cerise said, "What are you waiting for?" I started the car and backed out into the street and to both our amazement Stanley came bolting out of the house like a damn jackrabbit! I drove slowly to the corner and stopped at the stop sign.

I said to Cerise, "Look in the rear view mirror, but before you do take a wild guess who's running down the damn street."

She said, "Stanley?"

I replied, "Yep."

Stanley ran a house and a half down the street to my car. As he approached the driver's side window, he was breathing extremely hard. I rolled the window down, looked over at Cerise, stuck my tongue out at her, and mouthed, "I told you."

Stanley approached the window, "Whew bruther...I need to work out!! Whew Hew Hewwww! Bruther....I just had to tell ya just in case I didn't see you for a few days about my night!"

Didn't see me for a few days? Could that even be possible? I just smiled and said, "Okay, what is it Stanley?"

He paused and took a deep breath..."WHEW! Bruther, I rode it like a bronco busting bull bruther...she's knocked out! Whew...I hadn't made love like that in a few years whew! That CD was Hewww Weee perfect." Stanley threw both of his arms in the air, turned, and walked away, calling out one last "Whew!" I drove off as Cerise and I laughed until our stomachs hurt and we had tears in our eyes.

The best place to get cheesecake was at Shelby's if it wasn't too busy or the fools didn't show up. Shelby's was in the heart of the hood. It didn't matter though because everyone knew this was the place to go to get the best cheesecake. I asked Cerise, "You up for going to Shelby's?"

She said, "Well...okay. Why do they always put the good black establishments in the hood? Makes no sense." She was right about that no doubt.

While driving to Shelby's we talked a little about the last few months of Cerise's marriage, how happy she was that she hadn't slept with her husband in over a year now that she knew about his down low activities, and how she'd taken an AIDS test when she first suspected something was up with him. We talked about the man who'd been on Oprah and outted a whole slew of men who were married or with someone, didn't consider themselves gay, but had sex with men whenever they could.

"Marcus, how could a man endanger a sistah or any woman with shit like that?" Cerise asked. I had no answers for her. "This is the reason why black women are getting aids faster than anyone else, down low men!" I agreed with her.

Cerise and I continued the discussion until we arrived at the spot to get our sweet tooth satisfied. I was sick with the whole thought of down low and the danger Mike Ivan could have put Cerise in. It was time to jump-start my mind with some cheesecake and my body later with some good lovemaking. We walked in to Shelby's and looked for the lemon cheesecake, by far the best tasting cheesecake in the world. I once ate an entire pie while watching a movie. I looked over to Cerise as she looked through the glass at the varieties of sweets. I couldn't help but stare at her booty as she leaned over. "Hey Cerise you know what?"

She smiled and replied, "Please don't embarrass me Marcus." I looked at her and turned back around because who knows how she would have taken the comment that popped into my head. She slowly strolled over to me and whispered in my ear, "What were you going to say? Something probably to the effect that I taste better than your favorite pie?

I smiled and whispered back, "You taste better than all the pie in here except that one." I pointed to the lemon cheesecake I'd just spotted.

She and I laughed and Cerise said, "We'll see tonight buddy." I smiled as I stepped up to the counter and ordered my slice of cheesecake. Cerise eventually settled for apple pie with a scoop of vanilla ice cream.

As we walked over to a table I said, "I'm glad you and I are getting to know one another. You are one cool ass woman Cerise. Can I call you *C*?

It's nice and short and it has a more intimate ring to it. Plus when I'm hitting it from the back....C is much easier to say when I'm huffing and puffing trying to bring the house down."

Cerise laughed and sat there looking at me for a minute. She said, "You need counseling to get that one track mind out of the gutter. You are insatiable aren't you? But anyway, I don't generally like nicknames but that's cool. I like it. You can call me C."

I smiled and replied, "Cool. C.... I like that! I *like* that!" Cerise and I noticed three nigga's walk in, talking loudly while waiting at the register to be seated. I don't like referring to our people as 'nigga's' but I gotta agree with my man Chris Rock, you've got black people and you've got nigga's and I call it like I see it. One of the three was white but he was a nigga too in my book because he was trying to dress and act the role. They were probably in their late twenties standing fifteen feet from us and all I could hear was bitch this, bitch that...motherfucka this and that.

Cerise waved her hand in front of my face and asked, "Marcus, where did you go? What are you staring at?" as she turned around to see what had captured my attention. Why did she have to turn around because as soon as she did they all happened to look in our direction.

Cerise turned back around and said, "Oh, I see," she said and looked at me. "That's a look I haven't seen before. I need to go to the bathroom. I'll be right back. Don't get in any trouble baby."

I relaxed a little and told her, "Come on now, I don't start trouble baby. I may finish it but I never start it." Cerise stood up and walked past me to the restroom and I could see the nigga trio looking at her. I wasn't worried about folks staring because Cerise was nice, definitely nice to stare at. The hostess approached the counter to seat them and one of them pointed in my direction.

The host escorted them to an open booth two seats away from me. I eyed them and they eyed me as they approached and passed by single file. Initially my expression was open to a nod or what's up but the white boy in front gave me a funny ass look. I rolled my eyes and finished eating my cheesecake! The second cat had his mean mug face going but the last brotha gave me a subtle nod as he passed.

I figured Cerise and I should bail to avoid the bullshit that I could sense these fools wanted to start. We were almost finished anyway. I stood up and walked to the front counter to get our bill, ordered another cheesecake to go, and stood waiting for Cerise.

As she walked out of the bathroom, she had to pass the knuckleheads. As she approached, they started in with the comments. Just as she passed by, the white guy grabbed her wrist to stop her progress. I started walking in her direction but Cerise shook her head with a look that told me she could handle herself. I stopped short and continued to speak with the hostess but I kept my eye on the situation. When Cerise started to pull and the white boy wouldn't let go I cut the conversation short, walked over and, and while en-route he finally let go. Standing by Cerise's side, I stared the thug trio down.

"Come on C let's roll," I said and started to lead her away. The cat who, nodded earlier did so again.

As we walked away, the white cat said, "Yeah, take your bitch and get on."

I stopped, turned around, and looked at the three of them before addressing the white cat, "What the fuck did you say? Who the fuck do you think you are talking too. The only bitch I see is you." I said this in a deadly calm voice and by the time I was finished speaking I was about 3 inches from him. I looked at the other two and said, "Ya'll got a problem?"

The one who seemed to be leading the pack said, "I was all down for him holla'n but not disrespecting. He got to handle dis on his own."

I turned my attention back to the white boy, put my finger on his forehead, and said, "Apologize to my woman." If he said or did the wrong thing, I was itching to bust him up.

"I am sorry. I'm sorry," he said, looking past me and addressing Cerise.

As I turned to walk back to Cerise I heard him saying, "Ya'll fools are wrong for putting me up to that. Got dis big ass brotha ready to whoop my ass. You two ain't shit!"

The other two snickered, and I heard one of them say just as Cerise and I walked out the door, "Fool we were just playing and you went there with that big ole nigga. Your lucky he didn't stomp yo white ass right in this booth."

On the ride, home I still had some adrenaline flowing so I stayed quiet for a few minutes until I calmed myself down. After about five minutes, I said to C, "Sorry about that baby but I can't go out like that. I may downplay the part and dress nice but I will not allow a knucklehead to disrespect me or my lady."

Cerise grinned and said, "What are you talking about, I had your back homey! Like Bonnie and Clyde!" She knew that would get me to laugh, and it worked. Cerise balled up her fist and showed it to me. She said, "What's so funny? I am not afraid to scrap Marcus."

I laughed some more and Cerise started laughing too when I told her to imagine the headlines tomorrow if we both got into a fist fight in the hood. "Two prominent African American business owners were arrested tonight for throwing blows with peanut and ray-ray at Shelby's," I said in my best newscaster voice. We both cracked up some more and continued our drive to the house.

As we exited the freeway, I said to Cerise, "How much you want to bet that Stanley is out in the yard waiting for us to return?"

Cerise replied, "I'll take that bet. I don't think he'll be out there this time."

I laughed and said, "Cerise, I'm not even going to take you up on that bet. It would be like taking candy from a baby. Stanley is always outside when I'm away."

She said, "He wasn't when we pulled up earlier, even though he came to the door a split second later. I'll still take the bet but he can't be running outside or in the garage."

I thought about it for a second, "You got it! Okay so what are we betting?"

Cerise replied, "You said you wanted to bet. What is it you want or are willing to lose?" I sat there for a second thinking about what my prize would be for such an easy bet.

I then said, "Okay, if you lose, I want you to run me some bath water, bring some coffee to me as I bathe, and a full body massage."

Cerise nodded, "Now what do I get out of it when I win?"

I replied, "Whatever you want! You aren't going to win."

We were a few minutes from the house and Cerise sat there with a huge grin on her face. "What's so funny?" I asked.

Cerise replied, "Ooh, you better hope Stanley is outside because what I want will have you up all night long buddy!"

"Oh don't worry this is a walk in the park win for me. You'll be up all night serving me." Cerise and I both went back and forth trying to clarify our bets. Then it happened. I turned the corner and I didn't see Stanley!

Once I turned into the court and didn't see him, I drove down the street and made a U Turn.

Cerise laughed and replied, "What are you doing Marcus? You always park in the driveway or in the garage."

I said, "Baby I have neighborhood watch duties tonight and it's the rule to drive up and down the street a few times."

Cerise fell out laughing, "Marcus, you are too much for me!" she said, trying to control her fit. "Turn this car around and go park in the driveway. You lose. You lose. You lose!" She danced in her seat to the rhythm as she sang 'you lose' until I parked the car. She had beaten me at a game that I shouldn't have lost. I couldn't wait to see Stanley but what was I going to say? Why weren't you out spying on me tonight? Where were you? Damn! I stepped out of the car and looked around for Stanley. I couldn't believe it! He let me down! I walked over to the passenger door and opened it so Cerise could get out of the car. As she gathered her purse and coat, I stood there looking in the direction of Stanley's home.

Cerise stepped out of the car and said, "Baby quit looking around. He's not out here and face it, you'll be my love slave tonight!" Guess I wasn't too upset about losing the bet.

"Just for future reference," I told her, "we don't have to bet for me to sign up for those duties. I'll be your love slave without the bet baby."

Cerise smiled. "Oh yeah? That's interesting. Let me tell you what I had in mind."

I smiled and said, "Yeah tell me baby cause I'll be ya love slave right now."

Cerise said, "So you wanna take care of this body huh?"

I replied, "Oh yeah, like a mechanic working on his favorite car!"

She laughed and replied, "Good okay first you serve me some wine, wash my hair, then soak and rub my feet, give me a manicure, and then a massage to top it off. Then I'd send you out to get me a movie which I'll fall asleep watching."

My mouth dropped wide open. I said, "Whoa, whoa…that's not a love slave that's a slave, slave!" We both laughed.

Cerise replied, "Well looks like you better get ready to pamper me because I don't see Stanley outside."

We walked towards the front door and out of nowhere we heard a quick and sharp "whew." We both turned around and Stanley was nowhere insight. This wasn't hide and seek but I know what I heard. It was Stanley's patented "whew." I began staring at his home and near his bushes where he normally hung out. I said, "Stanley?" There was no response and Cerise looked around because she heard the call too.

Cerise said, "Did I hear a whew? Come on, let's go in before you start trying to change the bet up."

I said, "Whoa tiger, whoa. You heard what I heard and it sounded like Stanley was outside."

She replied, "I'm giving you 20 seconds and if Stanley isn't visible you lose."

I laughed. This was hilarious so I yelled, "All the all the outs in free!" Cerise jumped up and tried to cover my mouth but it was to late I got the words out and I got the bonus of holding a wiggling Cerise in my arms as she tried to shush me. I was laughing and calling the outs in and dodging Cerise. Finally, before my 20 seconds were up I called out, "I know I heard you Stanley!" Cerise started a countdown. When she reached 5, I said, "Okay, maybe he opened the door and yelled. You win." We turned around to walk in the house and Stanley gave me another, "whew hew!!" I said with a loud voice, "Stanley where are you? Why are you playing hide and seek?"

Then for some reason I couldn't explain I looked up and there was Stanley sitting on top of his roof. As soon as we made eye contact he said, "Yeah bruther...Yeah! I knew you'd see me! Damn! Whew!" Stanley waved to Cerise and said, "Hey biscuits and gravy. I see you. You are looking scrumptious." Cerise nodded her thanks but continued to look perplexed.

I had to do it. "Stanley, what in the world are you doing up there?" I asked. Stanley pointed towards the side of his house. As Cerise and I went to the side of his house to see what he was pointing at I said to her, "you lose I told you he'd be outside!" and stuck my tongue at her.

On the side of the house was the fallen ladder Stanley had used to get up there. "Stanley why are you on the roof? I see the ladder slipped. How long have you been up there?"

He said, "Cleaning the gutters bruther...I've been up here almost an hour whew, I'm glad you came home!! I didn't want to wake up my lady! Whew, bruther whew I'm glad you are back at the stable. Now, grab that there ladder and walk towards the front of the barn. It's easier to get down in front of the house."

I looked at Cerise and said, "I can handle this you should go get the Kings bath water ready!"

Cerise laughed and said, "Don't show out Marcus. See ya Stanley."

Stanley replied, "Okay Sista!"

I said, "You see how you have to talk to your queen Stanley." I did my best Mandingo voice and said, "Me King Marcus, fetch my water for my washing!"

Stanley's mouth dropped wide open. He stood there on the roof with a perplexed look on his face and said, "Yeah bruther....Yeah, uh whew!" Cerise overheard the interaction as she walked away and just laughed as she gave us the whatever hand up in the air.

Stanley began making his way down from the roof and said, "My woman, I mean my queen well she's been asleep the last hour because I rode that thang like a Pony!" Once Stanley was on the ground, he pumped his fist and yelled way too loud, " Whew Hewwwww...Go, Go, Go!" and hopped around smacking his ass as if it were the horses ass.

As soon as he did the front door opened up and the Ramona called out, "Get your crazy ass in here Stanley, and leave that man alone. Hi Marcus." She then put one thumb up and closed the door.

Stanley gave me a real low "Whew! Bruther Thanks. Well time for me to go." Stanley grabbed the ladder and walked into the garage.

I walked across the lawn but looked back when Stanley called my name. he has never used my name since I've known him, its always brother or bruther or something.

"Yeah?" I asked.

Stanley gave me a one-thumb deal and said "Hey bruther, she'd be a good ranch hand if ya know what I mean. Don't mess it up! Whew!"

I smiled and said, "I'll do my best buddy!"

As the garage stopped Stanley yelled, "Yeah bruther, Yeah!"

I walked in the house and I could hear Cerise running the bath water upstairs. I yelled, "That's what I'm talking about! Handle yo bizness baby!"

Cerise had a scowl in her voice. "Hush up Marcus," she fussed.

I laughed and called up, "Would you like me to pour us a glass of wine?"

She replied, "Sure but nothing too heavy." I chose a white merlot since it is not too strong seeing as it was getting late and we both had to get up in the morning for work and considering I planned to put in some more work tonight. I headed upstairs.

Cerise was standing there watching the water run. I walked up behind her and handed her a glass of wine. I wrapped my arms around her and said, "Mmm you smell delicious! That perfume is making me horny baby!"

She replied, "You like? You want to taste it"

"Oh yes, I do. I want to taste it baby."

Cerise said, "Oh I forgot, you won the bet, get in the tub!" We laughed as I slowly kissed her left shoulder and we stood watching the tub fill with water. The perfume that Cerise was wearing kept luring me back to her neck. I continued to gently kiss wherever the smell of perfume rested. I began swaying with Cerise as if music were playing. She caught the groove and we were moving in a rhythm that allowed our bodies to feel one another. I was hard and she was soft. What a combination! I grabbed the remote and hit the random play button. I turned and sat on the edge of the tub and Cerise straddled me.

Cerise said, "Don't fall in the water!"

I said, "Oh this feels to good to mess it up by falling into the water." I took a sip off my wine and began kissing her along her neck and chest.

Cerise exhaled and said, "Marcus…Marcus is this your part of the bet? Or are you making this up as we go along?"

I said, "Oh yeah this is what I had in mind baby."

She laughed and replied, "Yeah right Marcus."

I took another sip of wine and began kissing Cerise's chin and neck. Cerise brought her hand up and touched my lips. I licked her fingers and nibbled at the palm of her hand. Cerise grabbed the back of my neck and whispered, "Hmmm that's nice. I like that baby. I didn't even know about that spot."

"Oh you haven't seen anything yet baby. I'll find spots you didn't know you had."

She grinned. "Well do your thing Marc baby."

I ran my hands along her thighs. What was I thinking? I had moved my hand that I was using to balance the two of us. As soon as I thought about it, Cerise leaned further into me deepening our kiss and just like that SPLASH! We fell into the tub with Cerise on top of me! She may have been trying to drown me because it took her forever to get off of me! The tub is huge so we fell in without hitting our heads or breaking anything. When I came up out of the water Cerise said as she laughed uncontrollably, "What are you doing crazy man, trying to drown us?"

I spit out the water I had taken in and said, "What took you so long to get up?"

She laughed and replied, "My leg was under you remember!" We laughed as Cerise grabbed her wet dress and tried to lift it up to take it off. I walked over to help, placed my hands on her waist, and slowly raised the dress above her head. I dropped the dress and Cerise jumped up and wrapped her legs around my waist as I carried her to the bed. Cerise and I made love for two hours and then fell into a deep sleep without making it back to the bathtub.

WHAT CAN A BROTHER DO FOR ME?

The alarm clock woke me at 5am the next morning. I looked up and Cerise was already getting ready for work. I sat up in bed, "Why didn't you wake me up?" I asked groggily.

"Baby you've been snoring hard the last hour. I must have put it on you something fierce last night because you rolled over, played dead, and didn't move the rest of the night." She said with a grin as she struggled into her heels.

"Oh you are talking mess early this morning I see. Don't make me get up and put it on you! I'll have you doing the funny walk at work today!"

She opened her mouth wide and said, "Oh no, you didn't go there Marcus." She busted up laughing and said, "Get in the shower!"

Cerise went downstairs as I jumped in the shower. When I got out, she'd returned with two cups of coffee. I could get used to this! I took the cup from her and gave her a good morning kiss. I said, "Mmm…Its nice to see you this morning." Cerise looked stunning in the blue business suit she was wearing. I said, "You have something important to tend to today?"

She said, "No I just wanted to look cute as usual."

I smiled, "Well you succeeded, you are looking sexy baby."

She reached up, placed her hand around my neck, brought my face down for a much more thorough good morning kiss, looked in my eyes and said, "Thank you, sweetie." She gave another quick peck and then dashed out the door for work. I didn't suggest she come back tonight because I knew she would need to spend some time acclimating to being on her own in that big house.

While driving to work, I checked my voicemail and Tyler reminded me of our scheduled appointment once again. I felt bad for Tyler because he treated Jasmine well, or at least he did in the presence of family and friends. She'd always seemed happy to be with Tyler every time I'd seen here. I called Tyler on the phone. "Hello T, what's up my man? You eat?"

He replied, "Oh yes boss. I ate. As a matter of fact I have a thermo of hot coffee waiting for you."

I said, "Okay now your talking. You know how to get some service from me! So where are you and where are we meeting?"

"Lets meet at Steven's Records and Books," he said.

I replied, "I'll see you in 40 minutes."

I arrived at Steven's Records and Books and Tyler was standing outside his car reading the newspaper. I pulled up next to Tyler and said, "Jump in lets roll. Don't forget the coffee." Tyler jumped in and handed me a full thermo of coffee. I opened it up and took a whiff. "Mmm where did you get this coffee? It smells very good. They use very good beans."

Tyler said, "Yeah boss, I drove to Davis to get that coffee from your friend that runs Covenant Cafe and Coffee House as a thank you."

I replied, "Okay, now you're working it right! Hook ya boss up!" We both laughed as we drove to his place.

Tyler and I drove past his house and at 7am in the morning Jasmine's car was still in the driveway. I found a good spot to set up surveillance as we sat and shot the shit for a little while. I still had a feeling that Tyler was wrong about his hunch again but I didn't say anything. As Tyler sat reading the paper, I sipped on my coffee and stared at his house.

"Tyler so how are things at home? Are you two talking or what's the deal?" I asked.

He replied, "Marcus, I haven't been home since Tuesday. I told Jasmine that I was going out of town until Friday evening and last night I sat watching the house."

"Did she leave the house or did anyone come to visit?" I asked.

He said, "No. It was pretty quiet, but I have a bad feeling about this." Tyler shook his head, "I can't think about it too much, it makes me crazy. Enough about me, word on the street is you and Cerise Ivan are a couple...any truth to that?"

How in the world had word spread so fast? I'm not even sure how it got out. But I couldn't lie to my man. "Yeah she's pretty special to me. I haven't had this much fun with someone in a long while." Tyler and I talked for about 2 hours, it was now 9am, and then we finally got some action. Jasmine came out of the house, jumped in the car, and began backing out of the driveway.

I said, "Tyler we have some action she getting mobile. Any idea where she could be going?"

He said, "I don't have a clue. She's never left the house this early and I doubt she's going to the gym. Now do you believe me?"

Tyler and I followed Jasmine until we reached a small town called Visalia. Visalia is located about 15 minutes just outside the city of Fresno.

Jasmine parked in the driveway, removed her overnight bag from the trunk of the car, walked to the door, and rang the doorbell.

A man answered the door smiling and Jasmine stepped inside. Tyler started to get out of the truck and I asked, "Where are you going?"

He said, "To get my girl boss. She is about to have an affair and I will not stand for this. I am going to go knock on the door and say my piece."

"Tyler you can't. If you go up there and things go wrong then what?"

He said, "Boss, I can't sit here and allow her to have an affair while I'm out here waiting. What in the hell do you want me to do?" I didn't really know what to say because I could imagine how he felt.

I said, "Okay. Let's think this through real quick. I'll take the…" I couldn't continue. "Shit!" I said. "Shit, shit! If it was my woman, I wouldn't be sitting in this car! Fuck it Tyler, lets go get your girl!" I said, "Okay, for the last time, you sure you want to do this?"

Tyler said, "Damn straight I want to do this! I have to let my presence be known or else I'm not a man about mine." Tyler and I sat in the car for 30 minutes not saying a word. I was waiting for him to make the first move.

I said, "You okay? We don't have to do this if you don't want to T. I am with you either way."

He said, "Thanks. I was just sitting here thinking about the entire situation and my first thought was to turn away and go home. I thought maybe your advice was good for me. I sat here and weighed the pros and cons of it all and it's on. Let's roll."

Tyler jumped out of the car and we headed to the front door. I rang the doorbell as we waited for an answer. I began knocking with a firm stroke and still no reply.

Tyler said, "Fuck it lets blow the door boss."

I grabbed him and said, "Oh hell no. We aren't going to jail. We are going to do this right or not at all."

Tyler walked around the side of the house and made his way towards the backyard. A couple of minutes later, I heard Tyler yell, "Jasmine, what are you doing? Come to the door now! Jasmine don't make me come in there and get you!" As soon as he finished the statement, the front door opened, and Jasmine rushed out, looking at me with shame on her face, clutching at her shirt to keep it closed, and ran to her car. She jumped in her car, backed out, peeled down the street. Tyler came around the corner a few seconds later.

"Tyler she just ran out of there a second ago and drove off!" I told him.

"Well why in the hell didn't you stop her?" he hollered. I gave him that freebie because I had a pretty good idea what he'd seen when he'd gone to the back.

I said, "For what? You have what you want, she's out of there now let's roll."

"Damn!" Tyler shouted and slammed the gate closed.

As the gate closed, the front door opened and the same man rushed outside with a baseball bat. "I don't know what the hell is going on fellas but I am about to start cracking some heads open!" The guy started walking towards Tyler and actually took a swing, which Tyler dodged. Tyler beat feet behind the car as the man turned on me.

I stood my ground. "Let me tell you something before you swing the fucking bat at me. You better hit me when you swing cause if you miss, I'll kill you." The guy stood there for a second contemplating if his next move was smart. I said, "I'm not running so if you swing you cant afford to miss. I ought to whoop your ass for the problems you've caused my man." The bat stayed where it was. I wasn't scared of no cat with a bat. Either he'd hit me or I'd whoop his ass, that was the gist of it.

He said, "Fuck you tough guy. And fuck him too!" He pointed the bat at Tyler. "He can't take care of his woman and she doesn't want to be with him anymore. She belongs to me now!"

I took a step forward, "Let me tell you something else, if she comes here again, I'll personally kick your ass each time her car is in your driveway." This fellow was bolder than I gave him credit for. He approached me with the bat, swung, and missed. It was my turn now. I whooped his ass for about 30 seconds, knocking this wanna be tough guy to the ground and straddled him as he lay on his back. His mouth was busted from the two times I popped him and a bruise on the cheekbone from other contact. I said, "I told you if you swung that bat and missed I'd whoop your ass. You didn't believe me?"

He replied, "Fuck you." I slapped him across the face and he began crying.

I said, "Lets start over. I told you that I would whoop your ass if you swung that bat and missed correct?" As I sat there on his chest, I looked around for Tyler and he was still behind the car staring in amazement. I looked down at this guy and said, "Do we have an understanding?"

He said, "You can't tell me what to...." SMACK! I slapped him again. I had to slap him because one he wanted to hit me with that bat and two he still hadn't recognized I was in control at this point.

"Okay sir, okay sir. I wont see her again. She's not worth this and I am sorry for swinging the bat at you!"

I stood up and handed Mr. Nobody his bat. "Sorry it had to happen like this. I asked you not to swing the bat!" I turned and walked away as Tyler and I got in the truck and drove off.

Tyler and I didn't talk the entire way home. Once we reached town Tyler said, "Damn boss. I don't know how to thank you. He probably would have bashed my brains in had you not been there."

I said, "Don't worry about it, Tyler. It's Friday and it's only mid-day and already look at the craziness that's happened. The good thing is we didn't go to jail. You were right though. I'm sorry I doubted your hunch." I told him.

I pulled in the record store parking lot and parked next to Tyler's car. "So what are you going to do man?" Tyler shrugged his shoulders. "I know there is nothing worse that unsolicited advice," I began, "but let me give you some unsolicited advice. Go home and talk to your woman. It's worth repairing. You and I both know she means the world to you. If you need some time to work things out, you can always crash at my place until you figure out what you want to do. Okay?"

I could tell my man was on the verge of tears. I sat in the car with Tyler and we talked for a while longer until Tyler collected himself, clenched his jaw, and stuck out his hand. I shook it. "You are gonna be okay man," I told him. "No matter what happens between you and Jasmine, you'll be okay.

"You are the best Marcus," he said. "I gotta go find my woman and work some stuff out. I'll let you know about the crashing offer after I talk to her." Tyler grabbed his things and exited my vehicle. I waved as I drove off. Poor man.

On my way home, I called Cerise to see how she was doing. We made plans to go to dinner but after, as I'd suspected she might, Cerise was going to go home and get rid of anything else that belonged to Mike. I wanted to offer my assistance but knew this was probably something she wanted to do by herself.

I'D RATHER

For the next several months, Cerise and I saw as much of each other as we could. Her divorce went through without a hitch and we both breathed a sigh of relief that she was now legally a free woman once again. I didn't give her a chance to look around at other options, because I occupied as much of her free time as I could. Plus, she didn't seem to want to explore any other options than me.

I took her around to meet my folks one Sunday after I'd let my mother talk me into going to church with her. I extended the offer to attend services to Cerise and to my surprise she accepted. At dinner at my parents house Cerise met my parents, Jeremy and Johnny and their spouses. Everyone loved her. Since then, we've been going to church together as often as we can.

We even doubled a couple of times with Tyler and Ashley. He'd left Jasmine after making an effort to forgive her. He couldn't and moved out. He stayed at my house for a couple of weeks and, with Ashley's help, found a nice condo on the river. I guess the two of them got closer during the time she'd been helping him and were casually dating, waiting to see how things went. I wholeheartedly approved of the relationship. I don't encourage office romances but when you find love, you can't just let it pass you by because you work in the same building.

Kevin had nothing but nice things to say about her as well. We doubled with him and whomever he happened to be dating lately. I could tell from the way he seemed to admire the growing relationship between Cerise and me, Kevin might be getting tired of his constant string of women. He'd never admit it so I never brought it up, but he did ask me if Cerise had any friends like her. Cerise tried to hook him up with her girl Bernadette but between her schedule and Kevin's, Cerise was never able to pull it off, and she eventually stopped trying. I wished my buddy could find someone as wonderful as Cerise and that he'd treat her right so she'd stay.

I met all of Cerise's family and friends and they all seemed to like me as well. Her girls were crazy and wild but they were cool. When I finally met Cerise's mom, I told her she reminded me of Diahann Carroll and she's loved me ever since.

But during those months, everything didn't always go smoothly and there was a time or two that I thought Cerise and I weren't going to make it. For instance, when Cerise told me she wasn't going to change her last name unless she got married again, I walked around salty as all hell for weeks, thinking maybe she wanted to hold on to that piece of Mike Ivan because she still had feelings for him. When Cerise found out what was causing my foul mood, she told me it was strictly a business decision. I tried to convince her that her business could survive a name change now and later if she got married. She wasn't hearing it and I finally had to suck it up and accept her decision but maintain my stance her business wouldn't suffer behind a simple name change. Later, when I found out Tammy was still working at Xellron, and still incompetent as hell, I told Cerise she should fire her. Cerise exploded and accused me of thinking she didn't know how to run her own damn company. After that argument blew over, we decided maybe it was best if we didn't discuss our respective businesses unless it was necessary.

Then there was the time Cerise thought I was cheating on her. She ran into Sheila at her doctor's office when she went to get her yearly physical. Just my luck the two of them would share the same OB/GYN! I'd spoken with Donna occasionally and let her know I was still with Cerise and happy. Donna claimed to be happy for me and had obviously shared the news with Sheila. Everyone in the city knew what Cerise looked like because her picture was plastered in the local newspapers and even some national magazines because a deal she'd brokered awhile back was turning out to be a huge business success.

Apparently, Sheila approached Cerise in the waiting room, told Cerise I was sleeping with her, described my house to a "T" and even threw in a lie about how much Stanley loved her. "I'm just telling you this so you know what kind of dog you are dating. He's going to make a fool of you!" Sheila told Cerise and stormed out of the office. Cerise sat there waiting to be called and fought back tears and humiliation. Everyone in the office had heard what Sheila had said.

When I saw Cerise that night she slapped me so hard I saw stars. I could tell from the blazing look in her eyes that if she'd had a gun I'd have been a dead man. I eventually got the story out of her and spent days trying to convince her that Sheila had been lying, without giving up too much information about what had really taken place with Sheila in the past. It was an ugly story, one I wasn't proud of, and if Cerise never found out about it I'd be more than fine with that. But it was impossible to get through to her since she wasn't even taking my calls. I copped an attitude behind Cerise's funky attitude and stopped trying to get in touch with her.

Kevin knocked some sense into me. "Man, if you are gonna kick that fine, rich ass honey to the curb because you got too much damn pride to tell her the truth, you're a *got*damn fool."

I waved my hand at him, "Just drop it man, it's done." I said.

Kevin got a huge grin on his face. "Word man? Hey, if that's the case, can I get her number? You think I got a shot?" Kevin knew the right thing to say to get my ass in motion. I told him if he even *thought* of stepping to Cerise he was a dead man. But I knew if it wasn't Kevin, the city was filled with men of all races lining up to try and be next in line behind me. I couldn't let that happen.

I broke down and showed up at her house a week into the stand off with two dozen, blood red roses, and a story I knew Cerise did not want to hear. She was disgusted with me when she found out I'd been with Sheila the same night I'd had Cerise to my house that first time. The worst part, the part that caused Cerise to slap me again and throw my roses back at me, vase and all, was when I came clean and told her I'd lied about Donna not being an ex of mine. I told her I'd been with Donna the very night before Cerise and I met up again at Bucks that second time. It hurt her so bad because she and I had been inseparable since then but she knew, and I didn't deny, that I'd never have told her the truth if Sheila's ass hadn't opened up my Pandora's box of secrets. It made perfect sense to her now why Donna had been so shocked when Cerise had opened my door.

It took a lot of time, and a lot of trust on Cerise's part, to work past that ugly episode and for her to know I really hadn't been screwing around with Sheila or Donna since that second meeting with Cerise at Bucks. Eventually she came to realize Sheila had just been trying to throw salt in my game because she was still pissed with me for passing her over *and* for being with Donna on the night of my birthday. It took a while but things eventually got back to normal.

Another incident occurred, right before Christmas, and I was the one who almost broke up with Cerise.

I was coming off a surveillance on a case I'd decided I wanted to work alone. It was around 6:30pm, I realized Cerise and I hadn't made any plans to see each other that night, and I wanted to see my baby.

I called Xellron Inc. to see if Cerise was still in the office but the phone rang and rang until the answering machine picked up. I tried to reach Cerise on her cell-phone but she didn't answer that either. I called her house. Again, no luck. I decided to stop by my office to make sure things were okay and to my surprise there was one car still in the parking lot. Not Tyler's this time. It was Ashley's.

As I walked into the office I saw Ashley and I asked, "Hey what are you still doing here so late on a Friday? Everything alright with you and Tyler? You two don't have plans?"

Ashley said, "I'm finished here and on my way out now, and everything is *more* than alright with Tyler. Umph!" She exclaimed, and trembled as a chill shook her.

"*Alright*!" I said with mock sternness. "Enough of that! I don't wanna hear stuff like that woman!" We both laughed as I asked her, "But if that's the case why aren't you with him instead of staying so late?"

"I just wanted to finish up a few files that will need your attention on Monday. Gotta earn that huge Christmas bonus you are going to be giving, right?" Ashley said with a sly grin. "Have a great weekend boss!"

"Hey, before you cut out, is there anything of importance that I need to take care of this evening?"

She put her hand on her hip and did the sista head roll. It always cracked me up to see her Buffy looking self pulling some b-girl moves.

"Come on boss," she laughed, "Are you new around here or something? You of all people know if there was anything urgent I'd be on it or I'd call you or Tyler ASAP. Nothing urgent. There is one case that you'll find interesting but it's not a rush. The client is out of town for two weeks and wants to meet with you when he returns. We handled one small fire drill and the paperwork is on your desk. Again, have a good weekend, now can I go?"

"You are getting too big for your britches" I shook my finger at her. "No there's nothing else. Thank you, now leave the premises, and go find my boy. Have a good weekend crazy chick." She grinned at me as she left. I was never ever going to fire her. That girl was the backbone of this company.

Since there was no need to go in I turned around and headed back to my car. I called my home phone and car cell-phone and there were no messages. I decided to swing by Cerise's house and see if she was home. I pulled up to her house and the Navigator was parked in the driveway. I jumped out and headed to the front door. As I passed, I touched the hood to see if there was any heat coming from the engine. The hood was still fairly warm. She may have been home twenty minutes at most, considering how cold it was outside.

As I walked to the door, I began thinking about where she and I would eat tonight. I didn't feel like cooking. Maybe I would ask her to cook since in all the time we'd been together I'd never tasted her cooking so I wasn't sure if she could burn or not. Cerise was always talking about how well she could cook but I had to taste it to believe it.

Laughing to myself, I had to check myself because my mind was in the gutter, as always. If her cooking tasted even half as good as she did, then I had struck gold and would have no choice but to marry her!

I rang the doorbell but got no answer. I laughed as I yelled out, "Hey Cerise answer the door, its papichulo, remember you called me that last night? Time for your dose of chocolate love!"

I stood there as the normal time for a person to answer the door had passed. Maybe Cerise was in the restroom doing a number two and I didn't want to interrupt. I sat down on the edge of a huge planter and waited, thinking about how I could please her mind and body tonight. Maybe I could handcuff her with a tie while I made a banana split on her body. I'd use some ice cream; whip cream, cherries, bananas, and nuts. Deez nuts! Cerise would bop me on the head when she heard my joke but I knew I'd be dining off a banana split later tonight. I laughed to myself as I continued to sit there waiting for Cerise to open the door.

It was taking her a long time to answer the door so I pulled out my phone and called the house phone and I could hear it ringing and then stop as it went to voicemail. I leaned over and rang the doorbell again. "Come on Cerise, get off the pot and come answer the door," I called out.

I called her cell-phone and it went straight to voicemail. I wondered if maybe she came by with a girlfriend and they drove off together. I walked to the car, grabbed a receipt from my wallet, and scribbled a note. "Hey lady, give me a call when you get a chance. Maybe we can still get a bite to eat if its not to late. Marcus." I went back, wedged the note between the door and the frame. I walked back to the car, turned to look to see if the note was in a visible spot, and noticed the blind snap shut. Someone inside had been watching me.

I stood for a moment wondering if I'd imagined it, but I'd been a cop and a PI for too long for my mind to play those kinds of tricks on me. The damn blinds had moved and I hadn't imagine it. I walked back over and rang the doorbell. Maybe Cerise had been sleeping and had peeked out to see who was making all the noise.

I stood there waiting for Cerise to open the door but she never did. I got a strange feeling in my gut. Maybe she couldn't open the door. Maybe Mike had shown up and decided to act a fool, demand some more money. Anything could be going on inside that house. I decided to walk around back to make sure things were okay. I downplayed the possibility of anything terrible going on in the house but I still walked over to the side gate and pulled the chain. The gate was locked.

I took hold of the fence, pulled myself up, and jumped over to the other side. Damn, there better be an emergency in there because this was some bullshit. What was I doing jumping a damn fence? I am way too old for this shit. I walked in the rocks along the side of her house, peeked into the kitchen, and noticed the stove was on. Cerise was home no doubt because I know she wouldn't put food in the oven and leave.

I reached the sliding back door and the screen was closed but the door open. As I approached the door to take a peek and see what was going on out of nowhere Cerise showed up. I smiled and said, "Hey, what's up. I was worried about you."

I reached out to open the slider and Cerise said, "Go away Marcus. Go away!" and the heifer closed the door. I heard the lock click, and then she slid the blinds closed! I started laughing of course because this was hilarious. I must have startled her or woken her and she was just joking around, paying me back. A few seconds went by as I stood at the door waiting for Cerise to open the door but she never did. I called on the cell-phone and house phone and Cerise ignored my calls.

Ain't this some bullshit, I thought. I called one last time on the house phone and said, "What's up? You have a brotha outside locked in and you wont answer the door. What's the deal Cerise? I wasn't in the mood to call her "C". She never picked up the phone.

Fuck! I had to jump that damn fence again. It wouldn't have been so bad if the fence was sturdy but it wasn't. It was old and rickety. I'd told Cerise a hundred times she needed to have it replaced but she was always too busy to get around to it.

I climbed up on the fence and fell off on the other side. I was pissed at this point because I was only back there in the first place just trying to make sure she was okay but now I'd busted my ass falling climbing back over her damn fence since she wouldn't let me in.

If she were not at home, shame on me for over reacting, but her ass *was* home and not in any apparent danger so I had big issues with this incident.

I sat in the car tending to my bruises and scrapes, before starting the car. I called Cerise on the cell-phone, knowing she wouldn't answer, and left one last message. "What the hell was that all about? If you've got company just say that, don't start treating me like shit. If you don't have company, why in the hell didn't you answer the phone or let me in? Damn, I thought things were good between us. I guess not."

I drove away with a battered ego and a million thoughts running through my mind. Was I wrong for climbing her fence? I didn't think so. In all the time we'd dated, I'd always been able to reach Cerise at one of her numbers. She'd take my calls even if she was in a meeting! And damn-it, I'd been concerned that she might be in some kind of danger or predicament, not trying to snoop!

On that long drive back to my house, I tried to figure out why Cerise had dogged me out so quickly once she'd seen me outside her glass door. If she was holing up with some other nigga, or white man, given that she'd married one, or even some other girl because, shit, you never know nowadays, my time with Donna had taught me to expect the unexpected, I could understand that. What I just couldn't understand was why she brushed me off as if I were some chump.

Replaying the incident in my head was making me crazy. I turned on some music and tried to chill. My mobile phone vibrated and played the island song I'd programmed it to play and the caller ID showed it was Cerise on her cell-phone. I pressed the button to ignore her call and drove to a liquor store in the hood looking to find peace of mind from a bottle.

Before I got out of the truck the phone vibrated once more and the happy island song played again. I checked the number. Cerise again. I clicked it to answer the call. "Hello?" I said with a wooden voice. Cerise said, "Hello. Hey Marcus, what's up? You startled me ya know. I was shocked to see you in my yard."

I didn't say anything as I sat there listening to Cerise tell me how I shouldn't have jumped her fence and invaded her privacy. I acknowledged what she said with a few "umm hmmm...okay...hmmm umm hmmms," and then for good measure, Cerise turned the knife in my back and said, "For all I know, you could easily be stalking me Marcus."

I couldn't take it anymore! "Who the fuck do you think you are talking shit about stalking? When I was between your legs sucking your clit, were you worried about me stalking you? When you screamed out 'fuck me papichulo' last night, were you worried about me being a damn stalker? Don't you ever come at me with some stalking shit *Cerise*. If you think you are that damn important, grab the phone book and count the women in there. Any one of them would be happy as hell that I was enough about them that I did what I did. Find Sheila or Donna's name in there! They'd have welcomed me in! I was concerned about *your* trifling ass. What in the hell was I to think? Your sorry ass ex husband hasn't been gone a year! He could have had you in a very bad spot and I wanted to be there for you if you needed me. But since you think I would or could stalk you...believe you me, you don't have to worry about me jumping your fence again or invading your privacy. Any parts of your *privacy*."

I hung up and threw my phone into the back seat of the truck. I walked into the liquor store and bought a bottle of Johnny Walker Blue Label. This was going to be a lonely weekend, obviously, and I might as well bust out the barbeque grill and cook a steak to go with my expensive whiskey. Damn the weather! Fuck the fog! My weekend plans were set.

As I turned the corner to my street the first thing I saw was Stanley, sitting in his lawn chair, sipping a soda, soaking up the few minutes of sunshine the winter offered.

Stanley! Now there was a person who knew about loyalty. He was faithful about his spying on me and was out there no matter what the weather. After that bet with Cerise so long ago, I had to admit to myself I'd grown accustomed to seeing him when I got home. His antics just caused me to realize this was one crazy as hell individual and I was just glad he was on my side. I'd hate to think of the damage he could do otherwise. Even Cerise could hardly wait to see him whenever we pulled up to my house. But fuck her and the horse she rode in on. I was just glad my boy was sitting out there drinking a generic supermarket cola waiting for me to arrive home. At least I could still count on some things.

There was a car parked in my driveway that I didn't recognize. I drove past my house, made a U turn, and parked in front at the curb. I could see that there wasn't anyone in the car. The only person who'd be dumb enough to snoop around was Donna or Sheila. I opened my car door and Stanley was right there with a report, bless him.

"Hey bruther! She went around the side of your stable, whew! I started to go in the house to get my pistol, but then she blew me a kiss so I knows exactly which pony was loose in the barn bruther even though I ain't seen her in a long time! After that airborne kiss, I recognized my baby from back in the day! The one who flashed those glorious ta-ta's at me! Whewee! Whew! You need any help? She's back there, sitting in one of your lawn chairs buddy. Bruther brotha," Stanley giggled, "She's hooked! She returned to the stable without even being summoned, right?" Stanley eyed me for confirmation that I hadn't called Donna. I shook my head and Stanley let out another, "Awhewee! Bruther you and John Wayne would have made one hell of a team!"

I stood there trying to digest everything Stanley was telling me, but he wasn't finished. "Now go get rid of her before my sexy biscuit gets here. Whew, Hew! Gosh dern right!"

I guess Donna heard Stanley making all that noise because she came walking up from the side of my house. "Hey Marc. *Hello again, sexy Stan"*

Stanley blushed from ear to ear and put two thumbs up in Donna's direction, then bolted. As he crossed the lawn he shouted over his shoulder, "Whew Bruther…You *are* the master rancher! Whew!"

In spite of my mood I took a second to laugh at my faithful friend's antics before turning to Donna and asking angrily, "What are you doing here? You're just popping up without calling again? What's up with that?

Ain't that some shit! An epiphany! Donna's showing up out of the blue caused me to understand what, I guess, Cerise was saying about me popping up without her approval. I called Cerise a thousand times though, damn it!

Donna said, "Have you moved her in Marcus? Is that why you are mad? I thought we were friends! I wasn't worried about if she was here or not. I stopped by to check on you like I've always done. After so much time I didn't think you'd mind."

"Hell no the bitch didn't move in," I told her, "But I also recall telling your ass not to pop up here unannounced as well. What are you up to? I told you if I wanted a booty call I'd call *you*," I said harshly.

Donna looked at me for a long moment and then said, "Damn Marcus! I thought we'd moved past that." She wiped a tear from her eye and said, "What are you being so mean to me for? What's got you all in a huff?" I started to speak, to apologize, but Donna blew right though my hesitant response. "Save it. I see you don't have time for me. I'll leave! See you later, *friend!*"

Too much shit coming all at me at once fried my brain. I watched as Donna threw herself into the car. I threw my head back and begged heaven for a moment of peace.

"Wait! Wait, goddamn-it!" Donna didn't slam her car door closed. I guess I was making progress on this shitty day. I told her, "Look, it's just been a long day and I'm tired. Wanna come in and have a beer?"

Donna gave me a teary smile. "Yes, I'd love that, but I can't stay long. I need to meet Shelia in a couple of hours for dinner. We're going out to eat tonight."

I smiled falsely, "How are you and bitch ass, trifling, trying to destroy Marcus' happiness, Sheila doing? Before you stomped off to your car you seemed to be pretty happy."

Donna laughed at my description of her partner and replied, "It's going okay Marc. It's okay. In spite of the salt Sheila tried to throw your way, she and I are good. I checked her on that bullshit and you won't have to worry about her again. Also, she won't ever lay another hand on me and I will never again have to show up here bruised and battered. I took a page from your book and told Sheila if she ever laid her hand on me again, I'd kill her. You were always quick to tell somebody you'd kick their ass if they fucked with you." Donna paused a moment then continued, "Now, are you still with Ms. big-shot what's her name, all over the magazines I ran into the last time I was here or can I call her a bitch now too?"

"Aren't *we* nosey," I said, avoiding her question. Donna replied, "Well its no secret Marc." Donna laughed, "Remember that time I showed up here looking for some comfort because Sheila knocked me upside the head? Your Ms. Thing looked at me as if *she* were ready to kick my ass when she opened the door."

That got me to laugh. "Her name is Cerise, Donna, I've told you a hundred times."

I knew having Donna here was complicating things but I needed the company and conversation at the time. It would definitely take my mind off the incident that had just occurred.

"So how are the two of you doing?" Donna asked again.

I replied, "We are doing cool. It's all good. Why do you ask?"

Donna said, "Never mind I see this line of questioning has you on the defensive." She folded her arms and leaned back against her car.

"My bad Dee, I'm just tripping a bit I guess."

A six-pack of beer and more than a few shots of JWB later Donna sat back on the couch and asked, "So Marcus, what have you done to mess things up with Ms. Perfect?" We both began laughing. I just shook my head. "Fine, don't tell me! Fuck you nigga!" Donna said, stood up, and burped extremely loud and blew her beer breath in the opposite direction and said, "Marc honey, whatever happened, whatever's wrong, fix it. I know that the ice queen is really the love of your life. You need her and I need you to be happy since it didn't work out like you wanted for us. Swallow your pride and forgive her for whatever she's done because next time I need you to hook a sista up I need you focused on me and not her."

I laughed because I knew this new attitude of just being concerned about me had seemed false. I wasn't even going to get into it with her right now; I'd already had my quota of arguments with trifling females for one day.

Donna grabbed her purse and keys and said, "Thank you for the beer but now I have to go. Shelia is waiting for me. It was nice to see you. Don't be to tough on her either Marc." Donna kissed me on the check and we walked outside.

Stanley *and* Ramona were now sitting in lawn chairs on the front yard. They had an ice chest between them, and a small grill going. Why were they facing my house? They weren't even trying to conceal their spying anymore! It was almost as if they were at the drive-in movies and my house was the screen. I whispered to Donna, "Be nice, that's his woman sitting with him in the yard."

She smiled and mumbled back, "I wouldn't mess his thing up Marc." Donna and I approached her car door; she turned to give me a hug, and one last peck on the cheek, and jumped in. I walked to the edge of the driveway as she backed out and waved as she drove off.

Stanley stood up and said, "Whew Hew! Whew Bruther! That was one hell of a quickie bruther compared with your usual overnights! Woo wee, you must have been ready bruther! Like a firecracker ready to go pop, pop, pop! Whew!"

I gave him one thumb down and replied, "We only had a few beers and talked Stanley." Stanley's mouth dropped wide open and he looked at his woman.

She stood up, gave me two thumbs up, and said to Stanley, "You owe me fifty dollars. I told you he wouldn't do her!" Ramona grabbed the lawn chair and walked inside the house.

I didn't even know where to begin. "Stanley! What's the deal my man! You two can't be betting on me? You gotta be kidding me!"

Stanley looked shamefaced. "Bruther…it was just this once…. I told her you'd do the ta ta lady and Romie said you wouldn't. She thinks you're head over heels with my biscuit. Whew! This is some action bruther! Whew!"

I couldn't even say anything. I was tongue-tied. I just smiled at Stanley and motioned towards my house. "Okay, I'm going inside now. I'll talk to you tomorrow."

Stanley replied quickly, "Hey bruther, is she coming over tonight?"

I played dumb. "Who?" Stanley gave me a look as if to say *you know who*. I said, "Who Stanley?"

Stanley said, "You know who bruther whew! The one that makes you yell cocka doodle doo bruther…cocka doodle doo! Whew!"

I couldn't keep up the front. I laughed and said, "Maybe tonight or tomorrow. I haven't spoken to her yet."

Stanley replied, "Whew! Okay! Well, I'll see ya later bruther." Stanley gathered up his things turned to walk away but turned back towards me. He said, "Bruther, don't mess it up! You go get her and bring her back to the ranch. If you need some advice…pinch, nibble, and bite! Hell, do whatever you have to do to bring that woman back to the ranch! Do your thing bruther, do your thing!"

"Thanks for the advice…. I'll keep that in mind."

I walked back in the house and sat down in my lazy boy chair. I wanted to call Cerise so badly but my pride just wouldn't allow me to pick up the phone. I sat there wrestling with the devil sitting on my left and the angel on my right. The devil was saying, "Her ass didn't have to do you wrong. Marc she left you outside like a puppy in the cold and to make matters worse she *told* you to go away. You don't need her or anyone! Look around, there are many women in the world, she's just another brick in the wall. In fact, call up one of your old bones and see if you can lick on it just for the night. Let's bounce outta dis mofo, go get a drink, holla at some ho's."

I leaned over to the left and gave him a *not today* look. The JWB was obviously taking its toll on me. I looked over to my right to see what was going on and there sat the angel. This was the sensible side of me. The angel said, "Now, now Marcus, don't listen to that idiot. You slipped up and I tried to warn you but you dissed me earlier when I was trying to tell you not to go invading her space. Now you have a little mud on your face and your thinking about getting loose. This is not Nike Just Do It. I'm telling you *don't* do it. Next time, I bet you'll listen. Now, let me tell you how to fix the situation. Say I'm sorry and say it again. Then go out and buy some roses, make reservations for dinner, and say I'm sorry again because you messed up. I'll take care of the rest."

I really didn't see a tiny little version of me dressed as an angel or devil but the liquor actually had me imagining this situation in my head. After my conversations with the best and worst parts of myself, I knew I was partly right and partly wrong but mostly I'd been in the right. Because of that, it wasn't easy to make a decision to apologize or just say fuck it and fuck her.

Deciding not to decide for the moment, I grabbed the JWB, a DVD to watch, and lit a log in the fireplace. As the liqueur continued to numb my mind, and the fire had me transfixed, staring into the flames, crazy random thoughts ran through my head, like, why do the extremely mean and ugly brothers get the good women? Has anyone ever noticed this but me? I see it all the time. An ugly ass brother with a fine ass woman. Do they approach em with the U GOT U GOT U GOT WHAT I NEED! YOU GONNA BE MY WOMAN! I don't want to hear that shit about well maybe he has a big dick because before you even get to the dick the ugly is right there plahdow! As soon as this thought crossed my mind, I started laughing out loud in my lonely house. I thought back to my college days and one of my boys who was ugly as all hell but who managed to get all the fine women. And why was I sitting here thinking about this shit in the first place? That was the last coherent thought I had before I passed out.

The doorbell woke me up. From the light in the room, I knew I'd been out all night because it looked like it was already late morning. My mouth was dry and smelled of the beer and JWB, I'd consumed last night. Thankfully, I had no hangover but I was still dragging as I went to look out the peephole. It was a delivery guy. I opened the door, told the man he had the wrong address, and started to close the door again.

"Excuse me sir, is this the Haley residence?" I opened the door back up. "Yes it is, can I help you?"

"We have a delivery for you." I walked out to see what was going on and saw Cerise pulling up. I'd deal with her later. "A delivery? I didn't order anything."

Delivery guy replied, "Sorry sir we were suppose to deliver this yesterday afternoon but it was taken to the wrong house. We have a new driver and he didn't read the memo in the purchase order, I apologize. Please sign here."

Cerise was standing near the truck smiling and looking fine as always. The delivery guys pulled down the ramp and wheeled out a 54-inch screen plasma TV.

Damn! Damn! Damn! That was a hell of a sweet apology gift. She must have been out early this morning searching for something for me. I looked at Cerise and mouthed, "Is that for me?" Cerise nodded her head yes and she stood there with her hands folded together and smiling. I had the guys place the TV in the living room and they began to set it up as Cerise walked towards me, said "I'm sorry, Marcus," and gave me a long kiss just in case her words didn't convince me.

When she pulled away she said, "You've been drinking and you haven't brushed your teeth. Eww," she said with a laugh before continuing, "I know you were going crazy last night baby. I'm so sorry!

When you came by earlier, this stupid TV was in my living room. The guys delivered it to my house. I told them it was the wrong house but they asked if they could leave it, unload the truck since it was on the front, and come back and drop it off at the correct address later that night. Needless to say, they never showed up until late this morning. That's why I didn't open the door baby. This is your Christmas present and I just wanted you to be surprised. I know I handled things badly but I panicked when you showed up. Can you forgive me?"

In spite of my bad breath, I grabbed Cerise and crushed her against me, kissing her for another long moment. When we stopped she said, "Dayummm, I like that! Can you go brush your teeth please and then I'd like some dessert with that kiss you just laid on me."

I love you. I didn't say it but I felt it. As I looked at my woman telling me to go brush my teeth after spending 5 minutes sucking up my funkiness, and because she'd screwed up so badly just trying to surprise me, I knew.

I stood there with the biggest grin on my face but focused my attention on the TV. "That's one hell of a nice gift C! Good thing I planned a trip for us to Cancun instead of buying you socks like I'd first thought about." I grinned as Cerise looked excited at my news. "Are you serious?"

"Yup, the travel agent has everything at the ready. All we have to do is schedule the date."

"Damn baby, you actually do listen when I talk huh? I've always wanted to go to Cancun." Cerise went to give me another kiss, backed up, and pointed to the stairs. "Teeth!" we both said at the same time. We both cracked up and I went upstairs to shower and brush my damn teeth.

I came back downstairs and Cerise was pouring over the manuals for the TV the installers had left behind. She looked up as I approached and told me, "Now you can watch the games and feel like you are right there in the front seats."

"Hush," I told her. "You owe me something." I grabbed Cerise, hugging her tightly and kissing her again.

Cerise pulled away finally and said, "Marcus, I'll be right back. I'm going to run to the store and buy the stuff to make some Jambalaya. Okay."

My jaw dropped. I said, "Are you serious? You are actually going to cook? For me? Well be gone then! Take your time! I'll definitely be here when you get back."

Cerise laughed and tapped my cheek playfully. "I know you will probably be stuck in front of the TV" she said, and turned towards the door and opened it. I smacked her on the ass and she gave a little hop, shook her butt at me, and headed down the walk waving at Stanley and Ramona, standing in the middle of their front yard.

A slow grin rose on Stanley's face and that crazy man actually smacked Ramona on the ass. Ramona cocked her head to the side and raised her eyebrows at Stanley, but she didn't seem to mind the love tap. Stanley said, "Whew…Bruther…that's one helluva picture tube you just bought! Suppose we'll be having a get together at the ranch soon bruther, watch some of the ESPN?"

I smiled at Stanley and said, "Oh yeah let me break it in, and before you know it you and I will be watching the games on *ESPN* Stanley. Of course you are always welcome as well Ramona."

She smiled and said, "Thanks, I might just take you up on that. Maybe your lady friend can tell me where she buys her shoes. I do love those shoes she wears."

Stanley gave me two thumbs up and said, "Whew.... well alright," then placed his hand in the rear pocket of Ramona's jeans as they walked back into their house.

Back in my house, I moved my old big screen into the guest bedroom, and sat down to play with my new toy. I knew Cerise had to pay at least a couple thousand for this gift. I was juiced! What a difference a day makes! Thank God I hadn't listened to my dark side telling me to go out and hook up with a hoochie momma last night. Some kind of one nightstand could never fill the huge whole I'd have in my life and heart if Cerise and I actually did split up.

I grabbed the phone and dialed her number, "Hello Marcus, what's up?" Cerise answered.

I said, "Baby, you are not cooking tonight. We are going out and I'm going to treat you to the finest dinner in town."

Cerise replied, "I wanted to make you a nice meal but I'll take it though! I'll see you in fifteen."

I hung up the phone and called Beth's floral shop. Beth and I went to high school together and still have lunch from time to time. "Hello, this is Beth's Floral how can I help you?"

I disguised my voice. "Uh, hello Beth, this is Rocky Balboa," I tried for a thick Italian accent. "Uh yeah, I need 30 dozen roses delivered to my business tomorrow. Can you handle that?"

Beth said, "Thirty doz... Marc is that you?" She laughed. "You are so crazy! I know it's you so quit playing and tell me what you want. I am about to close and go to lunch."

I laughed and replied, "Hey Beth how are you doing pretty lady? I need two-dozen roses delivered to Alicia's Seafood on the Bay by 7:45pm. I'm meeting a special someone there."

She laughed and said, "I haven't heard from you in months and now you call with a special order? Negro please! Why should I?"

"Cause I'm yo boy! Now hook me up, we both know you are going to so stop arguing and just agree. Come on, please!!!"

"Lord knows I love to make a grown man beg," she laughed again. "Okay but you owe me." I told her the message I wanted written on the card and prepared to hang up.

Beth said, "By the way, Joseph has been trying to get a hold of you. He's ready to start fishing again so give him a call. Bye!"

Beth hung up the phone before I could respond. I scrolled down my phone list of numbers for Alicia's to make reservations. It's nice to have grown up locally. Friends of mine from way back owned most of the businesses I frequented, and it helped when I needed a favor and friends of mine often got a special discount for HiCi's services. I ran to the bathroom because all the beer from last night was dying to be released into the wild. I came back and called the restaurant.

"Hello? This is Alicia, What do you want Marcus?"

"Now why did Beth call you and tell you my business? That's not right!"

Alicia replied, "Hush up, what time are you arriving so I can save you a table."

I said, "We should be there around 8pm. I owe you big time. See ya soon. Bye"

I heard Alicia's voice saying' "Hold on buddy!" before I clicked the phone off.

"What?" I asked when I placed the phone back to my ear.

Alicia asked, "Is she the one? I haven't seen you in here in at least six months Marc. In fact, the last time you were here you were wining and dining some woman that wasn't funky Donna if I'm correct. Is it the same woman?"

"Yup!" I told her grinning.

"Well damn man, she must be special. And by the way, you owe me big time. I'll set it up. See you later." Alicia hung up the phone before I could reply.

I sat back down and turned on the television set. I couldn't believe I was watching a 54 inch plasma screen. It was like being at a sports bar! It's amazing how an observant woman can easily have a man eating out of the palm of her hand. I have heard that the way to a man's heart is his stomach but I believe there are a lot of ways to get there, all you have to do is find out what makes him happy. I guess that works both ways for men and women. Cerise and I were talking one evening, and plasma TV's, stereos, and digital cameras were the topic of discussion. I told Cerise that I was looking into buying a plasma TV and video camera soon. I had always wanted a plasma television but I wanted to catch one on sale.

Cerise rang the bell and walked in. "Hello baby, I'm back. I see you have your new toy up and running. That didn't take long."

I walked to the entryway to greet Cerise and said, "C, what are you ringing the bell for? My house is your house so cut that shit out." Cerise grinned and gave me another big kiss.

We walked into the living room and she said, "Wow the television looks very good. Do you like it?"

Now what kind of crazy question was that? "Do I like it? I love it! I love it, C! And by the way, we're having dinner at Alicia's Seafood on the bay at 8pm."

Cerise said, "Are you crazy? We can't get a reservation on this short notice."

I smiled, "I've taken care of all of the small stuff you just make sure you are ready to roll on time."

Cerise said, "Ha, ha, I'll be ready. What are you wearing out to dinner tonight? I don't want to be over or under dressed."

I replied, "I don't know, probably a pair of slacks and a silk shirt nothing major."

She got that look on her face and asked, "Are you wearing that black shirt?"

Pulling her to me again, I kissed her on both cheeks. "Oh you like Marcus in the black shirt huh?"

Grinning she said, "Oh yeah, you look *very* sexy in black Marcus."

"Is that right? I'm glad you like." I began to walk Cerise backwards until we came to a stop at the wall. Our bodies pressed together so tightly Cerise couldn't help but feel the affect her compliment had on me.

She shocked the hell out of me when she reversed our positions against the wall, grabbed my wrists and held them against the wall, reached up on her tip toes and asked while punctuating her words with kisses, "What can I do for putting you through a seconds worry about me last night? Can I kiss you like this? Can I make love to you? Can I hold you? Can I fuck you?"

Damn! My baby blew my mind with that one. UMPH! I reversed our positions again so that her back was to the wall again, grabbed her hands, and placed them above our heads against the wall. I was breathing erratically when I whispered, "You can do whatever you want as long as you scream my name out loud when I'm inside of you."

Cerise buckled at the knees and moaned deep in her throat as I slowly, with a promise I intended to keep, gyrated my hips against her pelvic area. Kissing her face, neck, chest, mouth, I told her gruffly, "I'll do anything, anywhere, anytime as long as it's with you." Cerise was damn near purring as she closed her eyes and arched her back, rotating and thrusting her hips in an answering slow hard grind.

Standing against the wall making love through our clothes we found a groove as I continued to press into her and she pressed back against me until I could feel the heat coming off of her in waves, through her jeans. I reached down and began to unbuckle them. Cerise slapped my hands away but I tried again.

"Uh-uh, baby, this is all about you right now." She said and again reversed our positions yet again, unbuckled my pants, and let them drop to the floor. She sank slowly to her knees, kissing my chest and stomach as she made her way slowly to the floor. Her hand rubbed and stroked me up and down until I couldn't stand it anymore. I was about to lay her down and take her there on the floor. Cerise put her hand on my stomach to stop me just as I felt her moist, warm tongue on me before her mouth fully engulfed me. I threw my head back so hard against the wall it would have hurt if she wasn't making me feel so good. My eyes rolled back in my head in ecstasy, as Cerise caused me to scream out her name in release.

Later, we stepped out of the shower and walked into the bedroom to get dressed. I grabbed the lotion from the dresser and sat down on the bed. "Come here ashy ass." I said to Cerise.

We started laughing and Cerise replied, "My ass is never ashy Negro." She crossed the room and positioned herself between my legs.

I put my arms around her waist and said, "Damn you look good. I'd love to just eat you up right now. I know we have to go but a quickie wouldn't hurt nobody right?"

Cerise said, "Nope. No quickies baby I'm hungry lets go eat. I began rubbing her body and released the towel that covered her. Cerise shook her head, laughing. "Do you ever get enough?"

"Enough? Please, there is no such thing as *enough*. Making love to you is something I could write a book about!"

She looked amused. "Is that right?"

"Damn straight. Chapter one would describe the sweet taste of your lips. Chapter two would describe the stimulating affects of you're skin against mine. Chapter three would make the readers weak when I describe how you feel when you slowly allow me into your world. Chapter four would cause the reader to sweat because I'd describe in detail how you moan and how you drive me crazy when I sample the fruit of your garden, and the final Chapter, Chapter number five, would show what love making is all about. It would capture how it feels to make love to you, from the moment our eyes meet, to the instant our mouths touch, to the moment we fall asleep in each others arms."

As I spoke, I slowly rubbed lotion on Cerise's stomach, legs, breasts, and arms. She made little noises in her throat to let me know she appreciated the words and the feel of my hands. I looked up and her eyes were closed as she listened to me talk. I smacked her on the ass lightly and said, "If we don't get out of here I'm gonna have you spread eagle on this bed so quick you won't know what hit you."

Cerise leaned over, laid me back slowly against the bed, and kissed me sweetly.

"We don't really need to go to dinner you know." I whispered.

Cerise cracked up laughing pulling me up by my arm. "Get up Negro. After you took all my energy away downstairs you aren't gonna feed me? Cruel!"

We finished getting dressed and on the drive to dinner we talked about nothing in particular until Cerise asked, "Marcus, have you ever thought about leaving the states?"

I said, "What do you mean leaving the states? Are you talking about moving out of the country?"

She said in her most enthusiastic voice, "Yeah, like living in Africa, Jamaica...Canada?"

"Nope, I like it here in California. Have you?"

Cerise replied, "I've put in bids with some overseas companies to bring my product under their umbrella. I've never heard anything back but I think it would be neat."

I smiled and said, "Baby, there is nothing neat about moving out of the States. This country certainly has its own problems but compared to most others, life here is a picnic."

She replied, "Have you ever traveled out of the States?"

I replied, "Only on business. At most 6 times."

She said, "Marcus you don't know what you are missing. It is a beautiful world out there. And it's too large not to travel and explore it. When I grow older, I don't want to think about or talk about the places I could have gone. I want to tell the stories of my adventures." I laughed at Cerise. "What's so funny Marcus? I'm serious." She said indignantly.

"You," I said, "You sound like a travel brochure."

I pulled into the parking lot at Alicia's. Cerise had been talking for the last twenty minutes trying to convince me there was nothing wrong with moving out of the country.

I said, "I'm not really looking to move but I guess if the right opportunity arose, I'd at least consider it."

She said, "Are you serious? Marcus, you serious?"

I replied, "Well yes, but it would have to be one helluva offer dear. One helluva offer." As I stepped out of the car to walk around to open the door for Cerise, I wondered where all this questioning was coming from? She had never discussed moving out of the City let alone the country. Why would a woman who has a thriving business, family, and a good man like me want to move?

I walked up to the main door of the restaurant and opened the door for Cerise. There were two huge mirrors in the entrance. I looked at our reflection and thought, damn, now that's what a nice looking couple looks like. Alicia noticed me out of the corner of her eye, walked over, and gave me a hug, "Hello Marc. Who is this lovely lady you've brought to my restaurant?

"Damn Alicia, you are looking just as good as always. Better each time I see you, in fact. This is Cerise. Cerise, this is Alicia." Cerise extended her hand and Alicia walked right around it and gave Cerise a big hug. "Any friend of Marcus is a friend of mine. Now you two follow me." As Alicia escorted us to our table Cerise looked back and blew me a kiss. She was obviously impressed by the welcome Alicia extended. As we approached the table, I could see the roses that I had ordered sitting on the table. My two ladies had come through for me again. Alicia positioned us at a very nice spot in the restaurant. We could see the flames from the fireplace and the sunlight dancing on the water. Cerise sat down at the table and I handed her the card in the rose vase before joining her.

Cerise opened the card and read out loud, "Cerise. You have made my dark days bright again. You have made my heart dance to the sound of your drum. You have shown me how to love again. Loving you is all I'm living for…. Marcus."

Cerise stood up, leaned across the table, and gave me a passionate kiss. She said, "Thank you Marcus. You are so sweet."

I said, "Okay enough soft stuff lets order so we can eat."

The waiter came by the table and I ordered a bottle of wine and a couple of appetizers. As Cerise and I looked over the menu, a man and woman entered the restaurant. I normally wouldn't position my back to the door in a restaurant but it was okay because of the mirrors surrounding the area. I noticed that Cerise continued to look at this gentleman and his wife. He was about 6'2, 240lbs, and a nice looking fellow. Actually, when I looked closer I noticed he could have passed as my brother. We had a lot of similar features. The Waiter escorted them to a spot table right across from Cerise and I.

"Someone you know?" At that very moment, he happened to look our way and Cerise looked away. I nodded because I was staring at the two of them and he nodded back. He continued to look at Cerise as if he knew her and then he excused himself from his date.

He walked over to our table, looked directly at me, and said, "Good evening. Is that you Cerise?"

She looked up and said, "Oh I thought that was you Tyrone. It's nice to see you. How have you been?"

I stood up, stepped between the two of them, and said, "I'm Marc, and we are about to have a little dinner. Maybe the two of you can pick this up some other time."

He replied, "I'm sorry brotha. I didn't mean to interrupt. Cerise it's nice to see you too. Maybe we can get together soon and have lunch like old times?"

I said, "Yeah you two can do that some other time." Tyrone looked at me, then at Cerise, and turned to walk back to his table.

"What was that all about?" I asked.

She said, "I am sorry Marcus. He and I had a thing about 4 years ago before I was married. It lasted about 2 months."

I replied, "It was pretty obvious you had a thing. You basically undressed him with your eyes."

Cerise said, "Marcus that wasn't the case come on now. And I don't know if you've notice but he looks kinda like you, except you are much more handsome. Lucky me!" Cerise patted my hand. "Look at you all jealous. Honey, I promise you, I was taken aback because it was weird seeing him and seeing you. I'm sorry for not introducing you."

"I'm not going to let a little deal that occurred years ago interfere with our lovely evening." I'd just finished speaking and wouldn't you know it? Tyrone was back.

"Excuse me, can I leave you my number Cerise?" He dropped his card on the table.

I was prepared to let the first interruption go but ole boy had obviously mistaken my politeness for stupidity or cowardice. I stood up and said, "Let me break it down for you *Tyrone*. Whatever you two had is over. I suggest you go sit with your woman before I put you through this window and toss you out in the river."

Tyrone squared his shoulders. "You think you could do that *partner?*" he replied.

"Damn straight, *Tyrone.* You better ask somebody," I said.

Cerise stood up and said in a hushed tone, "Tyrone, I definitely do not like your style. I didn't then and I don't now. Take your card and leave. If not, Marcus will definitely be delighted to put a can of whoop ass on you. I'm sure you can see he's for real. Oh and if you rode with the pretty lady you've been dissing since you walked in, you might have to walk home. She just left."

I'd removed my jacket while Cerise was talking and my arms were blazing and my chest was squared. My body was ready for combat. I stepped closer to him and said, "So what do you wanna do?"

Tyrone chuckled and said, "I'm going to go," turned around and hurried out after his date.

Luckily, I didn't have to take it there. Alicia would have killed me if I'd broken her place up, whether I had a reason to or not. And since we'd all been speaking in hushed tones no one had even noticed anything unpleasant was taking place.

We sat back down and Cerise apologized again. "I should have just brushed him off as soon as he walked over here. I'm sorry."

"Don't worry about it," I told her. "We came to enjoy our dinner and that's what we are going to do. Later, I'm going to enjoy the hell out of you."

Cerise clapped her hands, "Goody for me!"

The waiter came by with the appetizers and wine and Cerise and I ordered a pound of Alaskan Snow Crab with an entrée' on the side and I ordered the catch of the day, which was Salmon. Surprisingly Tyrone must have some kind of game because he'd managed to convince his date to return to the restaurant and they went back to their table. I asked the waiter if he could send Alicia over and a few minutes later Alicia stopped by the table.

"Marcus what do you want now? I gave you the best table in the house, you have a beautiful lady on your side, and dinner is on its way. What do you want now, I know you see I'm busy."

Cerise said, "Daang, Alicia, don't hold back, tell him how you really feel."

We laughed Alicia said, "He knows I'm just messing with him. Now what is it you wanted Marcus?"

"Alicia, you see the brother over to your left. Well, that's one of my beautiful lady's old flings. I can't enjoy my meal with his ass watching her. Can you move us? Or, I can go dot his eye and not have to worry about him watching us anymore."

Alicia looked at me and then at Cerise and said, "You still look for any excuse to fight huh? I don't want you getting niggerish up in my spot but why should I move you?" Alicia smiled and put her hand out for some green.

I said, "Oh okay, it's like that tonight Alicia?" We started laughing again. I reached into my wallet, pulled out a fifty-dollar bill, and said, "This is for all your trouble tonight now. Now hook me up Alicia."

Alicia snatched the $50.00 bill and said to Cerise, "Honey, I normally don't do business like this and Marc and I go way back but he's got to pay for his favors."

Cerise said, "I know that's right sister girl." Ain't that something, I'm paying to get away from her fling and she's agreeing with Alicia that I should pay. Whatever, I thought as Alicia escorted us to a private area on the patio. Cerise said to Alicia as we were sitting, "Thank you for moving us. I appreciate it."

Alicia said, "Girl I know how you feel its no problem. I'll see the two of you later. I hope you enjoy the meal and let me know if there is anything else I can do for you two."

I said, "Thanks Alicia, you are always taking care of a brotha."

She replied, "Don't worry about it, just have a good time. I'll be in touch with you Marc, bye." Alicia signaled to one of the waiters to have the food we'd left transferred over to the new table and sent another to check on our food.

Dinner went smoothly after we'd changed tables and we drove to my house making plans for New Year's Eve. The second the door closed behind us, to my surprise Cerise turned around and jumped in my arms, wrapping her legs around my waist, and kissed me hungrily as she hurried to unbutton my shirt. We spent the rest of the day in bed. Sometime during the night, I woke up to find Cerise laying in bed with her eyes wide open, just watching me.

When she saw my eyes open she mouthed, "I love you Marcus" I pulled her closer, snuggled against her, and went back to sleep with a smile on my face.

ALL MY TOMORROWS

Over the next several months Cerise's business kept her busy and it was hard for us to see each other. We did make it to Cancun and had such a great time Cerise asked if we could make it a yearly event. I loved that she thought we'd be together long enough to have yearly events. After we got back from Cancun, it was back to the grindstone but Cerise made every effort to spend all her free time with me, which I appreciated.

One night over dinner, the first time Cerise actually cooked, she sat toying with her food but practically inhaling her wine. I didn't blame her for not wanting to eat. It was horrible! But I know when someone is looking for liquid courage so I asked if she was okay.

Cerise said, "*Sooo*, what if I told you I'm trying to set up a deal that will take me out of the country for a long while? What would you think?"

"I guess I'd be packing my things cause I'd want to be with you." The moment I said it, I wished I could take the statement back.

Cerise jumped up and hugged me. "Oh my goodness Marcus you are so sweet. I'll remember that, if this thing goes through." She sat back down and took a bite of food. "This sucks doesn't it?" I nodded my head sadly and cracked up laughing.

In the back of my mind I had to wonder what in the *hell* had I been thinking to tell her that I'd pack my bags to be with her? I wasn't moving to Africa or anywhere outside this country. My life was here. All I could do was hope her chances of making the deal were slim. I knew that it was a terrible thing for me to wish her bad luck but I couldn't help it.

We decided to drive out to Shelby's again later that night and have some cheesecake to drown out the taste of Cerise's nasty dinner. Once we made it back to the car, Cerise said, "I'll drive Marcus I know you are tired from playing ball with Kevin all day."

I tossed her the keys and said, "Be gentle with my baby now."

Cerise said, "I'm always gentle baby. Don't you worry your pretty head, I haven't had an accident in years!" We both started laughing.

I replied, "Well I don't want my baby to be the first."

She said, "Okay, Okay. Now where are your CDs? Can you grab me Letni's Jazz on the Boulevard." I handed her the case, leaned over, pulled Cerise's head down, and kissed her for a long moment. Cerise gave me a peck on the nose and I smiled as I sat back in my seat and closed my eyes.

"Marcus, oh Marcus. Wake up we are here. I know you don't think I'm going to carry you in the house. Come on, come on get up."

I looked around and said, "Wow I must be tired. How long was I asleep?"

Cerise said, "You were snoring before I pulled out of the parking lot. Marcus you snore *loud* when you are tired."

I said, "Ah, I wasn't sleep I was just meditating."

Cerise and I walked in the house and prepared to relax the remainder of the evening. Just because I took a nap earlier didn't mean I wasn't ready to get busy before the night was up. If anything, the rest only rejuvenated me. Cerise went through the DVD's and put in Love and Basketball, one of her favorites. She snuggled next to me on the couch and we watched in silence for a while.

"Do you hear fire engines?" I asked.

Cerise said, "Yeah and they seem like they are very close. I rarely hear them in this area." The sirens became louder, and louder, then stopped.

I said, "Lets go outside for a second because the sirens are very close."

We headed towards the door and could see the illumination from the red lights through my window.

I said, "Oh snap that's here on our street." I opened the door and the paramedics were walking towards Stanley's home. I said to Cerise, "Baby can you grab my shoes? I need to find out what's going on." Cerise rushed back in the house. I was worried about my good neighbors. Did one of them have a heart attack? A stroke? Injure themselves somehow? Cerise came back to the door with my shoes and she struggled into hers as well.

We walked onto the lawn as Cerise asked, "What do you think is going on?"

I said, "I don't know he's never had the fire department or police at his home in the years that I've known them."

I approached the first paramedic and asked, "Are they okay in there? What 's going on? I'm a neighbor."

The paramedic smiled and said, "Oh he's okay, but I'll let him explain what's going on." That was a huge relief. Cerise and I walked up the path and approached their front door. A paramedic stopped us and he said, "He'll be out in one second, are you family?"

I said, "No but..." The paramedic interrupted me and said, "Well you'll have to wait outside for now. I'm sorry."

As Cerise and I waited on the porch for Stanley and his wife, I tried to figure out what in the world could have happened.

Cerise said, "Well at least he's okay according to the paramedic. Oh here he comes now." When she said that, her jaw dropped wide open, she blushed, patted my arm, and walked back into my house.

I turned to see what could have caused that reaction from her and there was Stanley being carried out on a Gurnee with a white sheet over him and a blood pressure sleeve on his arm. The sheet was tent poled. It was such a crazy sight I started to laugh but I didn't know what was going on. How could Stanley be aroused by a trip to the emergency room?

I walked up to Stanley and said, "Are you okay buddy?"

Stanley looked down at his erect penis that had the sheet sticking up and said weakly, "Whew bruther! I was only supposed to take one little blue pill to get Theodore going" but I wanted to bring the cows home bruther. I took three, and I've had this hard on since 4 p.m. It's been rock hard ever since. Whewwww! Betcha wish you had one of these. Anyway, it wasn't me who called cause, I didn't mind it at all. I felt 21 again! I stood up to take a quick break and started stumbling and Ramona blamed it on the Viagra and called the ambulance folks. Whew bruther this thing is rock hard."

I fell out laughing. I couldn't help it. Cerise came back out on the porch and I could see she was struggling not to laugh.

Stanley yelled as they carted him away, "I'll be back Romie! Whewee I'll be back!" The paramedic who was assisting Stanley told him to try and relax. They closed the door and drove off, sirens blaring. One of the paramedics from the other truck was packing up his equipment with a big grin on his face when Ramona came to the door and headed for her car.

"Hello Marcus" she said, with an embarrassed grin on her face.

I said, "Hello, he's going to be okay right?"

She said, "Yes, I was informed that they just want to give him something to counteract the pills because he's had IT to long." She started laughing and that's all it took to get myself, Cerise and the other two paramedics laughing. Cerise had to go back in the house again because she couldn't control her laughter. I advised Ramona if she needed a ride or anything to come knock on the door.

She replied, "Baby after I go pick up Stanley, all I am going to need is some rest."

I walked back into my house to find Cerise leaning against the wall laughing. I said, "You know you are off the hook!"

She said, "Marcus I am so sorry but I had never seen anything so funny in all my 35 years! When the gurney came from around the corner feet first I noticed this rise in the sheet and realized oh my goodness he has a erection sticking up the sheets." Cerise began laughing again. She had me busting up all over again. "And then the look on his face once he saw me looking at him was the icing on the cake. He didn't even have to say anything because he looked down at it and was proud!"

When I heard that, I laughed so hard my stomach hurt. For the next 20 minutes, we laughed over the entire incident. I said, "Damn, he may have an erection until the morning."

That's all it took and Cerise was back laughing hard again, "Marcus please stop I'm getting cramps in my stomach and it hurts."

I said, "Well what about poor Stanley with the everlasting hard-on!" I couldn't take it anymore so we walked out into the back to get some fresh air.

Cerise said as we walked outside, "Ya see, doctors couldn't leave it alone, they had to devise a pill for sex, now look at poor Stanley. Has an erection that everyone in the hospital will see!"

Cerise and I stood there on the porch laughing at Stanley when she suddenly said, "Hey why don't you take me in the greenhouse and show me around. I haven't been in there since we first met ya know?"

I said, "Anything for you. Let me run in the house, grab some wine and a blanket so we can watch the stars, and turn on the music.

Later, while we made love under the stars in the greenhouse she or I would suddenly burst out laughing and set the other off all over again! I've never laughed so much during sex in my entire life. Cerise laid her head on my chest after we'd exhausted ourselves, and we both looked up into the heavens and saw a shooting star. The first one I'd ever seen. I thought to make a wish but things between the two of us were perfect, so maybe I didn't need to wish upon a star. Maybe she had beaten me to it!

Cerise and I walked back up to the house at 1am in the morning. We both looked at each other and tired was written all over our faces. We jumped in the bed and fell asleep.

The next morning I awoke with Cerise spooning my back. I looked at the clock and it was 7:30am. It was Sunday and we had no major plans that day. I wasn't sure if Cerise wanted to go to church. Lately she'd seemed less inclined to go and I wondered if it was because she was starting to feel guilty about having sex with me without the benefit of marriage. Whenever the minister preached premarital sex Cerise would get squirmy in her seat or start picking at her nails. Guess I'd have to talk to her about it.

I quietly got out of bed, washed my face, brushed my teeth, and headed downstairs. I poured myself a cup of coffee and decided to make breakfast a big breakfast. French toast, scrambled eggs, bacon, hash browns, and I even squeezed my own orange juice. I walked upstairs with breakfast on trays and Cerise was sitting up in the bed watching television.

I said, "Good morning sleepyhead. How did you sleep?"

She replied, "Good morning Marcus. I slept great. Oh, you made breakfast...I am hungry too. Thank you, honey. Menz can learn from you!" We both laughed as I set the tray down. Cerise hopped up, washed her face, brushed her teeth, then came and gave me a kiss.

I said, "That's all I have to do is make breakfast to get this kind of attention? I should do this more often."

She replied, "That's all you have to do baby."

Cerise and I sat back down on the bed and discussed what we were going to do the remainder of the day.

Cerise said, "I don't think I want to go to church today," she looked at the ground when she spoke then turned her eyes up to me and said, "Hey, do you think we could go to Marine World?"

I told her, "Of course. Guess our day is planned."

We finished our breakfast and showered, and headed out. Cerise tried to pep me up as we drove to Marine World. She was determined to get me on a roller coaster and damn if she didn't manage to convince me to try one ride. I should have stuck with my initial no because the closer we came to Marine World the more my adrenaline pumped. I hadn't been on a roller coaster since I was a kid. Regardless, this was going to be a very nice day. We were both excited about just walking around the park, trying to win a huge stuffed animal, and getting theme park food. She was the only one excited about the rides! Cerise and I walked around, and went to every animal show, and by 1pm, I was ready to go. I said, "It's been a long day baby. My feet are tired."

She replied, "Come on follow me."

We walked over to an area and sat at two booths to get our feet massaged. Cerise placed a dollar in the machine and it was total relief. I sat there for two sessions and when we finished Cerise said, "Time for that ride, right there!" She pointed to the Medusa!" I thought Oh wow. Oh wow.

I said, "Why can't we start small?"

Cerise said, "Come on don't be scared."

Now why is it that she had to use the word scared? There's something about that word that makes me take on whatever challenge is presented. Cerise and I made our way over to the line and took our place. The sign outside the entrance said the wait was 30 minutes.

I said, "Wow that's a long line you sure you want to wait?"

Cerise said, "30 minutes is nothing. This line is normally around the block. Don't try to chicken out on me now."

I smiled and looked around and a couple of fellas were standing to my right looking directly at me. I said, "Please, I could ride this thing in my sleep."

She replied, "Oh yeah?"

I said, "Oh yeah lets do it." Cerise and I stood in line talking about other rides we'd be venturing to next. As the line slowly moved forward, I continued to try to persuade Cerise to exit the line but she wasn't buying it.

"Is Marcus scared to go on the ride?" I noticed a different group of guys in line behind us watching me to see if I'd chicken out.

I said, "Please, I could ride this ride over and over again except all these kids would be mad!" Cerise smiled. It was finally our turn, and boy did I want to step right over the seat and on to the ramp to exit but I couldn't. Cerise was watching me and laughing her ass off. We sat down on the ride and the attendant came and checked all the harnesses before the ride started its ascension up the huge track. I was breathing hard and started talking shit to Cerise because I was nervous, "Baby what did I tell you. I am not scared. I could ride this thing all day and night."

Cerise replied, "Yeah baby, I knew you could! Here we go we are almost at the top."

I grabbed Cerise's hand as the roller coaster started on its downward path, "Awwhhhhhhhhhh, Awwhhhhhhhhhhhhh, Awwwwwwwwwwwhhh." I had to scream. I was scared. Cerise looked over at me and I must have looked terrified because she kept laughing.

She laughed the entire ride as I yelled and screamed my way through it. I was just glad the guys who were behind me weren't on the ride to hear me screaming.

We exited the ride and Cerise was still laughing at me. She said, "Baby you did alright! You almost broke my hand but I'm okay!" She knew that I wasn't getting on another roller coaster that evening.

I put my arm around her shoulders, "Sorry about that C but an almost broken hand is the price you had to pay for dragging me up there." We both started laughing.

Cerise and I arrived back at my home as it was getting dark and Stanley was outside. I pulled up in front of his home and rolled the window down, "Stanley you okay."

He smiled and said, "Hello bruther.... hey biscuit how you doing? Bruther, come talk to me after you get that there sunflower in the house. Whew come see me!"

Cerise said, "Hello Stanley, have a good evening." I hit the button for the garage to open and parked, telling Cerise I'd be inside in a few, and walking over to talk to Stanley.

"Okay, let me tell you about my missile the other night. Oh Bruther, where art thou? That sucker was ready to come through the skin. I guess I took two pills too many! Whew I tell you what though, the nurse at the emergency room touched it just to see if it were real! Yeah bruther...yeah...I gotta watch it though because it had my pressure up."

I couldn't stop laughing from the moment Stanley started talking. I said, "Stanley follow the instructions.... Please follow the instructions. Now I gotta go because I'm due! Its time to put it down tonight.

Stanley smiled and said, "Whew hewww bruther...do it! Do it! Hey? Hey Marcus, you need any pills?"

I smiled and said, "Stanley my missile has too much fuel and energy, if I ever get low though I know who to go see!"

Stanley gave him two thumbs up and said, "Damn straight bruther yeah!!"

I walked in the house and didn't see Cerise. I thumped my chest and said loudly. "Unhn, C, me black Tarzan and me want to make love."

Cerise heard me and said, "I'm up here Tarzan come rescue me." I smiled and ran upstairs. Cerise was lying on the bed with a royal purple teddy on! I looked over at the shower and noticed that she had quickly jumped in and out. I snatched my clothes off and headed towards the bed.

Cerise said, "I know you are kidding right. Get them funky balls scrubbed up." I laughed and walked over to the shower.

I washed up, jumped out of the shower-soaking wet, ran, and jumped on the bed. I stood over Cerise with water dripping everywhere, "Abulaca....King Marcus is in town. Abulaca dunn, dunn de de...abulaca...dun, dun, deraybe...eyekeee keee keeeeee" I began popping my pelvis and penis all over as water dripped and flipped everywhere. I had my African bambata dance going on!

Cerise laughed and laughed, ran to her purse, took out a twenty-dollar bill and tried to stick it in the crack of my ass while I was dancing. As she screamed, "OWW! Shake it baby. That's right make it clap!" I grabbed her hands as she followed me around with the $20 and fell down on top of her. I couldn't believe how good she smelled as I began caressing and kissing Cerise all over.

I couldn't even wait for her to remove the teddy. I just licked and bit on top of it. We were in sync because as I licked in an area she'd slowly remove the garment so I could get to the skin. I stood up and helped Cerise up because I wanted us to be on the same playing field. Naked. I slowly removed the purple teddy, which she wore so well, picked Cerise up off her feet and walked to the wall. She wrapped her legs around my waist as our tongues danced and I ran my fingers through her hair.

Both of us were too excited for foreplay. I entered Cerise with a grunt and she sucked her breath in as she moved to my rhythm, one hand hanging onto my shoulder the other above her head holding onto to the light fixture. "Baby, you know if I were a wolf I'd be howling right now. Grrrrrr," I panted.

Cerise said, "Go ahead baby growl if you want to, I'm not scared. Can you hear the unh cat purrrrring?" Cerise made the sound of a cat purring in my ear and that was all she wrote. I staggered away from the wall and carried Cerise back to the bed.

It felt so good. Let me say it again. It felt so damn good; I might have lost my damn mind for a moment. I said, "UNH! Baby, baby, hot *damn!* Who's is it?" I slipped up and said it.

I hadn't meant to but it felt good to say it because Cerise said, "Its all yours. It's all yours, baby you know that. You like the cat purring I see."

She purred in my ear again and tightened those glorious kegel muscles and I couldn't take it. I was out of control. "Grrrrr, grrrrr...Ohhhhhh, Ohhhhh.... I gotta let it go baby...I gotta grrrrrrr brrrrrr.... burrrrr.... Awwwwh!" Just as I shouted out my release Cerise let out a holler I'd never heard from her. She and I were in sync as we exploded together.

We lay there panting, sweating, and pulsating. I looked at Cerise and she looked at me, put her hand in the air for a high five, and said, "Way to go big dawg. Got DAMN!" I fell asleep laughing at my crazy ass woman.

COMING HOME

I woke up lying on the small of Cerise's back as she lay on her stomach. For some reason I find it comforting lying next to her soft ass. She was still asleep and I shook her with my head. "Baby its time to get up."

She rolled over and said sleepily, "Damn, that was good last night. Okay. Its time to get up."

Cerise and I jumped in the shower together and washed one another's bodies. Damn, I started to get turned on but Cerise said, "Oh bunny rabbit save some for tonight." I smiled and finished washing her sexy body. I stepped out of the shower as Cerise finished up and dried off.

I went downstairs to get a couple of cups of coffee and when I returned Cerise was standing in her panties and a bra. Wow, she looked good.

She slipped into a black fitted dress and asked, "How do I look?"

I said, "Marvelous. You look stunning."

I walked into the closet, pulled out a Versace suit, and got dressed as Cerise finished getting dressed herself. I looked in the mirror as I kissed Cerise on her shoulder.

She said, "Marcus, look, we make a cute couple don't you think?"

I said, "Yes we do. We look good together now lets go downstairs before you make me slide this dress off."

Cerise and I walked downstairs and had another cup of coffee.

"Baby will I see you this evening?" I asked.

She said, "Of course, but maybe we can hang out at my house tonight. I might as well sell the place. I'm never there."

I almost choked on my coffee but managed to hold it back. Did Cerise just propose what I thought she did? I think she did! I wasn't tackling that one so early in the morning so I just said, "Gotta run baby."

Cerise took one last sip of coffee, grabbed her briefcase and said, "Me to, I have a big deal to square away today."

"Good luck," I told her, and kissed her check before opening the garage. I wasn't sure what the deal was but she seemed pretty excited about closing it so I hoped it went well. Cerise tooted her horn at me and I waved before jumping in the Ram, backing out, and heading into work.

Tyler was the only one in when I arrived as usual. I checked the board to see if anyone was out in the field today. A few investigators had appointments for later on that afternoon, so it was a good time to call an all staff meeting. I needed to know what was being worked and the status of pending cases. I called in an order for a couple dozen donuts and coffee from down the street.

I intended to review prospective client files during the quiet time before the office started buzzing but when I walked to my desk, I noticed a thick manila envelope stamped with CONFIDENTIAL on both sides with big red letters. In smaller letters under each stamp, someone had hand written, "For Marcus Haley Only."

Intrigued, I sat down to find out what the envelope contained. It was a handwritten letter regarding a man named Mr. Beauvias, an inventor. I had never come across someone who invented things for a living so this was a first. The letter didn't disclose much about what he invented but indicated that if HiCi took the case on assignment all business ventures would be disclosed after legal arrangements could be made insuring the legality of confidentiality agreements.

Apparently Beauvias, an inventor originally from New Orleans, owned a company that had lost out on a couple of very lucrative patents for the exact products currently in final trials with Beauvias' company. The products that made it to the market first were exact duplicates of those he'd invented. The first time it happened his internal investigative team went undercover in the factory to determine if someone was stealing secrets. Unfortunately, his team was unable to find a single person they even suspected of being a mole. Shortly after that investigation, the same small start-up company, Buckstar, beat him a second time to patent a product Beauvias had in it's final testing stages and again, it was exactly the same as the one Beauvias had designed. Both the legal team and the investigators checked out Buckstar but couldn't find a single link to Beauvias' company.

Mr. Beauvias' closest legal advisor advised him it was time to bring in outside investigators because it was possible the mole had infiltrated so deeply even his own legal staff and investigators were now suspect. Mr. Beauvias played golf on a regular basis with a man named Arthur Washington. Arthur Washington, recommended HiCi because the company had done excellent work for him and many of his contemporaries through the years.

Beauvias came back from a round of golf one day and told his legal advisor and confidant to contact HiCi, hire the company, no matter the cost, and arrange for one or more of the investigators to go undercover to find out who, if anyone, was selling his secrets to Buckstar. Attached to the file was a personal check for $250,000, presumably so even his internal office staff would not be able to determine an outside firm had been placed on retainer. The file indicated other required fees would be negotiated at the initial meeting, should HiCi choose to accept the case.

I sat back at my desk and exhaled slowly. This kind of case could sky rocket HiCi into a higher level of business success than even I'd dreamed about. There was no question we were taking the case. I had several highly competent ex detectives on staff, not even counting Tyler and myself, who could do the job. All I had to do now was figure out who I would choose. I had no doubt everyone of them would volunteer for the assignment, no matter how long it took.

Before the staff meeting, I had Ashley send three cases of aged scotch to Arthur Washington thanking him for his referral through the years. The man had been my benefactor, no doubt. Then I pulled Tyler aside and told him about the Beauvias Company and how they wanted to utilize HiCi. Tyler was excited as I was to continue discussing it but I told him to keep it under raps until I'd had a chance to consider it further. Secrecy might be the best course for now, considering the amount of money Beauvias was willing to pay to find the mole.

Around ten o'clock I was welcoming David to the staff of junior investigators, a promotion he'd worked hard to earn, when the temp who worked reception during Ashley's absence, walked quietly in the room and spoke with Ashley, who left the room.

Moments later, as the staff congratulated David on his promotion and sat talking while enjoying the last of the coffee and donuts, Ashley walked back into the room and quietly told me I had a call. I asked her to take a message but Ashley shook her head and pointed towards the door. She knew something I didn't, obviously.

I picked up the phone in my office and before I could even speak Cerise screamed through the line, "I GOT THE OFFER! I GOT THE OFFER BABY!" The words started tumbling from her mouth so fast I could barely keep up. "The Australian company, Diatronics, has been buying up a lot of American companies poised to make the Fortune 500 list. They want to buy Xellron Inc and make me a full partner. Oh my goodness Marcus this is the best news in the world! I'll be working with some of the leading software companies in the world, let alone the states!"

I was excited for Cerise and told her so. "Congratulations! That's my baby! Kicking ass and taking names! Was this the big deal you were waiting for?"

Cerise said, "Whew, let me sit down before I pass out. Yes! Yes, this was the deal. And Marcus…They offered a $350,000 signing bonus to be partner and my *salary* will be $1,400,000 a year. Can you believe it! Ohhhhhhh, my goodness! I'm shaking with excitement!"

I said, "Wow! That's great baby. That is wonderful. I see you are rolling with the big dawgs now! We need to celebrate tonight!

Cerise said, "Okay, Okay. Let's go out to dinner. This is so great. Marcus, I love you. Talk to you later." Cerise screamed and then hung up the phone. I was very excited for Cerise. In a flash, she'd become a multi-millionaire. Cerise was already worth a million on paper but now she was really a millionaire.

The rest of the morning I used to catch up with my investigators and discuss the Beauvias case with Tyler. I described the particulars of the case to him. Signed payroll checks for my employees. I couldn't stop thinking about how much money Cerise had made on that deal. It was exceptionally sweet! I was a little surprised she wanted to merge her company since we rarely spoke of our respective businesses after that huge fight and decided business discussions were taboo.

Around 2 o'clock, I decided to head over to the mall to buy something nice for Cerise.

While in route, I called Beth and before I could even get a word out, she said, "Okay Marcus, give me the low down. By the way, you never told me, did your lady friend like the flowers that last time? You never let me know."

"Thank you baby girl, the flowers were beautiful as always, you know you my girl!

Beth laughed, "Okay enough of that tell me the good part. Is she the one? Alicia told me she almost looks as good as me! So, when's the big date?"

I had to laugh. "You know there's no one in the area more stunning than you Beth, and slow down with the marriage thing. We are just good friends."

Beth replied, "I know good friends and good friends don't get to eat at Alicia's Seafood on the Bay."

We laughed. I said, "You are right about that baby. My bill was $250.00 by the time we walked out of that place and that didn't include the $50.00 she hit me up for. Can you believe her?"

Beth laughed and said, "Please Marcus don't even try it. Alicia is always hooking your ass up. I know you shame!" I snickered into the phone. I hadn't heard that expression in years!

"You're right. You're right, I'm bad. Okay, hey listen I need 5 dozen mixed roses delivered to Xellron Inc. within an hour do you have enough?"

"She must have really laid it on you the other night. Damn!" Beth said and we both laughed.

"You ain't lying Beth, but she's been laying it on me for a while now. You are the best. Thanks."

"Okay, she knows how to work it, huh? Good for you! I'll send those flowers in an hour. Same bank card as always right?"

I told her, "You got it! Talk to you soon." I laughed at Beth's crazy ass and hung up the phone.

I walked around the mall for a couple of hours looking at clothes, perfume, and different trinkets. I bought Cerise a heavy marble pen holder for her desk and had inscribed on it, in 24 plated gold, "To Cerise, A Phenomenal Woman!" I stopped by a business furniture store and purchased a high-end heating and massaging leather desk chair for Cerise as well.

I called her cell-phone to see what she wanted to eat. "Hey C. I'm trying to set up reservations what do you have a taste for this evening?"

She replied, "Hey honey. I'm so excited! This opportunity only comes once in a lifetime. Okay. Okay. Lets go where you and I can have steak. Let's see, how about Texan's Steak House? It's right down the street from my place so why don't I meet you there in an hour. Or is 5:30 to early?"

I replied, "Sounds good to me I haven't been there in quite a while and with the size of those steaks, I'll need some time to digest that monster meal."

She said, "Okay honey. I'll see you in an hour and a half."

For the next hour, I walked around the mall looking at suits and shoes. I hadn't bought a new suit in a few months and I needed a blue one. I ended up buying a Kenneth Cole suit and shoes. I was paying for my items when my phone rang. It was Cerise.

She said, "Marcus, you are so special. I am speechless about the floral arrangement you just had delivered. Thank you."

I said, "Okay, enough of the sweet stuff. I'll see you soon, and you are more than welcome baby." I hung up the phone, finished my transaction, and headed to Texan's Steak House. I arrived at 5:20 and Cerise was sitting in the parking lot on her phone. I parked two stalls over and she stepped out of the Navigator and headed in my direction. I could see she was still excited because the grin on her face told the story. I stepped out of my car and Cerise came and gave me a kiss. I said, "Congratulations baby you did it! Damn I'm proud of you!"

She replied, "Thank you. Now lets go talk and eat."

While Cerise and I waited to be seated I asked, "Okay, so tell me what you'll be doing? Give me the details on your new position. I know we agreed not to discuss business but I think in this instance we can bend that rule"

Cerise smiled and said, "*Thank* you. I've been dying to discuss the details, let's wait to be seated then I'll tell you all about it. Oh Marcus this will be so exciting."

I said, "Okay. I can't wait to see the size of the office you'll have and perks that come along with being a partner, dear. I hope you can get some floor seats to the Kings game." Cerise examined her shoes and didn't respond.

The waiter escorted us to our table and we ordered without looking at the menus. I was excited for Cerise to hear about the job and the perks. I knew that major corporations usually buy season box seat tickets to sporting events and that would be real nice. My business was doing well enough that I could afford it, now that I thought about it, but why buy when my baby could get them free?

Cerise said, "Okay let me begin. I have to move to Sydney for a year because all partners receive in house training to become familiar with the daily operations of the 150 companies Diatronics manages."

"Excuse me? Did you just say you have to move to Sydney? Australia! Whoa, whoa. I didn't know that was part of the deal. Did you accept the job?"

Cerise looked shocked. "Yes Marcus. I made a verbal contract to accept the job! An opportunity like this only comes once in a lifetime. Did you want me to say no?" She was starting to look angry.

"Yes. I mean no. I mean *I don't know*." I collected my thoughts and finally asked, "What about us, Cerise? You're just going to leave me for a year and you are excited about that?"

"Marcus, baby, you know I'd never leave you. You'll come with me of course. We just talked about this the other day remember? You said if I had to leave the country you'd come. I think it would be fantastic for us both."

I said, "Oh baby, I'm so sorry if you accepted the position because I told you that." I took her hands. "But baby, I can't just up and leave my business in the drop of a dime. We need to talk about this."

Cerise gave me a stern look and said, "*Baby*. There is *nothing* to talk about. I'm taking this job with or without you."

"Wait a minute now hold on, how are you g..."

She interrupted, "I'm sorry Marcus I should not have snapped at you like that. It's just that I've dreamed of this happening and now the opportunity has finally presented itself and I don't want to not jump on the chance of a lifetime."

I said, "Oh I know baby. I know you didn't mean to snap. Wow. This is one helluva crossroad."

Cerise said, "Baby come on its simple, I make enough money now to support the both of us. Maybe you can just shut down for a bit or sell the business. We can make it on my salary can't we?"

It was my turn to get angry. "I'm going to pretend you didn't just suggest I be a kept man." Cerise gasped and stammered to retract the statement. My anger faded as quickly as it had flared. I interrupted her, "Baby its not about the money its about me doing what I enjoy. I'll support you in anything baby but I'm not sure if I can move right now."

We were both silent for a long moment. The waiter brought our steaks but we'd both lost our appetites and only picked at our food. Finally, Cerise said, "Well, anyway that's the stuff we can work that out later. I am scheduled to fly out tomorrow for two weeks. I'll be back for another month to get my affairs in order before I leave again. During that month, we can work out the details. Let's enjoy dinner and each other tonight." Cerise smiled because I knew what she was talking about.

I smiled and said, "Oh baby you don't have to worry about that, and I'm going to take care of that tonight." We laughed.

Cerise and I didn't discuss the Sydney deal anymore even though it weighed heavy on both of our minds. I felt like a first class heel for putting a damper on what should have been the most exciting night of Cerise's life. We finished eating and went to her house to pack some clothes for her six o'clock flight. By the time we finished packing clothes and getting all the essentials for her trip, it was eight. Cerise and I decided to get a hotel close to the airport in the downtown area. The traffic in the morning was always horrible and she didn't want to chance being late for her flight.

We held each other and made love for hours. I didn't sleep at all but I could tell Cerise was tired as she snored while lying on my chest. I sat up the next four and a half hours just thinking about the bomb that Cerise had dropped on me. What was I to do? Was I supposed to follow her and support her dreams? Or was I just to let her move away without me leaving all that we had shared. What was I to do? What would happen if I stayed and she moved? I didn't have much faith that we'd be able to maintain a long distance relationship for two years. I held Cerise until morning.

I got up around 4:30 and sat on the edge of the bed watching Cerise sleep for a few moments, thinking about how far our relationship had come, all the things we'd been through. As Cerise slept, I walked over to crack the window to let in some fresh air. The cool morning air was crisp and refreshing. I listened as two lovebirds sang songs to one another as the sun slowly peeked over the horizon. I thought about Cerise getting on a plane to Australia and how I really didn't want her to go. Things were working so well between the two of us, I didn't want her to interrupt the flow of things with this trip and I knew that was a selfish thought and I just didn't care. I wanted to tell her not to get on the plane.

But I couldn't do that. Cerise had worked her ass off starting that company and building it into what it was today. I knew from experience that it took so much hard work and sacrifice to build a profitable company. And she'd worked and sacrificed so much so that she could broker a deal like this, who in the world was I to ask her to give up that dream? This was a perfect opportunity for her and if our roles were reversed I'd think she was crazy and be pissed as all hell if she had the nerve to ask me not to go. Maybe I should take a few weeks off and go to Australia with her? If she gave more of an advanced notice, I probably would have. Not to move there but just to be there for her when she got her feet wet.

It was time for Cerise to get up or else she'd miss her plane. I walked over to the bed and shook Cerise lightly. "Baby come on it's time to get up. Hey, baby come on now, its time to get up or I'll climb on top of you and make you miss your flight." She woke up slowly, ran her fingers down my face, smiled, and tried to roll back over to go back to sleep. I shook her legs, "Hey baby come on now. Today is your big day." I sat on the bed and Cerise rolled over on her stomach and pulled the covers over her face. I said, "Oh I see we have to do this the hard way." I crawled on top of Cerise and began humping her through the covers.

She snorted and laughed, poking her head out from under the covers. "Marcus…just five more minutes. The longer I lay in this bed, the longer…." Her voice broke. "The longer I get to avoid saying goodbye to you." Her lip trembled and I knew she was about to lose it. If she lost it, I would too. I humped her through the covers again to make her laugh. It worked.

"You want five minutes? I'll give you five minutes lady."

Cerise laughed, "You are something else Marcus. Damn baby. I lo… I gotta get ready. Now get off me so I can get in the shower." I rolled off Cerise, she threw the covers back, and said, "I dreamed about you all night honey. Why don't you fly to Sydney with me? Take two weeks off work and come hang out."

Now that's strange. I was thinking the same thing a few minutes earlier. As much as I wanted to, it was just too short a notice. I said, "Baby I have some big cases coming up and I need to be in the office. I'll check my schedule this afternoon and see if I can at least get down there for a few days."

Cerise walked into the bathroom and started the shower. She turned and said, "I have to brush my teeth, and then I have something to ask you okay."

I said, "Oh yeah do that because I'm not trying to get a whiff of that so early in the morning."

Cerise laughed and threw her diaphragm case at me. " Okay Mr. hot breath in the morning. My breath may be foul, but its not so hot I can actually see the steam coming out of your mouth when you yawn!" I grabbed my chest like I was wounded and fell on the bed playing dead.

Cerise laughed, threw her diaphragm foam at me, and grabbed my toothbrush. "Okay, Negro your bristles aren't even wet." She tossed me my toothbrush and said, "You definitely need to join me cause your breath is foul too."

I put my hand in front of my mouth, blew into my hand, and sniffed. "Did you burn your hand or your nose hairs?" Cerise asked.

"Oh you are trying to clown this early in the morning huh?" I walked over, stood beside her at the sink, put some toothpaste on by brush and began brushing my teeth looking at Cerise in the mirror as she brushed hers.

She looked up at me, made a face, and mumbled "Quit staring at me. You should take a picture if you are going to stare that long."

She was really bringing it this morning! I played it cool because my next move had to be quick and unexpected. Cerise bent over to fill her mouth with water to rinse out her mouth. The moment she did so, I stepped behind her and put my hand on her head. I gave her two quick pumps and said, "Who's da Master?" She didn't respond as she laughed and spit the water out. I had her head over the sink and she couldn't stand straight up. I gave her two more quick pumps and said, "Who's da boss?" Cerise was laughing so hard she couldn't respond. I let her head go, grabbed her hips, and fired off two more quick pumps. "Who's da Master," and walked away out of the bathroom.

Cerise couldn't stop laughing. "Marcus, oh my goodness you took that line from that movie we saw the other night. You *ain't* original and you *ain't* da master. You are just crazy."

I jumped up on the bed and stood in an "X" position with one arm crossed over the other. I did a quick thrust of the magic stick and asked again, "Who's da Master?"

Cerise bent over she was laughing so hard. "Okay, Okay, you are the Master."

I jumped down from the bed and crossed the room, took Cerise in my arms and kissed her passionately for a long moment. "I'm gonna miss you baby," I whispered as I pulled away.

"Me too," she said softly. "That was some nice kiss Marcus maybe I need to go away more often."

"Baby you don't have to go nowhere to get that" I told her.

Cerise replied, "Okay, I have to say this and please don't interrupt. Marcus Haley, I want you in my life. Don't ever say you didn't know. You are so special to me and I have and am enjoying every bit of you."

I cleared my throat because I was afraid it would crack. "I've been happy since you come into my life too Cerise. I have, and hope to continue to enjoy everything about you."

She grabbed my head and kissed my cheeks, forehead, chin, and lastly my lips. She said, "You are a good man, Marcus. I don't know why you hid from me for so long. I needed you back in the day man!" We both laughed as we got into the shower and as Cerise washed up I stood behind her the entire time just watching her. Her body was so lovely. Her feet, calves, thighs, ass, stomach, back, neck, face…everything. For some reason, I felt as if I hadn't had a chance to just look at her body. I had licked, rubbed, massaged, and caressed her body but I never took the time to just study it. I did now.

Cerise handed me a bar of soap and asked me to wash her back. I started with Cerise's neck and washed her back and legs too. Her skin was so soft and I started to get excited. Cerise said, "You are pretty quiet. You okay?" She turned around and looked at me.

I said, "Oh I'm cool. Just thinking about you."

Without even looking down, she grabbed my stuff and said, "Oh I know you are but you have to wait two weeks. I can't miss my flight. And you better wait."

Cerise pulled me close to her as our bodies touched. I could feel her soft hair brush against me as we kissed. Damn it felt good just to be up against her and wished we had just a little longer. I needed to be with her one more time before she left me. But we didn't have time. We stood in the shower holding each other until the water was almost cold.

I grabbed the towels, turned the water off, and said with a heavy voice, "Just don't forget to come back to me C." Damn if my voice didn't crack too.

Cerise massaged my head and said, "Oh you don't have to worry about that baby." I began drying off as Cerise took the towel and began drying my back. When she was done, she stood behind me, hugging me, and I could feel her soft breasts against my back. Cerise reached around, grabbed me again, and said, "Are *you* going to miss me as much as he's going to miss me?"

Immediately, I was hard as a rock. I butted her away from me. Laughing, I said, "Ya know ya wrong for starting something you can't finish."

She smiled, "I know we've never had one in all this time but you know, I think we have enough time for a quickie baby."

The moment the words left her mouth, I was on her. Cerise dug her nails roughly across my back as I pulled her closer than close. The beads of water that remained from the shower dripped to the floor as Cerise freed herself, turned around, leaned over, grabbed the bathroom counter, looked back at me, and wiggled her butt.

I didn't need any further invitation. I held Cerise's breasts in my hands as I entered her almost savagely from behind. She moaned so loudly I was afraid I'd hurt her but she began to rock her hips to my motion and I lost all track of rational thought.

There were tears in my eyes when I leaned down to whisper, "I'm going to miss you baby."

Cerise strained her head backward to kiss me and said, "I know. I'm going to miss you too" She leaned forward against the counter again. I thrust myself further and deeper with each stroke until Cerise screamed out her pleasure. Cerise and I moved back and forth in a motion that made us feel as if our parts were completely lost in each other. I heard a moan start deep in Cerise's throat grow as she neared explosion. I thrust myself into her pouring out all my love, all my sorrow at her leaving. She screamed and I roared as we reached a climax that was off the chart!

We fell to the floor and lay there for a few minutes. I held her in my arms as she lay on my chest rubbing my head. I said, "Damn! That felt so good to be so quick. Shit!"

She replied, "Marcus, you are one incredible lover!"

We quickly re-showered, got dressed, and headed to the airport, arriving just in enough time for her to check her bags and board the plane. I kissed Cerise briefly and hugged her so hard I'm sure she couldn't breathe. I didn't want to let go.

With tears in her eyes Cerise whispered, "Listen if you change your mind and decide you want to come, call me. You have all the numbers. I love you Marcus Haley." The tears started flowing freely now.

I wiped my eyes, cleared my throat, and said, "Okay, I'll call you." I pulled her to me to embrace her one last time before she boarded the plane and whispered in her ear, "I love you too."

Cerise whispered something to me that I couldn't quite make out because the blood was pounding in my head. It sounded something like, "lasminipitch ciao!" I couldn't make it out because her voice was thick with tears.

The attendant reminded Cerise her flight was boarding. She turned away reluctantly and headed into the terminal.

I willed her not to look back as she walked away from me so she wouldn't see the look on my face. I knew if she did, she'd never get on that plane and I knew she had to go. Cerise's shoulders were shaking and I knew she was sobbing as she rushed to catch her plane. I'm in the business of investigations, I know all the security measures in place since 9/11, and still, I attempted to catch up with Cerise and tell her one last time how much she meant to me and how much I loved her. The attendant's stopped me and I watched as Cerise rode up the escalator and out of my life. My heart felt like it had been shattered in a thousand pieces.

I walked away slowly, telling myself I'd only gotten a tear or two in my eyes because Cerise started crying, not because I was really missing her in my world already. I sat in my car until the plane I knew she was on lifted off, banked to the west, and flew towards the ocean. Taking deep breaths to collect myself, I slowly reached out, started the car, and headed into the office.

The drive into work was shorter since I was so close to downtown. I reached the office and tried to get into the swing of things, as if the love of my life wasn't flying a thousand miles away from me.

Tuesday mornings at the office were usually slow and today I knew I wouldn't mind everyone dragging in after eight o'clock. It would give me that much more time to put on my business face and get ready to deal with everything. It was just about seven o'clock when I pulled into the parking lot. It was no surprise to see Tyler's car because he usually arrived an hour or so before everyone else.

I walked into the office and yelled, "Tyler, what's up? I know you are at it bright and early. You should be at home in bed, or is Ashley here too?"

Tyler laughed and yelled across the room, "Hey boss, yeah I'm here. I wanted to get started on that new case you told me about last week."

As I headed towards his office, I yelled, "Where's my breakfast?" He was quiet. I said, "I know you can hear me. You are the only person at work."

Tyler called out from his office, "And for what reason would I want to buy your breakfast when you make the big money?"

I quickly replied, "Because I sprung for beers the last time you and I went to the bar."

I entered his door just as he yelled out again loudly, "Oh yeah, I remember…when beer was a quarter! That was how long ago boss?"

"You don't have to shout at me. I'm standing right in front of you. And it hasn't been that long!" He laughed and I gave my own attempt at a laugh even though Cerise was still heavy on my mind.   He stood and said, "Yes it has," as we greeted each other with our handshake, pound/pound, and pat on the back.

I glanced around Tyler's office and realized he had been working for awhile. I said, "Tyler let me give you some advice. Are you up for some early morning advice or are you going to ignore the wise Love Wizard of Oz?"

Tyler laughed sarcastically, "Oh wise and wonderful love wizard, please enlighten me with your wisdom." Obviously, he really didn't want to hear what I had to say but he was going to get a piece of knowledge anyway. I couldn't fix my love problems; why not drop some wisdom on him so he could avoid another mistake like with Jasmine.

I said, "Lets jump in the car and go get something to eat. I'll spring for your breakfast and kick you some knowledge in the car."   Tyler said, "As long as I get some free food and a fresh cup of coffee out of it I'm down."

"You're down?" I asked with amusement.

"Ashley," we said together, and laughed.

As we headed towards the door, Tyler asked, "Okay Mr. Love Wizard, what is it you have to tell me this morning?"

I said, "You know I appreciate your work around the office. You are here on time all the time, hell, you're here before time even starts."

Tyler laughed and said, "Oh boy, I thought you were a wizard? What's up with the mushy speech?"

I said, " Hush up now, I'm serious." I locked the door to the office and asked, as we approached the car, "So how are you and Ashley doing?"

Tyler replied, "I thought you were going to give me some wizard advice, not pry into my love life. But for the record, we are doing well, thanks for asking. Why? Have you heard something different?"

I said, "No, not at all. Tyler, let me ask you a question. Why in the hell are you here so early? You've probably been here since six. I know you are sleeping with and seeing a lovely piece of work. You could be spending that extra time with her, no doubt. Don't misunderstand what I'm saying either. You ran through a shit storm for that other woman and I saw how that crushed you. But you moved on and I know that now Ashley mean's everything to you so you need to take care of home first. This job needs to come second."

Tyler quickly responded with a smart-ass comment by saying, "Since you are all in my business, to be exact, I was here at five thirty!" I gave Tyler the look and he cleaned it up a bit. "You are right to an extent boss, but why are you coming at me like this? I have tried to…fuck it."

I said, "No go on. I gave you that look because last year, things were crazy for you, remember? Listen T, I'm not trying to tell you how to live your life. I respect you and would do anything for you but come on now, things can't get better when you are here two hours early. A woman would take that two hours and be happy. Feel me? I know you don't want to hear a sermon from me but I had to whoop a man's ass having your back. Take care of home so that shit doesn't happen again. I know you will take care of work. That's all I have to say about it, and I'm sorry if you are angry, but I had to say what was on my mind. Ashley deserves a man who is more concerned about her than a time-clock."

Tyler looked at me and said, "You are right and boss. You know, I'm grateful for all you've done for me." I started to speak and Tyler interrupted me, " Let me see if I have this straight boss. You are saying that I should be at home right now lying next to my woman."

I said, "Damn straight."

Tyler said, "I probably should have been holding her until at least seven or seven thirty right?"

I said, "Yeah, Yes! Now ya feeling what I'm saying. Yeah brother, whew!" I couldn't resist adding Stanley's tagline even though I knew Tyler wouldn't get it.

Tyler held his head down low and I thought his eyes began to tear up. What the hell was this all about? Please, Lord, tell me Ashley wasn't stepping out on him. He looked up, smiled, and said, "I started romping at four this morning boss. I didn't finish until five thirty. Then she went to sleep!"

I put my hand up and Tyler gave me a high five. I said, "Man I thought you were about to cry! Shit! I was about to say just forget it!"

Tyler laughed, "I should have been an actor boss! That's why I'm your number one man.. ain't that right?"

We both laughed and I told him, "Yeah right don't quit your day job."

We pulled into the parking lot at Wynona's and Tyler said, "I'll run across the street to grab a paper and a cup of coffee. The coffee here is worse than it is across the street."

I said, "Cool and grab me a lottery ticket."

Tyler returned with the paper, coffee, and my lottery ticket. We walked into Wynona's and Tyler said, "Boss, I was thinking…what's up with you and ole girl you've been seeing. It's been a while since I saw her. You've been spending a lot of time with her. In fact, you were hanging with her since before Jasmine and I split up."

I said, "Yeah I have, she's cool… we kick it, what's your point?"

Tyler gave me the same look I'd given him earlier. It was odd to have to take that coming from him. "Shit! You better give me more than that! You've been all up in my love life for the last half hour. Now it's your turn to be in the hot seat. So give me the 411."

Tyler picked the wrong day to come at me about Cerise. Or, maybe I picked the wrong day to come at him about Ashley? I'd just gotten all up in his business. I owed him something.

"She's a little something I've been working on," I said simply. Cerise would pop me upside the head if she'd heard me describe our relationship that way but she couldn't she was flying off to her destiny as we spoke.

Tyler said, "A little something? Please! We used to have a drink or two after work and now at five or even earlier you are in the wind with Cerise. I ain't mad at cha but it definitely ain't a little something."

"Damn!" I said, "Ashley is really rubbing off on you. I don't know if I can take to white breads talking more street than I do. And anyway, now you are going to jam me up about it after I gave you all that advice?"

Tyler smiled and said, "Damn straight. Plus, you've been jamming me up since you walked in the office. I think that's what you educated folks call projection?" I couldn't help but laugh as Tyler said, "So give me the scoop."

I didn't even realize that I had started grinning from ear to ear the second I thought about Cerise. Tyler said, "Damn boss, she must be something special because you haven't said a word about her yet and you are grinning from ear to ear." He'd broken me down. I finally had to give him the straight dope.

"Tyler," I said, "The woman is incredible. I have met some women in my time but none like Cerise. I could spend the rest of my life just getting to know her. She's smart, funny, sexy…." my voice trailed off as I remembered our hotel bathroom incident this morning.

Tyler tried to use the same tone of voice I'd used with him earlier when he said, "Well why aren't you still in the bed with her then?" The boy was good. I had to give him his due.

More sadly than I wanted to I said, "She just flew to Australia on business. Tomorrow their time she has a meeting with some CEO who is going to seek to merge her company into their conglomerate."

Tyler looked at me for a long moment and quietly asked, "So, Marcus, why the hell are you here with me at Wynona's?" I looked at him as if I hadn't heard him correctly and Tyler added, "Every time you mention her name, your eyes get big like a deer's in headlights. You must really like this woman."

"Like! Like doesn't even cut it close. I…never mind."

Tyler said, "That's just what I thought. Boss, this is the first time you've ever really talked about anyone except Donna. I've asked you in the past about women and you've completely ignored me. She must be a winner!"

"She's something special and I miss her already," I admitted. "Cerise is a woman of character, charm, beauty, intellect, and is the text book definition of sexy."

Smiling, Tyler said, "Damn, does she have a sister, oops, forgot I have my own one of those back at the house." We both laughed. Now that he'd gotten me to open about Cerise, I couldn't stop. "She keeps me happy Tyler. And that's what I want for you, man! Tyler, you know I depend on you for a lot of shit. I need you happy at the office."

Tyler said, "Oh no, not the mushy shit again."

I said, "Oh no, but I need you smacking, flipping, licking, and rubbing it up and down."

Tyler laughed and asked, "Why so? What does my sex life have to do with this job?"

I said, "Shit you've got to be kidding me! Every man feels better after he puts it on his woman and leaves her with the happy face on! He busts out those squigglies and comes to work a happy man, ready to conquer the world!"

Tyler went into another rage of laughter but was able to mumble, "Boss, you are crazy!"

After things settled down and we both stopped laughing he asked, "Have you called to see if she made it safely?"

I said, "The flight takes at least twelve hours. Cerise said she'd call me once she got things in order. I look forward to hearing about her flight and what she called her 'last minute pitch to the CEO' or listening to the pitch about the chow...or something to that effect. I couldn't quite make out what she was saying because...cause the noise in the terminal was too loud."

Tyler asked, "The noise in the terminal was going full steam at five something this morning?"

I didn't respond.

"Yeah whatever, don't answer me...that's cool but tell me this, why you didn't go? Don't tell me you're afraid to fly or worried about HiCi. You know I'd keep things in order while you were gone. I had a minor slip up awhile back, which resulted in you meeting the woman we are sitting here talking about I might add, but a minor slip up nonetheless. Since then and before then I've been rock solid. So, what's up?

Taking a moment to think about what he'd said, I finally had to answer truthfully, "To be honest Tyler, I just didn't want to leave all that responsibility on you."

Tyler said, "Boss, don't be offended but I know more about the cases than you do. You know that I run this place like a captain on a ship. You sign checks and take point or back-up when it suits you but I'm the one who makes sure the other investigators are doing their jobs. With Ashley's help, I'm sure I can manage things till you get back."

"You are right." I said. "Damn-it, you are right!"

Tyler interrupted, "You should heed your own advice sometimes boss. I think you need to call the airport and get your ass on a plane so you can be there with Cerise. You can be there to celebrate with her, or fuck around with these cases that you know we'll handle."

"Okay!" I almost shouted out to Tyler. "I get your point. But I would have to go pack and make reservations, it's too much of a hassle."

"Boss, get your ass on a plane! And, and that's all I have to say about the matter," Tyler mimicked me once again.

We'd finished our breakfast and were heading back to the office as I gave serious thought to Tyler's advice. I was used to being the one to hold Tyler up, give him advice. It was humbling for me to realize it was my turn to take his.

"Boss." Tyler said quietly. "You are thinking about going, huh? Go. I'll run the show until you get back. At least go for a few days so you can be there for her big pitch or whatever it was you said. Damn boss! Go surprise that woman! I could see you not going if money was an issue but we know that's not the case."

I said, "You sure, you can handle it?"

Tyler said, "Handled like a masseuse on ya body 24/7! Just be back in time for the meeting with Bueavias." I sat there for a few minutes thinking about leaving the business in Tyler's hands.

Then it hit me! If I couldn't leave the business in his hands for a few days, I wasn't doing my job properly. Tyler was my main man and I knew he had the best interest of HiCi at heart. What was the point of working so hard to build something into a success and once it was, never taking the time to enjoy the fruits of your labor? I thought about the idea for a few more minutes as we continued our drive back to the office.

I looked over at Tyler and he said, "If you scared call the police!" I didn't even have a comeback this time. To think I actually encouraged his relationship with Ashley. "What's it gonna be Wizard?" he insisted.

I said, "I'm bouncing for a few days and I'll be back next Monday. You have the numbers if anything comes up."

Tyler replied, "Just have a good time. I will take care of things at the office."

I dropped Tyler off at the office and headed home to pack a bag and arrange for my trip to Sydney.

While driving home, I called the airport and scheduled a last minute flight. I couldn't believe the cost of a last minute ticket! It was $6200 dollars!! I had to ask the woman on the phone again, "Can you repeat that price again? Did I hear you correctly? $6200!"

She replied, "Yes sir. It will actually be $6300 with taxes and other fees."

I said, "Damn!! Damn!! Damn!!" Love will always cost something. It's not free. It's time, patience, money, understanding, and the list goes on. I guess it wouldn't have been so bad had I made reservations in advance but Cerise was worth every penny! I told the agent to book the flight.

A plan formulated in my mind. Since I had Cerise's hotel information already I decided instead of calling to tell her I was on my way to meet her, I'd surprise her instead. I wanted to just show up at her door, wheel her out to a wonderful dinner, and ply her with flowers and gifts. I called the hotel Cerise was staying in, secured a room of my own, and inquired about the best place to eat. The receptionist informed me that one of the finest restaurants, Silks, was next door. She explained that the only way to get a reservation for dinner tomorrow night was through someone with connections and since she was connected, for a fee of $50.00, Thias, the manager of Silks, would take care of everything I told her I needed. I agreed to pay her and upon my arrival. She gave me the number to Silks and specifically told me to ask for him and to say, 'Raelene made the arrangements.

I called the restaurant and asked to speak to Thias. When he came on the line, I explained to him exactly what I was trying to do and that I needed the evening to be perfect. After listening to my requests he said, "It can be done for $475 U.S." he told me. "I will pay the others involved and you will reimburse me when you arrive, plus a small fee for my intervention, is that right mate?" I agreed to the amount Thias claimed he'd need to make sure my requests came off without a hitch. Raelene had told me he would be willing to accommodate my needs and she'd been right.

I wanted to make the evening when I surprised Cerise in Sydney with my presence one she'd never forget. I'd wine and dine her, present her with flowers, serenade her, and we'd take a tour 'of our lovely city at night' as Thias had described it. I was excited about how things were turning out! Money didn't matter at this point. Once I was in, I was in!"

I pulled up to my house, drove into the garage, and hit the button for it to close. Not surprisingly, as I stepped into my empty house, my thoughts turned to Cerise and the love we'd made this morning; about the last year we'd shared together.

My cell-phone vibrated. It couldn't be Cerise checking because her flight was still in the air. What did we do before cell-phones? I was having a good vision of Cerise and I sitting on the back porch sipping on some wine until I was interrupted by this call.

I didn't recognize the number but I answered it anyway. "Hello? This is Marcus Haley."

It was Donna, "Hi Marc. How are you doing, baby?"

I replied, "Hey Donna, how ya doing? I'm good. I'm good."

"I called you on the office phone and it went straight to voice mail,' Donna said. " What are you still doing at home? You're breaking with your usual MO of being out the door at the crack of dawn."

"Well Donna, I didn't know you were that concerned, and you know I don't report to anyone, including you. But actually, I'm home packing some clothes."

She interrupted, "Business or pleasure?"

I quickly replied, "Business. So what's up Donna, How have you been? I haven't talked to you in a while. Do you mind if I put you on speaker phone?"

She replied, "Is you lady friend present? If not, go ahead."

I laughed and put her on speakerphone. I said, "No my lady friend, Cerise is not here. I just need to get stuff together while we chat."

She interrupted, "Well what time are you leaving? Can I see you before you leave? I haven't seen you in awhile Marc and its nice to talk while you pack if that's okay with you?"

I said, "I'm leaving in a hour, so lets just hook up when I get back." I hadn't planned on leaving for a few hours but I didn't want to be bothered.

I wasn't thinking...I wasn't thinking...Donna was way ahead of me. The first thing I should have asked was, 'What are you doing up so early and where are you heading?' because she replied, "Oh that's more than enough time and since I'm down the street getting coffee. I'll see you in a few minutes."

I yelled, "WAIT, WAIT!" but it was too late, she had hung up the phone. I hit star69 but Donna knew I'd call back and it went straight to voicemail. She had turned the phone off.

Donna was only minutes away. I ran downstairs and opened the door just as Stanley's garage door slid noisily open.

I walked outside and pretended as if I were looking for the paper, realized I was in front of my home and had nothing to hide, and laughed at myself.

Stanley greeted me. "Hey brotha... damn you are looking sharper than a porcupines pricks in that suit... Whew wee!"

"Morning to you Stan. You are the man. I'm just trying to be all I can be."

He replied, "Hewww...Hewwwwww. Shit bruther.... I didn't know you could wear a suit like that! So where's that lovely ranch hand of yours... whew!"

I said, "She's on...."

Stanley interrupted me and yelled, "Cerise…you pretty desert rose come on outta there and see your Stan Man." What the hell? Stan Man now?

"Stanley, she's on her way to Australia."

Stanley, replied, " What in smoking hogs head is she doing in Australia brotha? Well I'll be a monkey's uncle. I didn't even see my flower leave this morning. I was doing the CD thing if you know what I mean brotha."

"She'll be back soon," I told him. I didn't add that she'd be leaving again soon after. To keep my mind off that fact I told Stanley, "I have a another CD labeled Happy Valentines Baby, if you'd like to check it out."

Stanley reached in his pocket, snatched his hands back out as if he had two pistols, Fired two imaginary shots, then blew on the ends of his fingers. He said, "Hell yes… bruther. Go head on and grab that for me! Whew Wee!"

Looking up and down the street to see if Donna's car was approaching and seeing nothing, I said, "Give me a second. I'll go grab you a copy," ran in the house looking for my extra copy of Happy Valentines Baby but couldn't find it. I quickly tossed the CD in the computer and burned a copy.

Stanley thought I was the man when it came to music to help his aging libido. Little did he know, I bought all my music from, "Spice Man." Spice Man was a local hustler who walked around town selling just about anything that was popular. When the African necklaces were in, he had them. When the tie-dye peace shirts were popular, Spice Man had them. Spice Man was able to get you just about whatever you needed at half price. Lately when I see the little dude, he's toting CD's, DVD's, oils, and throw back Jersey.

I walked outside and handed Stanley the freshly burned CD. "Whew…I gotta take it slow bruther…I may mess around and have a bun in the oven after all this time, if ya know what I mean." I cracked up laughing and Stanley said, "Yeah…brotha, used to be I could make a baby breathing on it bruther…whew!"

Laughing, I said, "I bet you still can Stanley. I bet you can." Stanley smiled and turned around heading towards his house.

Why did Donna choose that moment to roll up with her music blaring? Once she saw Stanley and me she turned the music down but it was too late. Stanley did an about face and tried to play it off by asking, "Bruther what's the name of this CD again? Happy Birthday?" He slowly approached me with that grin on his face. He whispered, as he got close, "When the heifer's away, the bull will play, huh? Whew!"

I said, "It's not like that Stanley, you remember…"

Out of nowhere he hollered, "Bulls eye bruther…that's my gurl…cocka doodle bruther. Damn she's back."

Before I could respond, Donna stepped out of the car with a white spandex body suit on looking like she where heading to or coming from the gym. Her body was banging and Stanley's eyes bulged out of his skull.

"Stanley! Stanley!" I tried to catch his attention and he held one hand up and shushed me! I tried again, "Stan…"

He beat me to it. "Shush now bruther…my brown sugar butter has just arrived! Whew!"

Donna stepped out of the car. "Hello Marc, Stan baby. You like my outfit?" she asked as she ran her hand along her body. Stanley stood there dumbstruck, then, spittle flying in all directions stuttered, "Uh, huh, hee-hee, whew damn-it girl…I cant even speak! Whew."

Ramona saved me. She opened up the door and yelled, "Stanley get in this house! Sorry Marcus," she said and nodded to me as she gave an unsmiling nod to Donna. "It's too early for you to be yelling out here!" Ramona yelled.

Stanley smiled with a crazy ass grin and began heading towards the house. He reached the garage, turned, and gave me two hard, quick thumbs up. Donna turned her attention to me and as she did Stanley grew serious and pointed his finger at Donna and then at her car and jerked his head towards it. Guess they liked Cerise better than Donna. I couldn't blame them; I did too.

I tipped my head back quickly to indicate I knew what he meant and to convey nothing was going to happen with Donna. Donna saw me looking in the direction of Stanley's garage and turned to see what I was looking at. He blew her a kiss and she blew one back. The garage door closed and we heard a muffled, "Whew! Hope the boy don't blow it! hew!"

I turned to Donna and asked angrily, "What the fuck did you come over to my spot wearing something like that?" I glanced over at the house and noticed Stanley and his woman peeking out of the window. Damn. Here we go again.

Donna was going to mess my good thing up if Stanley, or more likely Ramona even remotely believed she was here for a quickie. Ramona might feel like it was her duty to sisterhood to hip Cerise to the fact that Donna had come over wearing another of her "come get me" outfits.

"Wait one minute Marcus, I don't know what your deal is but fuck you for talking to me like that, it's not like I didn't tell you I was coming. That was one of your rules wasn't it? I'm not your…"

I cut her off, "Hey, Hey, I'm sorry its just, you know how Stanley is and I don't need you messing up my stuff. I don't need your bullshit right now." I glanced back at Stanley's and Donna followed my gaze.

"I thought we were closer than that! How you going to refer to me as bullshit? Fuck you Marcus."

Donna started to get in her car and I said, "Come on now. I wasn't calling you bullshit. I just don't need any misunderstandings, you know?"

Donna flipped me off, started the car, and then sped off down the street. I looked over at Stanley's place and of course, the two pair of eyes was still watching the show.

I didn't have time for this drama. I had to pack. I walked in the house to finish packing clothes for my trip when I heard a tap at my bedroom window.

Keeping still for a moment I waited to see if I heard the sound again. Nothing happened so I walked to the bathroom to grab my toiletries when I heard the tap again.

Walking to the window, I opened the blinds and looked down. Donna was in my backyard with a handful of pebbles.

I mouthed, "You are crazy!" held up a finger to indicate 'wait a second' and headed downstairs. If she wanted to apologize, why didn't she just use the front door?

I opened the sliding glass door and said, "What the hell are you doing? You are crazy!" She walked in and jumped on a barstool. "Yeah I got that when you said it upstairs. I didn't want to mess your stuff up with your girl, so I put on a show for the folks next door."

"But you are back! They will still talk shit."

Donna said, "Damn Marc, you know I'm smarter than that! I parked at the vacant house in back of you and came through their yard and climbed the fence to yours."

I couldn't even say anything because that was some ingenious shit she had just pulled. I chuckled softly and went to the kitchen with Donna following.

As I poured a cup of coffee, Donna asked, "Stanley told me how much he liked the outfit, what do you think?" I laughed and pretended to ignore Donna's remarks. She continued on, "Come on Marcus, turn around and take a look and let me know what you think."

Taking a sip of my coffee without looking at her, I said, "Donna, you know you look good in just about anything you put on. Don't go there with the crazy questions!"

I turned to move past her and head back upstairs to pack and couldn't help but take a good look at her. Damn! Donna was looking good. The material pressed against her toned body, outlined every curve, and made her look BAD!

Donna noticed me noticing her and flourished her hand up and down her body like a game show model showing off a car. With a grin she asked, "You like?"

I knew what she was trying to do. It wasn't going to work on me this time. "Yeah its nice. Where is your woman?"

Quick as a flash she came back with, "Where is your woman?"

"Doesn't concern you where Cerise is right now. Does it?" I told her.

Donna replied, "I guess I could say the same thing but I don't want to go round and round with you. Why the attitude? I'll leave if you'd like."

Relieved, I said, "Okay. That's cool. I'll catch you when I get back. I have to pack."

Donna looked as if she couldn't believe what I'd just said. "Oh, we are on those terms again? You know what? I'll leave! But let me say this, I can remember a time when it didn't matter what else you had going on, my phone rang off the hook with you calling. I didn't treat you like shit Marc. Have a good trip."

"Are you joking?" I yelled at her. "Look Donna, what do you want from me? Why are you here at 8:49, huh? I haven't heard from you since the last time you showed up ready. You have on a tight body suit that's making my dick hard, and your nipples are about to rip through that outfit and you demand that I look at you? You came over here so I could fuck you before you run back to your girl right?"

Once again, my mouth was out there all on its own before my brain even knew what it was about to say. "I told you I'd call the shots if I needed a booty call but, admit Donna, if that's what you need so badly then let's do it, take your damn clothes off! If this is what is going to be, you and I just fucking from time to time…come on let's do it. My girl is gone yours is wherever, lets do it." I pulled my pants down and began taking my shirt off.

Donna had remained silent throughout my tirade but when I dropped my pants, she quickly crossed the room and slapped the shit out of me. She said, "What has gotten into you? You and I were friends and what the fuck do you mean showed up ready? Fuck you, Marcus Haley!"

Donna turned and ran out of the house. I didn't give chase because I had no intention of taking it to the skins with her. Thank God, she hadn't taken her clothes off when I'd lost control and demanded she do so. My mouth was putting an end to something my brain hadn't figured a way out of yet. I was done to the highest order of done with that woman. I had bigger and better things to attend to.

Cerise was my only priority. I rubbed where the sting still lingered from Donna's slap. Good thing I'm a chocolate brotha because had I been light skinned, there would be a handprint on my face.

Putting Donna and everything to do with her from my mind, I finished packing my suitcase and headed for the airport.

Cerise had been able to run through the airport at the last minute because it had been so early. My flight wasn't till 11 so I knew the airport would be more crowded. Nowadays, with the 9/11 checkpoints in place I knew that the more crowded flights would require a longer check in time.

Parking my truck in the long-term parking lot, I caught the shuttle and made my way to the terminals. I figured I'd grab a bite to eat and watch TV at the bar until it was time to board.

I find it interesting how the moment you have a woman, it seems like other women come out of the woodwork with propositions. When I didn't have a woman, it seemed like there was only a handful on this earth. Then, the very moment I find someone I'm excited to spend time with, it seems like I'm the flavor of the month. Donna trying so hard to be all up in my space was one example, but I'd checked that.

One of many other instances occurred when Cerise was probably just changing flights in LA on her way to Sydney.

I was in the airport Starbucks adding sugar to my coffee when I heard a soft voice say, "Excuse me. Excuse me. Good Morning. You must have a lot on your mind because you have been stirring that coffee for quite some time. Can I sneak by you and grab some cream for my coffee?"

I turned around and to my surprise a very beautiful woman was standing, holding her cup of coffee waiting to get to the counter.

"Hello, Oh excuse me, I didn't realize you were standing behind me." I said. The cream, sugar, and napkins were kept in a narrow corner.

I stepped to the side as she politely slid past me. Her perfume permeated my space and drove my senses wild. I must have inhaled loudly because she said, "You like my perfume, huh?" Trying to play it off, I raised an eyebrow and said, "Excuse me?" She laughed, "I caught you inhaling my perfume."

Giving her a little smile, I shrugged my shoulders. I said, "Okay, you caught me."

"It's okay a lot of people ask what I'm wearing." I smiled and said, "You are right. You caught me. It smells excellent. May I ask what the perfume is called?"

"It's called Naedirrej."

"Nada who?" I asked, trying to wrap my tongue around the name.

She laughed and slowed it down for me. "Nah-due-rouge."

"Damn, sexy name for a sexy smell," I said, shaking my head. She reached into her purse and handed me a card. "It can only be special ordered through par fume dealers, like myself, because it's hand made from special plants only found growing beside the Nile River in Egypt."

I smiled. "Thank you for the card and the pleasure of smelling you. I mean getting to smell 'Nah-due-rouge'," I pronounced slowly. Okay, get it together Marcus, I told myself. "The perfume is lovely."

She laughed and replied, "I understand. It's titillating once the fragrance hits you, yes?"

I nodded, took a sip of my coffee, and realized I hadn't added enough sugar. "Can you pass back the sugar please?"

She smiled as she handed me the sugar. I poured more sugar in the cup and thought about how good that scent would smell on Cerise.

"You sure are pouring a lot of sugar. Not to be in your business but you might want to give it a taste. You poured quite a bit while you were daydreaming."

I came to and chuckled. "I like my coffee sweet like my woman."

She threw her head back, looking at me with appreciation. "I know that's right," she said. "Can I ask what you were daydreaming about? Or let me guess. A woman, right? She must be very special for you to be daydreaming about her like that."

I smiled and replied, "You are good! I am on my way to see her and I could only imagine the sweet smell of that perfume on her. It would be delicious."

She caught herself laughing at me and said, "Excuse me. It's not funny. I've heard funnier remarks about how this scent makes men feel. But delicious? She is a lucky woman."

"She sure is," I told her and we both laughed.

Curious and wanting to prolong this chance encounter I snuck in, "Why do you think she's so lucky?"

"Well, first of all, you didn't sneak that by me. Let me tell what I mean but before I do, I don't even know your name."

"How rude of me. I am Marcus Haley. It's a pleasure meeting you."

She smiled at me coyly, "How do you know it's a pleasure? I haven't even told you my name."

"Doesn't matter. It's a pleasure anyway. Now, if you choose not to tell me your name, I'll call you Nah-due-rouge."

She smiled and said, "Good come back. Very good, Mr. Haley. And by the way, my name is Trinity."

"Trinity? Like I said, it's a pleasure," I said, as I shook her hand.

She eyed me with appreciation and asked, "Are you in a hurry Marcus Haley?" I glanced at the clock on the wall. It was 9:45. My flight wasn't scheduled to leave until 11:00. I shook my head. "Good. Care to join me for breakfast?" she asked.

"Well, it would be a pleasure, but only if you give me a discount on that perfume."

Trinity smiled and opened the small case she carried next to her purse. It contained several bottles of thick, dark colored liquids. She handed me a bottle and said, "Breakfast is on you, and this is free. Now, lets get a table."

We walked over to the airport café and found a table. Before I could even get comfortable, Trinity asked, "So Mr. Marcus, are you a Sacramento man born and raised?"

"Yes. I'm a local boy just trying to maintain. What about you?"

Again, Trinity looked me over with appreciation, smiled, and said, "Well, you appear to be doing more than maintaining."

I felt like popping my collar but managed to check myself. "Thank you. You are maintaining very nicely too."

Trinity was wearing a sand colored business suit that complimented her complexion. I'd noticed standing beside her at Starbucks that she was about 5'5, maybe 125 pounds. Trinity had sandy brown hair and light brown eyes. She had that Caribbean Island look that you'd see on the cover of a travel magazine enticing you to come back to Jamaica.

"So where are you from? I know you can't be from around here."

She replied, "I'm from Belize. I moved to the states about 7 years ago. I met my husband when he was on a business trip in Belize. We fell in love and have been married since."

"Well that's nice." I replied. "I've heard a lot about Belize, but I've never had the time to visit."

"Oh, you'd love Belize. It's the most beautiful place in the world and the locals are very friendly to tourists."

I smiled and said, "You sound like a spokesperson for the Belize tourism board."

Trinity laughed. "I just believe everyone must visit the Caribbean at some point in their life. It's a big world out there and Belize is a place that must be seen before one dies."

The waitress approached our table and asked for our order. Trinity quickly ordered one egg, one strip of bacon, and toast.

The waitress turned towards me and I realized I hadn't even glanced over the menu yet. Quickly, I scanned it, and asked for the breakfast special. I'd already eaten breakfast with Tyler earlier but didn't mind eating again just to spend a bit more time in the company of this lovely woman.

Trinity and I spent the next 40 minutes laughing and talking about current events, politics, and other matters. It was strangely comfortable and yet again uncomfortable at the same time.

Trinity must have been feeling the same way I was because out of nowhere she said, "Marcus, I feel as if I've known you forever. It almost feels as if we had met somewhere before today. I am just telling you all my business and comfortable with it too." We both laughed just as the bill came.

It was almost time for me to get to my terminal. Trinity and I walked to the counter and I paid for the breakfast as we'd agreed.

"Thank you for breakfast. It's been a genuine pleasure meeting you," Trinity said.

"Likewise." I told her. "The pleasure was all mine."

As we walked our separate ways Trinity turned back and said, "Thanks again. You have my card. Call me. If my husband answers just let him know you want to order the Naedirrej par fume and he'll put the call straight through to me."

I said, "Thank you for the sample. I'll call to order more if she likes it." I said as I patted my breast pocket to show that I had her card close to me.

I continued toward my terminal and Trinity walked towards hers. I had to turn back to get one final look at her just as Trinity turned to get one last look at me. We were both caught peeking! In unison, we both laughed, embarrassed, as we continued on our way.

So far away I could barely hear her, Trinity called out, "You have the number, right?" I nodded and again touched my breast pocket. Trinity smiled alluringly, turned, and continued on her path.

I smiled and headed to my gate. Now that was refreshing! I met a very beautiful lady and managed to get some perfume for my baby, C.

I had to admit, if Cerise were not in the picture I'd have called Trinity right away and asked her out, husband be damned. She came on to me!

But Trinity quickly evaporated from my thoughts as I approached my terminal. I held the small sample of Naedirrej in my palm and planned to wrap it up and present it to Cerise tonight when I saw her, along with a few other things.

I smiled as I thought about the other things I wanted to present to Cerise tonight, but my thoughts quickly turned again to the woman who'd given me the perfume. Trinity was fine as all hell. I didn't go there, but I had to admit, a part of me enjoyed the hell out of flirting with her. I'd have to make up an alternative to the truth about how I'd come upon the tiny perfume bottle I planned to present Cerise with. She'd never understand that flirting was just flirting but flying 3000 miles to surprise my girl trumped any chance encounter in an airport.

I took my seat on the plane and pulled down the blind. It was going to be a long flight and I wanted to work on the plan I was going to present to Beauvias next Thursday. With that done, as the plane touched down in San Francisco, I settled back in my seat and put my notes away. I wanted sleep as much as possible for the rest of the long flight so I'd be fresh and wide-awake when I surprised Cerise.

Contrary to my plans, I didn't sleep the first 6 hours. My mind was busy with thoughts of Cerise, the year she was going to be away from me, and whether or not our relationship was strong enough to last the duration.

"Excuse me sir. Excuse me sir."

A hand reached out to firmly shake my shoulder. I awoke slowly and yelled, "What? Back up!"

Trying to focus on the owner of the hand on my shoulder, I saw a male and female steward standing over me. The woman looked amused but the man looked upset. While still trying to orient myself, the woman said, laughing, "I told you he was hard to wake up."

"Oh I'm sorry, I was knocked out." I said, "How much longer do we have?"

The male steward looked at me as if he were going to do something. He said with much attitude, "We are arriving in thirty minutes. Please pull your seat up."

He stood there, staring hard at me for a second, like he wanted to get something started. I was about to set it off until I realized I had hold of his arm. I let go and apologized again.

He walked down the aisle, mumbling under his breath something I couldn't make out. I'd guess he didn't like me very much.

The female flight attendant, watching the entire exchange, laughed, and said, "I rarely have so much trouble waking people up! You must have been very tired sir." She motioned her head in the direction of the man whose arm I'd grabbed. "Don't pay him any attention, he lost a bet with me that you would wake up the moment he said, excuse." She smiled widely. "Thanks to you I have next weekend off," and called out to her coworker as she followed his path towards the back of the plane.

As the airplane lowered, touched down, and taxied down the runway, I pulled the blinds up to catch my first glimpse of Australia. I gathered my luggage from the baggage claim area. I couldn't believe I slept so hard. Wow! I was in Sydney!

I made my way to the taxi area at the front of the airport and signaled to a cabbie. There was an immediate barrier because although everyone spoke English, the dialect was almost like a foreign language.

One of the cabbies approached and spoke with a thick middle-eastern accent but I understood him because most of the cabbies back home spoke with the same accent. "I'll take you where you want to go." I told him and he said the ride was about 15 minutes from the airport and gave me a card before opening my door to the cab and storing my luggage. I sat down, and we were on our way.

Fifteen minutes later, we pulled up in front of the hotel. I tipped him ten dollars, and he told me to call him if I needed another taxi during my stay. Time was flying. I left the States on Tuesday, flew all day and night, and arrived in Sydney on Thursday!

I checked into the hotel and inquired into which room Mrs. Ivan was residing. The man behind the counter wouldn't give me the information but told me he would place a message in her box. It was a stupid thing to say because the boxes with the room numbers on them were directly behind the counter.

Using my left hand, I scribbled a message for Cerise that didn't make any sense. I didn't want her to recognize the writing and ruin the surprise. Folding the paper into a triangle, I handed the note to Mr. Attitude behind the counter and walked away slowly before bending down, pretending to tie my shoe, even though I was wearing loafers. Straightening up, I quickly scanned the message boxes to see where my triangular missile had landed. Room 1130.

A line formed behind the counter as I walked towards the elevator. I'd go to my room first, freshen up, and then knock on Cerise's door. The clerk called out through the swinging door behind him. "Raelene, I need some help here please."

Raelene! I had almost forgotten about her! She came from the back room and I cut in front of the other waiting guests. "Excuse me, Raelene. I'm Marcus Haley." She immediately smiled and said, "Ah Mr. Haley, I'm glad you made it. Was your flight okay?"

"Yes. Thank you," I told her. She said, "Thias told me you made arrangements for your special dinner next door. Very good. Everything is set just as you requested."

I reached into my wallet and placed two travelers checks inside the envelope the male clerk had given me totaling fifty dollars for her, and another $500 for Thias. I handed Raelene the envelope with my room information and card keys.

"Can you check to make sure I have a non-smoking room please?" She quickly glanced into the envelope and switched out the travelers checks for another map of the area. "Everything is just as you asked Mr. Haley. Have a wonderful time in Sydney. Call if you need anything."

I took the envelope back and headed to the elevators. I knocked on Cerise's door but there was no answer so I backtracked to the elevators and headed to my own room.

The suite was perfect. It was much larger that I had thought it would be. There was a king sized bed, refrigerator, Jacuzzi tub, extra large living room/kitchenette, and a large television. I unpacked my bags and hung up my clothes.

Jumping into the shower to wash away my traveling grime, I dried off and lay spread eagle on the bed. Jet lag kicked in. I napped for about 2 hours, dressed, and then headed downstairs to get a bite to eat in the hotel's restaurant. I picked a seat where I could see people coming and going without them seeing me. I guess all the years of police and investigative work funneled over into my daily practices.

I looked at the menu and didn't really care for the offerings so I chose the buffet. I grabbed my plate and headed to the line. There was so much food and to my surprise, it didn't look that much different than what's served at my local Hometown Buffet back at home.

I sat back down to eat and began thinking about how surprised Cerise would be about me being in here.

Taking a forkful of food, I looked up at the crowd passing through the lobby. Oh, shit! Was that Cerise that just passed by? It was. I started to get up and run to give her a hug but instead, I crouched down in my seat so she wouldn't see me. Cerise walked to the counter and said a few words to the young hostess. I couldn't tell what they were saying but she stood at the counter after they finished talking. Was she waiting for someone? I sat there with my heart racing in excitement just from seeing her beautiful smile again.

I'd picked up the local paper and kept it in front of my face, pretending to read it and occasionally peeked around to see if she were still standing at the counter. A few minutes later, a man walked up to Cerise said "Hello" and kissed her on the cheek.

They walked to a booth two rows over and five spaces up from where I was sitting. And what was that kissing shit all about?

I checked myself. I knew this had to be a business meeting because Cerise opened up her briefcase and removed some papers. I sat there hiding behind my paper and taking peeks for the next hour.

Then the man grabbed both of Cerise's hands and held them for several seconds. Cerise looked uncomfortable, but she smiled and pulled her hand back tactfully.

Again, she appeared to be trying to go over the documentation in front of them but the man didn't seem to be paying attention. He again reached out, grabbed one of her hands, and gently stroked her arm. What was this fool all about? What has she gotten herself into?

Cerise hadn't eaten anything from her plate because she'd been trying to talk to the man about the papers in front of them. This cat and mouse deal went on for a few more minutes. Finally, he stood up. He was about 6'0, blonde, with slicked back greasy hair, medium build, and I noticed with a slight twinge that he wasn't an ugly man.

I was going to rearrange some things on that Adonis face of his if he didn't slow down with the touching. I knew Cerise could handle herself, though, and as long as there was no force going on, I could maintain my composure. The Australian man, wearing his Armani suit, red tie, and alligator shoes, leaned over the table to kiss Cerise on her cheek.

She was becoming inpatient as she leaned back and he sat back down. They both wrote something on the document in front of them and Cerise began packing her items, said something to make him frown, stood up, and walked out of the restaurant. The guy looked around, dropped some money on the table, and followed in pursuit. I figured what the hell, I might as well do the same.

I waited behind for a few minutes so I wouldn't be noticed, then made my way to the elevator and rode to Cerise's floor. I stepped off the elevator and, from the arrows posted in front of me, noted Cerise's room was down the hall and around the corner. I headed in the direction of her room and could hear a heated conversation.

I heard him say, "Come on. It'll make the deal even sweeter." I stopped short at the end of the hallway and continued to eavesdrop. Quickly peeking around the corner, I saw the man standing outside her doorway. He continued to try to talk his way in for a few minutes, then out of nowhere he pushed his way in and the door slammed shut.

I ran the length of the hallway as I heard Cerise yell, "NO! I wasn't flirting with you! Are you crazy? I have a man and even if I didn't I wouldn't fuck around with the likes of you! Now please get out of my room!"

I wanted to kick the damn door down but Cerise sounded as if she were handling the situation well. She might not appreciate me busting in like the Calvary if it could screw up the deal she'd come here to make.

Continuing to eavesdrop at the door I heard the man say, "You have been coming on to me all through dinner and now you want to play shy? Come on, loosen up, take your clothes off and let me properly welcome you to Diatronics you little BAP tease!"

With those words, I politely knocked on the door. I heard Cerise tell the man he'd better be on the other side of the door as soon as she checked to see who it was. I waited for her to open the door but a long second went by and she didn't. Worried, I kicked the door once. It didn't budge. Gathering more strength, I kicked it again and it flew open.

The man staggered backward holding his face, and an angry imprint of a tiny fist was on his tanned skin. Cerise may be little, but she obviously packs a punch! Her eye's lit up in surprise and delight when she saw me. "Marcus! Oh my God! You're here! How? Why?"

I walked into the room, kissed Cerise on her cheek, and stepped in front of the would-be rapist as he tried to escape the room without my notice. He obviously saw the rage in my eyes!

He said, "Listen I don't want trouble. I got the message from Sheila here. I just want to leave." I raised my fist to smash the guys face but Cerise caught my arm before it connected. Holding on tight, she pleaded, "Baby please don't do it. Don't get into a fight here. It's not worth it. I can't have you in jail in Australia! And don't worry! If you hadn't have come in I'd have kicked his ass myself!"

I put my arm down but I was ready to spring into action if this guy made any sudden moves. Giving him a stare that let him know he'd be a dead man, I asked Cerise, "Baby you okay?"

She replied, "I'm fine now! But how did...?"

I interrupted her, "One second baby."

Pointing my finger at the man's forehead, "Today was your day to die mate. Thank the lady for your life and don't you ever come near her again. Goodbye." He looked at me to be sure I was actually letting him go, then rushed from the room.

Cerise began to cry as he walked out. I wasn't sure if they were tears of joy or sorrow because she was in a fucked up position for a minute. She threw her arms around me and said, "I wasn't sure I'd really be able to fight him off if it came to that Marcus, thank God I'll never have to find out!" I held her trembling body in my arms and said, "It's going to be okay baby. I'm here. I'm not going anywhere."

Over the next few hours, Cerise had a chance to calm down and take a nap she'd wanted to take since she'd arrived. During that time, I didn't question her about the man who'd tried to attack her but definitely intended to find out who he was and what she planned to do about him. She couldn't work with him anymore if I had any say in the matter.

Cerise still had no idea of my dinner plans for her. We walked into Silks and Raelene must have described me to Thias because he knew exactly who I was. He approached me and said, "This must be the beautiful lady you told me about sir. Your table is ready."

He led us to our table as Cerise looked at me with surprise. Thias then clapped his hands and a violinist came from behind a secluded area and began playing the song that I'd played for Cerise the first night she came to my house.

Cerise's mouth dropped open and she tried to speak but couldn't find the words. She started crying all over again but this time I knew they were tears of joy. As the music played, I reached in my pocket and handed Cerise the Naedirrej. She wiped her eyes and opened the bottle to sniff the contents. "My goodness! Where did you get this perfume from Marcus? It smells…It smells wonderful."

I smiled but didn't respond. Just then, a large bouquet of roses of every color was brought to the table and handed to Cerise. She leaned across the table and kissed me for a long moment, just as the dinner I'd ordered on the phone arrived.

We ate dinner and Cerise couldn't stop talking about my surprise trip and how she thought I was going to kill Blaise. Turn's out he was the son of Diatronics CEO, who'd sent Blaise to solidify the deal.

Amazed, I asked what she planned to do about the bastard. Cerise assured me she'd talk to the CEO personally, tell him about what had happened, and demand that she never have to work with Blaise again. That could only mean one thing.

"So you signed the deal? You sold Xxellron?" I asked. I felt sorry for her employees, even Tammy. They would all be out of a job soon if she'd taken that contract. Cerise smiled but didn't respond.

"Cerise, did you sign away your company?" I asked again, impatient for an answer now.

She smiled and said, "They bought Xxellron Inc. for 7.5 million dollars. I sold them the whole kit and ka-boodle!" Cerise and I yelled in unison, "Hey!" Even though I felt bad for her ex-staff, that was too much money to be mad about. I was sure Cerise would give each of them a letter of recommendation, even Tammy, so that they'd have a good chance to find other employment before Diatronics moved the company out of the country in search of cheaper labor, as I was sure they would do.

Now that the deal had been made Cerise was bursting to tell me all the details. Turns out my sympathies for her staff had been misplaced. Cerise stipulated in the contract that her employees could not be laid off or have their salaries or duties reduced in any way. In addition, the company had to remain on American soil. I was proud of my baby for that. She probably could have gotten a few million more if not for those conditions. I'd been worried that she'd been so blinded by the money that she hadn't taken into account how selling her company might affect others. My worries were misplaced; at least as far as her staff was concerned. She didn't seem the least bit concerned about what selling Xxellron would do to us.

But I wasn't going to ruin her moment. As long as Cerise was happy, I was happy for her. However, mixed with the happiness came the sadness and grief I'd felt yesterday morning before she'd left Sacramento. I didn't think our relationship would survive her yearlong absence. Cerise was beautiful, smart, funny, and now, certifiably rich. I knew men would be all over her and truthfully, I didn't know if I'd be able to wait for her. Temptation was strong I thought, as the image of Trinity floated before me.

If we'd be in the same city for the next year, I had no doubt that I would never leave her side and she'd never leave mine. Now…I just didn't know what was going to become of this wonderful relationship we'd found. All I could do was make the most of my time with her here and now.

Silk's piano player soon accompanied the violinist and I held Cerise close as we swayed to the music playing especially for her. We danced; enjoyed Crystal champagne and cheesecake for dessert, and then danced to a few more tunes. One final surprise awaited Cerise as we exited Silks after a wonderful meal. She held the flowers in her arms as we walked outside just as Thaïs's father approached, wearing a top hat and tuxedo. He bowed before a surprised Cerise and reached out for her hand.

Cerise looked at me curiously and I nodded my head for her to take his hand. He led her away, and I followed behind, as they approached a plush horse drawn carriage with a placard that read, For Cerise, A Phenomenal Woman. For the next hour, we were treated to a view of beautiful Sydney at night. Cerise was amazed and tearful about my carefully laid plans to show her how much she meant to me and the trouble and expense I'd gone through just for her.

As the carriage rolled through the city, Cerise, nestled in my arms, turned her face up to me and whispered, "Marcus, I have to tell you something. You aren't the only one who knows how to surprise someone. And I hope you will be as happy as I am."

I was so busy enjoying the vibe of the entire evening that I barely heard her. Absentmindedly I responded, "Okay. What is it baby?"

"I'll tell you later. But you are happy right now, yes?" I nodded and kissed the top of her head. "Good. Because I'm overwhelmed with joy." Cerise said, her voice thick with unshed tears.

I told her, "I'm just happy that I was here when you needed me to be and that I could share in this special day with you." As my mind wrapped itself around what she'd just said I continued, "Okay. Now what was it you were going to tell me?"

"It can wait until later." Cerise said coyly.

Chuckling softly as I pulled Cerise even closer I replied, "How are you going to throw a partial declaration out there and leave me hanging?"

Cerise pulled herself out of my embrace to look me fully in the eye and replied, "Oh, but it's a surprise. One I hope you'll be happy about."

She had my full attention now. "What is it?" I asked again.

Cerise kissed me until we were both breathless, patted my cheek, and said, "In time baby. I'll tell you in time. Just be open to a change in plans, okay?"

"Okay." I told her as I sat there confused. What the hell was she talking about? Did she think I was going to move to Australia with her? Was she pregnant? Did she want to get married?

I looked down at Cerise for some answers but she seemed content to snuggle in close to me as she laid her head against my chest and smiled as if she had the whole world within the palm of her hand.